GW01111655

NOT THE SAME RIVER

NOT THE SAME RIVER

Stories

W. A. Polf

atmosphere press

© 2024 W. A. Polf

Published by Atmosphere Press

Cover design by Ronaldo Alves. Cover photo by Martin Sanchez.
Author photo by Robin Eisner.

No part of this book may be reproduced without permission from the author except in brief quotations and in reviews. This is a work of fiction, and any resemblance to real places, persons, or events is entirely coincidental.

PUBLICATIONS
"Banjo" won second place in the 2018 Doris Betts Fiction Award of the North Carolina Writers Network, published by the North Carolina Literary Review Online (2018). It was nominated for a Pushcart Award and for The Best Short Stories Online of 2018. "Banjo" was also among the top three winners of the 2018 Short Story America fiction award and is reprinted in the 2018 edition. "The Gun Rack" was published in the Tishman Review in 2016. "Arlen/Arlene" (under the title "Compton's Cafeteria") was a 2018 Screen Craft Short Story Award semi-finalist. The editors of the *New Yorker* wrote in an email that there is "much to admire" in the story "The Taste of Gasoline" (under the title "Two Sixpacks and A Pint"). "Lunch at the Dahesh" was published by *Still Point Arts Quarterly* in 2015. "Chickens" was a finalist for the 2013 Glimmer Train Short Story Award for New Writers and received an honorable mention. "Chickens" was published by the *Milo Review* in 2014. "Stepping Off the Curb" was a semi-finalist for the 2019 Doris Betts Fiction Award of the North Carolina Writers Network. "Marge and Maybelline" was a semi-finalist for *The Black River Chapbook* of St. Clarence Press in 2018.

Atmospherepress.com

FOR ROBIN

CONTENTS

BANJO
1

THE GUN RACK
19

THE ELEPHANT TRAIN
43

ARLEN/ARLENE
67

THE TASTE OF GASOLINE
91

LUNCH AT THE DAHESH
101

CHICKENS
113

STEPPING OFF THE CURB
141

THE SAWMILL POND
153

WITNESS
171

MARGE AND MAYBELLINE
189

A RIDE HOME
217

THE WOMAN IN THE CLOSET
231

DON'T YOU KNOW?
251

THE MAN ON GANU MOR
279

No man ever steps into the same river twice
For it is not the same river
And he is not the same man

Heraclitus

BANJO

Someone found Kate's mother standing in the shopping center parking lot, frightened and clutching her handbag tightly against her chest. She stood there, trembling, unable to speak. When the police asked her name, she just stared at them. They found her driver's license in her bag, along with an address book. The female officer who called Kate had been kind. "We figured you must be a relative since you had the same last name."

Her mother was sitting in the security office when Kate came in. Someone had placed a styrofoam cup of water next to her, but she ignored it. She sat slumped down, deflated, as though she had been caught shoplifting. Kate had never seen her look so defeated. All her life, she had been a proud woman, her shoulders square, her chin up, her curly red hair bright around her head like a crimson helmet. The red hair had long since turned gray, but her mother never lost her haughtiness, her sense of entitlement. Now she sagged like a bag of dirty laundry thrown on a chair.

"I forgot where I parked my car," she said, looking pathetically at Kate. In her mother's eyes, Kate saw fear so deep, so primal, that her stomach sank, and she inhaled deeply to control the churning. Later, looking back, she realized her mother had glimpsed her end—and it terrified her. Neither of them knew it at the time. That day at the mall, her mother finally remembered her name. Now, eighteen months later, she couldn't recognize herself in the mirror.

Kate stood at the sink in the kitchen washing dishes. She could hear the birds outside in the courtyard, chirping and quarreling around the bird feeders. She and her mother often sat together, watching the birds through the window. What does she see now? Kate wondered. For a while, early in the decline, her mother had struggled to remember things from the past. Kate helped by telling her about memories they shared, good things to stimulate her mother's mind. Kate searched her memory: there wasn't a lot to tell. Thirty-five years as a high school science teacher in her hometown, and what did she have to show for it? A teacher's pension and whatever would be left when her mother died. She decided not to speak about most of the memories that came to her; memories dredged up like sodden weeds from the bottom of a pond. Keep it cheerful, the neurologist said, so Kate tried to do just that.

Her mother did nothing to take care of herself anymore. When she awoke, she no longer reached for the robe Kate laid on the bed. She sat, slouched on the edge, until Kate put it on her. "She no longer seems to know what to do next, how to do the smallest thing," Kate told the doctor. A loss of executive function, he called it. Kate liked the term. Somehow, it elevated the disease above the mere inability to remember the details of the past, the ordinary events that make a life.

Now, her mother rarely spoke. Kate could only wonder what she was thinking. "Tell me what you see, what you hear?" Kate would sometimes ask. Her mother would give her a blank look and say nothing. When she did speak, the words came from nowhere, blurted out abruptly, sometimes making sense, often not.

Her mother was talking in the bedroom. Kate strained to hear her.

"Birds. There were birds, big birds. Green and red. We saw them."

She's remembering the parrots at the zoo, Kate thought. Her mother loved those parrots. "Sassy things." She laughed. "Maybe I'll get one for the shop. Keep the customers entertained." Her mother talked about it for days. Bernice, her partner in the beauty salon they owned, let it ride for a while before putting her foot down. "It would just be a noisy mess," she said. Bernice was the levelheaded one; she held the business together. Sometimes, she held Kate and her mother together.

Kate returned to the dishes in the sink. I'll leave the rest of them, she decided. A new nurse's aide was coming, a man this time. All the others had been women, well-meaning but lacking the mental or physical agility to manage her mother. Her mother turned passivity into resistance, fighting the helpers at every step until they quit in frustration. The agency diplomatically suggested a man. They think a man might be able to handle her, Kate thought, not certain whether to be offended. Then she said, "Sure, why not?" Her mother always had men around when she was younger. She seemed to need them, even the ones who beat her or walked out on her. Maybe a man was needed now.

Kate poured the remaining coffee from the pot into a cup and sat at the kitchen table where she could look out at the yard. Let the new guy do the dishes, she thought. Her mother was quiet now; there was no reason to check on her.

That day in the parking lot wouldn't leave Kate's mind as she sat, fingering the cup on the saucer. Maybe there had been clues before, but Kate hadn't caught them—or had ignored them. Her mother had no soft side, no obvious vulnerability. Together, the two of them blocked out any sign of the catastrophe taking shape in her mother's mind. Later, when the neurologist quizzed Kate about early warning signs, incidents came back to her: her mother forgetting the name of Tillie, the woman who had come in to clean for years; misplacing her handbag and Kate finding it among the garden tools in the garage; throwing away the mail, along with her social security check, before it was opened.

She and her mother deliberately overlooked these incidents. Her mother could laugh off anything, a survival skill she had learned from a lifetime of disappointments. Minor mistakes, her mother called them. Kate had no ability to contest her, so she went along. Now, in Kate's mind, they clanged like fire alarms in the night.

The front doorbell chimed, jolting her.

Kate opened the door. A man stood there; he was shorter than average but muscular, like a tumbler in a circus she had once seen. His forearms bulged. Popeye's arms, Kate thought. He wore a light blue smock, the uniform of a nurse's aide, and brown trousers, loosely rumpled. He's not American, Kate concluded. A foreigner. But what kind?

"I am Pavel Panchelevsky," he said. "Please call me Pancho." He raised a finger like a teacher calling for attention. "Not Pauncho, as the Mexicans say. But Pancho. Like a frying pan." He laughed lightly. Kate could not place his odd accent.

"I am here to care for Mrs. Marva May," he went on, sounding quaintly formal. His odd manner charmed Kate. For a moment, it seemed as though he might reach out and hug her. His eyes never looked away from her face. He's certainly not overly deferential, Kate thought. Then he smiled, and the smile drew her in. Even before she replied, Kate was persuaded.

"Well, come on in, Mr. Pancho," she said, pulling the door further open. "You've arrived just in time."

Kate walked back toward her mother's room, the man following at a respectful distance. He's probably sizing up the furniture, trying to get a sense of how well-off we are, she thought. How well-off her mother is, she corrected herself. This is her house, not mine. Kate would get it when her mother died. She had already decided to sell it when that happened; she had no desire to live in it.

Her mother sat as before, looking out at the bird feeders.

"Mother, this is Mr. Panchelevsky," Kate said. "He said we should call him Pancho." After a long moment, her mother turned to look at the man. Kate could see her incomprehension.

Her mother stared at him.

"Banjo?"

The man laughed. "Yes, Mrs. May, Banjo. Banjo will do fine."

He looked at Kate, and again, she felt like he might hug her. She had a sense that he understood everything, that she needn't worry anymore.

"Oh, Mrs. May, let's get you dressed," he said cheerfully. "You'll feel so much better."

Kate heard this and felt guilty. She had gotten into the habit of letting her mother spend the day in her robe. Dressing, undressing: it all seemed so pointless now.

Pancho asked, "May I look through her clothing?" Kate nodded. He moved through her closet as though he knew it already and selected a frock with roses, something her mother hadn't worn for years. Kate barely recognized it.

"This will make you look so pretty," he said to her mother.

Pancho hummed as he dressed her. When he asked, she stood and raised her arms so the dress could slide over her. Kate was surprised at how easily he did it—and her mother's lack of resistance. Pancho talked as he worked around the bedroom. "I took care of my mother, too," he said to Kate. "I helped her when she needed to be taken care of."

He needs no guidance from me, Kate thought as he moved about. He understands her and dying old ladies. Kate had a feeling of expectation, a sense of music for a new dance just getting underway.

"Banjo," she heard her mother say. "Banjo."

She hadn't said Kate's name for months.

Pancho slid smoothly into the household. Soon, it seemed as though he had always been there. He called Kate "Miss Kate" and her mother "Mrs. May."

"I can't believe how easily he has connected with her," Kate told Bernice. "I mean, it's like they're related. Like they've known each other for their whole lives."

Bernice agreed, "It's amazing." They watched as Pancho guided Kate's mother around the room on her morning exercise. When Kate did it, she almost had to drag her mother along.

"It's like they're dancing," she whispered to Bernice.

"Yes," Bernice answered. "A waltz."

Every day, Pancho arrived early, earlier than scheduled, to prepare her mother's breakfast. He talked to her as he fussed around the bedroom. When she refused to eat, he fed her. He stayed until she was ready for bed in the evening. Quickly, he took over the housekeeping so efficiently that Kate barely noticed it being done. When Kate offered to pay him for the additional hours, he wagged his finger and shushed her.

"Nothing matters but her care," he said. "Do not worry."

He left her mother alone only to do his other work. "Banjo!" her mother would call out. And he would return to her, sometimes putting her in her wheelchair to keep her close by as he worked about the house.

Pancho even planned their weekends when he wasn't there. Food was prepared in advance, her mother's clothing selected, television programs she might like marked in the guide. Just follow the directions on the box, Kate thought whenever she studied the meticulous notes he left each week. She sat with her mother as before, looking out at the birds, the television murmuring in the background. She sensed the vacuum created by Pancho's absence. She still tried talking to her mother about the past, things they both remembered. Sometimes, she even sang her old songs. When she couldn't recall the words, she simply hummed the tune. But her mother did not respond. When Kate grew tired of talking, they sat in silence, awaiting his return.

"He's taking care of the whole house now," she told Bernice as they sat under the canopy in the backyard, where they could hear Pancho busy inside. Bernice nodded; she had noticed the tidiness of the house.

"Your mother was no housekeeper," she said.

"And I learned that from her," Kate added before Bernice could say it.

Kate's bedroom remained an untidy mess, an outlier. She had been neater in her own apartment. But in her mother's house, she often forgot and was surprised when she entered her own room to find the bed still unmade from the morning. When that happened, it felt like a kitchen spill she had neglected to clean up, something she stumbled across after it dried into a hardened mess.

One day, she walked in and found Pancho making her bed.

"I had a few minutes while Mrs. May is resting. So it is no problem." He fluffed the pillows. "I shall change the sheets and pillowcases when I do laundry."

From that day, Kate remembered to make the bed herself.

Pancho's presence swelled inside the house. Kate felt him in every space and corner and herself being squeezed out. Things had slipped from her control without her knowing it. But she didn't care. As Pancho smoothly filled every niche, it felt like a mild narcotic taking hold, and she was drifting into dependence.

Kate also sensed a new awareness within her mother, an ability to perceive, which had been missing for months. Pancho had restored her mind in a way that nothing else had done. Her mother's movements, her attention span, the way she sat more erect in her chair—it all seemed to indicate a renewed ability to connect. But only for Pancho. With Kate, her mother lapsed into withdrawal until Pancho brought her back with a laugh.

Bernice felt the change, too. "Her mind's in there. And she knows it. But she only comes out for him."

Kate took to spying on them. She would stand outside the open bedroom door, just out of view, straining to hear what was being said. She heard his voice, speaking softly and confidentially. Was her mother responding? Kate couldn't tell, at least not from a distance. What was he saying? she wondered. One day, she asked him.

"Oh, I tell her stories. Mostly stories about Romania. When I was a boy."

"But does she hear you? Understand, I mean."

"Yes. Oh, yes. She hears. She knows what I say." He paused. "In her own way."

"And she answers you?"

Pancho waited a moment. "She says what she can say. What comes to her. She does not answer so directly. Not always."

He held a dust cloth in his hand and shifted from one foot to the other as though impatient to return to his work.

"Well, at least you're reaching her," Kate said. "When I talk to her, I can't tell if she knows what I am saying." And she no longer answers me, she could have added.

Pancho nodded as though clarifying a distinction between them, a distinction he understood but that she did not yet grasp.

Kate still shopped for groceries. Pancho swore he could do it easily, but she resisted: she wasn't sure why. So, instead, Pancho prepared a detailed shopping list and made sure she followed it, checking each item as he took them from the bags. He would have the groceries put away before she could finish hanging up her coat.

One day, he was not waiting for her when she returned from the market. She hefted the groceries onto the counter and listened. Nothing. Maybe they're out for a walk, she told herself. But Pancho would have left a note: he always did. She walked into the bedroom. Her mother's wheelchair was missing, so they must be out. He just forgot to leave a note, she told herself.

Then the thought struck her: they don't need me anymore. They don't even know I'm here. The feeling chilled her, and she stood for a while, looking at her mother's empty bed.

The next day, a laugh came from the bedroom—throaty, almost a bark. It startled Kate. Her mother's laugh. She'd know it anywhere. She hadn't heard her mother laugh for months.

She asked Pancho, "Did I hear my mother laugh?"

He nodded. "She is quite happy this morning. Very happy."

"Did you do it? Make her laugh, I mean."

Pancho hesitated. "Oh, I only told her a story. It amused her."

A story—to make her laugh. What could do that? Kate wondered.

"Tell it to me. I want to hear it."

"It is only a simple tale of my boyhood. Not important."

"That's okay. Tell it to me anyway. I want to know what she heard."

He shrugged and told her.

"When I was a boy in Bucharest, my father would take us to the country, to the farm where he grew up and where his mother, my grandmother, and my father's sister still lived. There, I would play with my cousin Ionela, who was very pretty, and I was shy to be around her. I was always trying to think up ways to impress her so she would like me. One day, as we played in the yard not far from the pen where the pigs rooted about, I got the idea of walking along the top rail of the pen, from one post to the next. In school, I was very good at gymnastic exercises, and I was proud of my athletic expertise—or at least as I saw it."

Pancho stopped talking and looked quizzically at Kate. She nodded. "Go on."

"'Watch me,' I said to Ionela. 'I will do something very hard—which I will do for you.' As Ionela watched, I climbed up to the top rail of the pen so carefully and stood, my arms out for balance, and then proceeded to step slowly, one step, another step, across the rail. Oh, I was doing so fine, my chest bursting with love for Ionela. Then, something, a little breeze perhaps, or a pig lifting its head, caused me to stumble. I struggled to keep my balance. And, as my arms waved, I began to wobble like a spinning top winding down. I fought for control, but it was too late. I felt myself falling backward into the pen, and as the pigs scattered out of the way, I plopped with a loud smacking noise into the sloppy muck. As I lay stunned, wondering what had happened, I could hear Ionela laughing merrily from the yard. Even the pigs seemed to be laughing at me, too."

Pancho had stopped for a long moment before Kate realized he was finished.

"My mother liked that story?" Kate asked.

"Oh yes. Oh yes."

"She actually laughed at his story," Kate said to Bernice as they sat on a bench in the park. "She won't even talk to me. Let alone laugh."

Bernice patted her hand. "She used to laugh a lot in the shop," Bernice said. "At jokes especially. Crude. The dirtier, the better."

Bernice was devoted to Kate's mother. She came every week and spent an afternoon talking about their years together when they were both single mothers struggling to survive. Their beauty shop was a female-only sanctuary, a place for curling hair, whispered tales of secret abortions, drunken husbands, and beatings at home. Marva and Bernice became famous listeners—Bernice, grandmotherly and sympathetic; Marva, tough love. Bernice talked endlessly to Kate's mother about it.

"It helps me remember, too," she told Kate. "Marva always liked to remember the old days. We would hear awful stories; women put up with so much." She sighed and looked at Kate. "Such memories."

The shop—Kate hated it, even the mention of it. She had never talked about it to her mother; she couldn't. When she was eight years old, the shop became a source of searing humiliation. She had rebelled against the long pigtails her mother made her wear in the summer. She took scissors and cut one off, close to the scalp. Her mother caught her before she could slice off the second one.

"So you're doing your own hair now," her mother said fiercely. "Let's see how well you did."

She unraveled the remaining braid, yanking Kate's head with each twist. Then she stood Kate in front of the mirror. "See how adorable you look."

Kate stared at the figure looking back at her, her eyes puffy from crying, her hair lopsided, long strands stretching to her shoulder on one side, haggled, weedy-looking remnants on the other.

"We'll see what the girls at the shop think of it," her mother said. She dragged Kate into the car, Kate sobbing all the way to the shop. She could still hear the sharp jangle of the bell on the shop door as her mother shoved it open.

"Look at my gorgeous daughter," she said, with that short bark of a laugh. The hairdressers and the customers in their chairs all turned to peer at Kate standing in the middle of the floor. She tasted the salt from the tears sliding onto her lips as she stood there, alone and mortified, gulping to hold back the vomit rising sourly in her throat.

For a long moment, no one stirred. Then Bernice knelt and squeezed Kate and said, "It's okay, honey. I'll fix it."

And she did. Kate's hair was short that summer, a tomboy look she grew attached to. Her mother mocked her, Little Miss Butch, and laughed. By the end of the summer, Kate's hair had grown out a little. But the shame of the salon never left her. The memory of it would flood back when she least expected it. And she would stuff it inside herself, reliving that lonely moment in the middle of the floor. From that summer, she resolved never again to cry in front of her mother.

There was nothing about the shop to love. Except for Bernice's kindness. And that seemed to have no bottom.

"I'd tell her a dirty joke if I thought she could hear me," Kate said.

Bernice chuckled. "I already tried that the last time I saw her." She touched Kate's hand again. "She didn't laugh for me either."

Pancho's presence began to wear on Kate. She could feel the mood in the house shift from when he had been so reassuring. Weeks now seemed to become longer. She found herself eager for the weekend and some privacy, as it had been with her mother before he came. Kate felt no connection with her mother now, beyond touching when she dressed and washed her. Her mother lived in another world, a world only Pancho could reach. Kate gave up on the stories from their past. What was the point?

One day, as she entered her mother's room, she saw a sight she could not have imagined: tears running down her mother's cheeks. Her mother never cried, not once that Kate could remember.

Pancho was making the bed; he did not look up.

"What's happened to make my mother cry?" Kate asked. "Did you say something to her?" She wiped the tears from her mother's cheeks with a tissue. And as she did, her mother stared directly at her for the first time in weeks. In her eyes,

Kate saw fear, the same fear she had seen that day at the mall so many months ago.

Pancho shrugged but did not stop fluffing the pillows.

"She's frightened. You scared her," Kate said, her anger rising.

"Only I talk. To make her mind work. To think," Pancho said.

"But she's crying. Why would she cry? What did you say to her?"

Pancho did not answer; he still did not look up at her as he pulled the quilt tightly across the bed.

"Tell me. Tell me what you told her." Kate was angry now. "I demand that you tell me."

Pancho stood without moving. The bed separated them. He looked at the bed, then across it to her mother sitting in her chair, gazing out at the birds, oblivious to the conversation around her.

Kate repeated her words. "Tell me what you said to her. This instant."

Pancho finally looked at Kate. She saw guilt on his face.

He told his story.

"When I was fifteen years old, the revolution came to Romania. My father was a government official, a traffic engineer, and no Communist. But it did not matter. The mobs formed in the street and in the great square in Bucharest, close to where we lived. All government officials were threatened and attacked. Men came to our apartment, men with guns and clubs, and drove us out into the street, where my father and other men from the government were jeered at and humiliated.

"There we were dragged to the very front of the crowd, near the great fountain. The crowd was screaming a mighty roar. I held my sister's hand tightly; I could feel her shaking. They put a rope around my father's neck and the other men and laughed and yanked them about. Then they made us look up, and there, above the crowd, were the bodies of the dictator

Ceausescu and his wife, dead, hanging by ropes around their ankles, upside down, the crowd jeering, laughing, throwing bottles and fruit at them. And things bouncing off their bodies, which were swaying in the air, back and forth, back and forth, pounded by all the things hitting them. It was a horrible sight, so awful that I wet myself. I could not stop it."

Pancho paused for a while, not moving, and Kate thought, maybe that's the end. But after a moment, he continued.

"We were forced onto buses and a long ride to the frontier. No food, no water, my sister and I clutching each other in fear. Some of the men and my father begged the border guards to let us cross. Finally, they did, but we became prisoners, not refugees, and they showed us little mercy. For months, we waited to be allowed to go somewhere—Germany, Britain, even the United States. The dampness and cold were too much for my sister, and she soon died of flu, I was told. My father's heart was broken, and soon, he, too, was dead. Only my mother and I survived.

"In time, a miracle happened, and my mother and I were sent to the United States. But the long time we were held in the pen and the death of my sister and my father had destroyed my mother's mind. She had become like a child, clinging to me, whimpering. I was now just sixteen, but I knew it was up to me to make my way in this new world. I worked and went to school sometimes, as I could, and took care of my mother. But she became a greater and greater burden. So dependent, so needful, so draining on me and my strength.

"As I became older—nineteen, twenty—I began to hate her, despise her even. And to wish her dead. My father, my sister, had died. Why could my mother not have followed them? Why could she not see how she was dragging me down?

"These thoughts plagued me, and after a while, I could not let them go, even in sleep. I dreamed about my mother and how she made me a prisoner in my own life. Because she would not die. I would waken, so full of hate and anger that I could not bear it."

He paused again, his shoulders slumping, still not looking at Kate. But he kept talking.

"And I began to tell her—to tell her that it was time for her to leave, that I could no longer carry the burden of her, that my life was being ruined by her, and that she was old and useless. Please die, I said. I repeated it. And I could tell that she heard me. And she understood. I could tell, oh, I could tell. I told myself that she wanted to die. That she would die if she could. I said it again, and again, and again. And soon she was dead."

Pancho stopped. Finally, he looked directly at Kate. "My words killed her."

The story had ended. As Kate listened, the shock of it grew inside her.

"My God, did you really say that to my mother, that story?" she asked when her voice came back to her.

Pancho nodded slowly. "She is losing all her thoughts now, and they will not return. It is my only wish to make her happy. But I can no longer make her laugh." Weariness replaced the guilt on his face. "I must tell her stronger things. Hard things. Things that can reach deeper. To keep her mind going. Where it is still alive." He paused. "Anger, hatred she can still feel. And fear."

He paused again. Kate waited, speechless.

After a while, he said, "With my mother, I learned how powerful hate is. And anger. They drive your mind and your soul like nothing else. Even love."

He sighed and reached up to rub the back of his neck.

"Is it not better for your mother to know these things, these horrible things, than to understand nothing at all?" He looked at her mother, staring out the window. "I know it makes her aware of her own dying. And she is afraid. But isn't fear better than emptiness?"

The question stirred Kate from her silence.

"No. No, I don't want her to hear such things." Kate's

anger shook her now. "I don't care what you think is best. Never say such things to her again."

She realized a threshold had been crossed. She could no longer wait.

Pancho nodded and resumed making the bed. As Kate walked from the room, he said to her back, "I loved my mother. So much. So much."

At least it's calm, Kate thought when she first entered the nursing home. Bernice drove them. Her mother came quietly, cooperating, as though her will to resist had finally faded. During the day, the nurses sat her in a chair in her room, music playing over the intercom. There are no birds here, Kate thought. Only the consoling prattle of the nursing staff. And nothing to terrify her.

Sometimes, as she sat while her mother drifted wherever the remnants of her mind had taken her, Kate thought about Pancho. He had wanted to stay on; he begged her. "I will go to your mother and take care of her at the nursing home. Speak only happy things," he pleaded. "And keep the house for you, as I do now. I can do it."

Kate thought about how he could pierce through the vacuum and reach into her mother's dwindling awareness. But she said no. And Pancho disappeared with Kate's blessing.

Sometimes, she worried that perhaps she had been wrong to change things. She talked to Bernice and told her about Pancho's story and his reason for telling it.

"Maybe he was right," Kate said. "Maybe any emotion, even fear or anger, is better than nothing but emptiness."

Bernice looked worried, then sad. "No." She shook her head. "Nothing troubles her now. Her mind is quiet. She should be allowed to slip away in peace."

So, doubt would take over once again in Kate's mind, and she would feel nothing at all.

Her mother stopped eating. The nurses could feed her, but it became harder. The doctors said it would take extreme measures to keep her alive. Kate refused. Her body's living, but she's gone, Kate believed. She knows she is dying, Kate told herself; she is only waiting for the right moment. Then she realized she wanted to believe that. She thought of Pancho's mother. Had she, in the end, wanted to go? Had she heard what her son said to her and simply given in?

Her mother stayed in bed now, staring at the ceiling. Kate sat, her hand on her mother's arm, feeling the bones inside the dwindling flesh as if her life was being peeled away layer by layer. And as she sat there, she knew she needed to speak to her mother one last time.

She began a story she had never told before—that she had never wanted to tell.

"Do you remember the time we went to the beach in Mobile when I was a girl?" she began. "It was so hot, hot even by what we expected from the Gulf. I had just turned thirteen, and we both had new bathing suits. Let's show them off, you said, and I remember your laugh. I was awkward, so shy about my body, afraid—ashamed—to look at myself in the mirror naked. I was flattered that you wanted me to come with you to the beach. You were so beautiful; men were sucked in by you. You used to laugh, 'Not bad for an old broad,' you'd say. We sat on the beach, you combed your hair, then mine. We giggled about the fat people, and I was embarrassed when you pointed at them. 'Don't do that,' I said, reaching to cover your hand. You just laughed. 'Fat people deserve to be laughed at,' you said. 'They shouldn't let themselves go like that.'

"You sat with your chin resting on your knees, looking out across the bay. I remember the sunlight on it, oh God, so hot. We huddled in the shadow under our beach umbrella. You sat that way for a long time, unmoving. You were so still that I thought you had dozed off. Then you bounced your chin lightly on your knee once or twice and said, 'We are nothing alike, you and me. Nothing at all.' You hugged your knees more tightly—I remember that so distinctly. 'I don't know who you are like. But it isn't me.'

"That was all, those few words. But they pierced me, slicing into me deeply. I panicked. If I was not like you, who was I like? I couldn't imagine anything else. 'Nothing alike,' you said. Nothing. Maybe that was it: I was nothing. I would never be anything. And fear came up inside me. A fear that has never gone away."

Kate stopped; the words no longer came. She had been looking toward the window absently as she spoke. It came back to her so clearly, that awful day.

"At that moment, I hated you." She couldn't look at her mother. "I've never stopped hating you."

Kate sat for a while without moving, feeling the silence in the room. When she looked down, she saw that her mother's eyes were closed. Was she still breathing? Kate touched her mother's arm, then her cheek. Cold. She realized that while she was talking, her mother had slipped away.

Kate stood and walked to the window. Above the neighboring building, she saw only a gray, uncertain sky. Her mother might have heard none of what she said, nothing at all.

THE GUN RACK

Old Jessup wanted his newspaper close to the front door, and Bradley had figured out a way to do it without stopping his bicycle. He would head up the rutted driveway, loop around the turning circle worn into the hard-packed dirt, and pedal back close to the porch of the cabin, tossing the paper next to the door as he rode by.

Today, as he approached up the drive, he saw Willard's pickup truck parked in the circle—Willard, old man Jessup's son, who came and went unpredictably and stayed in the shack by the garage when he was around. The truck sat slightly cockeyed; Bradley would have to slow down to maneuver by it. When he did, he noticed something against the shack: an unruly pile of wood, old boards, gray from weathering in the sun. The pile had clearly lain there for a long time, which surprised him. He had ridden past this point dozens of times without seeing it. Now it jumped out at him, like the dog next door lunging from the bushes.

Today, Bradley didn't need to throw the paper on the porch. The old man was sitting there in his rocker, dozing. They had become friends, and sometimes Bradley would stop for a while to talk. Old Jessup came from the Oklahoma Panhandle, where Bradley's father grew up before his family fled the Dust Bowl for California. Bradley had a powerful curiosity about his father's boyhood. Sometimes, old Jessup talked about Oklahoma, about growing up on the Plains, where life was hard. Bradley would try to picture his father there, a young version of the man in the photographs his mother kept on her dresser.

Talking about Oklahoma made Bradley feel peaceful and calmer somehow, and he liked old Jessup for it. His mother was from Missouri. She called it "back there" and never talked about it. She knew nothing about Oklahoma. Bradley was grateful for what he learned from old Jessup. His father couldn't have told him. He had never known his father, he explained to the old man.

Old Jessup nodded as though to say, Go on.

So Bradley said, "He died in the war. At Iwo Jima."

The old man nodded again. The nod seemed to make it all right that Bradley told him: that the old man now knew about the empty space inside that Bradley could not fill.

Then old Jessup spoke. "The Japs killed my oldest boy." He sat, not speaking for a while. "Roger, that was his name. But we called him Buster." He chuckled and repeated, "Buster."

He fell silent in his chair, rocking slightly, his eyes closed. Bradley waited for a while in case there was more to tell. But the old man had said nothing else. Bradley left quietly, not wanting to disturb him.

Today, Bradley stopped his bike and got off.

"Hello," he said.

"Hello back."

The old man did not open his eyes. Bradley walked across the porch and extended the newspaper in his hand.

"Here's your paper," Bradley said.

Finally, old man Jessup opened one eye and looked at Bradley. He said nothing but took the paper. He closed his eye.

"That pile of wood by the shack," Bradley said. "Could I take a couple of pieces?"

The old man looked at Bradley. "What wood pile?" His eyes sat deep in his face, like a boar's, sunk into his fleshy cheeks.

"By the shack. It just looks like waste wood."

At that, old Jessup sat straighter in his chair. "There ain't no such thing as waste wood," he said. "Wood's always good for somethin'."

"I just meant it doesn't look like you need it. I could use some."

Mr. Jessup rocked a little; the comment seemed to need deep consideration.

"Fer what?"

"At school. I'm making a gun rack in woodshop."

It sounded ridiculous when he said it; he didn't have a gun. But the shop teacher included a gun rack on the list of possible projects, and it looked pretty easy to build.

"For my room."

Mr. Jessup started to cough. Bradley had seen this happen before. Fits would seize the old man for long moments. His red face turned purple as he hacked, and fluid rattled in his throat. Talking seemed to bring it on. "Gassed in the trenches," he gasped once as Bradley watched, startled by the violence of the coughing. "In the Big War." Bradley knew he meant the First World War; he had been too old for the Second.

The old man's cough finally calmed down.

"You got guns, boy?" The spasm had reduced old Jessup's voice to a hoarse whisper.

Bradley yearned for a gun. It seemed like every kid he knew had at least a twenty-two. His friend Jay had a four-ten shotgun. Bradley pressed his mother on it, provoking an argument. All his friends had guns, he said. His mother stood firm; she had gotten rid of his father's guns after he died. Guns have murdered enough people, she said, like your father. But that was in the war, Bradley protested. His mother laughed, a mocking sound. "They kill each other around here, too," she said. He wanted to say, "My father would have said okay."

But his nerve failed him. That ended the discussion, but the ache never went away. He was older now and more responsible. His mother liked his initiative in doing the paper route. She might change her mind if he asked again. It seemed possible. But he didn't know how to bring the subject up. Maybe building a gun rack would help break the ice.

"My mom says I can get a twenty-two when I'm sixteen," he lied to old Jessup. "Next year." Two years, really, he said to himself. The old man didn't need to know that. The two lies bothered him a little. But he felt the need keenly.

"I want to build the gun rack now. To be ready."

Old Jessup wheezed for a while. He looked down at the empty coffee can he used as a spittoon but did not spit into it. He looked back at Bradley.

"So what's stopping yuh?"

Bradley stood there, uncertain what the old man meant. The response was vague. Had Mr. Jessup said yes to taking the wood or not? It was one of those ambiguous responses adults used to deflect questions. His mother did it a lot. "We'll see"— that was her most discouraging answer when he asked for something. It meant waiting until the desire wilted, stalling to make the question go away.

The stack of wood pulled him; he would have to decide for himself.

Bradley walked down the porch stairs and headed toward the shack, past Willard's pickup. The wood pile sat on the sunny side of the shack, the sun glinting on the surfaces of the boards. They had been thrown haphazardly into a pile, so Bradley studied them to figure out how to move the pieces. He approached it cautiously: a snake might have crawled underneath. He kept his muscles tense, ready to jump back as he gingerly handled the boards. But there were only some small snails sticking to the damper boards deeper in the pile. Bradley shifted the wood until he found four short planks, all about the same size, all relatively smooth and unmarked. Just what he needed, he thought, and pulled them loose.

"What the hell do you think yer doin'?"

The voice startled Bradley; he turned and saw Willard standing there. Willard's shirtsleeves had been cut off at the shoulder. A dark, serpentine tattoo twisted up his right arm. Bradley stared at it. Even at a distance, he could smell whiskey on Willard's breath.

"Mr. Jessup said I could have some boards," he said. His voice broke a little; he tried to control it. "I need it for school."

Willard looked toward the porch where the old man sat watching.

"It don't belong to him," Willard said. "It's mine." He glared at Bradley, his eyes bloodshot from the whiskey.

The boards in Bradley's hands grew heavy; he wished he could drop them and leave. But his muscles failed him, and he just stood.

"It ain't for giveaway," Willard said. A wad of tobacco bulged in his cheek. "But I'll sell you some. For them boards you got two dollars. And that's a good deal."

Bradley searched his brain desperately for a way out. Maybe he should just run, get on his bike, and speed away. But still, his strength failed him; he stayed rooted in place. He looked back to the porch, at Mr. Jessup sitting there, and silently begged him for help. Willard slouched, sucking the tobacco in his cheek, waiting.

"Let the boy be." Old Jessup's croaking voice rumbled across the yard. "I told him okay." He peered fiercely at Willard. Bradley felt the intensity even though it was not directed at him. Then, the old man's eyes shifted to Bradley, and the ferocity faded.

"Take yer boards and git, boy," the old man said.

Bradley hefted the boards, getting a better grip, without looking at Willard. He hurried toward his bike, trying not to stumble on the uneven ground.

"You still owe me two bucks," he heard Willard saying

behind him. "Don't you fergit."

Bradley got to his bike, breathing hard. He shoved the boards into the paper delivery bag hanging on the back and rode away as fast as he could toward Mr. Foster's house.

Mr. Foster lived in the house beyond the empty Zerstell home. Bradley pedaled toward it, the boards in his delivery bag clicking against each other. Mr. Foster often waited by his gate so he could talk about politics and the upcoming presidential election. He was a Democrat and supported Adlai Stevenson. "The second time around now," he said. He thought Eisenhower was a fool and Nixon a crook.

Years before, Mr. Foster had taught Bradley's father in high school: algebra and chemistry. He took the local Boy Scout troop on camping trips and hunting for doves and quail. Your daddy was a good student, Mr. Foster told Bradley. And good with a gun. You are a lot like him. Bradley tried to imagine what being like his father meant. Nothing came to him but a blurry image, like an old photograph of himself.

"What are the boards for?" Mr. Foster asked as he took his paper from Bradley.

"A gun rack," Bradley said. "I've got to build something in shop."

"A gun rack. For your daddy's guns?"

"No. My mom got rid of them. We don't have any guns."

Mr. Foster considered this, pausing as though deciding whether to go on.

"What do you need a gun rack for?"

"I thought maybe if I made it, my mother would let me get a gun." As soon as he said it, Bradley sensed the futility of the idea. "Just a twenty-two." The skepticism spread through him, but he kept at it. "She doesn't like guns. But I'm saving my paper route money to get one. In case she changes her mind."

Mr. Foster said nothing for a while. His old poodle dog, Candy, sniffed at Bradley through the fence.

"Well, maybe she's worried you'd get hurt," Mr. Foster

said. Again, he paused. Candy wagged her long tail. Mr. Foster didn't have the heart to bob it when she was a puppy. Now it gets full of burrs, he complained.

"I'd be happy to take you out for some shooting. To ease her mind," Mr. Foster said finally. "Your daddy used to go with me when he was your age, you know." He looked at Bradley for a while, and Bradley imagined him recalling the eager, towheaded boy from the Oklahoma Panhandle.

"I've got a twenty-two and a shotgun I don't use much," Mr. Foster went on. "You could shoot them if your mother said okay." He paused again. "I could ask her for you."

Bradley thought about this. A new wrinkle: Mr. Foster asking his mother. Bradley's mother liked Mr. Foster. The only man in town with any brains, she said. Maybe it would lower her resistance to letting him have a gun. The idea played around in Bradley's head. For a moment, it felt as though it might work. But the thought died: his mother would be angry that someone else came into the discussion, even Mr. Foster. Meddling, she might call it. She would become even more stubborn.

"Naw. But thanks anyway," Bradley said as he straightened up to leave.

"Keep it in mind. I'll help if you want," Mr. Foster called after him.

A few weeks later, as he started up Mr. Jessup's driveway, Bradley heard Willard's pickup turning in behind him. He moved out of the way fast; the track was too narrow for him to stay on as the truck passed. He could hear the gears grinding toward him as he wobbled off onto the grass, struggling to keep the bike steady. He fell over, and papers spilled from the bag. Willard rattled by. Through the back window, Bradley could see him holding up two fingers.

By the time he reached the old man's cabin, Willard had

already disappeared into the shack. Bradley rode straight for the porch, not circling Willard's truck in his usual way. Old man Jessup was sunning himself in his creaky rocker. He watched Bradley walk up the steps and said nothing as he reached for his paper. Bradley stood for a moment, not moving. Willard being so close worried him a little. But he had been thinking about Oklahoma, and the urge to hear about it was strong. Maybe he could get old Jessup to talk about it. But he couldn't think of a way to do it. Sometimes, the old man spoke without prompting. Maybe he would now.

Bradley waited while Mr. Jessup studied the newspaper. He lingered long enough that the old man finally motioned toward the bench sitting against the wall and said, "Why don't-cha siddown. Take a weight off."

Bradley backed up until he felt the bench behind him. Together, they sat, not speaking, watching an afternoon shadow creep across the front of the shack. As they sat there, the door opened, and Willard stepped out. He glanced at them sitting on the porch but looked away without speaking. At the door of his truck, he waved his arm and wiggled two fingers. Then he climbed inside, and the truck moved off, stirring up the dust.

Old Jessup gave Bradley a puzzled look. "How about that? I ain't never seen Willard wave to no one."

"I think he meant me," Bradley said. "He says I owe him two dollars for the wood I took."

Old Jessup snorted. "Two dollars, my ass. Them boards ain't worth two dollars. Anyways, that wood's on my property." The subject roused him; he sat forward. "He don't even live here. Just holes up in that shack when his old woman kicks him out. He don't help much. Groceries sometimes. That's about it."

He leaned down to pick up the coffee can and let loose a long dollop of amber juice into it. "He thinks I got stuff—stuff he wants. Money. Gold things, maybe. That's the only reason he hangs around." He grunted. "What would I be doin' with gold?" He stayed silent for a while, then went on. "He pokes around inside when he thinks I ain't lookin'."

The speech exhausted him, and he collapsed back into the chair. "He jest wants me gone so's he can have it." His voice gurgled slightly now; he closed his eyes. "Well, I ain't dead yet. And I ain't plannin' to be any time soon."

They sat quietly again and watched the shadow on the shack. Bradley needed to get moving, but still, he stayed. He thought about what might be inside the house. The idea that it held something valuable seemed ridiculous. Mr. Jessup didn't seem to have much of anything, certainly nothing worth stealing.

"How is them boards anyway?"

The question caught Bradley by surprise; the old man was looking at him.

"Okay. My gun rack came out real good."

Mr. King, the woodshop teacher, liked the boards. "They'll give it a rustic look," he told Bradley. He had shown Bradley how to cut the boards to size and make the notches for the guns to rest on. When Bradley finished putting it together, Mr. King handed him a small can, sticky with varnish on the outside. "This'll finish it off real nice. Like an antique," he said.

"I got an A for it," Bradley said.

"Well, damn that anyway. That's a good thing." Mr. Jessup rocked a little, fully awake now and feisty. Talking about Willard had stirred him up.

Bradley stood; now, he had to hurry. He had stayed longer than planned. People might gripe about getting their papers late.

"Maybe I'll see it sometime," the old man said.

"I don't know. Maybe," Bradley answered as he rode off.

Bradley left the gun rack in the shop at school. When Mr. King asked why he hadn't taken it home, Bradley said it was a surprise for his mother's birthday, some weeks off. Mr. King put it on a shelf where anyone could see it. Every day, Bradley looked at it and wondered how to take it home. Sooner or later, he would have to take it there; he knew that. Maybe his mother would think it was a good job, and it would soften her up about a gun. But it was hard to convince himself. If he surprised her with it, she might just flare and dig in her heels. He waited: it was the safest course.

One day, Mr. Foster stood by his gate, his fingers drumming on the fence railing. He seemed anxious to talk, like he was worried about something.

"I ran into your mother at the grocery store," Mr. Foster said as soon as Bradley stopped his bicycle. "I mentioned that you were interested in doing some shooting. And that I would be glad to take you out to do it. No problem."

Bradley felt his stomach tighten. He wasn't sure it was a good idea to ask his mother, especially in a public place. He knew she would feel awkward about it. But maybe Mr. Foster knew best.

"She didn't say anything," Mr. Foster said. "I hope I did the right thing."

Bradley said nothing as he left to finish delivering the papers. When he came into the yard after completing his route, he saw his mother waiting for him by the back door.

"Hi," he said. He dropped the empty delivery bag on the porch floor.

"Have you been talking to Ben Foster?"

"Sure, we talk a lot. About the election. All that."

She dismissed this with a wave.

"You know I don't mean that. What else did you talk to him about?"

"I had some old boards in my bag. He asked me about them."

"What boards? Why would you have boards?"

"I needed some for woodshop. At school. Mr. Jessup let me have some from his wood pile."

She studied him silently.

"For my project," he said. "We have to have a project."

"And what is your project?"

Bradley squirmed; he could think of no other way to stall.

"A gun rack," he said weakly.

His mother gave him a look he recognized, a look that said, Have you lost your mind?

"A gun rack. Why in the world would you build a gun rack?"

In the universe of possible reasons, none seemed adequate in Bradley's mind. The truth was as good as anything else.

"I thought if I built it. And you liked it. We might get a gun for it. Just a twenty-two."

Should he add something else, something to support the idea? Nothing came to him. He could say only, "Sometime, maybe."

His mother's face told him nothing.

"I ran into Ben in the market," she said. "He said the two of you talked about guns. Shooting. He would take you if I said okay. You could use his guns."

"I didn't ask him to. He offered."

His mother stood, looking at him. Bradley could not sense where the discussion had wound up. She continued to look at him for a while.

"You know I don't want guns in the house," she said finally. "I told you that."

He had learned to hide his disappointment when she said no.

"Okay," he said and walked by her into his room.

The gun rack shook on the handlebars as Bradley rode up the driveway to old Jessup's cabin. It was hard to keep a grip on. He held it awkwardly, afraid it would fall and break on the ground. On Sunday, he had no papers to deliver, so the old man would not expect to see him. Mr. Jessup was sitting there, wearing a shapeless sweater, even in the warm sun. Willard's pickup was not around.

"What's that you got there?" Mr. Jessup said as Bradley mounted the stairs carrying the gun rack. If Bradley's arrival surprised him, he didn't show it.

"The gun rack. You wanted to see it."

"Well, damn me. I didn't mean for yuh to lug it here on your bike."

The old man took the gun rack and examined it, turning it around and looking at it from several angles. He wheezed and gurgled; the effort seemed to bring it on.

"That's real good. Real nice. You done a good job with them old boards." He coughed and grinned. Bradley had never seen him do that before. "I'll bet your mama's real proud."

"Sure," Bradley replied.

His mother had not seen it; he had never taken it home. What's the point? he thought. It weighed on him, sitting on display in the school shop. One day, passing it, the thought occurred to him: why not give it to old man Jessup? It was made from his boards, after all. The more he thought about the idea, the more logical it seemed. His mother's mind hadn't changed. The gun rack would only remind her that he wanted a gun—and remind him that the answer would be no. He wanted relief from the drag of it, the burden it imposed on his hopes.

"I thought you might use it. Put your guns on it," Bradley said.

Maybe he doesn't have guns, Bradley thought. The idea hadn't occurred to him before.

Old Jessup chuckled. "We had guns back in Oklahoma. My brother and me used to shoot critters. Rabbits. Squirrels. Once, I even shot a skunk. We had to clear out fast when it let loose." He laughed again, the gurgle rolling with it. He continued to look at the gun rack in his hands, rocking a little now. He shook his head. "There's good shootin' in Oklahoma.

When I was a boy, we'd hunt all day sometimes. Back then." For a while, he sat, remembering. "But later, the dirt started blowin'. Big dirt storms. They blew all that away. Blew everything away." He looked past Bradley into the yard.

So my father must have learned to hunt there, Bradley thought. He had been fourteen, Bradley's age, when his family came to California. By then, he probably knew how to shoot. It would make sense for a farm boy.

"So why ain't you gonna put your own gun on it?" the old man asked.

"I don't want one anymore," Bradley replied. Another lie. The gun rack seemed to bring them out. "I just built it because it looked easy."

The old man nodded. "Well, I ain't got guns no more neither. Too old. But I'm gonna hang it on the wall anyway. Jest to look at it."

His red eyes were friendly, but he didn't say "thank you." Bradley hadn't expected him to, so he didn't miss it. He waited. Maybe the old man would say more about Oklahoma. Once, he had talked about harvesting wheat across the vast, open plains, hurrying to stay ahead of the huge storms that could wipe out an entire crop in minutes. In those days, farmers drove ten-horse teams, pulling huge reapers through the golden fields, praying for good weather.

"I was twelve when I learned how to handle them horses," the old man had said, his eyes moist in recollection. But today, he didn't speak of Oklahoma or anything at all. He just sat, fingering the gun rack in his lap and musing in his old-man way.

They heard a vehicle approaching in the driveway and looked up to watch for it. Willard's truck appeared, bouncing on the hard-packed surface, the gears groaning. He stopped next to the porch and revved the engine once, then twice. Bradley could see scratches on the side of his face like he'd been in a fight or had fallen and hit his head on the ground.

Close up, Willard never looked you in the eye, but now he was far enough off to stare at the two figures on the porch without looking away. The engine idled, and he kicked up the gas every now and then as though making a point.

"What's that shit you're holdin'?" he asked.

Old man Jessup pulled the gun rack tighter against himself.

"Somethin' the boy made. He just give it to me."

Willard said nothing but kept staring at the old man. Then his gaze shifted to Bradley, and Bradley winced at the anger in Willard's face. Thank God he hadn't encountered Willard in the yard. It felt better sitting on the porch with Mr. Jessup. But the sense of safety was slight: the old man wouldn't be much protection if Willard erupted.

Willard kept revving the engine, then said, "Them boards. Bullshit."

He slipped the clutch; the truck shot ahead. He looped around the circle, spraying gravel, and headed out the driveway. For a while, the odor of gasoline lingered as the dust settled.

Mr. Jessup sat holding the gun rack. He had stopped rocking, and Bradley could feel tension settle on them. He could think of nothing to say, so he simply waited on the bench, his hands still by his sides. Finally, the old man got up from the rocking chair, limping a little, holding the gun rack in one hand as he opened the screen door to go inside.

"You jest stay here for a bit."

Bradley stared out across the yard, waiting for Mr. Jessup. The sun-bleached weeds reminded him of the dead flowers he saw in the cemetery when he and his mother visited his father's grave. His mother always brought fresh flowers. In time, they withered and died, too.

Minutes passed as Bradley waited for the old man to return, and he began to shift restlessly on the bench, feeling its hardness. Sitting there so long made him nervous: Willard might return at any moment.

The creaking screen door broke the silence as Mr. Jessup pushed it to come back outside. In one hand, he carried a package about the size and shape of a brick as he limped back to his chair. He wheezed from the exertion and coughed when he sat, not speaking until he caught his breath.

"Come on over here, boy."

The old man lifted the small package, poking it toward Bradley.

"Take it," he said.

Bradley looked at it, hesitating; he couldn't tell what it might be. Then, he reached out and took it. He felt its weight. It wasn't heavy, but it had some heft. Not a brick. Not even wood or glass, he guessed. It was wrapped in plain brown paper, black electrical tape binding it tightly.

"You should take this here. And hide it somewhere's." Old Jessup looked at Bradley intently. "You'd be doin' me a favor. I'll tell you when to bring it back."

He hadn't blinked since he started talking; now he did.

"Keep it to ourselves. Jest you and me. Willard don't need to know."

The package seemed heavier in Bradley's hands.

"What is it?"

"No matter what it is. It's somethin' of mine. Somethin' Willard don't need to know about."

The small package pressed into Bradley's hands, its importance mattering more than its weight to him. For an instant, a desire seized him to drop it on the porch and run. Anything involving Willard scared him. Hiding the package seemed risky. What if Willard found out? What if Willard pressured the old man, and he gave in and said the boy was hiding a package? And Willard came looking for it, maybe even to Bradley's house. He imagined Willard demanding the package, his voice a snarl. His mother would be frightened and angry that Bradley had withheld something from her. The urge to escape swelled in him.

But he didn't run. He stood holding the package, the slickness of the tight electrical tape smooth in his hand. He felt himself teetering on the brink of an unknown, something he could sense but not grasp. The old man just looked at him, saying nothing. For a while, they stayed like that, silent and unmoving.

"Okay," Bradley said.

He walked quickly down the steps, gripping the package in one hand as he grabbed his bike with the other. He pressed the package tightly against his chest so it didn't loosen in his grip as he mounted. Hurry, he said to himself, feeling pressured to escape. He didn't look back as he rode away, straining against the pedals, splashing through the potholes, ignoring the mud spotting his pant legs.

At home, he hid the package behind a stack of old canning jars in the garage. His mother would never look there.

"Where have you been?" his mother asked when he went inside.

"Just riding around. That's all."

Fall brought rain, making the paper route seem longer and the papers heavier. Sometimes, they got wet in the paper delivery bag, and the people at the end of the route were handed soggy masses. No one complained; everyone liked Bradley and understood the problem. It didn't rain a lot anyway. Mostly, it just got colder. Bradley peddled harder to stay warm and finish sooner.

With the colder weather, old man Jessup stayed inside more. Bradley wouldn't see him for days. He would circle at the top of the driveway, throw the paper next to the door, and speed away, grateful that Willard wasn't around. His truck hadn't been there for weeks. Each day when Bradley arrived, the previous day's paper would be gone, and he would toss a new one.

One day, as he circled toward the porch and drew back his arm to throw, he saw the paper from the day before lying there on the porch. He stopped his bike. Maybe old Jessup was away; maybe he had gone somewhere with Willard. Bradley stood for a few moments, straddling his bike. Then he threw the new paper next to the old one.

The next day, both papers sat there, undisturbed. If Willard had taken the old man somewhere, it could be that they hadn't returned yet. No one had told Bradley to suspend the deliveries, but that didn't surprise him. People forgot to stop the paper when they were away all the time. Sometimes, they wouldn't pay for the days they weren't home. Bradley stared at the papers. Mr. Jessup couldn't be around—the old man always picked up the paper. So why not now? No answer came to him. He dismounted, walked up the steps, and placed the paper next to the other two, moving them all closer to the door.

All three papers were still in place the next day. He didn't add a new one. Instead, he rode slowly back down the driveway. Mr. Randolph, old man Jessup's neighbor, was working near the fence separating the two properties, trimming rosebushes, whistling as he clipped the bare branches. Bradley stopped beside him.

"Mr. Jessup hasn't picked up his paper for three days," Bradley said.

Mr. Randolph looked at him, his hand suspended in place.

"Have you seen him?" Mr. Randolph asked.

"No. Not for a while. Days."

"Maybe he's away. With that boy of his."

"I haven't seen Willard for a long time. His truck, or anything."

Mr. Randolph took this in without comment. Finally, he lowered his hand and dropped the clippers into the toolbox at his feet.

"Well, I'll walk over in a bit and knock on his door. See how he is. You can go on."

A half-hour later, Bradley came back along the road after finishing his route. A sheriff's car was parked by the old man's cabin. Bradley rode slowly on, his mind empty, thinking only of covering the three long blocks home.

He didn't see them take Mr. Jessup's corpse away later that day. Mr. Randolph had found old Jessup dead in his chair. A bad heart, Mr. Randolph said to Bradley later. Just gave out on him.

Bradley told the newspaper circulation department to stop sending a paper for Mr. Jessup.

The hidden package haunted him.

He could see it in his mind, its surface shiny from the black tape, waiting behind the canning jars in the garage. Once, he dreamed that his mother had found it and placed it on the kitchen table to confront him when he awoke. Sometimes, panic would sweep through him, and he would check on it to calm himself. It hadn't moved. But who knew what might happen? Willard might still appear, a dark menace haunting Bradley. The image of the package would come to him, surfacing in his mind as he tried to pay attention at school. He would fight it off, knowing it would reappear of its own will.

Sometimes, when his mother was away, he would take the package out and examine it, turning it slowly in his hands and hefting it. What was it anyway? It might be money, bills in a stack. He even took a dollar from his paper route savings and laid it against the package. Sure enough, it seemed to be the same size. He had an impulse to tear open the package and see. No one would know; no one knew he had it. He could rewrap it easily. It would be a lot of money, especially if it was big bills—tens, twenties. But where would old man Jessup have gotten money, especially a lot of it? He seemed to be poor, as far as Bradley could tell. And he had scoffed at Willard for suspecting there was something valuable in the house.

Yet the package was important enough for the old man to want it hidden. How could Bradley find out except by opening it?

But still, he did nothing. It nagged at him, pressing on his conscience, like telling a lie and covering it up. He should show it to his mother; he felt guilty for not having done so. But he couldn't do it. She wouldn't understand about Mr. Jessup or why Bradley had taken the package.

Another idea occurred to him: maybe it belonged to him now just because he had it. Maybe the old man meant for him to keep it all along. By asking Bradley to hide the package, maybe old Jessup was telling him to keep it, giving it to him in the same ambiguous way he let Bradley take the wood. The thought played around in Bradley's mind but wouldn't take hold. There just didn't seem to be a clear answer.

So, he did nothing.

One day, as he stood on the baseball field at school, pounding his mitt and waiting for the batter to swing, the answer finally came: his father would give the package back. His father would never take something that didn't belong to him. No one had ever told Bradley that; he just felt it in his gut. His father would give it to the rightful owner, whoever that was.

The batter swung and missed. Kids yelled, and Bradley ran toward the team's bench, considering this new idea.

With old man Jessup dead, the package must belong to Willard.

Still, no matter how hard he tried, Bradley couldn't give in to the idea of taking the package to Willard. At night, he agonized in bed, twisting in the covers. The thought of facing Willard, with the tattoo snaking up his arm and whiskey on his breath, terrified Bradley. Maybe he could sneak up to the cabin at night and just leave it on the porch. Or mail it to him.

One day, as he rode past the long driveway to the cabin

where he no longer left a paper for old Jessup, he realized that the old man's death had changed everything. He stopped his bike and stood as the new idea came to him: it wasn't only about the mysterious package anymore.

It was also about the gun rack.

He looked up the driveway at Willard's pickup sitting there. Willard must have moved into the cabin now that old Jessup was gone. Bradley looked at the other houses along the road, at Mr. Randolph's well-groomed field, where his pet donkey Belle once cropped the grass and dozed in the shade of an oak tree. Belle died last year, curled in the corner of the yard. Mr. Randolph didn't replace her.

Most of the houses along the road were smaller and drabber than Mr. Randolph's, like the Zerstell's empty house. No one here is rich, Bradley thought, but they all have things they value. Just as old Jessup valued whatever was in the tightly wrapped package. Bradley thought about the gun rack. He realized it was valuable, too. Valuable to him.

Bradley looked again at where Willard's truck sat skewed in the driveway, as it had that day Willard confronted him about the wood. Today, sunshine poured hotly down from the relentless blue sky, and Bradley could feel sweat inching down his sides from his armpits. On a day like this, old Jessup would have been sitting in the shade of his porch, hoping for a breeze that never came. Bradley wondered if Willard now sat on the porch, in the old rocker that creaked with every movement.

Bradley thought about Willard in the old man's house, the gun rack somewhere inside. Maybe Willard was searching for things like the old man said. Maybe he was looking for the small, brick-like package that old Jessup wanted to keep hidden. Maybe he would even figure out that Bradley had it and come for it.

Things needed to be sorted out.

The package for the gun rack. A fair exchange. It made sense.

*

Bradley rode one-handed up the bumpy driveway, holding the package in his left hand, bracing it against his chest. Willard's pickup truck sat parked in the circle. Bradley's stomach tightened. His confidence wavered: maybe he should just leave the package on the porch and sneak away. Let Willard figure it out. But the desire to retrieve the gun rack surged inside him again, and he kept moving, gripping the package tightly.

At the porch, he dismounted and walked up the steps toward the door. The wood planks didn't creak as he walked across them—that relieved him. He knocked softly on the doorframe, and the screen door rattled slightly. Nothing happened inside, no sound, no movement. He tried again, this time knocking louder. Suddenly, he hoped to get no response so he could just leave the package inside the screen door. Maybe Willard knew it was him and wouldn't open the door. Maybe he was dead.

Then, the inside door opened. Willard swayed there, his bleary eyes staring at Bradley through the screen. He stood shirtless, his feet bare on the wood floor. Bradley could tell he was drunk.

"The hell do you want?" Willard said, gripping the doorframe.

Bradley took a step back.

"I brought this package. Mr. Jessup told me to hang on to it. Until he said to bring it back." His dry mouth loosened a little as he spoke. "He never said what to do with it. But with him dead, I figured it must be yours."

He didn't say that the old man wanted to hide it from Willard. That fact no longer mattered.

Willard stared at the package in Bradley's hand.

"How come you didn't jest keep it?"

"It isn't mine to keep."

Willard swayed slightly in the door.

"What's in it?"

"I don't know."

Willard looked at Bradley, trying to focus.

"Didn't yuh even open it?"

"No."

"Why not? You little shit. You sure stuck your nose in my business before."

He must mean the boards, Bradley thought. Maybe he won't give me the gun rack.

"I guess Mr. Jessup would have told me if he wanted me to know what was in it. Anyway, I'm just bringing it back."

Bradley felt more secure now. Being drunk made Willard seem weaker.

"And I want the gun rack. I just loaned it to Mr. Jessup. So he could look at it."

Maybe Willard had a gun and was using the gun rack, Bradley thought as he spoke. He might not give it up.

"So I want it. It's mine."

Willard said nothing as he stared at Bradley. Then he opened the screen door a crack and held out his hand.

"Gimme it."

Bradley handed Willard the package. Willard grabbed it and turned away inside. Bradley stood there. Through the open door, he could hear Willard rustling around. He couldn't make out what was happening, so he just waited, on edge, uncertain of what to do.

Willard appeared at the screen door; in his hand was the gun rack. Bradley felt a surge of relief. Willard staggered as he moved through the door, steadying himself against the wall. He stood for a moment, swaying slightly, his eyes not focused anywhere.

Then, without warning, he raised the gun rack and smashed it against the porch railing. The wood splintered; pieces flew in every direction. Still holding a notched board in his hand, Willard lifted his knee shakily and broke the board across it.

He threw the pieces into the yard. The other notched board had fallen to the porch, the wood strips of the back still nailed to it. Willard stooped to pick it up and ripped off the strips one by one, throwing them into the yard. Another large piece lay under his foot. Willard reached down, nearly falling, grabbed it, and began swinging it wildly. It flew from his hand as he fell back. Only the wall stopped him from collapsing.

Bradley flinched as the board sailed past him. But his reflexes held, and he stood his ground. His body knew instinctively that the board wasn't aimed at him. Something inside him said, "Don't be afraid. This is not about you." He watched calmly as the board twisted through the air and slammed into his bike, knocking it to the ground.

He realized Willard no longer frightened him.

"So now you got it," Willard said, breathing hard. "Go fuck yourself."

He turned, lurching, yanked open the screen door, and went inside. The porch shook when he slammed the inside door.

Bradley studied the scattered pieces of the gun rack. It was ruined beyond repair—he could see that. Now, it amounted to nothing. But he knew what it had been. And he would remember it. He built it; he gave it to old Jessup; now it was gone. Things begin, exist, and finally end. Even people. His father. Buster. Old Jessup.

He leaned over to pick up the bike and swung his leg over it without looking again at the shattered wood on the ground.

He peddled slowly, avoiding the potholes and the ruts, feeling no urge to hurry. Another thought came to him: maybe the boards had belonged to Willard, as he claimed. Maybe the old man gave them to Bradley just to provoke Willard. It could have happened that way: they were piled by Willard's shack.

Bradley considered this as he rode slowly along, feeling the rough pavement under the bike.

Everything, all possibilities, lay there, waiting for him to put them together.

THE ELEPHANT TRAIN

On the day Tommy and Virginia died, Guy had already decided to quit his job. The idea had been with him for a while. Something would trigger it, and it would bounce around his brain like a pinball. Today, as he raised his head from the book in his lap, he knew without looking around that the other passengers had gone. He would be alone to the end of the streetcar line, where he would get off and walk the final three blocks to the zoo. Through the window, he watched the fog—the wet, sticky kind this close to the ocean. The streetcar glided through it like a ship at sea. It wouldn't burn off until noon or so.

Or it could be Donlon's failure at the dartboard last night. They had taken on two Scottish merchant seamen who had heard about Haight Ashbury and came into the bar looking for action. Donlon swayed as he studied the dartboard, the dart poised in his hand. He could have won it with any of his three darts. But didn't. Too drunk; anyone could tell. When he could see the board clearly, Donlon had a sharp eye for the kill. Now, Guy had to try. Three chances to double out; no wiggle room. I'm going to blow it, Guy knew in his heart when he stepped up to the line. And he did. The Scots were on the verge of winning now. Henny, the shorter one, a fireplug with biceps like burls on a chestnut tree, flicked his wrist, and the dart sank into the double six. Guy and Donlon were down another pitcher of beer.

"These guys are good," Donlon whispered as he poured himself another glass. He belched. His breath had a sour beer smell, recycled from his gut. He and Guy had been in the bar for an hour before the two Scots walked in. Donlon explained Haight Ashbury to them as he played. "Forget that counter-culture crap." The dart flew. *Thwack!* "That's television news bullshit. It's really about smoking weed." *Thwack!* "And fucking teenage girls from Cornbread Iowa, who got here on a Greyhound bus and think it's a big deal." Horny old men get off on it, he explained. *Thwack!*

Donlon. His Irish charm carried a whiff of menace, like slapping you on the back with one hand and picking your pocket with the other. Guy felt it when they first met. Donlon's real world was North Beach before the hippies and the Summer of Love across town in the Haight. People were serious about writing and poetry, Donlon explained to Guy. Donlon had a reputation around North Beach, not well known exactly, but people knew him. Berty Apple, the poet laureate of Columbus Avenue, praised Donlon's poems after Donlon read several at a coffee house on Broadway. That's good shit, the Great Man said. At least, that's how Donlon told the story. He told it whenever he could. He didn't write poetry anymore, but he talked about starting up again.

As Guy walked through the zoo gate, he finalized the decision to quit. He had been accepted to graduate school at Berkeley and would have left the zoo at the end of the summer anyway. Now, he was moving things up a few months. He could tell Frances wasn't keen on leaving the Haight, moving across the bay. They would have to work it out.

Warren arrived fifteen minutes after Guy got to the zoo,

ten minutes late and in a foul mood. "We're down a driver," he said as he fiddled with the lock. "I'm trying to get someone to come in early." Guy decided to wait until the end of his shift to tell Warren he was quitting. Why stir things up right now?

Four zoo visitors, a family, had already lined up to buy tickets for the tour train. Everyone called it the Elephant Train because the tractor pulling the cars was covered by a huge paper-and-plaster elephant head. Guy and the other drivers would weave the trains through the zoo, past the animal cages and grottoes, as they delivered monologues to entertain the customers. The drivers were supposed to talk about the animals, but mostly, they made up comedy routines, pushing the edge and making gags.

Guy liked the zoo early in the morning. The animals were quiet; the big cats hadn't been released from their cages into the grottoes yet. The monkeys on Monkey Island hadn't started chattering. Early singers in the birdhouse had started, but the squawking cacophony of morning hadn't begun yet. Guy liked the birds. They gave the illusion of being free as they flitted from branch to branch. Trapped in a world of wire and windows, but it seemed sort of like freedom to Guy, just like the real world.

Last night, the Scots had wanted another game. Donlon said sure before Guy could stop him. They were down two pitchers already. Both pitchers stood on the bar, one of them almost empty after everyone filled their glasses. Guy's cash had fallen to the crisis level. He couldn't afford his share of another loss. He wondered if Donlon could. It didn't matter. Being broke wouldn't have stopped Donlon from playing on, figuring that it would get paid for somehow.

A loan from Frances, perched on a barstool watching the action, was Guy's only hope. A ten-dollar bill dangled from her hand as he walked over.

"I assume you need this," she said before he asked.

"Thanks. I'll pay you back."

Frances said nothing, nodding.

"Donlon sucked us into this," Guy explained.

"What else is new," Frances said without looking at him.

"Maybe we'll win."

She snorted.

The game took less time than the first two. Guy got two turns before the Scots blasted them away with triple scores, going out on a double nineteen at the first opportunity. A third pitcher stood on the bar; Guy had to cover Donlon's share. Guy stuck the change in his pocket. When he looked around, he realized Frances had left.

Frances had balled herself into a cocoon, the blanket pulled tightly under her chin, when Guy came into the bedroom. He took off his clothes and crawled in behind her, feeling the cool sheet on his side of the bed. She might be asleep; then again, she might be faking just to make a point. He reached his arm over her, but she didn't move. Did it make more sense not to disturb her or to talk and just get it out in the open? It would come out anyway.

"I didn't see you leave," he whispered.

She wiggled a little within the tightly wrapped blanket. Like a chrysalis trying to hatch, Guy thought.

"I didn't mean for you to," she said, her voice muffled through the blanket.

Guy's hand searched under the blanket, trying to find her soft spot. She stiffened and pushed it away.

"Thanks again for the loan," Guy said.

She didn't respond. For a long moment, Guy thought she might have fallen asleep. Then: "Did he pay his half?" The question filtered out through the blanket.

Guy considered his response. Maybe he should lie and say yes. But he knew she'd catch him; he felt too guilty to be convincing.

"He couldn't help it. He was broke. It's almost his payday. He'll pay me back."

Finally, she rolled over and looked at him. In the dark, he couldn't read her expression clearly. "It's always 'almost payday' with Donlon," she said. "When are you going to figure that out?"

He wanted to reach over her again, pull her to him, lose himself in her. He reached up and touched her cheek. She took his hand away.

"It's just Donlon," he said. "That's the way he is. You should know that better than I do." Instantly, he regretted saying it. They avoided discussing her time with Donlon before she came over to Guy. It helped keep the tension down. She had been with Donlon longer than Guy had known either of them. She knew Donlon's faults; both of them did.

Frances had turned back toward the wall, pulling the blanket tightly under her chin again. "I just can't stand seeing him take advantage of you," she said.

They lay wrapped together like that until they dozed off.

Guy met Donlon in a North Beach pub where he had gone seeking a dart game. He had just completed his two years of military service. The Army sent him to a NATO intelligence unit outside of London because he had two years of college and could write complete sentences. He learned to play darts at a local pub. When his time in the Army was up, he hitched a ride back to Dover Air Force Base.

Inside the hangar, he sat on a bench, his feet propped on his duffel, and considered his next move. Back to Indiana? His family expected that; everyone did. He did himself. He also knew that he would never become a writer in Indiana. Guy watched crews loading the big, olive-drab jets. A sergeant with a clipboard stood nearby, checking a list. Guy walked over to him and asked, "Where is this plane headed?" The sergeant didn't look up from his work. "Alameda Air Base, California." So Guy hitched another ride. When he got there, he crossed the bay to San Francisco and North Beach. He found a room with a hot plate and a small refrigerator in Chinatown. He stood out, a lanky, blond Midwestern kid, conspicuous among the busy Chinese along Grant Street.

Darts weren't easy to find in San Francisco bars; there were pool tables and television screens instead. Guy wandered North Beach and the fringes of Chinatown looking for a game. His search didn't feel aimless. He hadn't been in San Francisco long enough to feel possessed by any part of it. He enjoyed scouting around, wandering into places and checking them out. Until he found Roses, where Donlon held forth. That night, when Guy first walked into Roses, Donlon needed a partner. He searched the faces around the bar, finally settling on Guy. He extended a dart confidently as though he knew Guy would take it. "Game?" That night, they became friends.

Donlon was the life of the party. He rarely stopped talking, telling tales and quoting poetry, sailing his darts to the board all the while. The onlookers in the bar took to him, laughing at his jokes and listening in studious quiet to his oratory, beer glasses in one hand, cigarettes in the other. Donlon and Guy became a team. Donlon played like a pro. Guy was pretty good, too. Together, they soon dominated play. When they won, Donlon would laugh out loud, clapping Guy on the shoulder and bragging, "We're the best." Guy soon figured out his meaning: "Because I'm the best." That's what Donlon really meant. Guy didn't mind. He liked winning, too.

That first night, a woman sat at the bar, watching, one leg draped over the other, her elbow propped against the counter with a cigarette between her fingers. Black hair and dark, liquid eyes sent a message Guy could not fathom. Like a Castilian Madonna, Guy thought. Between turns, he sidled up to her at the bar just to check her out.

"Donlon doesn't speak," she said as Guy approached. "He expresses himself." She smiled. Guy studied his new darts partner. Donlon had a relaxed throwing style, back on his heels, nonchalant. The woman seemed to read Guy's mind. "You won't be able to ignore him. There's no point in trying," she said. "He sucks you in. Everyone listens to him, even when they don't hear him." She laughed and introduced herself. "Frances. I'm with Donlon."

Her dangling earrings sparkled in the dim glow. A soft light exploded inside Guy. For a moment, he felt the future.

Early in their friendship, when Donlon learned about Guy's efforts to be a writer, he placed his hand on Guy's shoulder and said, "Good man." He needled Guy to read something he had written. You call yourself a writer, Donlon said. Show the world your talent—if you have any. He goaded and pushed until Guy overcame his reluctance and gave in. One night in Donlon's apartment, Guy read them a story he had written.

Guy's story went like this: a young officer in the American military is stationed at a NATO unit outside of London in postwar England ten years after the war. At the local pub, he befriends an old man, a local, who is full of tales about the English countryside. The old man also talks about the swarms of American airmen during the war, young rowdy lads at the nearby airfields, where the B-17 bombers lumbered into the sky to blast the Germans. In the pub, the locals kept their distance, polite but not friendly. But the old man liked the Americans for their exuberance and enthusiasm for their deadly work.

One American in particular became the old man's friend: a young pilot, fresh from a farm in Nebraska. In Guy's story, the old man talks about the pilot. One day, a cook discovers a small dog rooting through the garbage behind the mess hall. It is a homely mutt, piebald, with a defective tail that wags crookedly. The young pilot promptly adopts the puppy and names her Molly, after a woman he met briefly in a New Jersey bar. The dog and the pilot became inseparable. When the pilot is away on a bombing mission, Molly sits as near as possible to the long concrete runway, her ears perked up, waiting for the pilot to return. She becomes the bomber's mascot. Each crewmember makes a point of patting her head for good luck before they depart.

One day, Guy's story continues, as Molly sits patiently waiting, watching each bomber stumble back to earth, one plane does not return. Night falls, and still, Molly waits. In the morning, she sits there as crews prepare the bombers for a new mission. She is still there when they return. One member of the ground crew tries to befriend her, to lure her away with a small piece of meat. She eats the meat but refuses to leave her post. Finally, the young Americans, busy with war, ignore her. She reverts to rummaging through the garbage behind the mess hall. But she always returns to the spot near the runway to take up her post. Somehow, she survives.

Guy paused briefly in his reading. He looked at Donlon quizzically. Donlon nodded: go on, his expression said, let's hear the rest.

Guy went on. As the old man in the pub told Molly's story, the young American could see tears in his eyes. The war ends, the man says, and the Americans quickly abandoned the airfields. In no time, it seemed, the English countryside retook the landscape. Silence settles in. The Americans are gone; the locals in the pub lapse back into their stoic solitude, sipping their warm beer and smoking their pipes. Soon, the airfield begins to crumble. The runways erupt into fractured slabs as vegetation pushes through the cracks. Tall weeds spring up where American boots had once trampled the ground. The metal barracks grow rusty, collapsing onto themselves, derelicts of war.

But still, Molly waits. Local farmers swear they see her by day, sitting in the same spot even as the runways crumble and the weeds grow up around her. She turns feral, just another of the wild creatures that gravitate into the empty space of the abandoned airbase. No one knows how she survives. But they insist that she does. For several years after the war ends, people claim to have seen her.

Then, one day, no one sees her again. Dead, the locals in the pub surmise, maybe killed by the foxes that had moved into the thick brush. Whatever the case, Molly is no more. Her story ends, the old man says, wiping his eyes. But she had her purpose, he says, and lived it. In some tiny way, she was part of the war itself. She gave some meaning, some brief happiness, to the doomed young men. We should respect her for that.

The old man had finished his tale. He sat looking at the last dregs in his glass. For a while, the young American sat silently, taking it in. Then he stood, touched the old man on the shoulder, and said, "That's quite a story. I'll get us two more." As he walked toward the bar, he couldn't decide whether he believed it or not.

Guy finished reading and looked up cautiously, wary about Donlon's response. Donlon said nothing for a moment as he tipped back in his chair. Then the chair thumped down.

"Marvelous writing, my boy. You're a talent for sure," Donlon said. He got up and stretched. He turned and walked into the small kitchen for another beer. "But the story. Sentimental drivel. Lassie-come-home bullshit." Guy could hear him from the kitchen. "Never put a dog in a story. If you do, that's all the readers care about. They focus on the dog and miss your point." Guy heard the refrigerator door open and close.

Frances spoke for the first time. "The story isn't about the dog, is it, Guy?" She gripped his arm. "It's about the old man's nostalgia for the war. He misses those times. He needs to tell stories about it." She looked at Guy earnestly. "Even if the stories aren't true. Is that right?"

"Yes," Guy responded. "That's right."

*

When Donlon learned about Guy's job at the zoo, he mocked it. "Zookeeper. Great White Hunter," he said. He needed to see it for himself, he told Guy. He came to the zoo and rode the elephant train all day, sitting in the last car, listening to Guy's monologue as they passed the animals. In the rearview mirror, Guy could see the smirk on Donlon's face.

Later, at Roses, Donlon said, "They're prisoners, you know. The animals. Captives. They could take over if they wanted to. You should let the big cats escape. The lions. They'd clear the place out and take over." Two people were challenging them to a game. Donlon and Guy took their place at the dartboard. "Someday, we'll liberate them." Donlon winked at Guy.

As Donlon rattled on, Guy considered the idea. "No, not the lions," Guy said finally. "The grown-up chimpanzees. They're smart enough to take over." He thought about the adult chimps hidden away at the back of the zoo. Small, scheming eyes and big brains in gross, obese frames. "They hold their shit in their hands, and when they think you're not watching, they sling it at you through the bars. That's why they're kept at the back of the zoo, away from the tourists."

"Excellent!" Donlon slapped the bar with his hand. "Slinging shit. The perfect weapon. They'll be the generals." He gave Guy an approving look. "But we'll still need the lions. For muscle."

For a while after Guy met her, Frances never spoke about herself. When he had the chance, Guy probed for details, carefully. She would deflect him. But he kept trying. In time, as they got to know each other, she talked about herself.

She grew up in Mill Valley, not far from the other end of the Golden Gate Bridge. But the way she told it made it seem as distant as Mars. "My dad was a San Francisco cop," she said, stubbing out her cigarette. "A detective." At the outset of WWII, he had enlisted and somehow got into the Army Air Force in China, where he spent the duration of the war. He learned Mandarin and became an interpreter. After the war, he joined the San Francisco police department, assigned to the Chinatown beat. There were lots of sinister figures, opium drug lords, smugglers, stuff like that, Frances told Guy. It hardened him as much as the war had. At home, he brooded. His moodiness permeated the house. Even the family dog avoided him.

Frances was a restless kid, an arguer, and rebellious in the classroom. She got suspended a couple of times, which upset her mother. Her father ignored her. "He had a partner named Marty, who used to come over to the house," Frances went on. Marty was the friendly type. He paid attention to her, becoming like a sort of uncle. "When I got in trouble in school, he would lecture me all about the importance of education and paying attention to my teachers, that sort of thing. It had an impact, mostly, I think, because it wasn't my parents talking. Whenever I made a snotty remark in class, I would immediately think I was letting Marty down." She found herself caring more about Marty's opinion than her parents'. "He used to tell me, you can be pushy and stand up for yourself without showing disrespect for people," she said. "Somehow, that made sense to me."

When she started her last year in high school, her father was arrested. He and Marty got swept up in a larger investigation into police corruption in immigrant neighborhoods. They had been shaking down Chinese merchants for years. Marty ratted on her father to save his own neck. "My father's case was kind of odd—a white guy who spoke Chinese. The newspapers picked it up and gave it a lot of publicity." The court sentenced her father to ten years. Marty got probation.

A year or so after it happened, just as she was graduating from high school, Marty sent her a letter apologizing for the trouble he had caused. I really liked your father, even respected him, Marty wrote. But I couldn't go to jail. I wouldn't have survived.

"I felt a bigger loss about Marty than I did about my

father," Frances said. "I was grateful for his letter. I guess I felt a kind of forgiveness. Not for what he had done to my father, but because he had remembered me." She gave a tight little laugh. "That's how kids think. In their self-centered worlds."

After Frances graduated from high school, she headed straight for North Beach. There, she found a community to take her in, young people like herself drifting and gauzy with ill-defined expectations. She loved it. She found work as a secretary in the financial district and moved into a two-room apartment on a North Beach side street, August Alley.

She met Donlon when a friend took her to the City Lights bookstore. He caught her eye across the room and wouldn't stop staring at her. It worked. She had been with Donlon ever since, four years before the night Guy showed up at Roses. Donlon and Frances made an odd couple, the babbling raconteur at the dartboard, the quiet beauty at the bar, sipping her glass of wine.

On another night, when she had the chance with Donlon out of earshot, Frances continued her story.

"A while after I had come to North Beach, the *Chronicle* did a follow-up story on the police scandal. In it, they mentioned that Marty was working as a security guard at the de Young Museum in Golden Gate Park. One Saturday, I went there, and sure enough, I found him. He was so surprised to see me that tears came to his eyes. On his break, we had coffee on the plaza. He asked about me, about my mother, and how I was doing. Neither of us mentioned my father. He appreciated his job at the museum, which kept him alive. But he wanted to return to the police force. He was convinced that he could go back when things calmed down and memories faded. I didn't want to discourage his hope—I wouldn't have known how to— so I didn't say anything."

She didn't speak for a while or look at Guy. Finally, she resumed.

"I gave him my address and telephone number, but he's

too shy to contact me. I know that. I don't know if he's still at the museum or if he managed to become a cop again. But it won't surprise me if he turns up eventually. We share a past that isn't going away."

She fell silent again, then laughed quietly to herself.

"Donlon doesn't know about this part. About Marty, I mean." She looked at Guy carefully. "Please, don't tell him."

Guy had listened silently. She's sharing her secrets with me, he thought. The idea sent a thrill through him, and he shivered. He nodded. "Sure."

One cold night, when Donlon and Frances were not at Roses, Guy left to search for them, shivering in the chill of the North Beach fog. He found them seated at a small table in Donlon's apartment. A gun lay on the table near the center. Six bullets stood in a row in front of Donlon, lined up like tiny tin soldiers.

Guy had never seen the gun before, although Frances told him about it. "He has a gun, you know," she said in a hushed tone one night as they watched Donlon from the bar at Roses. "A guy in New York sold it to him. As a kind of joke, I think. Donlon used to brag about shooting himself. So, the guy said, 'I'll get you a gun.'" She watched Donlon for a while. Then she said, "He plays with it. Twirls it around and points it at things. At himself. He always says it isn't loaded."

"What's that?" Guy asked, nodding toward the gun as he sat. Under the table, he could feel Frances's foot jiggling nervously.

"That, my friend, is a pistol," Donlon said, reaching for it. "It's for blowing things away." He waved it around. "Don't worry. It's empty. See, there are the bullets on the table. Little tykes for ripping through things." He laughed. "You know. Tin cans, beer bottles." He laughed again and placed the revolver in the middle of the table. "Let's see who it chooses." He spun the gun around. It stopped twirling, the barrel pointing somewhere between Frances and Guy. "Ha!" Donlon said. "It can't decide which of you to pick. What a predicament."

"I told him to put it away," Frances said, looking at Guy for help. "I don't like it. It scares me."

"It should, my dear. That's what it's meant for," Donlon went on. "It is meant to intimidate. The enforcer. To dispense justice." He drank from the beer bottle in front of him and set it down noisily. "Let me tell you a story to illustrate my point."

Donlon grew up in Bayonne, New Jersey, a gritty industrial town across the Hudson River from Manhattan. "The Irish kids ruled," he said. "Tough as steel rivets. We fucked over the Italians, the Jews." He laughed. "The toughest kid was Lawrence O'Flynn. Loony Larry, we called him. Or just Loony most of the time. He would do any crazy thing—swim in the sewer wastewater from the tannery, where there were sometimes dead animals floating in the water."

Loony's old man was the meanest asshole on the block, Donlon went on. Came home drunk every night and beat Loony's mother senseless.

"Loony finally got tired of watching the beatings. Somewhere, he got his hands on a rusty .22 caliber pistol, a seven-shot, that could shoot long-rifle bullets. Those babies are big enough to do real damage. One night, as his father was pounding away on his mother, Loony loaded up the pistol with the long-rifle bullets. Then, he plugged his father seven times. As his old man lay there gasping, dying, Loony shook out the empty shell casings from the pistol, reloaded, and pumped seven more bullets into the old bastard. Fourteen bullet holes. 'I wanted to make sure the fucker was dead,' Loony told the cops."

Donlon paused, a benign look on his face as though remembering a picnic in the park.

"Loony's lawyer did his best to paint Loony as a dimwit, too dumb to know what he was doing. The judge gave Loony three years. People on the street mostly supported Loony. The son of a bitch deserved to die, they said. Loony got out on parole after eighteen months and came back to the neighborhood. He lived with his mother like nothing had happened. No one gave a shit. So, you see, justice."

Donlon finished, and for a while, none of them spoke. They looked again at the pistol lying on the table. Guy had an urge to hold it.

"May I?" he asked, his hand reaching halfway there. Donlon nodded, watching him. Guy placed his hand on the pistol and circled his finger onto the trigger as he hefted it. Its weight surprised him. How could someone hold it steady enough to aim? he wondered. He twisted it in his wrist a time or two, then placed it back on the table.

"I agree with Frances," Guy said, not looking at her so Donlon wouldn't think they were ganging up on him. "It's a little scary. Why don't you put it away, and let's go to Roses."

Donlon reached forward and picked up the gun. He moved it around as though admiring it from different angles.

"It's worthless without the little guys," he said. He stood and opened the top drawer of a battered chest behind him. He placed the gun inside, then turned, scooped up the bullets, and threw them in too.

"Roses. Why not?" Donlon said.

A week later, if Guy hadn't asked Frances about the bruise on her left cheek, swollen, she would not have needed to answer, and everything that came after would not have happened. Guy considered saying nothing. A black eye could come from anywhere, any small mishap. She might be embarrassed about it; maybe she felt foolish.

But he needed to know.

"That's a serious bump on your cheek," he said as casually as he could. The blueness of the bruise blended into a reddish swelling, reaching to her bloodshot eye, the lower lid puffy and spongy-looking.

She looked directly at him as she smoked a cigarette, defiance on her face. "Why don't we just say I walked into a lamppost," she said. "Or better, that a taxicab door swung back and hit me in the face." She stubbed out the cigarette. "Then we can talk about something else." At the dartboard, Donlon had the onlookers fixated with some tale about something or other.

Let it drop; that's what she wants, Guy told himself. But he persisted.

"It looks ugly, like someone slugged you," he said. The word "someone" hung there, dangling in front of her.

Frances had looked away, studying the glass of wine in front of her, her head turned slightly so that Guy couldn't see the lump on her cheek. For a few moments, she said nothing. Then she turned and faced him again, the bruise now in full view.

"Guy, please don't press me about it. I can't tell you." She reached and laid her hand on his arm; she had never done that before. For the first time he realized he had become Donlon's rival. He had no idea—not a clue—where that might lead them.

The next day, Guy decided to move to Haight Ashbury. The possibility had been on his mind for a while. Cheap rents, a friend told him. Guy checked it out, riding the N-Judah streetcar down Market Street through the tunnel. He walked along Haight Street, looking at the storefronts. In one window, a sign read, "Stop the War." The store sold colorful T-shirts and bell-bottom jeans. Next to it was a shoe repair shop, giving off a leathery odor through its open front door. A few doors down stood a bar, the Sherwood Forest. On an impulse, he walked in. Through the darkness of the bar, at the back, a light illuminated a dartboard. Guy didn't see a pool table. This place has promise, he remembered thinking.

"I'm moving to the Haight," Guy announced the next night when he saw Donlon and Frances at Roses. Neither of them responded. "Closer to work. And to the college," Guy went on. He had wondered how Donlon would react. They had gotten used to each other.

"Well, have fun," Donlon said finally. He left to take his turn at the dartboard. As he did, Frances leaned toward Guy and said quietly, "I'm coming with you." She touched Guy's arm. He hesitated for a beat, then two, then placed his hand over hers and said, "Okay." It was as simple as that.

The next day, Guy went to Frances's apartment, and they discussed how to tell Donlon. Guy worried that Donlon might blow up and get violent.

Frances shook her head. "No. He's too proud to do that."

How about the bruise? Guy wanted to say. But didn't. "Let's tell him together," he offered.

Frances shook her head again and touched his arm. "No, Guy. I'll do it alone. It's the only way."

For his final days in North Beach, Guy avoided Roses. He regretted not saying goodbye to his friends there. But it seemed best. Frances had been right: Donlon's reaction had been mild. When Guy asked her what Donlon had said, she replied, "Not much. Just 'Have fun.'"

Guy and Frances found two rooms in a large Victorian house on Cole Street, just off Stanyan, across from the park. Frances could commute to her job in the financial district; Guy went to his classes at San Francisco State and worked on the tour train. Guy liked the ambiance of the Haight, the laid-back, easygoing street style. People in the bars were friendly, blue-collar beer drinkers from the neighborhood. Outside, more and more windows had signs that read, "Make Love Not War." Young people began filling the streets, different from the working-class types who were already settled in the Haight. The shoe repair store next to the Sherwood closed, replaced by a shop selling psychedelic ornaments and pipes for smoking dope. Frances loved it, too. North Beach seemed remote to them now, like another world. "I'll become a hippie," Frances laughed.

One night, about six months after they moved to the Haight, Guy and Frances walked into the Sherwood. Guy heard the voice, piercing the smoke, before he saw him: Donlon at the dartboard. The same old Donlon in a new setting: ebullient, loud, entertaining. The drinkers and dart players were gravitating toward him. He found us, followed us here, Guy thought. Frances didn't react.

Donlon greeted them cheerfully. "Hello, folks. Good to see you," he said, waving his hand holding the darts. "These are my friends from North Beach," he announced to the crowd in general, as though Frances and Guy were the newcomers. "We go way back." People looked at Frances and Guy as though they were strangers. Donlon's friends: they must be okay. He already has them in his grip, Guy thought. He felt the world shifting around him, like Roses, with Donlon at the center. Frances must have felt it, too, but she said nothing. She and Donlon looked at each other for a moment. "Hello, Terry," she said. Guy had never heard her call Donlon by his first name.

Donlon had moved to a room across from St. Mary's Hospital. North Beach had become unlivable; that was the excuse he gave. Columbus Avenue has gone topless, he said. Just tits and tourists. All the action's in the Haight now. Guy and Frances didn't challenge him about his reasons. Donlon seemed no different. Was anything different now? Guy wondered as he watched Donlon regaling the crowd, pitching darts flawlessly—when he could stand up. Only Guy and Frances were different. They had shed Donlon for good. At least, Guy wanted to believe that.

One night, not long after Donlon's appearance, as Guy and Frances walked home along Haight Street, alive with hippie panhandlers and teenage girls with jangling, looping earrings, Frances said, "He's come for me." Guy looked at the psychedelic posters in the store window and said nothing. Swirling colors decorated everything. Haight Street was a harbinger of something new.

Later, in the dark of their bedroom, Guy said, "Yes, I know."

They lay there silently, their world dissolving around them, the new one not yet fully formed.

After Warren arrived at the zoo train ticket booth to open up, the day settled into its routine of trains and tourists. Guy couldn't get Frances out of his mind. She had said nothing when he hinted that he might go to Berkeley early to get a feel for the place, to get ready for the fall semester. In her eyes, he could see the reluctance. Was it Donlon? "He's come for me," she had said. Guy thought about her words as he steered past the animals. Maybe she had known it all along. For an instant, he felt uncertain of her and of himself. Maybe the move to the Haight had been a kind of game, a way of punishing and enticing Donlon at the same time.

Noise from up ahead shook him from his musing. The tour train had just passed the birdhouse with its squawking mayhem. Guy could see a crowd gathering in front of one of the lion grottoes. Urgent voices were attracting more people; they hurried toward the low fence on the edge of the deep trench separating the lions from the crowd. Tommy and Virginia, a young mating couple, were in this grotto. The depth and width of the trench were designed to prevent the lions from escaping. Guy stopped the train and climbed down.

"He's down there," someone yelled, pointing into the trench as Guy walked up. Guy's safari-like jacket apparently looked official; people moved to let him push up against the fence.

"He must have fallen!" someone yelled.

"No, he climbed down there," another voice shouted. "I saw him. He was standing at the edge of the pit, shouting at the lions, 'I'm setting them free! Free the lions! Free the lions.' Then he tried to climb down. He hung from the edge and fell the rest of the way."

Guy leaned across the metal fence as far as he could to try to see deeper into the pit, but the edge of the surface obscured the figure below. People were pushing to see; Guy could hear others running up behind. A muffled voice rose from the pit above the mayhem, "I'm setting the captives free! Freedom for the animals!" The crowd pressed against Guy; he pushed back to maintain his position. Finally, the figure in the pit moved enough that Guy could get a clear look.

Donlon! Donlon was in the pit. Drunk as hell. Guy struggled to take it in. Oh my God! That crazy son of a bitch! Donlon leaned heavily against the wall. He couldn't stand on his own. There was blood on his pant leg; a sharp edge of bone poked through. His leg must have shattered when he dropped into the pit. In his hand, Donlon gripped his pistol. He began waving it and yelling gibberish nonsense about the animals, the lions. He pointed the gun to the sky. "Let's go! Out of jail," he shouted.

"He has a gun! He has a gun! Watch out," a woman behind Guy cried.

Suddenly, the blast of a gunshot exploded in the air. The crowd shrank back from the sound. Donlon was firing into the sky. One shot, then two, another one. Someone screamed, "He's dangerous! Get back! Get back!"

Guy frantically searched his mind for something to do. The trench was too deep for Donlon to climb out. Ladders—we need ladders, Guy thought. Donlon continued to babble, yelling and laughing like it was a great lark. "Donlon! You idiot," Guy yelled, trying to make his voice heard above the clamor of the crowd. "Lie down. Be still so the lions don't notice you."

Tommy and Virginia were attracted by the commotion.

The lions smell the blood, Guy thought. Virginia crouched on the edge of the pit, looking down at Donlon, moving her big head to catch the scent. Tommy stood next to her. At first, Tommy seemed more interested in the crowd along the fence than anything in the trench. But then he apparently caught the scent. He opened his huge mouth and shook his mane. He crouched next to Virginia and studied the figure a few feet below him in the pit.

Then, carefully, Tommy extended his front paws downward on the sloping wall of the pit and began to half-jump, half-slide down the wall into the trench. He landed awkwardly but quickly righted himself on his four feet. The crowd swayed and gave a low moan as Tommy's tail twitched, and he gazed directly at Donlon. Donlon finally seemed to grasp the danger. He stumbled backward and fell to the ground, the pistol still gripped in his hand.

"Oh my God! Oh my God!" Guy heard voices in the crowd. "The lion's going to kill him!"

"Stay still!" Guy shouted, the sound of his voice lost in the noise.

"Look there," a voice yelled. "Someone with a rifle."

Guy looked up across the grotto. An animal keeper had emerged from the cage entrance door at the back of the grotto, a rifle in his hands. He was proceeding cautiously toward Virginia. Guy knew rifles were kept in the zoo as an emergency measure. The keeper moved slowly, cautiously, the rifle ready to be used. Virginia, focused on Tommy and Donlon at the bottom of the pit, had not yet scented the figure creeping across the grotto. Then, suddenly, she turned her massive head slightly; the man had raised the rifle toward her. *Crack!* The crowd gasped at the shock of the loud bang. Virginia flopped to her side, her hind legs kicking. The bullet caught her directly in the eye.

"He killed her! Shot her in the head!"

Down below, in the pit, Tommy had jumped at the sound

of the rifle. His head jerked upward momentarily. Then he turned back toward Donlon and crept closer. He sniffed the air, smelling the blood on Donlon's broken leg. He stuck his snout close to the leg and seemed to nuzzle it. He opened his jaws, clamped them onto the injured leg, and began to drag Donlon backward.

"Shoot him! With your gun," someone yelled down into the pit. But Donlon had dropped the pistol as he squirmed away from the lion.

Up above, on the grotto surface, the keeper with the rifle crept closer to the prone figure of Virginia. Down below, Tommy still had Donlon's leg gripped in his teeth. Suddenly, he released Donlon's leg. He stepped forward and straddled Donlon's body, lowering his huge head down toward Donlon's face. His jaws opened, wide, wider—and Tommy clamped his yellow fangs around Donlon's skull. Donlon's entire head was now encased in the lion's mouth.

A sensation surged through Guy's brain: *Kill him! Do it!* His mind recoiled, repulsed. *No! Please, God, don't let him die.*

Crack! Tommy's body jolted; he collapsed, then flopped over to the side. His jaws reflexively released Donlon's head. *Crack!* A second shot. Tommy quivered, then lay still. Donlon, free now, managed to drag himself away from the lion carcass. Guy could see him gasping for air. Blood covered the ground, some of it from Donlon's broken leg.

"It's okay! It's safe to come out now," the man with the rifle shouted over his shoulder. "They're both dead." Carefully, other figures began to appear from the doors at the back of the grotto. "He's alive! Thank God," someone shouted. Guy struggled to take in the scene: two dead lions, Donlon in the pit, crippled, zookeepers running around, shouting directions.

Firemen appeared; a huge fire truck had lurched up, disrupting everything. Ladders materialized; rescuers had reached Donlon, hovering around him. Guy looked down at the figures around Donlon. Nothing to do now except clean up the mess.

Kill him!

Guy turned and worked his way through the crowd, past the ambulance. Blood pulsed in his temples. Kill who? What had he meant, "Kill him"?

He passed his empty tour train, still idling where he left it only minutes before. He no longer cared what happened to it. *Kill him?* Tommy was dead; the keeper with the rifle killed him. That would have to be the answer.

Guy walked toward the tour train ticket booth. The fog had burned off—it always did. Guy's lungs sucked in the cool, salty air in the ocean breeze. He felt the sun warming the skin of his face. He still had to tell Warren about quitting today. Tomorrow, he would cross the bay to Berkeley and look for lodgings. Only a few miles, at the other end of the Bay Bridge. On a clear day, you could see the campanile on the campus.

Who knew what would happen after Berkeley? He remembered a saying from Heraclitus: "No man ever steps into the same river twice, for it is not the same river, and he is not the same man." In his gut, Guy knew that once he crossed the Bay Bridge, he would never return to San Francisco. Frances could decide for herself.

ARLEN/ARLENE

Arlen ran into the store. "Gunner's after me," he gasped. He needed to hide—fast. Boyd shoved aside the cardboard boxes on the floor behind the counter. He pulled up the basement door in the floor. "Down here," he said to Arlen. "Hurry." Arlen stepped carefully down the steep steps. The railing wobbled as he gripped it; his heels clicked on the stairs.

"Don't turn on the light," Boyd whispered. "And don't smoke down there." He quickly closed the door and pushed the boxes back onto it. He resumed stocking the cigarette counter. A minute later, Gunner, the detective, strolled in. He never hurried, he told Boyd once. He didn't need to; he knew all the places where the queers hid. Did he know about the basement? Boyd couldn't be sure. Gunner had been in the Tenderloin so long he might know. Boyd's stomach suddenly felt queasy.

Gunner's suit jacket hung open; Boyd could see the handle of his gun. Gunner liked for people to see it. He leaned against the counter and gave Boyd a hard look. Gunner's stare could intimidate anyone. The psycho cop, Arlen called him. Gunner grinned when he heard that. "Makes the faggots pay attention," he said. He was a tail gunner over the Pacific during the war; that's where he got his nickname. "Firing from the asshole," Gunner joked. "A perfect job for an asshole," Arlen said.

"A pack of Camels," Gunner said and put a dollar on the counter. He tore the cellophane from the cigarettes, crumpled it, and dropped it on the floor. "Tell your fairy scum friend if I see him turning tricks again, he'll regret it," he said.

As he left, Tom walked in. "What's the tail gunner up to?" Tom asked as he watched Gunner walk out. Tom was old-school San Francisco. He had lived in the Tenderloin his entire life. Every day, in all weather, he wore a snap-brim hat, and a full-length, dark wool overcoat buttoned up. A cigarette dangled from the corner of his mouth.

"Chasing Arlen," Boyd said. He wouldn't mention hiding Arlen in the basement until he could be sure Gunner was out of earshot.

Tom laughed. "They deserve each other. Cops and queers are wrecking the place. Not like in my day."

In his day. Tom loved to tell Boyd about it. He had been in the Tenderloin through two world wars, Prohibition, the Depression, and Korea. Now, nothing's the same; everything's changing, he complained, flicking ash on the floor. He knew the store from way back. During Prohibition, there was a speakeasy in the basement. On the cellar walls, Boyd could still make out faint blue paintings of mice dancing a jig. Now, they used the basement to store the stock—and, right now, to hide Arlen.

"Arlen's hiding in the cellar," he said.

Tom laughed and flicked his ash again. "We didn't have 'Arlens' in my day. Regular people lived here," Tom went on. "Good people, working people." He shook his head. "Not the hippie trash we have now. And the queer whores." He shook his head again. He lapsed into silence, nostalgic for the old days. Boyd didn't disturb him. Tom's San Francisco was long dead. Now, in 1966, Vietnam had put everyone on edge. Body bags were lined up in neat rows at Travis Air Force Base north of San Francisco, more of them every day. Tom fretted about the war. Boyd just tried to stay out of its way. He took classes at the University of San Francisco to avoid the draft, trying to make as little progress as possible toward graduation. He hated the war and blamed the government for it.

At first, he respected the soldiers, the unfortunate grunts who bore the brunt of it. Then, at a party where there were several Vietnam vets, one sailor who served on a ship that patrolled the coastline told a story. Through his cannon lens, he saw a woman riding a bicycle. He blew her away with one shell. His comment: "Just one less gook to fuck." Everyone laughed. After that, Boyd wasn't sure how he felt except empty.

Tom and Boyd stood there for a long time, looking out at the sidewalk scene, when Boyd heard Arlen tapping on the basement door. Boyd flushed: Arlen had slipped his mind. He quickly moved the liquor boxes and lifted the door. Arlen poked up his head carefully. Like a prairie dog, Boyd thought, checking things out.

"Is the asshole gone?" Arlen asked.

He came cautiously up the stairs, looking around. Tom's presence didn't bother him. He and Tom came from different planets, too far apart to collide. Arlen was decked out in purple tights, white sandals with medium heels, a silk, thigh-length Oriental jacket with peacocks on it, and a red sash. Around his head, he wore a tiara with rhinestones glittering in different shades. It held back his short, dark hair. Sometimes, he wore beads drooped around his neck, giggling as he twirled them. "Just like a Haight Street hippie," he would say. But he wasn't wearing them tonight.

"Thanks, Boyd—you saved my life," Arlen said. "I don't know why that prick pesters me so much." Arlen had a prissy way of speaking. He thought it sounded refined.

"Maybe he thinks whores should lift their skirts and spread their legs," Tom said. "Not drop their pants and bend over." He grinned.

Arlen ignored him. "Look, Boyd, why don't you come to a party at my place? It's Mitzi's birthday. Everyone will be there."

He saw a cobweb on his jacket sleeve and picked it off. "We're all going to dress up."

Boyd thought about what "everyone" would mean at Arlen's—a collection of queers, queens, cross-dressers, and lesbians. Mitzi called himself the Mean Queen. No one disputed it.

"You can bring someone," Arlen said.

Who? Boyd thought. Angie, the Greek girl he knew at the bank? Too shy for the crowd at Arlen's. Maybe Sheralee, the black Jamaican cocktail waitress he met at a Geary Street bar where the sports crowd hung out. Sheralee wore dresses so tight she looked sewn into them. In heels, she was an inch taller than Boyd. His curly blond hair stood out against her black afro. She would know how to hold her own at Arlen's place. She had held Boyd off for months.

Boyd was working as a clerk at Woolworths on Powell Street when he met Arlen. Arlen shopped for cheap, frilly women's underwear. The other clerks snickered and avoided waiting on him. Boyd wouldn't do that. Arlen was different, no question. San Francisco's diversity hit you in the face, especially if you were a small-town kid like Boyd. You had to deal with it, he thought, like it or not. He was cordial when Arlen came up to him, and Arlen always sought him out.

One day, as he was about to leave after Boyd handed him his change, Arlen said, "These are really very good quality, you know. Especially at the price." The remark struck Boyd. It was something anyone might say. It had never occurred to him that someone so different could say something so ordinary. Arlen was just being a typical shopper, looking for a bargain.

"We appreciate your business," he said as Arlen left. He could think of nothing else to say.

A few days later, as Boyd sat on a crowded bench in Union Square, eating a sandwich for lunch, he saw Arlen approaching. Arlen saw Boyd, too, and hesitated. Boyd slid over to create space on the bench. After a moment, Arlen squeezed in beside him. Boyd felt the firm pressure of Arlen's thigh. Most of his friends would hate that pressure and would probably get up and leave if Arlen sat next to them. He often thought about guys back home who bragged about going to San Francisco and beating up homosexuals. In time, he realized that people like Arlen scared them. They felt threatened and uneasy about their manhood. Homophobia shielded their vulnerability; violence validated them. Boyd searched inside himself and discovered that he did not have that fear and didn't need that protection. Arlen's thigh was just another squeeze on a crowded bench.

Boyd extended half his sandwich. "These things are so big. I can only eat half."

Arlen looked at it, then smiled and took it. "Thanks."

The sandwich bonded them.

So, there was nothing unusual about Arlen inviting Boyd to a party.

"Sure, I'll come," Boyd said.

Arlen primped his hair, then looked up and down the sidewalk before leaving the store.

Sometimes, as their friendship deepened, Boyd and Arlen would ride the Geary Street bus all the way to the end at the Cliff House and take walks on the beach. Arlen would dress in jeans and sweaters. He was small, three inches shorter than Boyd, and dark against Boyd's lanky blondness. They told each other their stories and surprised themselves by how similar they were.

Arlen described growing up in a small town on the Oregon coast, where he always felt different and alone. In high school, his difference was apparent to everyone. The girls teased him; the boys called him names: queer, fairy, faggot. Some threatened him. Much of the time, he was scared. His family offered little consolation. Only his mother showed some understanding. "It's a sickness," she told him. "It will go away in time."

Arlen knew better. He left before finishing high school when his father offered to send him money each month to stay away.

Boyd listened to Arlen, and something stirred inside him. He felt Arlen's loneliness. He grew up in a small lumber town and knew what isolation meant. As he reached his teenage years, he sensed that he stood outside the small, confined world around him, the life he could see his high school classmates drifting toward. Their ambitions lacked imagination; their horizons were close by. Most of them would not escape lifetimes of drudgery, living at the margins, frustrated by the limitations of their universe.

"Fighting in dance hall parking lots. That's what they did best," Boyd told Arlen. "Beating each other senseless." They used guns a lot, he said—on animals, on each other, on themselves. They were so used to cruelty that it seemed normal to them. Once, when he heard some of his friends laughing about dousing a stray cat in kerosene and lighting it, his stomach turned over. From then on, he felt like an outsider.

When Arlen spoke of his lonely isolation, Boyd felt it with him. They realized the sameness of their feelings and felt more alike than different, as friends do.

At first, for a long time, they did not discuss Arlen's trade. Boyd was curious but could think of no way to bring it up. One day, as they sat together, the only passengers on the bus, Arlen spoke of it: "They're not so bad, the johns, really. At least not the normal ones."

"Normal ones?" Boyd asked before he could stop himself.

Arlen laughed. "I mean the ones who just want sex. Mostly, they're trying to have a feeling of some kind. Something to make them feel good, not miserable." He searched for the right words. There were bad guys, of course, Arlen explained, but not as many as you might think. He mostly stuck with regular clients, people he got to know and could trust. He picked up tricks on the street only when he needed the money, and he had learned how to be careful.

"Gunner's a bigger threat than they are," Arlen said ruefully.

Boyd could not fathom any of it—wanting to touch another man's body. When he had sex, he wanted to have the only dick in the room. But Arlen had brought the subject up, and Boyd realized he wanted Boyd to know. He listened and said nothing. From then on, it seemed less important to him.

Mostly, they talked about themselves, their aspirations, their fears. Boyd described his efforts to avoid getting shot at in Vietnam. He spent a lot of energy fretting about it. Arlen talked about his body, how he yearned to have it changed, transformed into the reality he felt inside himself. Only "the operation" could do it, he told Boyd. The operation: the ultimate step, over the cliff, no going back. It surpassed anything hormone shots could do. It meant that clothing didn't have to hide a secret; life didn't have to be an act.

"A full commitment to yourself," Arlen said in a quiet moment when they shared a bottle of cheap red wine. "To be yourself, your true self." Arlen kept repeating it like a mantra.

"I should be Arlene," he said. He sipped the sharp wine and brooded. "Someday I will be."

But it seemed impossible. American surgeons wouldn't do it. Mexican doctors couldn't be trusted. No one had the money to go to Europe. Mostly, Arlen and his friends just talked about it. Maybe someday.

The idea fascinated Boyd and scared him. He could not imagine what was happening in Arlen's mind, what it felt like to want something so drastic, so irreversible. Somehow, because it came from so deep inside him, it made Arlen seem more human, Boyd thought, surprising himself. The straight world saw the opposite: a sex change was perverse, the reverse of being human. Only Christine Jorgensen existed as an example. And everyone regarded her as a freak. It's against nature, the argument went, so how could it be right? Dressing up in women's clothes—that might be okay. That's just a game, showing off for entertainment, kinky but explainable. But slicing off your manhood? It's disgusting, people said. No one could really want that. No one could be that way in their mind or in their soul.

Yet Boyd felt its reality for Arlen and other of Arlen's friends, trapped in the wrong bodies. He accepted what they yearned for, just as he accepted Arlen. Or Arlene—whatever his name was or would be. Boyd did not pretend to understand it in his gut.

"Do it," Boyd urged, slurring his words. "Find a way." His drunken savvy made him brave for Arlen.

At the party, Arlen opened the door when Boyd knocked, Sheralee by his side. Arlen stood at the door, wearing a blue gown that reached nearly to his ankles. It had a low neckline, revealing his shoulders, and short puffy sleeves, the edges tight around his arms. The bodice fitted snuggly around Arlen's chest just under his breasts (such as they were), then hung loosely around his body, down to his feet. A pair of shiny blue slippers peeked out from under the edges of the gown. It's from a Jane Austen novel, Boyd thought.

"This is my Alice Blue Gown," Arlen said and did a full turn so Boyd and Sheralee could admire it. Sheralee took it in. What's going through her mind? Boyd wondered.

"Very nice," Sheralee said after a moment or two. "Have you considered a blue bow in your hair?"

Inside the room behind Arlen, the party had already reached a level of boisterous intensity. Loud music competed with people talking, and the volume of each rose to counteract the other. Here and there, Boyd caught a whiff of marijuana smoke, an odor still new enough to be noticeable. "We'll probably be the only straights," Boyd had warned Sheralee. Then he realized that he didn't know whether Sheralee was straight or not. Maybe she was a lesbian. Maybe that explained her indifference to his advances. The possibility hadn't occurred to him before.

Boyd could see Arlen's friends scattered throughout the crowded room. La Madame: famous as one of the cross-dressing creators of North Beach bawdiness. He retired when Broadway and Columbus went topless. How gauche, he said, absolutely tasteless. Mitzi, the star of the evening, sat on the couch, drinking in the attention. Mitzi wore a sleeveless blouse to show off his muscles. A tattoo on his arm read, "Life is an open wound." He led a gang of tough queens who straddled Harleys and fought with the straight motorcycle gangs who harassed them. Mitzi liked a good brawl and wasn't above starting one. Benny Boy, dressed as Little Lord Fauntleroy, pretended to be a girl dressed up as a boy. He does it because he's confused about his own identity, La Madame had explained to Boyd.

Over in a corner, Boyd saw Louie-Louise, Arlen's roommate. Louie-Louise wore white. He always did. Because I'm a virgin in my soul, he said archly when pressed about it. Certainly not in his butthole, Mitzi snickered. Louie hated his name—and his gender. I should be Louise, he pouted. Everyone started calling him Louie-Louise. He took to the name: he liked the hyphen.

"It's like Oz in here," Sheralee whispered in Boyd's ear. "Where's the Wicked Witch of the West?" She seemed to be enjoying herself.

From across the room, Boyd saw Betty Beat-Me approaching. Of all Arlen's friends, Boyd liked him best. Betty Beat-Me was secure in himself; Boyd admired his self-assurance. It was not common in the cross-dressing crowd.

"Boyd, where did you find such a gorgeous date?" Betty said, giving Sheralee an admiring once-over.

Betty was decked out as an early nineteenth-century dandy, Byron or Shelley, with silk flourishes, tight breeches, and knee hose. Regency England must be in this year, Boyd thought. He introduced Sheralee to Betty, and they chatted.

Sheralee told him that she worked at a sports bar; Betty said he had jock friends, too—and clients. They laughed. Maybe he would stop by one night and talk some football. Sure, I'll buy you a drink, Sheralee said.

"Why is he called Betty Beat-Me?" Sheralee asked Boyd as Betty melted back into the crowd. Boyd explained. As a teenager, he started calling himself Betty; it felt more normal than his real name, Arthur. Betty's father was a minister who tried to beat the habit out of him with a belt, quoting scripture the whole time. "Skip the sermon. Just beat me," Betty said and took the whippings. When he finally escaped to San Francisco, and the street people who took him in heard his story, they called him Betty Beat-Me.

The racket in Arlen's apartment grew louder. Someone cranked up the volume on the stereo, and the temperature rose with it. Boyd absorbed the garbled noise and felt the salty sweat leaking from his pores. Sheralee had squeezed onto the couch next to Mitzi, who was admiring her dress. Arlen swayed over. Mitzi was in a playful mood. He examined Arlen closely. "Arlen, your gown is divine. If only your eyes matched it." Arlen had hazel eyes. "You're breaking the law, dearie," Mitzi said, grinning. "Cross-dressing is illegal, you know." He patted Arlen's cheek. "You'll give us all a bad name."

After the party, Boyd and Sheralee strolled boozily along Ellis Street toward Boyd's apartment, the hot night pressing on them. After the party, the world seemed new to Boyd, hopeful almost.

"A nightcap?" he asked Sheralee.

"All right," she answered and smiled. In his apartment, he had to wash a wine glass for her.

"My zipper's stuck," she said when he returned. "Help me with it."

Two weeks later, late one night, Boyd's brain swam up through the murk of sleep, struggling to the light—he jumped awake.

The phone woke him, ringing urgently. He groped for the receiver and held it to his ear. Arlen's voice was on the line. Boyd tried to focus. Something about jail. Arlen rasped into the phone, "Gunner beat me up. Put me in jail. Would you come to the police station and get me?" Someone had to vouch for him, or they would keep him locked up until morning. "Bring some clothes, some of yours," Arlen said. "And shoes."

Boyd looked across Sheralee at the clock on the nightstand. One o'clock. Sheralee hadn't stirred. Her arm rested on Boyd; he extracted himself carefully to avoid waking her.

Light blazed around the Howard Street police station. Glowing like a spaceship in a Ray Bradbury story, Boyd thought. He rode the elevator to the jail on the top floor, where a guard poked through the shopping bag of clothing he had brought. He had to pass through three locked iron doors with barred windows. All this to hold one puny cross-dresser, he thought as he went through.

Arlen sat alone, slumped on a bench in a holding cell. If they had thrown him in with the riffraff, he would have been assaulted. Arlen stood and walked over to the bars.

"I'm a mess, I know," he said. A sleeveless, waist-less dress draped down from his shoulders to the top of his knees: a chemise, Jackie Kennedy style. Blood and grime speckled it. Mascara ran down Arlen's cheeks, and a big purple lump bulged on his forehead. Dried blood from his nose caked his upper lip. He was barefoot, but Boyd could see a single high-heeled shoe under the bench. He had seen cops beat up drunks behind the Greyhound bus depot. Arlen's battered face brought it back to him.

"I don't suppose you have a cigarette. No, you wouldn't, would you," Arlen said, answering his own question before Boyd could respond.

"What happened?" Boyd asked.

Arlen gave him a look of injured innocence.

"Gunner busted me. They put handcuffs on me, behind my

back." Ray, Gunner's partner, had shown up. "Gunner told him, 'Let's have some fun. Hit the fucking fairy.'" Arlen gripped the bars. "That moron Ray banged my face against the wall." He gave Boyd a sorrowful look. "I wet my pants when he hit me." He looked away. "They were laughing at me." Arlen gingerly fingered the swelling bump. It had started to look like an Easter egg. "It hurts like hell. Not that they give a shit."

He had been on his way to Compton's Cafeteria, a few blocks from his apartment, where the cross-dressers and transvestites hung out. The homosexual bars wouldn't let them in. Cross-dressers attracted the cops. No one needed that. Compton's became the alternative. He had almost reached the door of the cafeteria when Gunner pounced on him. "I just wanted a cup of tea," Arlen explained. "And I wasn't doing anything wrong."

Boyd sighed. The moment seemed more pathetic than frightening now.

"You know the rules, Arlen. No dressing up when you go outside. The cops don't like it. High heels, short skirts. It just pisses them off." Arlen never seemed to get it. "And wiggling your fanny doesn't help," Boyd added for emphasis.

Arlen looked defiant. "I was only going into Compton's. I was right at the front door. They could have left me alone."

"But you know they're watching the place," Boyd said. "There's more trouble these days."

Compton's had become a lightning rod that summer. Fights broke out inside, then spilled into the street. Management hired private guards—vicious thugs—to watch the doors. Beatings took place in the alleys. Someone inevitably called the police almost every day, it seemed. Arrest them, not us, the cross-dressers demanded; they're harassing us. No comment, said the cops, and they busted the customers who complained. Pickets on the sidewalk carried signs that read, "Stop the Brutality." Onlookers taunted them: go to hell, faggots. Both sides got louder; the shouts became more threatening.

Arlen dressed in the clothes Boyd had brought. "They lost one of my shoes," he pouted. "My best heels." At the front desk, Boyd had to sign a paper accepting responsibility for Arlen. The cop in charge warned him, "Take that fairy straight home. Keep him off the streets." He gave Arlen a disgusted look.

Three o'clock in the morning, and no cabs in sight.

"Great," Boyd said. "We'll have to walk to the Greyhound station to get a taxi."

They turned and walked up Seventh Street. Arlen moved awkwardly in Boyd's pants. The cuffs were turned up three times, but they still dragged on the sidewalk. He gripped the waist with both hands to keep them from falling. He looks pathetic—like Charlie Chaplin as the Little Tramp, Boyd thought. Boyd felt sorry for him and tried to cheer him up.

But Arlen had receded inside himself and didn't reply. He just kept repeating, "Motherfucker, motherfucker; I'll get that motherfucker."

An hour later, Boyd crawled back into bed with Sheralee. She roused a little. "Where were you?"

"Gunner threw Arlen in jail. I had to get him out."

"Poor Arlen," Sheralee murmured. She flopped her arm across him and fell back asleep.

The Tenderloin sweltered that summer. The Asian war got nastier. Body bags mounted up at Travis. Napalm blasts in the jungle lit up the television news. They showed images of Vietnamese children caught in the horror of war. It sickened Boyd; he turned off the television. Haight-Ashbury was ground zero for the so-called counterculture. Hippie antics fascinated the public. Tourist buses cruised Haight Street; long-haired kids on the sidewalk held up mirrors to the gawkers inside the buses. Drugs were everywhere. Streets in the Tenderloin got scarier because of the dealing. Sheralee took cabs to work; she felt safer. All Tom could do was grouse about it. "It's turning into a shithole, the Tenderloin, the whole damn city," he said. He flicked his ashes and went on playing the horses at Golden Gate Park.

Ten days had passed since Boyd got Arlen out of jail. Arlen hadn't been in the store, and Boyd hadn't heard from him. It surprised Boyd that Arlen hadn't returned his clothes yet. That's not like him, he explained to Sheralee. She worried about Arlen. She liked Arlen's determined pugnacity. "He's tough," she told Boyd, "Stronger than he looks. He has to be more than we do. He has more at stake." Boyd couldn't remember Arlen staying out of sight for so long. Maybe we should check on him, Sheralee suggested, to make sure nothing's wrong.

No one answered at Arlen's apartment. Sheralee rang the buzzer over and over, then tried the lobby door. As someone left the building, they went in and climbed the stairs to Arlen's apartment. Boyd banged on the door. "Arlen, are you in there? It's Boyd and Sheralee." Down the hall, someone opened the door a crack to check on the noise. "Have you seen Arlen?" Boyd asked, walking toward the door. It closed quietly. "No," the muffled answer came back. They went down to the street.

"Where else can we look?" Sheralee asked, frowning. Boyd didn't know many of Arlen's hangouts; Arlen and his friends mostly stayed in their apartments. It's safer that way, he told Boyd.

"There's Compton's," Boyd said finally. The thought of going to Compton's made him nervous, but he couldn't think of anything else.

Sheralee agreed. "We need to find him," she said urgently. "Before something happens to him."

To Boyd's relief, the street around Compton's was quiet. As they approached the front door, a cab pulled up. Betty Beat-Me and Benny Boy got out. Betty saw Boyd and quickly looked away.

Boyd moved to stop him before he went inside. "Wait," Boyd said. "We're looking for Arlen. Have you seen him?"

Betty gave him a cautious look. "The cops beat him up. He's scared. He's hiding." He started to move toward the door.

Boyd grabbed Betty's arm. "I know. I got him out of jail. He's my friend too. I want to help him."

Betty Beat-Me shook off Boyd's hand. "I don't know where he is."

And wouldn't tell me if you did, Boyd realized. If Betty wouldn't tell him, none of Arlen's friends would. They were Arlen's friends, not his. Betty Beat-Me had disappeared into Compton's. Benny Boy followed him.

They didn't find Arlen that night. Three days later, they walked along Turk Street toward Arlen's apartment to try again. Up ahead, through the descending darkness, they could see a crowd gathering. Sheralee gripped Boyd's arm tightly. "Something's happening," she said. Someone ran by them toward the scene. Then another, then more people rushing through the street. Boyd and Sheralee walked ahead slowly, approaching the growing crowd. Out of nowhere, the sound of shattering glass pierced the air.

"The fairies broke the window at Compton's," someone yelled. A police car sat in front of Compton's, halfway on the sidewalk, its doors open, its radio squawking. Three policemen were struggling with someone near the door. Some of Arlen's friends were involved. Boyd could see them.

The crowd pressed toward the scene.

"Stay back," Boyd said to Sheralee. "I'll try to see if Arlen is here."

He pushed forward, barely staying erect in the push and pull of the crowd. More police arrived; Boyd could hear their cars skidding to a halt, doors slamming, cops shouting. They faced the crowd, pushing it away from Compton's. More sirens screamed in the distance, shattering the growing darkness. Broken glass covered the ground; the cops slipped and slid on it. Boyd managed to fight his way to the front.

Now, he could see the action. Mitzi struggling with the police; they had hold of him, one of his hands in a handcuff, fighting to get his arms behind him.

Someone screamed, "Don't let them arrest Mitzi!"

The crowd surged against the police. Blood covered Mitzi's face and ran down his arm across the tattoos. One of the cops had lost his cap; Boyd could see blood on him, too. Mitzi managed to swing his free arm with the handcuff dangling; the loose end hit one policeman on the cheek. More blood. At the edge of the crowd, Boyd saw Gunner run up and join the police line. His partner, Ray, pushed in behind him.

People in the crowd—Arlen's friends—began tugging Mitzi away from the police. Boyd recognized them from the party: Benny Boy, Louie-Louise, Betty Beat-Me, even La Madame, and a bunch of others. Many of them were in drag. La Madame's wig had fallen off; his thinning blond hair stood out against the glaring light of Compton's neon signs.

The mob had taken on a life of its own, swaying and twisting as the momentum shifted. Then Boyd saw Arlen, just behind the people around Mitzi. The cops kept pulling Mitzi's arms. One of the queens had his arms locked around Mitzi's waist, trying to yank him in the opposite direction. Others joined in, dragging Mitzi backward. The tug-of-war went on, the cops pulling one way, the queens the other.

Suddenly, the cops lost their grip—Mitzi fell back into his rescuers. They quickly surrounded him, trying to hide him in the crowd, blocking the cops from getting at him. Now it turned into brawling, the police swinging their sticks, dragging people away.

Boyd lost sight of Arlen. Then, off to the side, he saw that Arlen had worked his way to the fringe of the crowd, to a little alcove where the garbage cans sat behind the police. He had a large wooden riot club in his hands; one of the cops must have dropped it, and Arlen picked it up off the ground. The tugging and hauling, the cops hitting and grabbing, surged in Arlen's direction.

Boyd saw Gunner in a group of policemen straining to get at Mitzi. Arlen stared fixedly at Gunner; the pressing crowd pushed Gunner backward, closer and closer to Arlen. Gunner hadn't seen him. Arlen rested the riot club on his shoulder like a baseball bat. Only a foot or two separated Gunner from Arlen now. Arlen gripped the club, then raised it.

Boyd struggled close; he yelled, "Don't do it!"

Arlen stepped forward and bashed Gunner in the back with the club. Gunner grunted and fell to one knee. Above the din, Boyd could hear Gunner rasping, trying to get his breath. The crowd's attention was focused inward, toward the melee around Mitzi. But Arlen focused entirely on Gunner, who was panting in front of him. Gunner hadn't looked back toward his attacker. Arlen took another step forward, swinging hard; the heavy stick slammed against the back of Gunner's head—crack! Boyd heard the crunch, even in the noise of the fight. Gunner collapsed on the ground.

The crowd tripped across his prone figure, stumbling as they fought to keep Mitzi from the pressing cops. Gunner lay still, Arlen hovering as the momentum surged away from them. No one had noticed Arlen. Boyd struggled toward him. Arlen raised the club again, poised above Gunner's head. Boyd was close now. The force of the crowd pushed him; he struggled toward Arlen. Boyd strained forward, reaching out; Arlen began to swing; Boyd barely touched Arlen's arm, deflecting the blow. It slammed down on Gunner's shoulder. Another blow to his head would have killed him, Boyd thought as he fought to stay upright.

Chaos had taken over; people were scrambling, tripping, trying to get away. The police were bashing anyone within reach, grabbing who they could, trying to hold onto them.

Boyd almost fell again, fighting to keep his balance. When he steadied himself, he looked around. Arlen had disappeared.

The riot at Compton's Cafeteria caused a sensation. Headlines went wild: Drag Queens Riot in Tenderloin! Perverts Pound Police! Tinkerbell Gets Tough! The editorial pages exploded: San Francisco is being ruined. Something has to be done. People blamed the government for not clamping down. Street violence wouldn't be condoned, the mayor proclaimed. The uproar went on for days. Even Tom couldn't find words to describe it. Maybe he hadn't seen everything that could happen in the Tenderloin, he told Boyd, shaking his head.

Twenty people were dragged into police vans. Three policemen were injured, one seriously. Boyd heard Gunner's real name for the first time: Detective George O'Teale. Gunner came out of a coma after two weeks but remembered nothing. The crowd had mostly favored Compton's clientele. No one could identify Gunner's attacker. People clammed up. Everyone acted confused. People said, "Who could tell anything with all the wigs and miniskirts?" Gunner's attacker got away.

But the police wouldn't give up. They searched relentlessly. "Anyone who saw anything should come forward," they said over and over, pressing for information. Some of the cops told Tom that Gunner would recover, but it would take time. He wouldn't be back on the street soon, if ever. When they found out who attacked him, there would be one less pervert around. Permanently.

Boyd knew the true story, and it haunted him. The image of Arlen bashing Gunner's skull was seared into his memory. He could still hear the thud, the cracking bone of Gunner's skull. Arlen's face had been determined, grim, as he swung the club.

"I tried to stop him," Boyd said to Sheralee. "But I couldn't." He told no one else what he saw. "I don't know what to do," he said as he sat, shaking. She held him to calm him down.

"You have to talk to Arlen," Sheralee said. "Tell him what you saw." But then her voice faltered; she didn't know what to do after that. It didn't matter—Arlen couldn't be found. He didn't respond when Boyd rang his apartment buzzer. No one answered his telephone. Boyd couldn't ask him, "What the hell were you doing?"

Two days after the riot, Ray came into the store. Ray was a bad character; he scared Boyd even more than Gunner. Ray had been a cook in the navy during the war; he laughed about spitting in the soup. He had a porcine face with small, mean eyes.

"I know you were at the fight," he said. "Tell me what you saw." He stared at Boyd through his pig-like eyes.

"Just a lot of brawling," Boyd replied. He could feel the sweat under his arms trickling down his sides.

"I saw your faggot friend, too."

He thinks Arlen did it, Boyd realized. And that I saw it. He said nothing, but panic began to choke him.

Ray stared at Boyd, trying to rattle him. It worked; sweat dappled Boyd's face.

"When I get that fairy, I'll make him talk. And you, too," Ray said as he left. "I'll keep checking in until your memory clears up."

Ray wouldn't back off. He brought other cops into the store. "College-boy here was at Compton's. He won't tell me what he saw," Ray told them. "I think he knows who slammed Gunner." In case they didn't get it, he added, "Like his buddy, that queer shit, Arlen. He was there, too." The other two cops nodded and gave Boyd a blank look. Boyd could feel their skepticism. They knew Arlen, too. They didn't see him as the violent type. He was just some streetwalker, easy to harass and beat up. But who knew? Maybe Ray was on to something.

They joined the pressure on Boyd.

Ray wouldn't leave him alone. He strolled by the open storefront just to let Boyd know he was there. Sometimes he would ask, "Heard from your faggot friend yet? Tell him hello for me." Other cops came in, nosing around. The stress weighed on Boyd. He had no idea what to do.

"Gunner's an asshole," he told Sheralee. "But Arlen nearly killed him. And I saw it." The tension pressed on him; it never went away. Finally, in desperation, he said to her, "Maybe I should tell them. Just to get them off my back."

He could see the doubt on her face. She didn't know what to do either. She hugged him. "Arlen should turn himself in. You should tell him that."

Boyd laughed. His voice cracked. "Okay. You tell me where he is, and I'll do it." Sheralee held him again tightly as he shivered.

Two weeks later, Arlen called.

"Meet me at the Buena Vista," he said.

Boyd rode the Hyde Street cable car to the end and went into the café across the street from the cable car turntable. Arlen sat there by the window, drinking an Irish coffee for which the Buena Vista was famous. Big, round sunglasses perched on his nose. He looked like a tourist enjoying the view of the Golden Gate Bridge and Alcatraz. When he saw Boyd approach, Arlen waved his hand, the cigarette in his fingers sending off a few sparks. Boyd pulled back the opposite chair and sat heavily.

"Where the hell have you been?" Boyd asked. "We've been looking all over town."

Arlen gave him a cheerful smile. "I'm taking a little vacation. That's all." He crossed his legs and dangled one of his sandals from his toes.

The smile irritated Boyd. "The cops are looking for you all over the place."

Arlen shifted a little in his chair and took a drag on his cigarette.

"No. They're looking for whoever bashed that shit, Gunner." He glanced at Boyd, then looked away. "They don't know it was me."

Arlen's friends must have found out that the cops can't pin it on Arlen, Boyd thought.

"Ray certainly thinks so. He won't get off my back," Boyd said.

"But he doesn't know it." Arlen stressed 'know.' "The cops can't prove anything."

"Arlen, I was there. I saw you hit him. Three times." Sitting there, Arlen looked so frail, too small and weak to do something so violent. If Boyd hadn't seen it happen, he wouldn't have believed it.

Arlen jiggled his sandal a little harder; Boyd could feel his nervousness.

"I know. I saw you, too." Arlen looked away, out the window toward the bay. "I heard you yell."

Boyd sighed and slouched in his chair. His neck and shoulders were stiff from the tension. "You heard me—and didn't stop?" He wanted to shake Arlen by the shoulders. "You nearly killed him, Arlen." Boyd rubbed his neck; it didn't help.

Arlen continued to look away. His sandal jiggled; he stopped it. "Some of my friends know about it, too," Arlen said finally. "But they won't talk."

Your friends won't talk, Boyd thought. Does that include me? For a while, they sat there, Arlen stubbing out his cigarette, Boyd slumped in his chair.

Then Arlen spoke. "The cocksucker deserved it." He took off his sunglasses. "He's an asshole. He hurt me."

Boyd looked at Arlen, who had hunched forward in his chair.

"It could have been murder, Arlen." The sound of the club crushing Gunner's skull surged back, burning in his gut. Like it or not, he was part of it. "And if Gunner had died, how could I live with that on my conscience?"

He turned to look out the window, away from the small figure sitting across from him. A cable car rotated on the turntable, briefly blocking Boyd's view of Alcatraz. "Sooner or later, they'll catch you," Boyd said. He wanted to be free of it.

For a while, Arlen sat, his eyes down. Then he raised his head; his expression was sad. He said softly, "Only if someone tells them. Someone who actually saw it."

The wind was beating up whitecaps now, and sailboats rocked back and forth, their hulls crashing into the waves.

Someone who actually saw what happened, Boyd thought. That was him.

"Yes, someone who saw it," Boyd said finally. "That would be me."

For a while, he did not turn back to face Arlen. When he did, he saw that Arlen's expression had hardened.

"I don't regret it," Arlen said. "I wish I had killed him. He deserves to be dead." He gave a little laugh. "I'd do it again."

Boyd flared. "For Christ's sake, Arlen, what do you expect me to do with that? Am I supposed to forget it, like you flipped him the bird or something?"

Arlen didn't respond. He just looked at Boyd for a while, then turned away.

"I thought you would understand," he said quietly. "I really did." He shifted in his chair. "Maybe you can't understand. Maybe no straight person can."

Boyd's temper had cooled, but the anger left a sour taste in his mouth. Straight person, he thought. Arlen had never called him that before. Boyd thought they trusted each other. Maybe he was wrong.

"You should turn yourself in, Arlen," he said after a while. "It might be best. For both of us."

Boyd sat back in his chair. He felt only the distance between them.

Arlen was silent for a long time. Boyd could think of nothing to say, so he simply sat and watched the sailboats beating against the wind. He jumped when Arlen stood, his chair scraping as he pushed it back.

"Well, now that prick knows there's one queer he can't push around," Arlen said.

He walked toward the door without looking back.

At least he still has his flounce, Boyd thought as he watched Arlen leave.

Boyd never saw Arlen again, but it didn't matter. Time took care of the problem. Gunner's beating became old news. Other things grabbed the public's attention. Haight Ashbury generated lots of action—dope busts, street crime, hippies to harass. Compton's was history. Boyd felt the pressure ease.

Even Ray finally backed off. "I don't know where Arlen is," Boyd told him the last time they spoke. "I haven't seen him for months." At least he could be honest about that.

Boyd and Sheralee moved to the Marina district where they could walk along the Marina Green in the late afternoon, watching the fog slide under the Golden Gate Bridge and listening to the bleating fog horns. The Marina felt pristine after the Tenderloin's grime. Boyd started law school. Despite the odds, it somehow kept him from being drafted into the slaughter in Vietnam. He quit his job at the liquor store. They lived on Sheralee's wages, loans, and Boyd's part-time work as a clerk in a local supermarket.

A year later, a postcard arrived addressed to Sheralee at Boyd's old address in the Tenderloin. Boyd hadn't left a forwarding address. The mailman gave it to Tom: he remembered Boyd and his tall Jamaican girlfriend and thought Tom might be able to get the postcard to them. Better than just dropping it in the dead letter bin, he told Tom.

The postcard was from Switzerland. Arlen sent it.

"This is a wonderful place," it read. "People are very understanding. The doctors are great. I'm happy. I won't be coming back."

He signed it—Arlene.

THE TASTE OF GASOLINE

Deke bribed old Billy to buy the stuff: two six-packs of beer and a pint of vodka. "Gave him a dollar," Deke said, "out of the gas money." "You boys be careful," Billy said. Deke grinned, showing his teeth. "Sure, old man." Deke's grin wasn't friendly—it meant "don't mess with me." The grin made Rusty uncomfortable, especially when directed at him. You could never tell what might irk Deke. Rusty kept quiet so Deke didn't notice him too much.

Bobby sat up front in the car with Deke. Rusty couldn't figure out whether they were really friends beyond being neighbors. Bobby seemed to prefer Rusty's company. Bobby sat next to Deke because, at sixteen, they took the lead. Rusty and Stevie, two years younger, fell into line. Stevie was a cut-up. Deke liked to provoke him so Stevie would hide out in his clown act. Rusty sometimes felt sorry for Stevie. But he didn't say anything out of an abundance of caution. Bobby mostly ignored Deke's bullying, except when it seemed to be drifting toward Rusty. Then Bobby would step in and deflect it. When that happened, Rusty felt so relieved the world seemed almost safe.

They stood grouped at the raised trunk lid of Deke's 1947 Plymouth, ten years old and clunky when he bought it. Deke had put the beer in a beat-up cooler in the trunk, along with the vodka. If we get stopped, the cops can't open anything to search, Deke said, like the trunk. Deke always seemed to have information like that. His father told him things—how to protect yourself in a fight, where to hide a loaded gun, how not to get a girl pregnant. Rusty didn't know how much of it was true. He didn't have the knowledge to question it anyway.

Deke had driven to a spot off the road to the lake where he could pull up behind some bushes. A ridge on a nearby hill provided a backdrop for pistol target practice. Random bits of trash lay littered about: shell casings, beer bottles, torn magazines. People used the bushes for a bathroom. "Smells like someone's shit house around here," Deke said. Everyone laughed. The full moon had edged past the trees, illuminating the boys brightly enough to see the light in their eyes.

Deke twisted the top of the vodka bottle; it opened with a pop. He held the bottle to his lips, tilted back his head, and took a long swallow.

"Ah, damn, that's good," Deke said with a gasp. Deke handed the bottle to Bobby. Bobby seemed to study it for a moment as if wondering what it was. Then he lifted it and swallowed, not as much as Deke, but a lot. He didn't gasp. Rusty admired that; Bobby could control himself. Bobby stood holding the bottle, looking at the two younger boys. Then he handed it to Stevie.

"My turn," Stevie laughed nervously. He held the bottle against the sky, and Rusty could see the empty space where Deke and Bobby had drunk some.

"Here goes nothing," Stevie said.

"In your case, nothing's a lot," Deke said, grinning. Stevie quickly brought the bottle to his lips, tilted his head, and sucked. The vodka hit his throat, gagging him, but he kept it down. Deke laughed. Stevie wiped his mouth with his sleeve as he handed the bottle to Rusty. If he can do it, I can, Rusty thought. Someone had told him that vodka didn't have a flavor; it just burned. The bottle still felt cool from being on the ice. Make it look good, he told himself. He wiped the top of the bottle with his hand and raised it. No odor, but a sort of presence penetrated his nostrils. He put his mouth to it, pressing his tongue against the opening to control the flow until he was ready for it. Then he drank. A warmth spread through him, first in his throat and belly, then to his whole torso, and out to his limbs where he felt it in his extremities, his fingers tingling. The vodka momentarily paralyzed him, a pleasure so intense he simply stood and let it take over.

"You okay?" Bobby asked.

"Yeah, sure."

"Give me the bottle," Deke said.

"Yeah, okay." Rusty watched his hand extend the bottle to Deke.

"Let's have a beer," Deke said. "If Stevie can keep it down." He and Bobby laughed. Rusty joined in, but the laugh rose from someplace he couldn't identify, which didn't seem to be coming from him at all but from somewhere outside.

"Yeah, a beer," Rusty said, and it made perfect sense to him, like something important he had said and then couldn't remember what it was. He had done it; Bobby would approve.

For an hour, they stood around, leaning against the car, gabbing, sipping beer. The vodka went around again, then again. Rusty took his share and prided himself on being able to stand while Stevie wobbled and finally sat on the ground. Stevie started to sing, off-key, some new popular song. He mumbled gibberish; Rusty couldn't catch any drift of meaning. Deke and Bobby ignored him. They were talking.

"We're out of money. And we need gas," Deke said.

"How so? We pooled our money for booze and gas," Bobby said.

"It's gone. I had to give Billy a buck. And the stuff cost more."

"Don't shit me. Are you holding out on us?"

Deke raised his hands in mock surrender. "Hey, I'm just

saying. The money is gone. And we need gas. Or we're not going far."

Rusty listened, drifting in and out. Billy, booze, gas. He heard it, most of it at least. His mind drifted, thought to thought, settling on nothing. Vodka, he said to himself, gas for the gut. Makes you get up and go. He giggled, then caught himself. Luckily, Deke and Bobby didn't hear.

"So what do we do?" Bobby asked.

"Siphon some." Deke's hands were stuffed in his armpits now.

"Steal some, you mean?"

"Borrow it." Deke laughed.

Bobby considered this; Rusty watched him, trying to focus. "How do we do it?"

Deke explained: a mile up the road, he knew a house where they parked their truck next to the road at the end of a long driveway. Deke had a five-gallon can in the trunk and a short hose. Someone would sneak up and siphon the gas while he waited in the car. When they filled the can, he would pick them up. Easy as hell.

"Sounds like you've been planning this for a while," Bobby said.

Deke shrugged and said nothing.

"Who's 'someone'?" Bobby asked.

Deke looked at Rusty and grinned. "Rusty can do it. He knows how."

Even in the dim light Rusty could make out Deke's bared teeth. He tried to focus on the words. He heard them, but his brain lagged behind his hearing. When it caught up, he understood what Deke had said. He did know how to siphon. He bragged about it after his father showed him how. Rusty's father thought there were things any man should know, like how to change a tire or unplug a stopped-up toilet. Siphoning gas fell into that category, something for an emergency. They took some gas from their boat's outboard motor for the lawnmower. Make sure the gas is higher than where you want it to go, his father explained, pushing the siphon hose into the boat motor tank. Then hold it with your thumb close to your mouth and suck the end of the hose slowly until you taste the gas. Then, fast, stick your thumb over the end of the hose to lock it in, lower it into the lawnmower, and pull your thumb away. It'll flow right in. His father chuckled: like magic.

Rusty tried it. "It worked," he told his friends at the time. Not even too much gas in my mouth. It tastes awful. My father thought that was funny as hell. Basically, you suck it out, Rusty explained, feeling proud because he got their attention. Now, it amazed him that Deke remembered something he had said.

As the memory of telling them came back, panic surged inside him. Steal gas. Holy shit. He couldn't do it. He struggled against the effects of the vodka and beer, trying to waken his brain, to resist.

Bobby jumped in. "Why the hell don't you do it?" he said to Deke. "It's your goddamn idea."

"No, I have to drive. Otherwise, we'll all get caught and wind up in the pokey."

Bobby fell silent, considering again. Rusty felt desperate. He gulped and swallowed. His stomach rose on him. Don't vomit, he thought, fighting it. Hold it in. Maybe he should sit like Stevie. But he couldn't move; he just stood, wavering slightly, propped against the car, waiting for Bobby. Bobby looked at him.

"Can you do it? Do you want to?"

Words backed up in Rusty's mouth. He shrugged. "I don't know. What do you think?"

Bobby continued to look at him. Then he said, "I'll help you."

Finally, Rusty's jaws seemed to work with his brain. "Okay, then."

"Just so long as it gets done," Deke said.

*

The moonlight no longer seemed friendly. Rusty felt exposed, like a spotlight had found him. He lagged along behind Bobby, the siphon hose gripped in his hand. Bobby had the five-gallon can. They crept along the side of the rough asphalt surface, loose gravel crunching under their feet. To Rusty, it sounded like a chainsaw blaring their arrival. It didn't seem to bother Bobby, who had reached the old pickup truck parked at the end of the driveway. Deke had dropped them off about thirty yards ahead and then pulled a little farther away to wait, the engine idling. A waste of gas, Deke complained when Bobby insisted on it for a quick getaway if needed. Bobby placed the can quietly next to the truck. Rusty watched him remove the gas cap and place it on the running board. Around Rusty, the dark, alcohol-blurred world seemed dreamlike.

"Just take it slow. You know how to do it," Bobby whispered. "I'll keep watch."

Rusty stepped forward. He looked across the pickup bed to the house, where lights shined in every window. It sat well back from the road, too far for them to be heard if they were careful. And thankfully, no dogs. Rusty cursed the moonlight. From the open gas tank portal, an acrid odor of gasoline brought his attention back. He inserted the siphon hose slowly into the tank until he felt it hit something. The bottom, he hoped. He held the other end of the hose to his mouth with his thumb an inch from the end, just like he had learned, and began to suck, tentatively at first, then with more confidence. He could feel pressure at the other end of the hose; that should mean the gasoline was coming. He concentrated, pulling in with his lungs, careful not to rush it. Slow and steady: that was the trick. Then, suddenly, an oily, burning taste. He spat and quickly sealed the end of the hose with his thumb. Lowering his hand to the opening of the gas can, he thrust the hose into it. And, blissfully, he heard the gurgling sound of gas flowing.

Bobby had watched the whole operation while keeping a

wary eye on the house. For a few minutes, they remained that way, Bobby watching, Rusty gripping the hose as it drained into the gasoline can. Then, abruptly, a sucking sound, once, twice, and the flow stopped.

"That's it. We must've drained the tank," Rusty whispered.

Bobby nodded. He replaced the gas cap on the pickup. Then he screwed the cap on the gasoline can.

"Let's get the hell out of here," Bobby said. He picked up the can and started off at a half run, Rusty close at his heels. A giddiness swept through Rusty: he had done it! By God, he pulled it off! He laughed to himself out loud. By the time they reached Deke's car, laughter had infected Bobby too.

"Jump the fuck in," Deke said as they ran up, laughing. Bobby and Rusty piled in, dragging the gas can with them. The car surged off almost before they could close the door.

Deke returned to the shooting range where they had started. Back behind the bushes, they got out, except Stevie. He had passed out.

"More beer. To celebrate," Deke said, lifting the trunk lid. He punched open a can and handed it to Bobby, then one to Rusty. As Deke handed him the can, Rusty thought he detected a certain respect in the gesture. A thrill rushed through him: damn, he had done it! Bobby had only kept a lookout. The triumph belonged to Rusty. No one could ever take that away from him. He lifted the beer can to his lips and felt the warm glow spread through him. What a good goddamn life.

Deke looked at the gas can on the ground.

"How much did you get?" Deke asked.

Bobby lifted the can slightly and shook it.

"I don't know. A gallon, maybe. A gallon and a half if we're lucky."

"Shee-it. That's nothing," Deke said. He spit on the ground. "We can't go anywhere on a lousy gallon. Why the hell didn't you siphon more?"

Rusty listened to this exchange. He should say, "That's all

there was in the tank." But he stood frozen, speechless, his old lack of confidence swimming back. Bobby saved him.

"That's all the bastards left in the tank," Bobby said. "It's not Rusty's fault."

"How the hell do you know that?" Deke said. "You weren't sucking on that hose."

"I know it because I heard it. That tank was empty." Bobby shifted his stance and leaned toward Deke. In the moonlight, Rusty could see that Bobby's fists were clenched. Deke stood his ground.

"Well, crap-ass, we need to find another car somewhere." Deke turned his head to look at Rusty. "Bright boy here will have to suck out some more." He grinned.

The words hit Rusty in the gut; he felt the beer he had just guzzled rising in his throat. Don't vomit, he told himself. He struggled to breathe evenly as panic returned. He felt his earlier triumph trickling away. One paltry gallon. Maybe he could have sucked out more. Maybe he didn't place the hose right. Desperately, he looked at Bobby. Bobby had been there; he heard the hose rattling like the tank was empty. But maybe he was wrong, too. Maybe they could've gotten more. Now Deke was demanding that he do it again, suck it out of another car.

Bobby stood, not moving, his fists unclenched now. Help me, Rusty pleaded in his mind, trying to signal Bobby, the emotion so forceful he felt it pulsing in his temples. But Bobby said nothing. Rusty felt his body trembling.

Then, something triggered a reaction in Rusty's brain, maybe the alcohol, maybe the tension of the theft. Something changed everything. Now he understood what to say.

"No." He looked directly at Deke as he said it.

"No, what? You twerp."

"I'm not sucking any more gas. We've got enough to get home."

Deke studied him. In the dim moonlight, Rusty could see Deke's puzzled expression as he sized up this new source of resistance. For a while, no one moved.

"Well, then, you won't be riding home in this car." Deke's grin came back. "You'll have to walk."

Finally, Bobby spoke. "For Christ's sake, Deke. What the hell are you talking about? No one's walking anywhere."

Deke had regained his composure. Rusty could tell he felt in charge again.

"This punk's not riding in my car. If you don't like it, you can take your ass and go with him."

Rusty heard this but no longer cared. He turned and walked away down the uneven track to the road, being careful in the dark. He would walk it. Eight, ten miles. It would take all night, but so the hell what? At least he wouldn't be swallowing any more gasoline. No one tried to stop him. Not even Bobby. As he passed the bushes concealing his friends, he could feel his separation from them. He didn't care. The moonlight barely illuminated the surface of the pavement when he reached it, so Rusty walked down the center of the road instead of along the edge. The effect of saying no to Deke had worn off. Now, he felt a creeping uncertainty. How far was it to the main road? It must be a mile, maybe more. There, he could try to hitchhike, but there were no cars along this lonely road. He told himself, just keep moving ahead. You'll get there eventually.

Behind him, he heard a car approaching. He turned to look. Deke's car. He moved off the edge of the pavement; Deke might do something funny as he drove past. Instead of going by, the car stopped beside him.

Bobby sat behind the wheel. "Get in," he said.

Rusty opened the back door. Stevie was still slumped against the opposite door, out cold. Up front, in the passenger seat, Deke sat staring straight ahead. In the dim dome light, Rusty could see a dark smear under Deke's nose and on his cheek that looked like dried blood.

Bobby looked at Rusty in the rearview mirror. "Deke was

drunk. I decided to drive." He pulled ahead.

For a while, Rusty gazed at the back of Bobby's head. He could hear Stevie snoring lightly. Rusty turned and looked out the window. The moon must have disappeared altogether. Outside the car, the darkness enveloped them, the darkness he had been walking through by himself. Could he have made it? Now, he would never know.

Maybe Bobby knew. He should ask him.

LUNCH AT THE DAHESH

Collin hurried along Madison Avenue as quickly as the crowded sidewalk allowed, late again for lunch with Glenda at the Dahesh. One last lunch before it closes, he thought as he maneuvered around the other pedestrians. The announcement of the museum's closing had been abrupt and unexpected. Glenda was in a state of shock.

He should have left the office earlier; he should have paid more attention to the time. He glanced at his watch—seven minutes past noon. His lateness would annoy her. She wouldn't say anything, but her face would show it.

At Sixtieth Street, the crowd eased, and he could step up his pace. But at Fifty-Ninth, a red light stopped him. He jiggled his foot impatiently and considered trying to dodge through the traffic. Too risky, he decided and relaxed a bit. Being a little late shouldn't matter so much. Neither of them had a lot of time these days. They should give each other some leeway. He looked at his watch as he pushed against the crowd crossing Fifty-Ninth. Fifteen minutes past. Still two blocks to go. At least twenty minutes late by the time he got there.

Glenda sat at the table reading the menu when he arrived. She didn't need to read it; she knew it by heart. But he supposed it deflected the awkwardness of waiting alone.

"I'm sorry I'm late," he said as he sat across from her. "The lab conference ran over."

"It's okay," she said without looking up from the menu.

Tony, their usual waiter, came over. "Have you come for the benediction?" he asked. "You're lucky there is any food left in the kitchen."

"It is so sad," Glenda said. "And closing after such a short time."

Tony shrugged his shoulders. "Maybe it will reopen somewhere else. Who knows? I just have to find another job." He walked away with their orders.

"I think it's a tragedy," she said, looking at Collin for the first time. She loved the Dahesh. It exhibited the nineteenth-century academic art she adored. In the late nineteenth century, academic art had been so completely supplanted by Impressionism that it became nearly forgotten as a genre. The Dahesh brought it back—here, in New York, where it could stand up against the collections in the great museums nearby. Glenda had been ecstatic when it moved from its cramped quarters into an expansive new facility near where she worked. Now, the Dahesh was closing after a brief life, and Glenda's sadness knew no bounds. Collin hadn't helped by keeping her waiting.

He had met her in Central Park as he sat on the curb rubbing his ankle. He twisted it when he stumbled during a race—not a real race, just a fundraiser for research in Alzheimer's disease. He took running seriously, and it annoyed him that he had injured himself slogging along in a crowd of joggers out on a lark. Glenda had approached him as he sat, silently cursing. She saw him from further back in the crowd; she watched him trip.

"Can I help?" she asked, leaning over him. Collin raised his head to look at her. The sun shining through her short blonde hair made it glow. She may be nearly as tall as I am, he thought, but he couldn't tell for certain, looking up at her from the curb. They both had blue eyes, hers tending toward teal, his toward gray. He could see she took running seriously; they wore the same brand of expensive shoes made for distance runners.

"It was a stupid move," he said. "I wasn't paying attention. I'll be all right."

She sat next to him on the curb and looked at the ankle with him. They could see the swelling and puffiness around the ankle bone. "It needs ice," she said.

"Yes, you're right. I live just over there—on Central Park West," he replied. "That's the only lucky thing about the whole rotten business," he griped as he stood and tested the ankle. He winced; it would take a while to get to his apartment. She stood when he did, watching him gingerly putting weight on the foot.

"I'll help you get there. Put your arm around my shoulders," she said.

Together, they moved slowly through the joggers to Central Park West. "That's my building on the corner," he said.

Glenda laughed. She lived in the building next door; she had lived there for five years, she told him as they hobbled along. "So typical of New York," she said. "Long-time neighbors who are completely unaware of each other."

"Yes," he agreed, "being so close but anonymous in the crowd." He felt the weight of his arm on her shoulders, his sweat mixing with hers. "We've probably been crushed together on the subway dozens of times," he said as he leaned on her, "but were oblivious to everything, our minds off in Turkestan or somewhere."

"Nice to meet you at last," she had said.

"Yes, even under the circumstances," he had replied as they limped into his building.

*

She had noticed him ahead of her in the crowd of joggers. His tallness stood out, his blond hair so light that it set him apart. He turned his face slightly; she could see his profile. He reminded her vaguely of Max von Sydow, the Swedish actor in so many of Ingmar Bergman's movies. His face had the same pensive look, almost gloomy, as though he had focused his mind on subjects more serious than fundraising events. In time, she recognized this as his usual demeanor—abstract, detached, thoughtful.

He had remained in view as they plodded along. When he stumbled and staggered to the curb, she went to him immediately, without thinking. Race officials nearby could have helped him. But she felt an instinctive attraction, a desire to make contact, a need to investigate what had captured her attention.

As they sat in his apartment, the icepack in place on his ankle, they talked about the chance encounter in the park. She laughed about how she had reacted instinctively when she saw him stumble. He told her how the sunlight shining through her hair had created a kind of halo. They discovered a common interest in brain research; she was an executive at a foundation that funded research, and he was a scientist at a well-known research institution. They worked only a few blocks apart on the East Side of Manhattan.

As they sat and talked, they each felt a growing connection and could tell that the other felt it as well. When she left, they both knew they would see each other again. When he called the next day, she had expected it.

So many things drew them together. She loved to travel, and so did he. He favored Paris; she preferred Vienna. They agreed that Italy had so much to offer, and they traveled there together not long after they met. A magical trip, they both said, as they began to fall in love.

They read similar books and argued about them. She believed in the continuity of ideas, that the accretion of time carried forward the most enduring universal principles, leaving the ephemeral and superficial at the wayside. He believed in the mutability of ideas, their ever-shifting shapes, adapting to new realities, and fashioning themselves to suit the times. They argued these positions with a passion that matched the passion they felt for each other. Ultimately, they concluded that their views were complementary, not contradictory, and they tacitly agreed to accept each other's perspectives.

Music, especially opera, affected them deeply. They listened to opera all over Europe—La Scala, Vienna, Berlin, Covent Garden. They discovered that they had both decided to live near Lincoln Center to be close to the Metropolitan Opera and laughed about it. She loved Wagner; he, Verdi. "Wagner distills grand cultural themes into intense musical expression in a way Verdi never could," she insisted. Collin responded, "No one, not even Wagner, can match Verdi's ability to channel a country's aesthetic heart into music, as he does for the romantic Italian soul." Back and forth they went without resolution and finally agreed to admire both of the great composers.

But above all, they loved art—that became the real bond between them. Art meant everything to them; we are artists at heart, they told each other. Glenda had been an art major in college and held a master's degree in art history. She volunteered as a docent at the Metropolitan Museum of Art. Collin had learned about art in college as well. Later, in medical school, he took a course on art in medicine and came to believe that art made medicine more humane. Yet their approach to art differed. Collin's artistic sense was intuitive and emotional; he felt it in his gut. As a student, he had wept on his first visit to the Impressionist gallery at the Met. Glenda studied art with a scholarly focus; her approach was more disciplined, relying on a deeper understanding of the technical aspects of artistic composition. She appreciated the skill it demanded. Artists are seeking perfection, she believed. She wanted to parse that perfection into components she could understand.

For nearly three years, they had been wandering through the museums in New York and elsewhere and had grown closer in the process. They are so much alike, their friends commented, almost a perfect couple.

They had heard two weeks before that the Dahesh would close. Something about rent and expenses, someone told them. The shock rattled the New York art community. The new quarters had opened only a few years before. No one could say what would happen next. Rumors flew. Some said there would be no museum at all, at least not in Manhattan, and not in the short run. The exhibits were already winding down.

"I still don't get it at all," Glenda said during lunch. "It's such a good place. I'll miss it." She looked at him, her face quizzical. Her expression asked, Will you?

"Yes, I'll miss it too," Collin replied.

But he said it for her sake. In truth, it mattered less to him. Academic art did not excite him; he came there because of her. For Collin, the museum's location in a corporate tower reflected the art itself: engineered, following a blueprint, creatively predictable. He realized that they went there for lunch so that Glenda could be close to the art she loved. At first, he had enjoyed strolling with her past the paintings as she analyzed and explained each one in detail. In time, the walks through the galleries began to wear on him. He found excuses for not joining her: a meeting, the press of work. Now, by default, he would no longer have to come here. He felt slightly relieved and also guilty for feeling that way.

Glenda had said little during lunch but now spoke. "After lunch, I want to take one last walk-through. You don't need to come along if you don't have time." But he said he would come. After all, they wouldn't have another opportunity. He knew what she wanted to see. They would find their way to Bouguereau's "The Water Girl" if it hadn't already been taken down. She liked it more than all the other paintings, and she could talk about it at length.

She had anticipated his thoughts. "I called ahead to see whether 'Water Girl' is still up," she said. "It is."

After lunch, they walked through the galleries to the place where "The Water Girl" was located. Already, vacant spaces appeared on the walls where paintings had been removed. They are leaving before the closing, she said, seeking new places to be admired. She smiled wistfully. Probably going into storage, he replied. They saw only a few people in the rooms. Maybe the public has already given up on it, Collin thought as they walked through them.

"The Water Girl" hung alone in the last gallery, surrounded by empty space, as though the curators had been reluctant to take her down. The painting mesmerized Glenda. She would gaze at it with no hint of leaving until Collin pried her away. In the picture, the water girl stands poised on the balls of her feet, one foot slightly ahead of the other, stopped in mid-stride. The water jug sits lightly on her shoulder, one hand balancing it against her neck. The other hand rests on her hip, which thrusts outward as though she is about to dance. She looks straight at the viewer, her eyes shaded but untroubled; she has paused and is waiting patiently to proceed.

"It is a point of tension, perfectly depicted, as though she has stopped just for you," Glenda had said. "You almost feel she will start walking as soon as you look away."

Early on, she had explained why she loved "The Water Girl" so much. "It is one of the most important paintings of the time," she had told him. "All the great techniques come together in this single painting. It uses classical forms; academic art often does. You can see that she is like an ancient sculpture, Greek or maybe Roman. The light along her arm and across her shoulders gives life to her shape, but subtly.

Everything about her is distinctive—the careful brushwork, the muted, precise colors, the quiet scene. She is so carefully crafted, so accurate, that she seems real." Glenda had paused, then continued. "She doesn't force herself on you or jump out at you," she said after a few moments. "She doesn't need bright colors or flashy details to get your attention. The whole point is to make her seem alive."

She had stood admiring the girl for a while. "She is so carefree, just doing her job, insouciant and alluring. Bouguereau has captured her charm perfectly. She is like a Beethoven Sonata: you can't imagine improving her."

Today, Collin studied the painting with her, as he had done many times before. Glenda saw life and spontaneity in the girl. To him, she seemed posed and stiff. In Collin's mind, the girl was not poised to move, but positioned by the artist and standing rigidly in place. She felt static, not mobile, exactly the opposite of how Glenda viewed her. She smiled vacantly, abstractly, portraying no emotion of any kind, he believed.

Collin couldn't help comparing "The Water Girl" to Monet's "Woman with a Parasol," painted at the same time in 1884 or 1885. Bouguereau and Monet were contemporaries, both highly visible in the Paris art community. But their worlds did not overlap. Already, Impressionism had begun crowding out academic art and setting the course toward Cézanne, Picasso, Cubism, and everything beyond. Collin had taken Glenda to the Musée d'Orsay in Paris to see "Woman with a Parasol" and explain the differences from "The Water Girl."

"The scene is so much more evocative," he had said. "'The Water Girl' is stationary; the 'The Woman with a Parasol' is surrounded by motion. The clouds are drifting; the tall grass around her is swaying. The scene is vaguely ominous. There is a sense of unease. Maybe a storm is coming, or the wind has suddenly turned cold. The woman seems pensive, anticipating something that is not seen, maybe apprehensively, like seeing an approaching lover who is about to tell her their affair is over."

He had glanced over at Glenda, trying to fathom what she was thinking, but could read nothing in her expression. He went on, "See, the sun is behind her. Her shadow spreads darkly in front of her. Her scarf and skirts are billowing forward in the wind, drawing her toward the shade. Her face is obscured by the shadow of the parasol; you can't make out her features. She seems worried, fearful of what lies before her, like she is about to step into the darkness at her feet, not knowing where that might take her." He had felt tears swelling in his eyes as he described the painting. Monet did that to him.

They had discussed the two paintings and argued about them many times. "Impressionism is okay, I guess, in its way," Glenda conceded. "But it's just superficial emotionalism. It can't compare with the demanding precision of academic art. With Monet and the Impressionists, you try to understand what you *feel*. The academics force you to understand what you *see*. Their paintings penetrate your psyche; they deepen your understanding—of art, of yourself, of everything. Monet's appeal is ephemeral, like a good meal, enjoyed and soon forgotten."

Not so, he argued back. "You say academic art is the peak of artistic expression, the highest attainable ground. But it's really a dead end. Monet and the Impressionists were leading the way to the future, to the art—and world—we now know. Your paintings are skillful and pleasant, but they lead only to the commercial art of the twentieth century—illustration, advertising pictures." Which is where they would leave the subject every time, each unyielding.

Today, as they stood looking at the water girl for the last time, he realized how different he and Glenda were, as different as the art they each admired, like Bouguereau in her world, Monet in his. He loved Glenda, and she loved him. But their differences sometimes came through and could be painful. Sometimes, his mind wandered when she was speaking, and that annoyed her. "You are out of focus, fuzzy around the edges like the Impressionistic art you love so much," she teased him once. She laughed, but her voice had an edge. Maybe she believes it, he remembered thinking—that I'm muddled and blurry. Not like her at all. She's lucid and direct, clearheaded about life in a way he could never be.

As they stood there, studying the girl, Glenda said, "She is still so beautiful. Almost perfect." Collin glanced over at Glenda. You, too, are like the painting in front of us—beautiful, exquisitely created, he reflected. He looked back at the water girl. Flawlessly crafted. "Almost perfect," Glenda said. Yes, almost perfect, he realized. But empty. Glenda said the girl seemed almost alive. But Collin felt no life in her, perhaps because of her perfection. Life isn't really like that, he thought. Life isn't perfect. It's more disorderly and uncertain, nuanced and vague.

He began to feel uneasy, unsure why. Nothing seemed different; they had been in this very place many times before. Yet the situation seemed changed, as though he had shifted his position and now saw "The Water Girl" from another perspective. His feelings about her became clear to him: no matter how hard he had tried to connect with her, she did not move him. All the art in this place affected him in the same way. It conveyed nothing to him, nothing that reached deeply into him.

A dawning sense of reality swept over him, and he accepted this truth in a way he had avoided before. He had tried to appreciate the art—struggled to do so, in fact—because Glenda loved it so much. But as he stood there, he realized he would never like it. There would always be a void between them. The thought unsettled him. Glenda stood there next to him, warm and wonderful as always. But the realization of the profound gap separating them would not go away.

"Yes, perfect, perhaps. But not alive." He could think of nothing else to say.

They left the gallery. She didn't slip her arm through his, as she often did, and didn't look at him. Passing through the rooms, she remained thoughtful, saying nothing, and he wondered what she was thinking. They hadn't argued as they sometimes did. Maybe the poignancy of the moment subdued them. But he couldn't help thinking that perhaps she also realized how different they were. And the depth of those differences.

On the sidewalk outside the building, the wind had turned chilly, and they pulled their coats more closely around them. They looked at each other. After a moment, he said, "So, no more lunches at the Dahesh." He kept his tone light; he did not suggest another place. Or another lunch date.

She looked back at him, her gaze steady as always.

"No, no more lunches," she said finally. "Maybe it's for the best."

CHICKENS

Tom Hustle decided to quit smoking as he crawled from the trash heap where the tornado had dumped him. He stood shakily and straightened up slowly until he was more or less perpendicular. The ground felt wavy under his feet. Just his addled brain playing tricks, he figured. He patted himself up and down: I'm intact, he thought. His vision seemed okay, although his eyes teared up and blurred everything. Dust hung in the air, so the world looked even fuzzier. Electric fireflies danced in front of him; the buzzing in his ears sounded like demented crickets. Probably just more mind tricks, he thought. At least I'm not dead, he said to himself, relieved. Or maybe I am, but my brain hasn't caught up to the fact yet.

From his woozy stance, Tom could see clutter scattered everywhere. The screen door lay about twenty feet from him; he had pulled it open to flee inside when the tornado yanked him from the porch and sent him cartwheeling across the yard into the trash pile. Over by the barn, the chicken shed had been blown off its foundation and rested on its side, exposing the racks where the chickens roosted. A hen perched on the rack, its head tucked under its wing, roosting in midday in the open air. Like trying to sleep off the memory of all hell breaking loose, Tom thought. Another hen picked its dainty way around the yard, pecking here and there as though nothing had happened on a typical Iowa summer day. Tom didn't see any other chickens.

Otherwise, things looked surprisingly normal. The house hadn't been torn apart; the roof looked okay; the barn stood in its proper place. Missing things slowly began to occur to him. His shoes had vanished, but he wiggled his toes and could feel his socks. His cap had blown away; he could tell without feeling for it. He didn't see Zeke, his dog, anywhere around. Zeke was pretty cagey. He's probably hiding somewhere, Tom figured, waiting to make sure that the storm has moved on.

Then it dawned on him—no pickup truck. As the tornado roared toward him, he had been racing up the driveway in the truck to get inside the house. Now it had disappeared, evidently sucked up into the void and dropped God knows where. Boy, he needed a smoke. Instinctively, his hand reached for his shirt pocket. But he remembered the decision to stop smoking, made just a few minutes before. His resolve came back, a consequence of penance and practical fact: penance because his doctor nagged him about it, and practical fact because, when his hand flew to his shirt pocket where his cigarettes should have been, it was empty. The twister must have been making a point. The cigarettes flew away with the shoes, his cap, and the truck. But not Zeke, he told himself. Zeke would have figured out how to survive and would show up when things settled down. Tom said it out loud, just to reassure himself.

A plume of dust roiled behind a pickup speeding along the driveway. His cousin Oscar, from the farm next door. Oscar slammed on the squeaky brakes and slid to a stop. His eyes bulged; he panted, short of breath. Excitement turned his face bright red. "I saw it hit your house," he said, gasping. "Looked like the whole damn thing would blow away." He surveyed the yard. "Your chicken shed's on its side." Tom's mouth twitched a little; restating the obvious was Oscar's main form of communication. Tom couldn't let it annoy him. "Look at that chicken roosting right in the sun," Oscar said. "I never seen that before." He studied the house. "House looks okay." Then he added, "But your screen door's off its hinges." He looked around some more. At last, he asked, "Are you all right?" Tom had been his boyhood hero. Oscar still modeled himself after his older cousin.

Tom nodded his head. "The tornado blew me across the yard, but I think I'm in one piece." He didn't mention the trash pile. "At least nothing has fallen off so far." Oscar's breathing began to slow down. He continued to examine the yard, trying to figure out what wasn't right. Then it occurred to him: "Where's your truck?"

"It's gone," Tom replied.

"Well, I'm damned. Your truck just blew away." The missing truck impressed Oscar even more than the roosting chicken. "Damn," he repeated. He continued to shake his head and look around, his hands stuffed in the back pockets of his overalls. He looked at Tom's feet. "Your socks are getting dirty," he pointed out. "You should get some shoes."

"Thank you for that," Tom said. "I hadn't noticed." Tom's hand reached for his shirt pocket. Nothing there. Inside the house, he had some cigarettes in a kitchen drawer. "Yeah, I need some shoes. Let's go inside and check things out."

They walked across the yard to the porch. Tom moved a little unsteadily; the ground seemed to wobble under his feet. Maybe it's the effect of walking shoeless on dirt, he thought. Or maybe the lack of nicotine made him woozy. Hadn't he read somewhere that withdrawal could do that to you?

As they mounted the stairs to the porch, Tom's cell phone rang in his pants pocket—at least he still had that, and it worked. His sister Marigold's name appeared on the phone. Marigold shared the house with Tom, which they had inherited from their father. Tom lived downstairs; the upstairs belonged to Marigold. She maintained it mostly for respectability. She really lived with their stepcousin, Phelps Stahl, east of town in the Lutheran section of Clay County. The Hustles settled west of town, where the Methodists had located in the 1850s, a decade after the German Lutherans took the better ground closer to the river. Marigold worked under Phelps, the president at the bank owned by the Stahls. No one quite knew whether living together as stepcousins constituted incest. The gossipy set murmured about it. Phelps and Marigold ignored the noise, but Marigold kept her mailing address at the Hustle farm anyway.

"We heard in town that the farm got hit," she said, her voice urgent. "Are you okay?"

"Word travels fast," Tom replied. "Must be the internet."

"No, Agatha saw it and called me," Marigold said. Agatha Applecross kept a close eye on the Hustle farm from her wheelchair in a window perch across the road. When her eyesight began to fail, she used her dead husband Jim's binoculars to monitor the comings and goings at the Hustle farm. She led the speculation about the illicit nature of Marigold's relationship with Phelps. She was their closest neighbor and best friend.

"I'll be there in a couple of minutes," Marigold said and hung up.

Tom and Oscar stepped carefully into the house. Tom felt a little uneasy: the place might be a mess. But everything seemed to be in order, except for a layer of dust forced through the nooks and crannies. It still hung in the air, slowly settling onto the flat surfaces. They walked into the kitchen; nothing seemed out of place. Tom had a faint hope that Zeke had somehow found his way into the house and would come out from under the couch or the bed when he heard Tom enter. He last remembered Zeke running beside him toward the house. But Zeke did not appear. For the first time, Tom felt a surge of worry. Zeke might have blown away, like most of the chickens. Maybe the tornado killed them all. His hand found his pocket again—still empty. He couldn't help thinking about the cigarettes in the drawer just in front of him.

"I'll get some shoes," he said to Oscar. "Why don't you go back into the yard and see if you can holler up Zeke."

As Tom walked from his bedroom with the shoes, he heard Marigold's car drive up. She walked in the door as Tom sat putting on his shoes. Marigold looked at him, then around the room. She resembled Tom, with the same pale eyes and graying hair. But she had a narrower face and higher cheekbones, giving her a vaguely Indian appearance, a possible affirmation of long-standing gossip that the Hustles had Indian blood, gossip that Agatha Applecross helped keep alive.

"What a lot of dust," Marigold observed as she looked around the room. "At least it looks like nothing's broken." She watched Tom as he put on his shoes.

"The wind pulled my shoes off," he explained. "It took the truck, too." He didn't mention the cigarettes. Marigold disapproved of smoking and kept her upstairs doors closed when she smelled cigarette smoke in the house.

Outside in the yard, they could hear Oscar calling and whistling for Zeke.

"Where's Zeke?" Marigold asked.

"I think he may be hiding until he's sure the storm is over," Tom said, trying to sound optimistic. They stepped out onto the porch, and Marigold looked over at the chicken shed lying on its side. She could see the hen pecking the ground and the other one roosting in the open air. "Where are the rest of them?" She gave him a quizzical look. "Why would the tornado take them but leave these two behind?" Purely a rhetorical question, Tom thought; tornados can be whimsical. His hand pawed at his pocket.

After they inherited the farm, Marigold wanted to add more animals: another milk cow or two, a few horses, maybe even a pig. Tom would have none of it. He had retired after thirty years of teaching high school algebra; he had no intention of taking up farming, he said. When he returned from the state university to teach, the high school had adopted him. The students and the parents liked his easy manner and his ability to make mathematics plain to all, even the dullest students. After thirty years, the uneasy conviction grew in his mind that algebra no longer served a purpose. Who needed it? In an age of cell phones and the internet, it had little value. These days, no one even had to balance a checkbook; their laptops did it for them.

The school administration begged him to stay. "You can teach social studies," the principal told him. "We don't want to lose such a good teacher." But social studies seemed even more useless than algebra. What could he teach adolescents who grappled with methamphetamine and marijuana, who had sex at an age when Tom was too shy to ask a girl to dance? Kids now had a universe of information at their fingertips, so information was essentially irrelevant to them. He thanked the principal for his kind words but left as he had decided to do. He quickly disengaged and never missed it.

Marigold came up with the idea of the chickens. Their mother had disliked the hens that clucked around the back door. The cackling drives me crazy, she said. More than once she threatened to make stew out of the roosters that competed endlessly to announce that the sun would rise eventually. She made Marigold and Tom collect the eggs in the henhouse, and Marigold took to it immediately. Marigold adored the chickens and named each hen. Tom remembered names like Henrietta, Bethany, and Louise. Even after Marigold grew into a local version of elegance when she returned from college and moved in with her stepcousin, she loved the operations of the farm. The old hens had died off as their father's health declined. Marigold decided to bring them back.

And not just any chickens: Black Jersey Giants, purebred prizewinners from a hatchery in Georgia that specialized in rare and expensive breeds. Marigold bought fertile hatching eggs, insured against breakage. They had a few tense hours when the eggs arrived and went into the incubator Marigold had rented from a hatchery. Only one egg had broken in shipping. Soon, they had almost two dozen prime chickens clucking, scratching, and crowing their way around the yard. They pranced like ballerinas; even Tom admired their beauty. "Black" was the name of the original breeders, but the chickens had adapted to the hue of their name. Their glossy feathers shimmered blue-black, blue-black, blue-black as the hens pecked and the rooster strutted.

Marigold fretted as brooding time approached. Brooding would be a tricky business since the hens were so big that they sometimes crushed the eggs in the nest. Most farmers favored incubating the eggs. But Marigold stubbornly refused. "We'll let them get broody," she insisted. "If they want chicks, they'll have to learn how to hatch them."

Oscar walked over. "Those are the only chickens we've seen," he said. "We thought maybe the others were around somewhere, but we don't see any."

"We've lost twenty-one pricey hens," Marigold replied. "And two roosters."

"And Zeke is missing, too," Oscar added helpfully.

Tom felt a knot in his stomach and reached for his shirt pocket.

"We haven't checked the barn yet," he said. "They could be there."

They walked together to the barn. Inside, everything seemed to be in place, pretty much like the house. Larry, the horse, raised his head when they entered, a puzzled look on his face, which seemed to ask, What the hell happened? Hattie, the retired milk cow, was dozing. Sleeping off the memory of the storm, like the roosting hen, Tom thought.

They searched the barn carefully—behind the rusting plow, inside the tool closet, up in the hay loft. But they found nothing; not Zeke, not the chickens. Tom's fear turned into resignation. By now, the dog should have surfaced if he had survived. Zeke would have wanted to check on the animals in the barn; the responsibility came with the territory, and he accepted it eagerly. The sound of the barn door opening would have summoned him. Deep down, Tom hadn't expected to find him inside since there was no obvious entry point unless the storm had blown open a hole, and Tom didn't notice any. But he had clung to hope, pointlessly as it turned out.

Tom's dogs had always been smart; farm dogs had to be. But Zeke superseded them all. He had the size and build of a perfect border collie, like his mother and father. They gave him his black fur. His white face and vest came from his father, his three white feet and the white tip of his tail from his mother. His grey, searching eyes always seemed to be asking, What next? He carried his tail limply, as his mother Nan had trained him to do. It helped maintain a dog's balance in the nimble moves needed for herding sheep. Nan also taught him how to circle a flock to drive the animals toward the center, her racing in one direction, Zeke in the other, the ring gradually shrinking until the sheep were condensed into a tight grouping. Tom had read that border collies in Scotland could execute this maneuver over a vast area where the sheep had scattered, around hills and valleys, out of sight of the herdsman.

When Tom's father got rid of the last of the sheep, Nan adapted the circling technique to the half-dozen cows Tom's father still had. The dogs hardly needed to do this since the cows made their way home every day without prompting. But it allowed Nan to teach Zeke that managing animals, wooly or otherwise, required patience and adaptability. Zeke's herding instincts compelled him to seek order; he fretted over disarray among the animals. Lacking sheep to mind, he gravitated to the others. The horse ignored him. The one remaining old cow plodded along slowly, too ponderous to be a challenge. With the barn cats, it was a standoff.

When the chickens arrived, Zeke took to them immediately. They presented challenges that baffled his herding genes. Unlike lambs, which could be maneuvered into tight bunches, the chickens defied group logic. They squawked and scattered when Zeke tried to round them up, running in all directions, almost never where he wanted them to go. At first, his frustration was palpable. He would lie on his stomach and give Tom a hopeless look: who are these weird creatures; why won't they behave?

In time, he figured out a tedious method that worked: he herded each chicken individually, nosing and goading it to the fenced-in hen house yard, where it tended to stay once there. The others continued their pecking, allowing him to pick them off one by one. It took time, but he got them into the chicken coop eventually. Zeke would then guard the gate to prevent any possible straying until someone thought to close it.

Tom, Marigold, and Oscar trooped back to the yard, uncertain what to do next.

"Maybe we should look for the truck," Tom suggested. "We'll need it for the cleanup."

"Yeah, for the cleanup," Oscar repeated. Then, for good measure, "We should find the truck."

Tom's spirit sagged; depression settled on him like a soggy sweatshirt. At first, the relative lack of damage left him surprisingly calm. Now, with the truck gone, the chicken house on its side, and Zeke missing, he could feel his mood deteriorating. Oscar was giving him a headache. Maybe it's the lack of nicotine, he thought, resisting the temptation to touch his pocket. He considered responding to Oscar's observation sarcastically. But then his cousin would become sulky; he had done that as a child when Tom put him down, making things even worse. He held it in; Oscar was just being Oscar.

"Thanks, Oscar, for pointing that out. You're right about the cleanup. Let's see if we can find the truck."

"I'm staying here to look for the chickens," Marigold said. "Maybe they found someplace else to hide. I'll put those two in the hatching coop in the barn." She caught them and tucked one under each arm. She headed for the barn and said over her shoulder, "Maybe Zeke will come back, so someone should be here."

As Tom and Oscar left, they could hear Marigold calling, "Here Zeke! Here Zeke!"

Oscar stopped at the end of the drive. "Which way?"

Tom thought about it: how far could a tornado carry such a heavy object? Probably not very far. "The twister headed roughly northeast," he said after a few moments. "Let's look along Comet Road."

Comet Road got its name from a meteorite that slammed into the area in prehistoric times. Comet Road was a misnomer; everyone knew it should have been called "meteorite" road. But nothing could prevent "comet" from creeping into local parlance. One story had it that a schoolteacher in the 1890s didn't know the difference between comets and meteorites. A generation of kids grew up confused about it. Or "comet" might have simply rolled off the tongue easier than "meteorite." In time, the name became official when the county government began naming section roads. Hustle property contained artifacts where the meteorite had impacted. People still came to search for fragments, as well as arrowheads.

A mile along, they spotted the truck in the deep drainage ditch by the road. It stood upright on its wheels but way down in the ditch, so slanted to the right that it could not be driven out, even if it still functioned.

"Well, it doesn't look too damaged, but there's no way we can drive it out," Tom said as they stood looking at it.

"No, there's no way we can drive it out," Oscar agreed. "At least it doesn't look too damaged."

Tom reached for his pocket. He patted it lightly. Nothing there.

"Maybe Buck could tow it out," Tom said.

Buck was their other cousin. His parents named him

Luther, but he had been called Buck since he shot a deer at age nine. He and his sister Annie owned the Hustle property east of Oscar and Tom. But Buck preferred his garage business to farming. Buck's snide manner offended many people. He couldn't resist a jibe, a verbal poke in the ribs, even at sensitive times like funerals. Every smart remark got followed up by a snicker or a chuckle. People found this annoying when Grandma was being lowered into the ground or when he told them that they would have to replace a truck engine or that a wreck couldn't be fixed. They put up with it because Buck did excellent work. He could also drag tractors out of the muddiest fields. Buck paid no attention to criticism. He chewed tobacco and expectorated wherever he chose. (Out of politeness, he only spat on the grass or dirt, never on the sidewalk.)

"I'll try his cell phone," Tom said. The number rang several times until the voice of Buck's wife, Connie, came on saying, We're not here; please leave a number. "He's probably towing someone else out," Tom said. "Let's go into town and see if anyone knows where he is."

"Yeah, maybe they can tell us in town where he is," Oscar replied.

Tom felt his pocket. Still empty.

Sure enough, no one responded when Tom banged on the locked door at Buck's shop in the county seat, named Hillyard after its founder, the reverend Lucas Hillyard, in 1852. Tom rattled the doorknob and called out, "Hello," just in case Connie had locked it so she could work on the books without being disturbed. The cardboard clock with the movable hands to indicate when someone would return hadn't been used.

"No one's here," Oscar observed.

"Let's try Melvin's," Tom said.

They crossed the street and walked around the corner, where Melvin's Café and Grill and Bar sat in the middle of the block, between the hardware store and a vacant office. Along the way, it didn't look as though the tornado had hit the town. It must've skipped right over, Tom thought. Thanks for that, at least.

"It doesn't look like the town was hit," Tom said as they walked.

"No, it doesn't look like the twister hit here," Oscar agreed as he tagged along.

Melvin's became a fixture in the life of the town in the 1920s, when the current Melvin Senior's grandfather, the first Melvin Sprock, established it. The three-part name came about after the repeal of Prohibition. The founding Melvin decided to add beer to the menu of fried steak and mashed potatoes. He planned to change the name to "Melvin's Bar and Grill." The name stirred great controversy among the churches in the community. The ministers pronounced their unanimous opposition to the substitution of "Bar" for "Café" in the name of Melvin's establishment.

The debate raged for weeks. On the west side of town, the anti-beer message evolved into a condemnation of sinfulness in general. The three Methodist ministers competed to outdo each other in raging against a mountain of sin in the town, a veritable hidden iceberg on which beer drinking was just the tip. They hammered away until the argument turned against itself. If we are doomed anyway, people reasoned, what difference could a glass of beer make in the overall scheme of things?

It took the levelheaded approach of Hillyard's most prominent black resident to eventually solve the problem. Bascom Beyond and his sister Beatrice lived on the north side, where the New Englanders had settled in the 1850s. Their great-grandfather, Bascom Beyond, came to Clay County after the Civil War with a local soldier who had befriended him. The "Beyond" name came about when the fugitive slave asked the young Iowa soldier where he came from. "Beyond the Mississippi," the soldier replied. "People call me Bascom Lonsdale," the slave told the soldier. "Lonsdale is the master's name; I have no affection for it. I'll take Beyond; it'll do fine."

In time, the Beyonds became established in Clay County, and a small community of African-Americans emerged, most of them related by blood, marriage, or kinship of some sort. They were tanners, then leather workers, then merchants of leather goods. The Beyond store has the best boots in the state, people said. Gradually, the Beyonds acquired land until they became one of the largest land-holding families in the county. By the second generation, they became respectable; by the third, affluent; by the fourth, prominent.

His prominence explained why Bascom Beyond could resolve the controversy over Melvin's name; people respected his common-sense judgment. Why not just add "and Bar" to "Café and Grill?" Bascom suggested. That way, the name "Café" will still be there at the start to show that it is a respectable place for families, while "Bar" will tag along at the end like an afterthought. People could see the logic of Bascom's proposal, even if it made the name sound a little odd. Melvin agreed to the idea: anything to get past the noise so he could just serve fried steak and pie—and beer—without controversy.

The name became "Melvin's Café and Grill and Bar." As the center of the town declined and businesses moved away, it became more of a bar and less of a café. Some people called it nothing more than a saloon now. But Melvin's had become entrenched in the community's mind. People accepted it as part of the established landscape, like Stahl's bank and Truffle's feed store on Acorn Street. It had existed for a long time, and people in Hillyard respected tradition.

Inside, the cool darkness made it seem more like a saloon than a café. Melvin Sprock Junior stood behind the bar, and he hurried over to Tom and Oscar. The Sprocks and Hustles became connected through the marriage of Melvin Senior's brother, Peter, to Tom and Oscar's Aunt Sarah, the mother of

Buck. Melvin Junior started running the place after his parents retired to Florida.

"Mr. Hustle, we heard your farm was hit by the tornado," Melvin Junior said, worried. "Are you okay? Is the farm okay?" Melvin Junior had been Tom's student in high school. He never outgrew the deference farm kids had for teachers in those days, so he couldn't break the habit of calling Tom "Mr. Hustle." "Call me Tom," Tom had urged, but Melvin Junior resisted. It doesn't feel right to call you Tom, he explained. It would be like calling my father "Mr. Sprock." So Tom gave up the effort.

Melvin Junior's rapidly receding hairline seemed to show more of his bare head every time Tom saw him. Male-pattern baldness ran through his family, all the way back to great-grandfather Sprock, whose rim of white hair clinging to his naked scalp just above the ears set the pattern for future generations. Melvin Junior's squat, square shape gave him an appearance of brute strength, but, early on, Tom detected a softer inner core.

Melvin Junior always tried out for the high school football team, even though he had no athletic talent, and didn't seem discouraged when the coach inevitably cut him. He tried hard in everything he did but fell short of the best. His destiny would keep him in Hillyard, running Melvin's. Tom had seen it in Melvin Junior's eyes and sensed it in his heart as he watched him make his way through high school. In time, it happened.

"I'm okay, and the farm wasn't hurt much," Tom answered. "But my truck's in a ditch about a mile from the farm, and we're looking for Buck to tow it out. Do you know where he is?"

"He went over to Beaumont to see if he could help out," Melvin Junior said. "The tornado skipped over Hillyard but landed at Beaumont. No one got hit around here." He caught himself. "Except you, of course."

Tom began to reach for his shirt pocket, then resisted the

impulse to check it once again. "Well, that's fate, I guess," Melvin Junior said philosophically.

Oscar helped: "Yeah, fate."

Tom grimaced. Fate, hell, he thought. Trouble gripped his place like a curse, a source of relentless bad luck. The urge to flee Hillyard surged in his chest; it had been there since he felt it as a teenager. But he had never yielded to it, even after four years at college had pried him away temporarily. Something brought him back and wouldn't let him leave again. I'm locked in, Tom thought in his darkest moments, to tend the increasingly dilapidated farm and become a local character. He and Melvin Junior had stasis in common; maybe that's why Tom liked him.

"Can I get you something? A beer, maybe?" Melvin Junior asked.

Tom shook his head. He really needed a cigarette but resisted the desire to ask for a pack from the shelf behind the bar.

Oscar chimed in, "I'll have one." His chubby face had a look of anticipation.

"Tornadoes do funny things," Melvin Junior said as the beer flowed into the mug. Everyone had tornado stories: single straws driven through tree limbs, barns that were emptied of their contents without damage to the structure, and toys that wound up in other people's houses. "My granny used to tell a story about an auntie of hers who was making egg salad in her kitchen when a tornado hit. The tornado peeled the eggs in the bowl and left them there. Nothing else in the house was touched. Once she got her wits back, she finished making the egg salad."

As he brought the beer to Oscar, Buck walked in.

Melvin Junior and Oscar tripped over each other to speak. "They're—we're—looking for you."

Buck grinned. "Beaumont's a mess," he said, chuckling. "No one killed, but livestock is scattered all over the place."

"Tom's place was hit," Melvin Junior offered.

"Yeah, it was hit," Oscar affirmed.

"I heard," Buck said. "Everything okay? You look all right."

"I got blown around a bit—across the yard, in fact," Tom said. "But my truck is in a ditch, and we need you to tow it out."

"A 'tornado tango,' eh?" Buck laughed. He wiggled his hips a little to show what he meant.

Tom pursed his lips. "Something like that," he said after a couple of seconds. He couldn't let Buck bother him: it would accomplish nothing. Buck's jokes had always been part of Tom's life, just like Oscar's childlike adulation. Buck had been a gagster as a kid, too, a persistent prankster, a nuisance to the teachers and entertainment for the students.

"It's on Comet Road, just off Route 22," Tom said.

Buck whistled. "Holy shit. That's at least a mile from your place. It flew that far?" For once, he didn't chuckle. "In Beaumont, some cows were tossed into the next farm. A couple of barn roofs are off. And the chickens have all disappeared." Now, he grinned. "But that's about it."

Tom felt queasy. Missing chickens—he knew about that. But he said nothing. If he had, he would have to mention Zeke, and he couldn't bring himself to do it. He figured Oscar would chime in about it, anyway. But, for once, Oscar kept quiet.

They found the pickup as Tom described it and clamored out of Buck's tow truck. Oscar joined them; he had followed in his own pickup. For several long moments, all three of them just stared at the tilted truck in the ditch. Buck stood meditating, Buddha-like, his hands tucked into his armpits. Tom knew it wouldn't be easy to get it out. Finally, Buck leaned slightly and let out a long stream of tobacco juice.

"Boy, she's down there," he said. "That twister did a hell of a job on 'er." He gazed over in the direction of Tom's farm, then back at Tom. "Good to stay away from tornadoes," he offered, grinning.

"I'll try to remember," Tom replied. "Do you think you can get it out?"

Buck pushed his cap back on his head. "It will be a challenge," he stated firmly. "But, what the hell, we'll give it a try."

While Buck and Oscar worked on hooking the tow line to the pickup, Tom called Marigold on her cell phone. "What's going on?" he asked when she answered.

She anticipated his next question. "I haven't found them yet. But I'm still looking. And Donna called. I told her everything was okay and not to worry."

Tom didn't respond. Donna: his ex-wife. He hadn't thought to call her. That must be why she called Marigold instead of him. He'd have to call her later.

"If that's it, I need to get back to work," Marigold said and hung up.

As Buck dragged the truck to the roadbed, the full extent of the damage became clear. The right side of the cab had caved in, and the back wheel canted badly. Probably a busted axle, Buck said. The truck clearly couldn't be driven anywhere. Tom looked gloomily at the damage; it would be a major expense. Buck had said nothing as he worked, and Oscar had the good sense to keep his mouth shut.

"I'll have to tow it from the back," Buck said after inspecting the off-kilter wheel more closely. For some reason, Tom felt a pang in his heart at the thought of the pickup being towed ass-backward. Just another indignity, it seemed, like him being thrown into the trash heap instead of a haystack. Buck said that he could tow it to his shop or take it to Tom's farm.

Tom thought about the options. At the shop, he would be faced with the reality of repairing it. At home, it would sit as dismal evidence of the farm's decline. He thought about how they also needed Buck to lift the chicken house back in place—that subject hadn't arisen yet. The thought of bringing it up depressed him too much to mention it.

Oscar helped him. "We also need the tow truck to put the chicken coop back up." Oscar explained how the chicken house blew over, and the chickens disappeared, except for two. He also talked about the hen roosting in the sun, but Buck didn't seem impressed. "Strange things always happen in twisters," Buck said, shrugging.

Tom stood silently as Oscar talked. Suddenly, he felt his hand jerk up and pat his shirt pocket like a conditioned reflex. He hadn't thought about a cigarette for at least ten minutes. Now, the need surged. Panic seized him for an instant; he shook it off. "Quit" might be too definitive a term, he thought. "Temporarily delayed by necessity" could be more accurate since no cigarettes were available. An image of the cigarettes in the kitchen back at the farm wormed its way into his mind.

They discussed whether to leave the pickup there so Buck could retrieve it on his way back or to take it along to Tom's farm, put it down, and re-hook it once the chicken coop was dealt with. Tom favored the former; he didn't want Marigold to see the damage to the pickup. But Buck and Oscar decided on the latter. Buck wouldn't have to drive the extra mile out of his way, and Oscar, getting fidgety with the proceedings, wanted to go home.

Buck scratched his head and considered the situation. "Well, as long as I'm out here, I might as well kill two birds with one tow." His joke tickled him; he chuckled. "Let's go to the farm first, then I'll drag the pickup over to my shop."

On the way to the farm, Tom decided to ride with Buck; he didn't like the idea of trailing along with Oscar behind the pickup, staring at its nose, tipped down until it nearly scraped the road. On the way, Buck evaluated the intensity of the tornado. "It was a pretty puny effort. Didn't really cause much damage anywhere. Nothing like the big one in '99." He added quickly, "Except at your place, of course." He didn't follow up with his usual chuckle.

Tom said nothing as Buck babbled on. Buck's cheerfulness and Oscar's repetition of everything Tom said wore him down. Weariness descended on him, pressing on him until his shoulders ached and his head drooped. The day had degenerated into a disaster, which deepened his gloominess. Even his happy surprise at still being in one piece had dissipated. He could think only about the pickup, the hen house lying on its side, the missing chickens—and Zeke, of course.

His whole body craved a cigarette; every fiber yearned for a nicotine jolt. He briefly considered asking Buck for some chewing tobacco but recoiled at the idea; he hadn't sunk that low yet. Besides, he could see the farm coming up, and he focused on the cigarettes in the kitchen.

As they came up the driveway, Tom could see Marigold sitting in a chair on the porch. Six large black garbage bags, filled and tied, sat on the ground in front of the porch.

"No Zeke?" Tom said as he climbed out of the tow truck.

"Not yet." Marigold would not give up easily. "I haven't found the chickens either." After a pause, "Yet."

"What's in the garbage bags?" Tom asked.

Across the yard, Oscar and Buck circled the chicken house, discussing how to get it back upright.

"I'm throwing away a lot of stuff from the closets and drawers," Marigold said. "The dust got into everything, even the refrigerator. We'll need to get a cleaner to come in."

Tom started up the porch stairs. When he reached the front door, Marigold said, "If you're looking for cigarettes, I threw them out. The place smells bad enough without your cigarettes stinking it up. If you want them, you'll have to find them in the bags." She didn't indicate which one, and Tom didn't ask. His irritation rose. *Why didn't you spend your time looking for Zeke instead of tossing my cigarettes?* he wanted to say. But he didn't. How could he—hadn't he just decided to quit? Maybe he should thank her.

Tom walked toward the chicken coop, where Buck had begun backing his truck into position. "She looks in pretty good shape," Buck said. "That's a damn good building." Oscar reaffirmed it: "She's in good shape. Takes a good building to stand up to a twister." That's the most original thing Oscar has said all day, Tom thought.

Buck extended the tow truck's boom and lowered the cable so that Oscar could hook it to the metal installation ring attached at the top. "The lift'll handle this fine," Buck assured Marigold, who watched dubiously.

Buck positioned Oscar and Tom to steady the structure as he lifted it slowly, first standing it upright, then moving it over the foundation, where Oscar and Tom could guide it until it settled into place. Buck maneuvered it so precisely that it lined up with the edges of the chicken yard fencing. The whole structure—hen house and fenced yard—was once again intact. Buck got out of the truck and admired his work. "The foundation mounts got yanked out by the wind," he explained, looking at Marigold. "I'll come back and fix that later." He grinned but didn't spit. "She'll be as good as new."

Buck started to reattach the tow truck's cable around the rear axle of Tom's pickup. Once again, the pickup's hind end rose, and its nose drooped toward the ground. Tom felt another twinge of empathy for the pickup; he imagined himself being lifted by the seat of his pants and dragged along, dangling like a sack of feed from a hook.

"How will I get around with the pickup at your shop?"

Buck rubbed his chin and scratched his ear lobe.

"Well, I guess I can lend you Connie's old Chevy for a bit." He paused and chuckled. "You should probably rent something. Fixing the pickup will take a while." Once again, he paused. "If we can fix it."

Tom climbed into the tow truck for the ride back to town. Marigold had gone into the house, and Oscar got into his pickup to go to his farm. He told Tom he would come over the next day to help clean up the yard and put the screen door back in place. No one mentioned Zeke. Tom didn't know whether Marigold had told Buck that Zeke disappeared in the storm. He certainly didn't intend to bring it up himself. The weight of the day's events dragged on him; he wanted to avoid thinking about Zeke as much as possible. Poor old dog: always trying to put things in order, just like his ex-wife Donna.

Donna didn't understand why Tom quit teaching, why he gave in to his disillusionment, why the students—most of whom loved him—disappointed him so deeply. Tom couldn't explain it either. It emerged from somewhere and buried itself inside him, gradually, like a lump growing in his body. In time, he surrendered to it: he could think of nothing else to do. At first, Donna sympathized, then empathized, then urged him to go back to work. Tom heard her but couldn't respond. The need to quit teaching had gone on too long and gotten too big to resist. After a few months, Donna's empathy soured, and her urging turned to hectoring. At the end of the year, she left and moved to Des Moines, and took a job as a secretary in a law firm. She filed for divorce. They talked once a month or so. Neither had a lot to say.

By the time Tom had driven back to the farm, the sun hung low on the horizon, about to depart from the long and vexatious day. The old Chevy rattled and bounced all the way; Buck didn't waste valuable business time keeping his own cars in shape. Tom found the jouncing oddly comforting, like a massage chair, shaking loose the tight muscles in the back of his neck and shoulders.

The tornado had stirred up enough dirt to create a lingering haze in the air, filtering the sun until it looked like an overripe tomato on the verge of turning rotten. When Tom got to the farm, he saw that Marigold had left. She hadn't closed the gate to the chicken coop, which surprised him. She probably saw no reason to close it with the chickens gone, Tom thought. And no Zeke to look after them, anyway.

In the kitchen, Marigold had left a note: "I'll be back tomorrow to help. The cleaners will be here at 10:00. You'll just have to cope with the dust. PS: I left the hen house gate open in case any of them wander back. But I've essentially written them off."

The note said nothing about Zeke.

Tom turned on the yard light to let people know that life went on as usual at the farm; he felt a need to assert the fact, true or not. At least the electricity worked. He flipped the switch in the kitchen on and off a couple of times, testing its reliability. Maybe it's a good sign, he said to himself. I could use one.

He sat at the kitchen table and ate a bowl of canned soup he heated on the stove. Random thoughts meandered through his head, and he couldn't concentrate as they picked at his brain. He kept thinking, what do I do now? How could he pay for the repair of the pickup? Buck's services wouldn't be cheap, even with a family discount. Tom had only his teacher's pension and the rent Oscar and others paid him for farming his land. Social Security wouldn't come for years yet.

He had canceled the comprehensive insurance on the truck to save money, against Marigold's advice. There might be damage elsewhere on the farm; he hadn't had time to look around. The farm insurance had also been minimized. Would it cover any losses? Costs would undoubtedly grow; the burden of the farm would deepen. And all because he didn't have the guts to leave thirty years ago when it could have made a difference.

Replacing the chickens would cost a lot. Technically, he supposed he could consider that to be Marigold's problem. But the chickens had become part of the farmyard milieu, and he found himself missing them. Replacing them should be a farm expense, he decided. Nothing could replace Zeke, of course. A sense of loss gripped him; he resisted the impulse to reach for his shirt pocket. Dogs had died on him before. Somehow, he had gotten past those departures, and new puppies eventually took their place. Maybe that would happen this time, too. He had to hope so, no matter what he really felt.

Some people had pushed hard to keep Tom from retiring. "Don't leave; we can't afford to lose you," Deborah Beyond, the school board chair, said bluntly. She pressed hard. The town is changing; there is more poverty, different from the kind we knew. The kids are lost. They need you. The pressure played on Tom's guilt, and he felt uncomfortable. But he could not go back. He had already gone too far.

"Too far" meant only back to the farm, where he could figure out his next move. But it wouldn't come to him. He felt his life grinding down as day after day, week after week, month after month passed, and he had no strength to propel himself into action. He thought about the farm: maybe he would sell his half. Land prices had slipped, and he would take a beating. But it would release him from the responsibility of caring for it—and about it. Maybe.

He thought about the cigarettes buried in the trash bags in the yard. Maybe he should search for them; he might get lucky. But the thought of digging through the bags depressed him. If he didn't find them, it would be a frustrating excess of useless effort. If he did, he would be succumbing to what he had vowed to give up. Inevitably, it was just another "maybe." Like everything else in his life.

Scratching. Scratching on the door. Tom grew aware of it as he struggled out of a deep sleep on the living room sofa: he hadn't wanted to go into his bedroom. Then a light thump, and another. Tom jolted up: Zeke! He stumbled toward the front door and yanked it open.

Zeke stood there. Twigs and grass stuck in his matted fur, but he didn't look injured. His tongue dangled from his mouth like he had run a long way and his journey had exhausted him. But his eyes burned bright. He looked up at Tom as though to say, here I am. He hadn't barked at the door—he could bark, he just never did. It didn't surprise Tom. Long ago, he decided

Zeke considered barking beneath his dignity, a crude form of communication.

Tom reached down with both hands and cupped Zeke's head in them. "It's good to see you, boy," he said as he scratched Zeke's ears. "You can't believe how good it is to see you."

Zeke slid past him and trotted into the kitchen to his food dish and water bowl. Tom hurried to fill the water bowl, and Zeke lapped it up noisily. As he drank, Tom opened a can of food, then another; why not give the old guy a treat? Tom said to himself. Zeke gulped the food, his snout stuck in the dish. Normally, he ate with fastidious indifference. "You must be starving," Tom said aloud. "Eat all you want." As he ate, Tom picked some of the junk from his fur. Where the hell had he been? He asked the dog, "Where have you been, you old devil? Where did the tornado drop you off?" He wanted to lift Zeke to his breast and hold him tightly to keep him from disappearing again. But that would've offended Zeke's sense of propriety. They were working partners, more colleagues than friends, who didn't hug each other. Tom satisfied himself by scratching Zeke's ears some more and rubbing him along his back and sides. When things settled down, he would get out the comb and clean him up. God, it was good to have him home.

Zeke went back to the front door and waited for Tom to open it. He wants to check things out, Tom figured, and to see how the animals had weathered the chaos. They stepped together into the brightly lit yard. The yard light illuminated the destruction, casting eerie shadows all around. Zeke ran to the chicken coop and checked inside: nothing there. He ran immediately to the barn and looked at Tom to open the door. Inside the barn, the cow drooped, asleep, and the horse barely acknowledged the anxious dog.

One of the barn cats surveyed the scene from the hayloft, its eyes glowing in the bright light from the yard. Zeke spotted the two hens in the hatching coop. He sniffed them, then sniffed the air. He turned back to Tom: where are the others? his eyes asked. "I know, boy, they're gone," Tom said. He wanted to explain: if the wind had blown you almost to perdition, how could the chickens have survived? The hens in the barn were an anomaly, a freak of the storm.

The two of them walked slowly back into the yard. Zeke kept looking from side to side, his nose in the air, sniffing for meaningful scents. Tom's own exhaustion came back. Even the joy of Zeke's return couldn't offset the drag of the day. He needed to go back to sleep. When they reached the front door, Zeke resisted going inside. Tumbling around in space must have made him leery of confinement, Tom thought. Maybe he wanted to be outside, where he could get a running start ahead of any new turbulence. Tom pulled over a kitchen chair and propped the front door open so Zeke could come and go as he pleased. He plopped down on the sofa and immediately fell asleep.

A rooster's faint crow woke him. At least it seemed like crowing—he could barely hear it. Maybe he dreamed it in his drowsiness. Then, it happened again, unmistakable but distant and slightly garbled. Maybe the chickens have come back, too, Tom thought as he swung his feet to the floor. The door stood propped open as he had left it. He walked out onto the porch. The sun rested just out of view, about ready to penetrate the horizon; the growing light brightened the objects in the yard: the barn, the screen door lying on the ground, and the detritus scattered about by the storm.

Again, he heard faint crowing from far away. It seemed to be coming from somewhere beyond the barn, out in the neighboring field of sweet corn. He looked over at the chicken shed, now standing upright, the fence gate open. Then, he heard a cluck—and a hen stepped carefully from the shed into the fenced-in area. This isn't one from the barn, Tom realized. It must be a new one, from God knows where. "So you found your way home," Tom said. "Welcome back: we missed you."

And as he stood looking at the hen, now stabbing at the ground with its beak, Zeke came slowly around the corner of the barn, carefully nosing another chicken ahead of him, checking it from veering off course as he coaxed it gently forward. When he reached the chicken house, he nudged it through the gate to join the other one. He looked over at Tom as though he had just seen him. Close the gate, you fool, Zeke's expression said, so I don't have to round them up again. Tom did just that. The hens blinked, oblivious. He would need to feed them soon; they must be starving.

Zeke watched this without moving. But when Tom finished closing the gate, the dog trotted back toward the barn. At the edge of the building, he stopped and looked back at Tom. As Tom walked toward him, the dog ran into the field, out among the fledgling cornstalks. Even though the storm had rustled the corn rows somewhat, Tom could easily see Zeke as the dog moved quickly. He had to hurry as he followed along.

About a quarter of a mile from the barn, a rickety old tractor bridge lay across a drainage ditch that ran through the field. Zeke reached it first; he turned again and looked at Tom. As Tom approached, he heard the rooster crow again, now much louder. Then he saw it, standing on the bridge, stretching its neck to crow again.

And there were the chickens, huddled under the bridge in a great pile, tucked up in the crevice beneath the wooden planks where they joined the ground.

The tornado must have carried the chickens here, Tom realized. In their terror and confusion, they sought out the dark safety of the bridge's underpinnings. Zeke found them and started the tedious process of herding them back, one by one.

Tom started to laugh. Tears ran down his cheeks. "Zeke, you are incredible," Tom said as he wiped his eyes with his sleeve. Zeke gave him a look that said, what are you waiting for—there's work to do.

Zeke slowly approached the pile of chickens and gently nosed one away from the others. Tom got the idea. "Okay, boy, we'll get them back to the hen house." He crawled under the bridge and pulled two more chickens from the pile. Tucking one under each arm, he stepped slowly along behind Zeke as the dog nudged his chicken forward.

It will take hours to move them this way, Tom thought. He could use the wheelbarrow to bring the hatching cage from the barn so he could move more of them at the same time.

But as he shuffled along, he rejected the idea. This was Zeke's operation. He searched for the chickens, found them, and enlisted Tom to help bring them back. Why disrupt something that worked? "If it ain't broke, don't fix it—right, boy?" Tom said to Zeke as the dog herded the chicken down the corn row. The hens clucked softly in his arms as he slowly followed Zeke. No reason to hurry; they had all the time in the world.

And besides, carrying a hen under each arm prevented him from checking his shirt pocket for his cigarettes.

He didn't need to—he knew they weren't there.

STEPPING OFF
THE CURB

If Henry Marlowe hadn't paused momentarily to study his wife's new pen and ink drawing propped on the dining room table, he wouldn't have been delayed on his morning walk and wouldn't have stepped off the curb into the crosswalk at precisely the moment Miriam Banks turned right. She didn't see him clearly through her cataract-blurred eyes until the very last moment when she accidentally stomped on the gas pedal rather than the brake, sending the car surging across the street and up onto the curb, striking the fireplug in the process, releasing a towering waterspout, and smacking into Burl Curtis as he walked his wire-haired terrier, Murphy. Murphy's leash flew from Burl's hand. The emancipated dog yapped happily as he disappeared up the street, dragging his leash behind him.

Marlowe watched this unfolding scene with a combination of befuddlement, incomprehension, and surprise. The blur of activity distorted his senses, playing out in front of him like the flickering images of a silent movie, except in color. People materialized out of nowhere. In his stunned condition, Marlowe struggled to understand what they were doing. Some crouched around Burl, who lay prone on the sidewalk. Others yanked open the door of Miriam's car. Two men in overalls struggled to open a concrete lid covering a valve next to the fireplug, trying to stop the fountain of water that was wetting down everything.

Marlowe stood riveted on the very spot where he had stood when Miriam almost ran him down. A sense of detachment descended on him as the frenetic activity battered his senses. Shock. He recognized it. Had he been sitting, he would have lowered his head between his knees to generate a flow of blood to his brain. But there was no place to sit, and his old knees would never have lowered him all the way down to the curb. He stood there, wobbling, feeling his heart race. The tension arched his neck and shoulders like a bowstring. He tried to relax them but felt his shoulders growing taut again.

Vehicles of all sorts arrived, compounding the sense of urgency. Police cars. A fire truck, unneeded, but a huge presence. The pulsing emergency lights dazzled Marlowe. The sheriff climbed out from the front seat of his cruiser and lumbered over to study the scene, his hand resting on his gun, just in case, although Marlowe couldn't imagine a need for it. A state trooper, an athletic-looking African-American man with a humorless expression, walked stiffly from his patrol car and began entering data into an iPad. Two ambulances pulled up, then a third. Paramedics helped Miriam from her car. Others tended to Burl sprawled on the ground. The two men in overalls had stopped the flow of water from the broken hydrant, which calmed things down. More people milled about, watching, speculating about causes.

No one noticed Marlowe. No one asked him what he had seen. As he watched, it dawned on him that he occupied a special status. He had been the first to arrive. He had seen everything unfold. Shouldn't that somehow be recognized and acknowledged? Should he speak up and draw attention to the fact? I saw it first, he could say. He turned to look at the figure on his left, a man, a stranger. On his right was a woman, also someone he did not know. He could see the questioning in their eyes, the puzzlement over the chain of events. Marlowe could answer those questions.

But he held back. Did he have a responsibility—a duty, even—to provide the answers they searched for? No, he decided after a moment. He had no obligation to feed their morbid curiosity. They would only pass the information along in some garbled form. Marlowe would speak only to the proper authorities to set the record on a sound foundation of fact. He looked over at the tall state trooper and thought to himself: he's the right person.

Then, a realization shot through him like an electric shock—the accident was his fault! If he hadn't been on that spot at that very moment, none of it would've happened. One step from the curb, a single shoe reaching the ground, had been enough to trigger the mayhem. All the blame belonged to him. He felt his hands sweat and his knees weaken. His breath quickened; he wondered if he was having a panic attack. His knees sagged. The facts were not kind to him. For a moment, he paused and considered staying silent. But the compulsion to confess pressed on him. Like it or not, he had to own up and admit his guilt. It was the right thing to do.

Marlowe squared his shoulders and stepped forward. He approached the trooper cautiously, taking care to do it respectfully. Hat in hand, so to speak.

"Officer," Marlowe said. The trooper turned slightly. In his face, Marlowe read strength, authority. A man accustomed to taking charge. He gave Marlowe a quizzical look without speaking.

"Sir," Marlowe began. "I know how it happened. I caused it."

The trooper's eyes widened slightly. "You were in the car?"

"Oh, no," Marlowe said hastily. "Not that. Not that at all. It was my morning walk."

He realized his words were rushing out, tumbling over themselves. Don't babble, he said to himself. He took a deep breath and continued. "I just meant, I mean today when I reached the curb..." How exactly should he put it? The trooper stared at him, stone-faced, and Marlowe felt sweat pebbling his armpits. He tried to continue: "I was thinking about a pen and ink drawing, and, as I stepped into the crosswalk..."

Abruptly, the trooper stopped him. "Thank you, sir, for the information. Now, please step back." He looked at Marlowe like a stern second-grade teacher. Then, he raised his iPad to his face and proceeded to photograph the damage at the accident scene.

Marlowe stood silently, watching the emergency personnel and policemen working to put things right. The firemen milled around, some of them chatting with policemen, most of them gazing at the toppled fireplug as though studying a new piece of art. The excitement, the chaos, and the frenzy of the collisions had dissipated. Everything was being straightened out, like standing up the chairs after a barroom brawl. Marlowe tried to focus on the scene to understand it better, to flush the haziness from his brain, to find a pattern that might leave him blameless. The trooper ignored him. Maybe that meant it wasn't Marlowe's fault, just a random chain of events. But Marlowe knew it hadn't been chance. He couldn't shake the cold, hard reality: he had caused it.

Across the street, Marlowe could see Miriam perched on a camp stool. Even from a distance, the dazed look on her face stood out. A bandage had been stuck to her forehead. She must've banged it on the steering wheel or the windshield. She stared directly ahead, oblivious to the bustling around her. Marlowe wondered how much, if anything, she could see through her cataracts. She had stubbornly resisted having them fixed. People gossiped about the hazards Miriam presented creeping around the neighborhood streets in her old car. Marlowe felt a sudden wave of sympathy for her. Now, someone would no doubt step in and take her keys away. Her daughter Ruthann, probably. Miriam had been a strong personality in her day. She reigned majestically over the local

Democratic Party, able to shout down any obnoxious grievance from the floor. Now, like Marlowe, she was just a leftover from...what? Just the past, he supposed.

Marlowe stepped gingerly across the pavement separating himself from Miriam. The crowd had backed up after a few commanding glances from the trooper. No one stopped Marlowe from entering the accident scene. Miriam seemed oblivious to him. Someone had placed a blanket around her shoulders. Still in shock, Marlowe thought. He leaned over and placed his hand on her shoulder.

"Miriam, I'm so sorry," he said. Her eyes had a glazed appearance as she lifted her head to look at him. She studied his face, squinting to make him out.

"Henry? What are you doing here?"

He braced himself to admit his guilt. "I was here. I saw it happen," he started. "On my walk..."

"She'll take my keys now!" Miriam blurted. "She's wanted to for a long time."

Her outburst caught Marlowe off guard. "Who?"

"That Ruthann, that's who." She spit it out like Ruthann was an alien, not her daughter.

Sympathy surged in Marlowe again. "Maybe, you know, your eyes if you had them attended to." He stopped. If he hadn't caused the accident, she wouldn't be in this fix right now. How could he blame her eyes? The unfairness made him pause. "But your eyes aren't to blame," he continued. He wanted to be on her side. Ruthann could be hard to deal with.

"Oh, she just thinks I'm a crazy old bag, a big nuisance," Miriam went on, still ignoring Marlowe. She shivered and pulled the blanket around her. Marlowe wanted to say something comforting, but only the urge to confess came to him. "Miriam, you know I had just stepped off the curb," he began.

She cut him off. "Next, she'll be trying to put me in the rest home. She wants to, you know."

A feeling of helplessness crept over Marlowe. She wouldn't

listen to him. Nothing got through to her.

Just then, one of the officers, a woman, came up. She leaned over Miriam and gave her a sympathetic look. "Ma'am, can you talk now? We have a few questions." She ignored Marlowe. "I guess so," Miriam replied, her voice resigned.

Marlowe sighed. No one would listen to his confession. He backed away as the officer began to question Miriam. The thought occurred to him: she doesn't know that anyone was in the crosswalk. She doesn't seem to know why it happened at all. Just that it did. As he mused on this, a sense of normality began to engulf him. Nothing about the accident seemed bizarre or extraordinary anymore. The initial sense of panic had dissipated. It did not seem unusual to see a policewoman leaning over his friend Miriam or to watch as paramedics loaded Burl onto a gurney. Seeing Miriam's car perched across the grassy strip and the sidewalk seemed quite acceptable now, almost as though she had simply parked it there as she went about her errands.

Marlowe realized that the shock of the accident had begun to wear off. Even so, the truth would not let go of him. The tension across his shoulders had returned. He tried to shrug it loose, but it held on, tight as the A-string on a violin. If he hadn't stepped off the curb at precisely that moment, Miriam would have either already passed by or would not yet have arrived. Burl would not have been standing at that precise point, pausing while his dog lifted his leg on the soon-to-be-demolished fire hydrant. It could be explained only in cosmic terms, Marlowe concluded, like the random chance of a particle splitting an atom and the ensuing explosion devastating everything. And he was the particle that triggered it.

Marlowe could hear Burl groaning on the gurney, speaking to no one in particular. He walked over and peered down at the man. "Murphy," Burl gasped. He tried to raise his arm, but it fell back feebly. "Where's Murphy?"

It took Marlowe a moment to realize that Burl meant

the dog. From the recesses of his memory, Marlowe dragged up the recollection of the small white dog, barking in joy as he disappeared up the street. It seemed so long ago. "Not to worry," Marlowe said, laying his hand on Burl's arm in what he hoped was a reassuring way. "He's on his leash. Someone will find him."

At least, he hoped they would. How could he know? Murphy was the kind of dog that strained against any restraint. Only the leash kept him connected to Burl. He seemed hell-bent on freedom the instant the opportunity arose. Marlowe had no knowledge of dogs or their ways. It seemed entirely plausible to him that the explosion of activity allowing Murphy's escape might have released him forever. "Burl, I'm so sorry this has happened," Marlowe said in his most sympathetic voice.

For the first time, Burl focused on Marlowe. "Henry, thank God you're here. Murphy has run off." The old man pulled against the straps the attendants had belted around him. "You've got to get him back."

"You just rest," Marlowe said, giving him the reassuring pat again. "Let them take care of you. You need to go to the hospital."

Burl groaned again. "But Murphy. Murphy's gone."

"Murphy will be fine. I'm sure of it," Marlowe said. He tried to sound soothing.

The dog's name, Murphy, reminded Marlowe of a clerk's name at the local supermarket: Murcaster. Marlowe had read it on the clerk's name tag. The name rang of gentility, an important name, Lord Murcaster. Yet it also seemed ordinary; the name of someone close to the simple realities of life, someone who worked for a living. Murcaster (Marlowe had forgotten the given name) had the sallow look of someone whose troubles weighed on him. He had none of the contrived cheeriness of a supermarket clerk. He grunted one-word replies when Marlowe tried to draw him out.

One day, Murcaster paused in his work, looked directly

at Marlowe, and said, "There is no kindness in the beauty of the desert. Georgia O'Keeffe said that." Marlowe blinked. The comment shook him and stayed with him for days. Murcaster disappeared from the market after a few weeks. Marlowe couldn't help wondering what happened to him. One day, he asked another clerk what had happened to Murcaster. "Who?" she asked as she scanned the items and put them in a bag.

"Murphy, Murphy," Burl moaned. "He ran off. You have to find him." He shifted against the belts.

Apprehension rose in Marlowe. Had he somehow unwittingly accepted responsibility for finding the dog? Throughout his life, he had often been surprised to find himself obligated for tasks he could not remember accepting. Murphy. Battered as he was, all Burl cared about was the dog. He didn't know that the blame for his condition—and, for that matter, Murphy's escape—rested squarely on Marlowe's shoulders. Marlowe had to tell him.

He patted Burl's shoulder. "Burl," he began. "I had just started my walk, and as I stepped off the curb..."

Two ambulance attendants pushed past Marlowe, interrupting him. They lowered Burl's gurney to the ground so it could be lifted into the ambulance. "Don't worry," Marlowe called out as they hefted Burl up. "I'm sure Murphy will turn up." Burl could not have heard Marlowe's reassuring words as the ambulance doors closed. Marlowe was glad he said them anyway.

The accident scene seemed to be dissolving around him. Miriam had disappeared; she must have been loaded into one of the ambulances while Marlowe's attention had been diverted by Burl's groaning. Now the ambulance bearing Burl pulled quietly away, sucking the urgency of the accident along in its wake. A tow truck backed up to Miriam's car still tilted across the sidewalk and latched onto it. The sheriff had gone, and the police officers were preparing to go. Even the state trooper now sat in his patrol car, talking on his radio. A few of the firemen hung around, puzzling over what to do about the broken fireplug. Then they mounted the fire truck, and it rumbled noisily down the block. In its absence, silence displaced all the remaining energy. Little remained of the original chaotic scene.

Marlowe stood, uncertain what to do next. He had played no role in the aftermath of the accident, even though he had been the star of the main event. Marlowe felt a certain pique, which surprised him. He should be relieved that he wasn't being blamed for causing it. Instead, he felt irritated that no one seemed to care about the truth that only he could tell. His insignificance hurt his pride. His white hair gave him away, he supposed: old, therefore unimportant. He took a deep breath and let it out slowly to calm himself. Another defect of old age: invisibility.

It dawned on Marlowe that he had been standing for a long time, much longer than usual, on his daily rounds. Thank God for his cane. With the distraction of the accident, he had forgotten about his weak and undependable knees. The damaged cartilage under his kneecaps now spoke to him. He needed to find a place to sit. But where? He usually rested on a bench in the small park at the town roundabout. If he headed south, he sat on the brick wall in front of the library. He could return home. But he resisted the idea. Why should circumstances upend his walk? Stubbornness gripped him, a pushback against the humiliations of aging.

Marlowe started along the sidewalk leading toward the library. He had gone half a block before he realized he meant to go toward the traffic circle. His aching knees and sore back would have preferred the benches in the oval park. He considered reversing his direction. But that would mean walking back through the accident site, which he didn't want to do. He cursed softly and continued along his way.

The spring day blossomed around him, with buds popping out on trees and the grass seeming to turn greener as

Marlowe watched. He felt the sun's warmth soaking into him and closed his eyes for a moment. Maybe the soothing air would calm him. But his brain wouldn't leave him alone. It kept replaying the accident over and over. Just a few steps would have prevented the entire catastrophe. If he hadn't paused in the dining room to admire his wife's new artwork, he would have been several steps farther along, possibly as far as the opposite curb.

As he brooded, he had a revelation: maybe the accident was not his fault. It could have been his wife's. If she hadn't placed the drawing on the table, he would've had no reason to stop. His footsteps would have been synchronized safely with Miriam's half-blind turn. His wife's decision to place the drawing where he could not avoid seeing it had caused the whole thing. A sense of relief moved through him. For an instant, he felt blameless.

But the feeling was fleeting. He imagined his wife's reaction if he tried this logic on her. She would laugh and say something like, "Henry, if the drawing hadn't been there to divert you, you could have been in the middle of the crosswalk, where Miriam would have run right over you. They would have hauled you to the hospital instead of her." Marlowe's shoulders slumped. She would be right, of course, as usual. Maybe the drawing had saved his life.

Up ahead, Marlowe could see the library. He felt an eagerness to get there and rest; even the hard brick surface of the wall seemed appealing. His legs ached, and the spasm in his lower back had returned. Old age: what a pain. Literally, he thought. He spent much of each day battling his debilities with various medications. Most proved futile, it seemed to him. Once, he muttered a petulant protest to his physician. If you don't like taking pills, the doctor replied testily, try living without them. Marlowe had no such courage. He did as he was told, meekly and without resistance.

Marlowe sat on the low wall at the library's entrance,

relieved at taking the weight off his legs. Even the hard coldness of the wall felt good. He rested his chin on the cane and began to doze, his mind drifting. An image of Burl's dog flashed in his brain. He snapped awake. Murphy. He should have been looking around as he walked. Another ripple of guilt made his cheeks flush. He hadn't promised to look for the dog, but he should have kept his eyes open to the possibility of finding him. But he hadn't. Murphy had left his mind entirely.

In fact, the memory of the accident itself had begun to take on a certain surreal quality, as though it hadn't really happened. Or at least not in the way Marlowe's brain interpreted it. Maybe it hadn't been so bad after all. Maybe Miriam would now see that the time had come to turn over her car keys to her daughter. Maybe Burl would realize that he could no longer live alone, with no more help than the companionship of a small dog. A disloyal dog at that. Perhaps the accident brought forth a reality every old person needed to accept and face up to: the end of independence, the onset of subordination. Maybe it's for the best, Marlowe told himself.

At least they're not dead. The sudden thought both alarmed and amused him. For a moment, the clarity of it erased his memory of the accident. In its place, Marlowe felt a wave of something between regret and fear. He shivered reflexively until the warm sun brought a sense of relief. They aren't dead. Neither is he.

Time to go home, Marlowe thought. He eased himself up from the cold wall a little unsteadily as he felt every joint creak into place. On the return walk, he decided to keep his eyes peeled for Murphy. The dog had run off in this direction, so he might still be somewhere in the vicinity. It wasn't much of an effort, he admitted to himself. At least he was trying to help. He felt a slight sense of satisfaction. Burl's house lay up ahead. When he got that far, his commitment could end. Someone was certain to find Murphy. Somehow, word would get back to Burl that Murphy had been found. Marlowe limped along, reviewing all the events of the day. By the time he reached home, he expected his wife to have heard the details of the accident from one of her friends. Marlowe hoped his version would hold up to her scrutiny.

A large azalea bush concealed the short sidewalk to the front door of Burl's house. As Marlowe passed it, the front porch came into view.

At the top of the steps sat Murphy, wagging his stubby tail. His leash trailed down the stairs. For a few moments, they stared at each other, two veterans of the earlier excitement, both blameless, both innocent bystanders. They understood each other perfectly.

"Murcaster," Marlowe said, limping up the walk to take the leash.

THE SAWMILL POND

On hot summer days, the odor rose from the murky surface of the sawmill pond and spread over the area like a suffocating membrane of decay. Sam Porter knew that stench of rotting wood pulp: a sickly, sweet, enveloping smell. He lived next to it in a cabin he built out of stray pieces of lumber from the nearby sawmills. The pond existed so that the logging trucks had a place to dump their loads, where the logs drifted in the dirty water until being dragged out to dry and be sawn into lumber.

Sam's neighbor, Mississippi Ed, said the pond smelled like the swamps where he grew up. Sam didn't see it that way. He figured the swamp cycled death back into life, plants and creatures, like a living thing. Nothing like that happened in the pond. Only a mossy fringe ringed the pond walls at the waterline, just a weak, yellowish-green coloring. Not real life, to Sam's mind. The pond produced only rottenness, no new life of any kind. To Sam, it did not resemble a swamp. It was just dead.

Sam stayed on in his shack after he stopped working at the sawmill because the pond reminded him of his big brothers, loggers who loomed so large in his life that they came to him in his dreams. He tolerated the odor and sometimes remembered it when he was somewhere else, as he did after the thing happened, and he lay in the hospital, silent, while the sheriff told him about the boy. The odor of the dead pond came back, even though the hospital smelled only of antiseptic and soap on the nurse's hands.

Sam quit his job at the sawmill years ago because he could no longer stand the scream of the big trolley saw ripping the logs into boards, a sound so intense that it threatened his sanity. His brain would barely return to him before the saw took another cut, and he had to steel himself against it again. Sometimes, panicked, he almost wet his pants. He stood it for most of his life until the day when he couldn't take it anymore. Sam left the sawmill and became a handyman. He had no trouble getting jobs patching roofs, painting sheds, and fixing old washing machines. He did good work, and people liked him and could trust him to show up and do what they hired him to do.

He got old and couldn't be sure how it happened. Even though he couldn't do sawmill work anymore, he couldn't quite separate himself from it either. Porters have sawdust in their veins, people said, and Sam thought it might be true. His lanky frame stooped a little now, and his sunburned face made him look older than his sixty-some years, especially when he didn't shave his gray beard. The razor nicked the wrinkles in his skin, so he didn't use it as much these days. He had gray eyes, too, like all the Porter men, and he couldn't see as well as he once could. But he wouldn't spend a lot of money on glasses just to read the damn newspaper, he said to Mississippi Ed. He could see well enough to know what was going on around him. He didn't need to see any more than that.

Porter men had strong backs and good minds. Sam came into the world long after his two brothers, Lucas and Harry. His mother called him her miracle from heaven. As the baby, Sam got more schooling than his brothers. It taught him to think, and all his life, he wondered about things. Sam kept going to school after his father died and then his mother while he was still a little kid. His big brothers took over his upbringing. Lucas became his new father, stern and strong, teaching Sam how to use the tools in the workshop and to spot deer antlers through the brush. Harry watched over him, making sure that he combed his hair and brushed his teeth. He saw to it that Sam did his homework and didn't act up in school.

To Sam his brothers seemed as mighty as the huge trees they cut down. As a boy, he watched them, awestruck, as they skipped across the slick, half-sunk tree trunks in the pond, sliding and swaying on them, pushing the logs with long, steel-tipped poles. In the woods, his brothers shinnied up the tall pines, wood cleats strapped to their boots, topping off the trees with the saws dangling from their waists, a job so dangerous that they both died from it. Sam had pretty much grown up by then, but their absence spawned a vacuum in his world that burdened him. When his brothers came to him in dreams, it felt like they were alive again, and that calmed him and gave him comfort. He liked sitting on the porch, looking out across the murky water, musing and remembering. Now that he had gotten old, the memories were good company. He stayed put in the little house next to the pond so nothing would be disturbed.

On the hottest day so far that year, Sam first saw the boys at the edge of the pond on the opposite side, distant figures, one taller than the other, but both young. Just like boys to be out in the hot sun while everyone else hides in the shade, Sam thought. Restless, curious, looking for anything to fight the boredom. He understood because he had been pretty much the same. Only when they came closer as they worked their way around the edge could he make them out more clearly. He had never seen either of them before. Must be new in town, he thought. One, the younger and smaller, trailed along behind, his sun-bleached hair shimmering in the blazing sun. He was a nervous-looking kid with washed-out blue eyes, and skinny, his bony knees pressing against his patched jeans. Maybe nine or ten, Sam figured. A towhead, probably an Okie kid. The town had a lot of them, and they came and went so often that no one really knew them.

The older boy stood several inches taller, with broad shoulders and strong-looking arms, on the edge of adolescence, thirteen or so, clearly the leader. His face and arms were weathered and blistered-looking, from sunburn. His dark hair had been hacked off and hung down raggedly. The boy flipped his head now and then to keep the hair off his face. He moved with confidence along the pond edge, carrying a long stick that he used to poke at the drifting logs or to whack the grass and bushes to see what he could stir up. A good-looking boy, Sam thought. Too bad they didn't cut his hair better.

Sam could see that the older boy held all the power and liked it. When Sam first noticed them, the bigger boy was jabbing at the little blond kid, teasing him, trying to trip him. As they drew closer, Sam heard the little boy whining to be left alone, but the bigger boy kept at it. "I'm gonna push you in the water," the dark-haired boy said. He laughed and used the stick to maneuver the younger boy toward the pond. "You'll float like a log." He laughed again. The younger boy scrambled to get out of the way and slipped, falling to his knees. The bigger boy poked at him some more.

Sam called out, "Now, don't you play too close to that edge. It's dangerous there. The ground is shifty. That little boy might fall in."

The older boy turned to look at him. A grin spread across the boy's face. "Ah, we're just playin' around," he said. "I ain't gonna hurt him." The boy gazed steadily at Sam, unafraid, as though calculating Sam's authority to issue a warning or enforce it. He flicked the hair from his face, the grin fixed in place. Sam saw the boy's dark eyes, almost black. The boy turned back to poking the logs with his long stick. He kept on doing that for a while, ignoring Sam as the younger boy moved up beside him. Not a brother, Sam guessed, just a little kid drawn to the bigger boy, as smaller children are to older kids.

Curiosity about the old man must have gotten to the dark-haired boy, and finally, he turned toward Sam to take another look. The boy grinned again. Sam sensed a certain craftiness in it as though the boy had decided a grin might make peace with the old man. For a minute or two, they stared at each other, the boy never looking away. Sam held his gaze. Then he said, "That's a mighty fine stick you got there. Haven't ever seen one like it. Where'd you get it?"

The boy said nothing; he stood motionless. Sam got out of his rickety old chair and walked slowly toward the boy. The boy stood his ground. Sam took another step, then another, until he stood face to face with the boy, who still hadn't moved.

"Yep, a fine stick," Sam repeated. "Could I take a look at it?"

Sam felt the boy's dark eyes sizing things up. He and the boy stood, waiting, neither moving. Then, the boy abruptly handed Sam the stick and stepped back, like he expected Sam to hit him with it. Sam hefted the stick. Its weight surprised him. Heavy to handle, although the boy seemed to lift it with ease. Hardwood of some kind, Sam thought, not oak, maybe hickory. No hickory around here, so it isn't local-made. The stick had been whittled by someone who knew what they were doing, tapering down from a butt-end about two inches across to a slightly slender end, but not a point. Sort of like a pool cue, Sam thought, but thicker and a lot heavier. The whittled marks made an intricate pattern, something only a skilled carver could do. Sam considered how someone might use such a stick. Prodding animals around, maybe big animals, like cattle or even bulls, something strong against the hefty resistance of the cows. You could kill someone with a stick like this.

"This here's a good stick," Sam said. "Where'd you say you got it?"

The boy had relaxed a little, apparently no longer expecting a blow.

"Someone gave it to me," he said. "An old man. Said he didn't need it no more."

Sam took that in. Almost certainly, the boy stole it somewhere, he decided; that's what boys do. He could imagine himself as a kid, yearning for such a fine stick, sneaking it away from the owner when he could and his brothers making him return it when they caught him. He handed the stick back to the boy.

"Well, you should check and make sure the old guy don't really need it. Just to make double sure." The boy took the stick without comment. Together, the boys contemplated Sam. Then, the older boy yelled, "Run!"

And they vanished into the brush.

Two days later, the boys came back. The boiling midday sun had heated the pond water until Sam thought the logs looked like turds floating in laundry scum. He stayed in the shade of his porch. Mill work had slowed down, so Sam had the pond mostly to himself.

The boys approached through the brush where they had run off before and went straight up to the edge of the pond, down the way a bit, without looking in Sam's direction. Ignoring him, he figured, because the older boy wanted to make a point. The dark-haired boy had his stick, and, for a long moment, he stood holding it, his arm outstretched, the slender end jammed against the ground. The younger boy held something in his hands, something alive. He struggled to keep it in his grasp as it wiggled to get free. Sam couldn't tell what it was. The dark-haired boy stood silently, looking at the pond as though meditating, paying no attention to the smaller boy's effort to hold the squirming something in his hands. That went on for a minute or two until the younger boy began to complain that he couldn't hold it much more and what should he do with it. Finally, the bigger boy broke his concentration and looked down at his companion.

"Throw it in," he ordered.

The little kid flung it as far as he could.

The something flailed as it arced through the air and then splashed into the water a couple of yards from the shore. As it flew through the sky, Sam made it out—a frog, a big frog, a bullfrog, probably. They must have found it somewhere else because Sam had never seen a bullfrog anywhere near the pond. The frog landed in the water on its back, quickly righted itself, and circled around to get its orientation as it searched for a place to hide. The logs had drifted away from this part of the pond—later, Sam decided the boys must have chosen it for that reason—so the frog had nothing to climb onto. Sam could see it struggle in the foul, hot water, desperate to escape. Frogs can't stand water that's too warm, Sam thought to himself; they won't even go in it. Water as hot as the pond under the baking sun would kill them after a time.

The frog headed toward the bank, stroking with its strong legs. The boys watched in silence. As the frog drew nearer to the bank, the dark-haired boy lowered his stick, placed the tip against it, and pushed the frog further back into the pond, away from the bank. The towheaded boy giggled. Again, the creature struggled toward the shore: once more, the boy pushed it away with the stick. Again, then again, and again, for twenty minutes or so, until the older boy finally let the exhausted, half-cooked creature struggle onto the bank, where it sat, too weak to move. The boy stepped forward, reversed the stick in his hand, and placed the butt end against the frog's skull, forcing the stick down, crushing the remaining life out of it.

He studied his work for a few moments, then turned to the younger boy and said, "Let's go." And they left the way they came.

That night, Sam lay awake and thought about the boys and the frog. He hadn't tried to stop them. He remembered his own boyhood when his brothers had taken him frogging along the creek beds where he grew up, carrying three-pronged frog gigs with sharp barbs to snag the bullfrogs. It's hunting, his brothers explained, like shooting a deer for meat. But what the dark-haired boy had done with his stick wasn't hunting; Sam knew that. He had seen creatures teased and tormented all his life. Boys sometimes killed things for sport—squirrels, blue jays. It seemed to be part of the world. He stared into the darkness as he pondered the right or wrong of it. Finally, he decided: boys do things that they don't do later in life. They grow up and change. Bullfrogs still make their way through the world.

But the image of the desperate creature dying slowly in the stinking water wouldn't leave him. He barely slept all night.

They had a dog with them when they came around the next time. A mutt, piebald, small and scruffy, somewhere between a puppy and a full-grown dog, trailing the younger boy and sticking close to him. Today, the boys emerged from the brush closer to Sam's shack. They had gotten used to him, he thought, and weren't so wary. But still not friendly: just tolerant of his presence, like he didn't matter at all.

"That your pup?" Sam asked as they got closer. The younger boy squatted to stroke the dog, which got so excited from the attention that it danced on its paws, its rear end vibrating from the thumping tail-wagging. "He ain't no one's dog," the older boy replied. "He's a stray. Nobody wants him." Sam watched a grin grow on the boy's face as before. The grin made Sam wary: he no longer trusted it. Sam watched the dog licking the younger kid's face, the puppy's butt gyrating from the tail-wagging.

"Well, it looks like your friend wants him," Sam said.

The older boy looked at the kid and the dog. "That's just 'cause he gave it some scraps. It'll follow anyone who feeds it." He stared at the wiggling dog for a while. Then repeated, "Nobody wants it." Abruptly, he turned and started walking away, sticking close to the edge of the pond—to show his independence, Sam figured as he watched. The older boy said nothing as he left. The towheaded boy jumped up and followed him, the mutt glued to his heels, pausing now and then to sniff something, then trotting to catch up.

The boys' presence had cast a gray mood over the day. Sam brooded as he watched the figures grow smaller. That dark-haired boy's got trouble, Sam thought. The little kid's too young to understand much; he just goes along. Across the pond, he could just make them out, playing, throwing stones and pieces of wood into the pond, but he couldn't hear them. Then he had another thought: the dog is the happiest one of them. He dozed off. When he awoke, the boys were gone.

The air had cooled a little overnight, and it had clouded up, maybe ready to rain, something rare in the summer. Sam hoped it would rain. He liked the sound when the rain splashed across his tin roof and ran over the edge, close to where he sat in his rocker on the porch. The coolness of the air gave Sam a charge of energy. Do something, he told himself; I'll take a walk around the pond, stretch my legs. The mill had shut down for a while, so the trucks had stopped coming, and it had grown quiet. The stillness made him jittery.

As he walked along, he could feel the quiet turn into emptiness, and loneliness began to take hold. Sometimes, the pond did that to him. He realized he needed to talk to someone: have some conversation. For more than a week, he hadn't spoken with anyone except the boys, and they weren't exactly good company. He might get into his truck and drive to Mississippi Ed's bait store on the road to the lake. They could chat if business allowed.

Sam saw it floating in the pond just when he reached the point where he had seen the boys playing the day before. At first, he couldn't make out what it was, but he knew it didn't belong in the pond. Sam studied it, squinting; then he knew: the pup. The piebald coloring had thrown him off at first. Sam moved cautiously to get a closer look, mindful of the steep side and loose dirt on the edge. The small body floated about five feet out in the water. As Sam looked at it, an idea chilled him: the memory of the dark-haired boy pushing the bullfrog away from the shore, tormenting it, watching it die. Sam shook his head; it didn't seem possible. No one would do that to a puppy, would they? The bank was high and crumbly. The dog must have slipped into the pond, and the boys couldn't get it out. Sam saw it in his mind's eye: the poor thing struggling in the water, the boys watching helplessly.

A sadness came over Sam: just a puppy, happy because he found a friend, now dead. He couldn't let it float there. He would go back to his shack for a shovel and bury the small body over in the brush.

The boys returned two days later. As soon as he saw them, Sam quickly got out of his chair and walked up to them. "How come I found that pup floatin' in the pond, dead?" he challenged the older boy. The boy stepped back like he did that first day when Sam asked to see his stick. The boy said nothing. The younger boy piped up, "It fell in, and we couldn't get it out," he said. "We tried and tried, but we couldn't get down to the water 'cause the bank's so steep—and crumbly like you said." He stopped for a moment. "So it drown-ded."

Sam looked hard at the kid, trying to tell if he had lied.

The explanation felt a little coached. The kid shifted nervously, but that didn't mean anything. Kids get fidgety when you stand over them. He looked at the dark-haired boy, who had kept silent. No grin today, Sam thought. He could read nothing in the bigger boy's expression. Sam remembered him pushing the bullfrog back out with his stick over and over. But a puppy's not a bullfrog, Sam told himself. He's smarter; he would avoid the stick and crawl out. If he could. They stood like that for a while: the smaller boy fidgeting; the dark-haired boy silent, holding his stick; Sam, alone in his thoughts, trying to imagine what had happened.

Finally, the dark-haired boy spoke. "It don't matter that it's dead. It's just a stray. Nobody wanted it." Sam shook out of his musing and stepped toward the bigger boy. The boy moved back, gripping his stick. "Don't you bring no more dogs up here," Sam said as sternly as he could manage. "I told you it's dangerous. One dead puppy's enough." The dark-haired boy stood for a few moments, then spun on his heel and headed away, walking fast. The towheaded boy had to scramble to catch him. As he half-ran to keep up with the bigger boy, Sam heard the younger kid say, "I wanted it." The older boy kept moving, even faster now, almost running, until he reached a point where he could step down from the bank and duck into the brush.

At the edge of the bushes, he looked back at Sam and repeated, "Nobody wanted it."

He disappeared, the younger boy right behind him.

The next day, three boys came. Across the pond where they emerged from the brush, Sam could see the two familiar boys, but now another one trailed behind the younger boy. The new kid had a chubby frame and a slightly peculiar way of walking, a kind of rocking gait. He had brown hair, but not nearly as dark as the older boy. No more than five or six, Sam thought.

As they drew closer, Sam could make out the new kid's face, and saw the difference from the other two. The new boy's eyes were alive but dull, like he couldn't quite keep track of the actions around him. He stayed locked on the towheaded boy, oblivious to everything else. Slow-witted, Sam thought. He remembered the polite term: backward.

"Who's your friend?" Sam asked as the boys approached, the new one following behind. The boys stopped and looked at him. "He lives next door to me," the towheaded boy said. "Barney's his name. Sometimes, I look after him when his mama wants me to." The older, dark-haired boy smirked; the grin returned to his face. "He's a dummy," the boy said. "He can't talk. He don't even go to school." He aimed his stick at the new boy, like he intended to poke at him, but didn't. "His folks is gonna put him in the loony bin. They don't want him no more."

Sam studied the three of them. The new boy gazed steadily at the back of the towheaded boy; he hadn't looked at Sam since they walked up. Poor kid, Sam thought, what a life he'll have. He had known slow kids before, plenty of them, kids who sat in school fiddling with their pencils or just looking out the window. Most of them could still do things—hunt or work in the sawmill. Sam couldn't imagine this boy doing those things. The kid would spend a lifetime being looked after, needing someone to take care of him. Sam felt a surge of sympathy for the new little kid. The two other boys had befriended him—or the towheaded one had anyway—and that made Sam feel better. At least they didn't have another puppy with them.

"Well, you kids, be careful," he said. "Don't let the little guy get hurt."

Sam dozed in his chair after the boys were gone. He fell asleep more often now, especially on these hot days. He dreamed about his brother, the older brother Lucas, and he didn't like the dream as he usually did. In it, his brother stood facing him in the deep, thick forest, calling out to him, trying to tell him something, something urgent and important. But Sam couldn't make out what his brother said. What? What are you saying? he wanted to yell. Even though his lips moved, no sound came out. His brother kept calling, his hands cupped around his mouth. Still, Sam couldn't hear the words. He tried to run closer, but with every step, his brother receded further into the woods. Sam struggled, held back by some invisible force, but couldn't get closer. His brother was disappearing deeper into the woods, calling soundlessly.

Sam jerked awake. The boys! His brother had been warning him about the boys! Something bad had happened. Sam could feel it. He rose from his chair; he had to get to the boys. Across the pond, he could see the dark-haired boy poking his stick at something in the water, poking and prodding something floating on the surface, while the towheaded boy watched.

Sam called out, "Stop that, stop that now!"

He started to run, but his panicked breathing dragged on him. He saw the towheaded boy turn and run into the brush. The bigger, dark-haired boy faced Sam now as the old man hurried forward. Sam didn't see the other boy, the backward one, anywhere. Sam panted, gasping, as he ran, half stumbling on the uneven ground. He tried to shout again, "Stop." Only a hoarse whisper came out. Sam could see the dark-haired boy concentrating on him, gauging the situation. The boy reversed the stick in his hands, like a baseball bat, and crouched, waiting. Sam half staggered, half lunged toward the boy, reaching for the stick. The boy stepped to the side, ready to swing. He's going to hit me, Sam realized. The big stick whistled through the air. Sam raised his hands to ward off the blow but saw only a blur. The heavy end of the stick caught Sam high up on his left side, making a thudding sound as it slammed into him. Some ribs cracked; he gasped as pain shot through him. He stumbled back, barely able to stand. The boy came at him, sneering, a wicked grin on his lips—and he swung the stick again, this time at Sam's head. Sam's hands jerked up, deflecting the blow. The stick glanced off the side of his head, knocking him to the ground.

Now he saw only the sky and realized he was on his back, defenseless. Dimly, through sparks of pain, he saw the boy raise the stick again. This is it—that'll kill me, Sam thought.

And he felt the world fade away.

He awoke, the sun blazing in his face, a throbbing skull. For a moment, he had to think about where he was. Then the boy's sneer, the stick flashing through the air, came back to him. At least he hadn't been killed, he thought, relieved. He lifted his head and tried to raise himself with his right arm. Pain shot through his left side as he moved to a crouch and stood shakily. His side hurt worse than his head.

The boys! He looked frantically around him. He didn't see the dark-haired boy anywhere, but the stick lay on the ground nearby. His head pounded, distorting his vision. Sam peered into the pond, searching for any sign of the little backward boy in the water. He saw nothing. That didn't mean much; the body might not have surfaced yet. Desperately, Sam shouted, "I've got to find him!" A spasm from his chest shook him and sent pain shooting through his body. He staggered to stand straight. He had to get help. Slowly, he made his way back to his shack, sitting on tree stumps to rest, crawling the final hundred feet. There was no telephone in his cabin, so he had to get into his truck and drive.

Climbing into the truck hurt like fire; pain flashed across Sam's chest as he tried to steer. When he reached Mississippi Ed's yard, he honked the horn twice, three times—that hurt too—then half climbed, half fell out of the truck, and sat on the running board as his neighbor ran out of the house toward him. "Sam, what the hell happened?" Ed yelled. "There's blood on your face." Sam reached up; he felt blood from the wound where the dark-haired boy hit him. His fingers came away sticky.

"That don't matter right now," Sam gasped. "There's a dead boy in the pond. I tried to find him but couldn't." He panted. "Call the sheriff. They've got to go find the boy. In the water." His words stumbled over each other. "And another boy hit me with his stick, bad, in my ribs, my head." A spasm of pain bent him over. "I think he broke a bunch of ribs."

"Let's get to the hospital," Mississippi Ed said urgently. He made a pallet with blankets so Sam could lay flat in the bed of the truck. Sam felt the truck moving, sensed the rhythm in the road, every bump. The thing flooded his mind—the boys, the stick. "Nobody wants him," the dark-haired boy said. Nobody wants him, Sam repeated over and over. A great sob swelled in his chest, hurting him. He could think only of pain. At the hospital, they eased Sam out of the truck and onto a hospital gurney. He kept trying to tell them about the dead boy: a little boy, his friends killed him. But the nurses shushed him. "Tell the sheriff. He's coming," they said.

Someone gave him a shot of painkiller, and the pain began to ease. A pleasant glow settled in as drowsiness washed over him. He struggled to keep awake—no sleeping until he talked to the sheriff. But he felt at peace.

He awoke to the sheriff standing next to the bed, watching him.

"The dead boy," Sam said hoarsely. "Did you find him? In the pond."

The sheriff waited a bit. Then he nodded.

Sam's heart surged; the news spread through him like poison. "The poor little tyke," he said, his voice catching in his throat.

The sheriff waited for a while before speaking. "Sam, what happened out there?" He pulled over a chair. "You've got some busted ribs. And a lump the size of an apple on the side of your head. Ed said you were babbling that someone clubbed you."

Sam moved his head from side to side, trying to clear the fogginess. He struggled to put it together in his mind: the bullfrog, the puppy, the little backward boy. The words were stacked up in his head, locked in his tongue. Slow down, he told himself, get the words out. "There are three of them," he finally managed to say. "A big kid, dark-haired, thirteen, fourteen. And a little towheaded boy, maybe ten. And, lately, the littlest boy, who was—I don't know how to say it—slow in his head, I guess."

The words choked him, and he paused. "The older boy is the boss. He orders the others around. He killed a bullfrog and a puppy with that big stick of his, pushing them out in the water until they drowned." He stopped to catch his breath again and felt his heart pounding. "I tried to stop him killing that little boy the same way. But I didn't make it in time." He could sense his breathing and suddenly wondered, what would it feel like to suck in water instead of air? "When I ran up, the big boy whacked me, and I fell. Knocked out, I guess."

The speech exhausted him. He settled back as best he could. His side hurt like hell, and his head throbbed.

The sheriff leaned forward in his chair. "The older boy is named Wes. Wes Mobley. We know about him. He's in trouble all the time. And we found the stick, just like you said."

The recollection flooded back through Sam's mind—the stick coming at him like a baseball bat. Did Wes beat the little kid to death, too, or drown him like the puppy?

The sheriff went on, "We found the other boys, too."

Sam stared at him. "Boys?"

The sheriff nodded. "The little backward boy, Barney. Evidently, he wandered off. And the blond boy, Toby, ran looking for him. They were lost in the woods for a while. Scared and scratched up a bit. But they're okay now."

Sam continued to stare at the sheriff. "The little one ain't dead?"

The sheriff shook his head. "No, Sam. The body in the

pond was the big boy, Wes."

Sam strained to hear the sheriff's words: maybe he misunderstood. "That boy who hit me—he's dead?"

The sheriff nodded. "We found his body in the pond, way out in the middle." He paused, considering his words. "We can't figure out how he got there, so far from the edge. If he fell in and drowned, he couldn't have drifted that far. The water's as still as pudding."

The sheriff sat back in his chair. "The boy shouldn't have drowned anyway. There were plenty of logs to grab onto." He looked at Sam for a while. "It doesn't make sense. That boy way out in the middle of the pond, dead." The sheriff fell silent for a while. Then he said, "Unless he got dragged out there. And held under." He paused again. "But how the hell could that happen? And who could've done it? Like you said, he was a big boy. He would've fought back. And grabbed a log."

Sam couldn't think of anything to say.

The sheriff rotated his hat in his hands for a while. After a bit, he stood to leave. "So we don't know what happened. We just know that boy is dead. Somehow."

Sam lay there silently, trying to take in what the sheriff had said. Someone killed the dark-haired boy. Held him under and drowned him. But who? Not Sam himself: he had been knocked out. The little boys? Sam dismissed the idea: they were too small. There was no one else around. Yet it happened right there with Sam sprawled out on the ground. Fatigue was settling in as he pondered it. He couldn't solve it right now. Fogginess returned to his brain: he needed to sleep.

He dreamed. In his dream, his brothers came back to him, Lucas and Harry, and that pleased him. Loggers to the heart, they were strong as bulls. They could do anything. As he slept, the warmth of his childhood flowed through him.

He knew there was nothing left to explain.

WITNESS

When Mason pressed the handle down, the toilet didn't flush. Jiggling the handle didn't help. "Damn," he said under his breath. He jiggled the handle more vigorously. Still nothing. The handle sat limp, useless. Sighing, Mason lowered the toilet seat, moved the box of Kleenex from the back of the toilet, and lifted the heavy ceramic cover from the top of the tank. Sure enough, the tank was empty. Mason studied the situation. None of the mechanisms looked familiar. He had expected to see a long arm with a floating bulb connected by a short, linked chain to a rubber flap. Instead, there was a plastic structure that looked vaguely like a miniature air traffic control tower. He could see no logical way for it to flush. He reached carefully for the top of the plastic structure and shook it tentatively. Nothing happened. He tried a little harder, still careful not to use too much pressure. But the toilet stubbornly refused to fill. "Damn," Mason said again, this time out loud. A toilet too complicated to understand. He shook his head. Most people worried about vicious tweets or Facebook frauds. He just wanted to flush the toilet.

Mason straightened up, grunting from the exertion. Old age. A bummer. He would have to use the one in the guest bedroom until he could get it fixed. The toilet had been installed less than two years before, during a remodeling. Fixing it would be a job for Pete the plumber—young Pete, not old Pete, young Pete's father. Old Pete was Mason's age and was weighed down by a variety of ailments, which he described in minute detail to anyone who would listen. Mason had no patience for old Pete; his bad-health monologue reminded Mason of his own mortality. Mason preferred young Pete. He had watched young Pete grow from a boy to a man, a neighbor's son who delivered the paper, mowed the lawn, and helped Evelyn in the garden.

Young Pete developed an attachment to Mason's wife, Evelyn, that Mason never quite understood. As a teenager, he would hang around just to talk with her. Mason would hear them conversing in the kitchen, Pete drying dishes, chopping vegetables, or helping however he could while they chatted. Evelyn must have exuded some schoolteacherly attraction that drew Pete in. Maybe he got something from her that his own mother couldn't provide.

Young Pete left college when his mother began her final decline. He never went back. His mother didn't take long to go. From that point, young Pete's presence grew in his father's business. Unlike his father, young Pete had a soft-spoken, reflective manner, probably induced by his two years of college. Even into middle age, he remained "young Pete." Old Pete still serviced a few clients, mostly people his age who could tolerate his garrulous piddling around. Mason preferred young Pete's serious-minded amiability. He always called Mason "Professor."

Fooling around getting the toilet fixed was a nuisance, but the fact that young Pete would be coming gave Mason an odd sense of relief. When he was still working, he had always enjoyed being in the house alone. He liked the quiet and solitude, which gave him time to read and think without disruption. Lately, being alone appealed to him less and less. Uneasiness would creep over him as he became aware of the silence in each room. At such times, he felt exposed and defenseless against some formless, dangerous threat. He would slip into an introspective funk, which turned into morbid soul-searching, until he snapped himself out of it, shaken, hollowness swelling inside him.

Somehow, his life had settled into a monotonous series of repetitions: daily pills, doctors' appointments, and household chores so mundane he barely knew they existed when he was a professor. Time passed relentlessly; differentiating the days wasn't easy. Before, his work had guided him along. Now, nothing did. Projects he had planned to pursue bogged down. He had a stack of research notes for a book, something new, with innovative ideas. He made a start shortly after he retired, but his energy waned, and he couldn't sustain his momentum. It languished in the messy pile on his desk. One of his former graduate students, now an assistant professor eager to advance himself, took the ideas and published a book incorporating them. Mason had been superseded by his own spawn. He didn't feel envious, just useless. He sent his young colleague an effusive email full of ironic praise for the book's originality.

At times, he reflected on his forty years with Evelyn, struggling to grasp their reality with clarity but finding it elusive, like trying to make out figures in a blurry photograph. He could not answer the question of whether their marriage was a success or whether they were happy. He thought of Evelyn as quiet, kind, and strong in a way that meshed well with the needs of her clients in social work, who drew on her strength to cope with their own misery. Once, he asked her how the two of them had stuck together for so long.

"You're my husband, and I love you," she said. "Isn't that enough?"

He supposed that must be right, and he wondered if he loved her in return. He realized he admired her and made respect a proxy for love. She had been part of him so long that his whole being knew when she was absent. She had left early this morning to join her friends on a daylong museum excursion. She wouldn't be back until dinnertime. She gave him a peck on the cheek. Only after she left did he realize he should have kissed her back. Now, she was away, and he would be alone. It would be better to have someone else in the house, even young Pete.

Mason managed to reach young Pete on his cell phone just as he was leaving home.

"Lucky you caught me, Professor," Pete said. "I'll make you the first stop. Shouldn't be more than twenty minutes or so." Mason made himself a cup of coffee and sat down with the newspaper to wait.

An hour later, Pete had not arrived. Mason's frustration grew as he sat, his knee jiggling impatiently under the newspaper. Waiting for people always agitated him. Why the goddamn delay? Young Pete was probably shooting the bull with someone, oblivious to the discourtesy of keeping Mason waiting. Maybe he had changed since Mason last saw him, becoming careless about time. These days, most service people acted as though showing up an hour or two late was doing you a favor. But that didn't seem like young Pete. Something could have happened. But he should have at least called to explain.

Another two hours passed. Mason's impatience had degenerated into a simmering anger. Wasted time ate at him; he felt diminished and impotent. Did he not even merit a call to explain the delay? Was he that unimportant? He had tried calling Pete's cell phone. Voicemail. Half an hour later, he tried it again. Still nothing. The more Mason fumed, the more his anger grew. This is how the younger generation treats old people, he said to himself. We barely exist in their minds; we're just useless ornaments cluttering the landscape, easy to ignore. He paced the living room. He couldn't even complain to Evelyn. It was just as well. It upset her when he ranted about the injustices that seemed to plague him uniquely.

Where the hell was he? Mason balled his fists, then flexed his fingers a few times. Waiting was becoming an agony. There was no escape from it. He walked from room to room, back and forth, trying to control his frustration. Nothing seemed to help.

At last, he saw young Pete's truck pulling up out front, more than three hours late. Mason stood watching through the front door screen, calculating how he should act. Pete would have some excuse, of course. Mason decided to project a certain coldness to reflect his anger but to keep his words civil. He watched young Pete take his toolbox from the truck. Something seemed different about him. He was acting nervously, his motions jerky and hurried. When he reached the porch, Mason could see his eyes bulging, with sweat running down his face.

"Oh, Professor, I'm so sorry," Pete said, his words rushing out. "I apologize for being so late. You'll never guess what happened."

Young Pete's agitation caught Mason off guard. "Happened? What do you mean?"

The plumber took several deep breaths. He spoke slowly, trying to stay calm.

He was driving along the road near his house just after he spoke with Mason. Traffic was always light on the two-lane road leading to the interstate. Suddenly, in the rearview mirror, he saw a car racing up behind him. It moved so fast that he thought it was going to hit him. He began to slow down and pull over to avoid a collision. At the last moment, the car swerved to the left and barreled past Pete's truck. Pete had slowed almost to a stop. He watched transfixed as the driver lost control of the car; it spun once, twice, and shot off the road across the narrow grassy strip, slamming head-on into a tree. It all happened in an instant. Somehow, through the blur of action, Pete noticed the driver as the car shot by and swirled in front of him. He remembered long blond sideburns.

Before he could react, a police car came roaring by with its siren shattering the morning calm. The patrol car raced past Pete and skidded to a stop on the grassy strip just behind the vehicle lodged against the tree. Two officers, one of them fat, climbed out and cautiously approached the wrecked vehicle. Pete could see their drawn pistols as they slowly approached. Inside the car, the driver had turned his head to look out the car window at the approaching patrolmen. One of the officers shouted, "He's got a gun!" Gunshots erupted, making Pete wince. He counted two, then three, then he lost track. He had reflexively ducked down. When he gingerly raised his head, the firing had stopped. The two patrolmen were yanking open the door of the wrecked car. The driver flopped to the side and fell halfway from the seat. He appeared to be dead. A young man, hardly more than a boy. His long blond hair fell forward over his sideburns.

Pete paused and took a breath, trying to calm himself. Mason stood mutely, stunned into silence. Anger drained from him like oil sludge from a crankcase. Pete stood peering at Mason, his eyes bulging, his story hanging in the air.

Mason searched for his voice. "What did you do?" he finally managed to ask.

Young Pete went on, "The cops. The fat one came over to me. I hadn't gotten out of the truck. Too scared. The cop told me to get out. I realized I had been gripping the steering wheel so tightly my hands felt frozen in place. I was shaking as I got out. My knees were weak, so I kept leaning against the fender. The fat cop's gun was back in his holster. He said, 'Did you see what happened?' I nodded. 'That guy shot at us first, right?' the cop said, looking at me hard. Made me feel guilty, almost like it was all my fault. I didn't know what to say. 'Well, it all happened so fast,' I said. 'It was hard to see what happened.'

"'Try to remember,' the cop said back. 'That guy shot first, that's all. I'll put in the report that you saw him shoot through the window.' He told me another officer would get my name and address and would write down what I saw: that the cops shot back in self-defense. He kept giving me that hard look. And I said okay."

Pete paused again, looking inquiringly at Mason as if to say, you get it, right?

Mason still had no idea what to say. The story was too incredible. All he could think about was young Pete as a boy, a shy but friendly presence, so polite and sensitive that Mason sometimes wondered whether he had the fiber to stand up for himself against other boys, to push back against bullies. He tried to imagine Pete's state of mind as he watched the terrible scene unfold. What must it feel like to watch someone die, shot to death before your eyes? Mason had only seen dead people groomed for burial at funeral parlors. None of them ever seemed any less alive than they did when they were walking around. Only momentarily sleeping. Mason had never felt an emotional attachment to any dead person primly displayed for viewing. But this. To watch someone die in front of you. That he couldn't fathom.

"I drove away then," Pete was saying. "The place was getting crowded. Cars all over. People gawking. TV trucks started to pull up. I didn't want to talk to anyone, to have anyone know I was a witness. So I just drove off. Didn't even tell the cops I was leaving. I drove about five miles to the shopping center parking lot. Then I just sat there, for a couple of hours at least, not doing anything, just trying to clear my mind, make sense of what had happened. It kept going around and around in my brain—the cars racing by, the crash, cops shooting, that dead boy slumped over. It made no sense to me. I was shaking so bad I couldn't hold my phone, so I just let it sit there, buzzing when someone called. I couldn't answer; I couldn't talk to anyone at that point. I felt like someone had beat the hell out of me. For a while, I just had to sit."

He stopped talking again, a look of desperation on his face. Mason shook his head in amazement.

"Which toilet is it?"

"Pardon?" Young Pete's question had come out of the blue. "The broken toilet. Which one? The master bathroom or the guestroom?"

Mason had forgotten about the toilet. Now, it rushed back to him. "Oh, the master."

Without a word, Pete turned and walked through the bedroom door toward the bathroom. Mason was left standing, his mind tumbling, still struggling to grasp Pete's amazing story. The abrupt return to reality—the reality of the broken toilet—disconcerted him even further. His knees felt weak. He walked shakily to his chair and grunted as he sat heavily. From the bathroom, he could hear the scraping and metallic jiggling sounds of young Pete working on the toilet. What a way to start the day—watching someone get shot to death. Mason tried to imagine himself as a witness but couldn't conjure up the emotions to match the situation. Maybe he had watched too many crime shows on television, where cops routinely gun down people, then go about their business as though nothing had happened.

Pete walked back into the room, holding the miniature air traffic control tower from the toilet in his hand. "Here's the problem," he said, waggling it in the air. "The toilet mechanism is shot. Cheap parts these days. Real junk. I'm sorry, Professor, I'll have to replace it." He gave Mason a sympathetic look. "I don't have one on the truck. But I'll stop at the plumbing parts store and get one. I have to stop at two other customers. But I should be back in a couple of hours." He held the toilet part up as if to validate what he was saying. "I'm real sorry. About being late. About the delay. But we'll get it back on track."

As he turned to go, he seemed almost like his old self.

Mason studied Pete's back as he walked through the front door. Even as a grown man, Pete had the willowy looseness of a teenager. For a while, Mason stood, remembering how things had been with young Pete hanging around: Evelyn, just beginning her social work practice, and her group of friends who were mostly still with her after all these years. Mason, focused intently on his academic career, blocking out almost everything else. There were no children; maybe Pete's teenage presence helped offset some vacuum in their lives. If so, they never acknowledged it to each other.

Pete's departure sucked the life from the room. Mason sensed the creeping emptiness enveloping him. He felt himself withering like a houseplant that hadn't been watered. He walked to the radio and switched it on: Beethoven filled the room. Of course, what else? The station repeated the same Beethoven pieces over and over because that's what the audience expected: something familiar, something soothing, never challenging their attention. He switched the radio off.

In the kitchen, the sunlight streaming in made the room almost too bright for comfort. He took a glass from the cupboard and ran the faucet in the sink for a while to cool the water. After filling the glass, he stood without drinking, looking out the window at the pond across the street where a family of ducks had taken up residence. Where they came from no one seemed to know. They simply appeared one day and acted as though the pond had been created for them. He poured the glass of water into the sink. In a few minutes, he would turn on the local news at noon to see what was being reported about the shooting.

Pete pulled up in front of the house shortly after three o'clock. Mason had made himself a sandwich for lunch while he watched the noon news. The newsreaders told the story in their usual excited way, stretching out the details to enhance the drama. Not that they knew much. The cops were tight-lipped, saying only that they had been pursuing a stolen vehicle. When they caught up, the driver shot at them, forcing them to fire back. Regrettably, the driver died. Neither Pete nor his truck appeared in the report. He had managed to escape, as he explained to Mason, just as the television cameras started to arrive. When the news switched to another story, Mason turned off the television and settled back in his chair with the newspaper to wait.

Young Pete came to the door carrying another miniature air control tower that looked exactly like the one he had carried out. He waggled it again, as he had done before.

"This will do the trick," he said. He seemed calmer than he had earlier, more subdued. He walked back into the bedroom and headed for the toilet in the bathroom. Mason followed him and stood watching while Pete tinkered with the toilet. After five minutes, he stood and pressed the handle. Water began to flow into the tank. When the tank had filled, Pete pushed the handle again, and the water flushed out of the bowl with a swoosh. The tank began to fill again, as it should. Pete gave Mason a satisfied look.

"Good as new," he said. "And there won't be any charge. I know my dad put this toilet in just a couple of years ago. It shouldn't have failed. And I shouldn't have been so late. I feel guilty now for letting that shooting bother me so much. Christ, you see the same or worse on TV every day. What's the big deal?"

He picked up his toolbox. The two of them returned to the foyer, where Pete paused to say again how sorry he was for the delay.

"Don't worry about it," Mason said in his most reassuring voice. "Things happen." Another wave of loneliness swept through him as he considered being in the house with Pete gone and Evelyn not yet returned.

"Why don't you sit for a few minutes," Mason said. "You've had a tough day. How about a beer?"

Pete had paused and turned halfway to leave. Then Mason could see him relax slightly as though a burden had shifted. "All right, that sounds good. You're right. I'm a little stressed.

I'll pass on the beer, though." He stepped further into the living room, a little uncertain, as though he didn't quite belong, or this wasn't something he should be doing. Mason motioned toward a chair, and Pete sat in it.

"I'm glad my clothes are clean, that I haven't been crawling under the house or something like that," Pete said. He gave a nervous laugh. Mason tried to think of what to say that might calm him down. Only the shooting came to his mind.

"I suppose the shooting has been weighing on you all day," he said finally, stating it not quite like a question.

Pete sat stiffly forward on the chair, his hands clasped between his knees. "You know, Professor, the whole thing has really made me think. It plagued me all day, thinking about what happened. Thinking about what I had seen. It happened so fast; everything just sort of—I don't know how to say it—swirled out, kind of exploding all at once. I was scared, but I was also fascinated. Like a rubbernecker at a car accident."

Mason watched Pete clenching his hands tightly between his knees. For a few moments, the plumber sat without speaking. Mason waited, feeling the quiet in the room. "One thing I did decide, though," Pete said finally. "I've been thinking about it all day. It's been pressing on me. I didn't know what to do at first. That's why I had to sit so long in that parking lot just thinking about it. Thinking about what had really happened—not the words the cop tried to put in my mouth."

Pete had been staring at the floor as he spoke, but now he raised his head and looked in Mason's direction. "I wanted to say what really happened. I couldn't just let it go by." He looked determined as he spoke. "That cop lied. That boy didn't shoot at them first. They just ran up to the car and started blazing away. They just killed him. Then they wanted me to say I saw him shoot first. For me to lie about it. Just to cover their asses." He stopped and looked around the room. "And I did. I let them say that. Even gave them my name and address. Even though I knew it was wrong." Finally, he slipped back into the chair. "Do you think I should go and tell the police the truth?"

Mason looked at Pete's face, the worried furrowing of his brow as he spoke. He had always been such an earnest kid. He considered what Pete had said. The "truth" amounted to a dead boy and two cops covering their asses. A story that repeated itself almost every day. Mason's first instinct was to leave things alone. Why stir them up? If Pete changed his story, the cops might retaliate. Find some way to get back at him or harass him. Why should he put his own security on the line just to get the story straight? Most people would support the police. He might even lose business. Young Pete would make himself a marked man for no good reason. Maybe it would be best just to leave things as they were.

"The cops probably wouldn't like to hear you change your story," Mason said carefully. "Maybe you're better off leaving it as it is."

Pete sat, hunching a little forward in the chair, still clasping his hands, staring fixedly at a spot on the floor. He stayed like that for a while, pensive, then gave a little sigh. "Yeah, I thought about that," he said. "It could even hurt my business. Most people would think I was bad-mouthing the deputies. My dad wouldn't like it either."

He fell silent again. Mason could sense the strain on him. An image of him as a teenager surfaced again in Mason's mind, a serious, bookish kid trying to figure out what the world—what life—was all about. Would he have given Pete the same advice then, just when the boy was trying to get reality to conform to his ideas of it? Would he have advised him to withhold the truth to avoid the possible repercussions of it? Mason realized he didn't have a good answer to that question.

"You should do what you think is right. Follow your conscience," Mason said finally. "You'll have to live with yourself for a long time."

Pete absorbed Mason's comment without responding. For

a long while, he simply stared into space. Then he stood, pressing his hands against his knees as he rose. Mason could see the determination on his face. "Thank you, Professor," Pete said. "That really helps to clear my mind."

He walked toward the door, picked up his toolbox, and turned the doorknob to leave. He looked back at Mason, pausing for a moment. "It's hard to keep the truth bottled up. Covered by a lie. Keeping it inside, eating away at your guts."

The screen door squeaked as he pushed it to leave. Mason watched him climb into his truck. But the truck didn't move; Pete just sat staring ahead, his hands not even on the steering wheel.

Mason went back into the living room and sat in his chair. Some of Pete's anxiety had spilled over to Mason as he tried to think things through. Something about Pete's sincerity, the conviction with which he spoke, had made Mason uneasy. Maybe it was just the fact that he spoke so openly, exposing the vulnerability he felt. Mason did not ordinarily expect that from a man. Maybe that was just Pete being Pete, Mason thought. But it had aroused Mason's sense of exposure, putting his secrets at risk. For a moment, he had doubted his own commitment to honesty. His instinct was always to protect himself before anything else. He felt jealous that Pete cared about the truth.

The doorbell stirred him. Pete was standing there; he hadn't left after all.

"Did you forget something?" Mason asked as Pete opened the door and walked back into the room.

"No," Pete said. He didn't go back to his chair but remained standing near the door. "There's something else I needed to say." He didn't seem to know what to do with his hands, finally dropping them to his side. "I'm going to go to the police headquarters," he said, "and tell them what I really saw. That boy didn't start shooting at the cops first. I don't even know if he ever shot at all. Maybe it doesn't matter. I can understand those cops. They were probably scared, I don't know. But I sure as hell know he didn't start shooting at them first." He looked around the room before going on. "It probably won't make any difference, but I won't be able to sleep if I don't say it the way I truly saw it. The truth, just like we were talking a few minutes ago. That's what will clear my conscience."

Mason thought about responding, saying something encouraging. But he held back; his doubts about telling the truth resurfaced in his mind. What good could come of it? The boy was dead. Pete would only create doubt.

"Oh God, this day. This crazy day." Pete raised his hand to his temple and rubbed it. "All day, it has felt unreal. Like none of this really happened. But it did. I've been thinking about everything—not just the killing—like it jarred loose a whole bag full of things, things that I needed to understand. And to let go of."

He stopped rubbing his temple and stood looking across the room like he didn't want to look directly at Mason.

"And there's something else," Pete went on. "Something that I've had inside me for a long, long time since I was a boy. Something I should have said to you years ago. But I could never bring myself to do it. Every time I came here, I thought of it—thought maybe this was the time to say something. Just to get it off my chest. But I didn't have the nerve. I just kept it to myself. Now, I want to get it out. Just like the dead kid in that car: I need to say what I saw. Even if it was so long ago."

Pete seemed to be staring at the grandfather clock in the corner where it had stood for forty years. "You know, I've looked at that grandfather clock my whole life," he said after a while. "It was one of the things I liked about coming here. You and Mrs. Webb were so nice. You seemed to take me seriously as a kid, Mrs. Webb especially. She was so different from my mother."

He stopped, apparently reluctant to continue. Maybe bad memories of his mother, Mason thought. She was a shrill, chaotic woman who intimidated the neighborhood and bullied her husband and son. An odd match for the affable old Pete, who was friends with everyone. Mason could never quite figure them out.

"Mrs. Webb would always listen to me," Pete continued, "and have something to say that made me feel better. I really liked her. I felt safe here, accepted." He paused again, his eyes closed. Mason could think of nothing to say, so he just stood, taking it in. "Maybe that's why I told her what I had seen. From my bedroom window." Pete opened his eyes. "And now I'm going to tell you. I realized it after we talked this morning about the need to tell the truth: that the truth is what matters. That I couldn't keep it to myself anymore. That it wouldn't be fair to keep it a secret anymore. That it hasn't been fair all these years."

Something in Pete's voice triggered a twinge of apprehension in Mason's stomach.

"Across the street where we lived," Pete said, "my bedroom window on the second floor looked out into the alley behind the house. I used to sit there in the dark, looking out at the night sky and stars. One night, I saw you walk down the alley and go into the back door of Mrs. Hurley's house. At first, I didn't think anything about it. You could've been going there for any reason to help her with something, maybe, since Mr. Hurley was always away on the road on his job. But then I saw you do it again a night or so later. Then again. Then, it became a regular thing. I was sixteen at that point, just beginning to be able to put things together. It finally dawned on me why you were going there, at night, through the back door, when Mr. Hurley wasn't there."

Pete's gaze had turned toward Mason as he talked. Mason's stomach churned, the painful memories forcing their way into his mind. Daisy Hurley. Tantalizing, seductive, and frustrated by her lot in life. Available when Jeff Hurley left her alone for days at a time. It didn't last long—nine months, a year. The Hurleys moved away, and that ended it. An easy and convenient ending, Mason thought at the time. He had almost forgotten it.

"I didn't know what to do with the information," Pete continued. "I wasn't the kind of kid who talked about such things with other boys. I was too shy. But I felt the urge to tell someone—I couldn't keep it bottled up. I guess kids have a hard time doing that, just holding things in. At least I did." He paused again as though reluctant to continue. But he did.

"So I told your wife," he said finally.

Mason was stunned. He felt woozy and reached back to find the arm of the couch, where he sat awkwardly. He realized his mouth had opened; he closed it and sat speechless.

"She said not to say anything to you about it," Pete said. "That she'd handle it. And that I should just forget about it. She was a very calm person, completely unlike my mother. I felt safe talking to her about it, telling her. I guess it didn't really occur to me how much it might have hurt her. Kids don't think like that, you know. They only care about their own feelings." He relaxed; some of the tension surrounding him dissipated. "After what happened this morning, and after I spent all day thinking about it, worrying about it, I realized I should tell you what I told Mrs. Webb back then. No more secrets. I should've talked to you about it at the time. But I didn't have the nerve. Maybe this can make up for some of it."

He turned as if to leave, then paused.

"I'm sorry, Professor. I just thought you should know."

He walked through the door, and it closed slowly behind him.

Mason remained sitting on the couch arm; he wasn't sure his legs would support him if he tried to rise. He felt his heart pounding like he had walked up the stairs too quickly. His mind raced around the details of Pete's words. It all happened so long ago. It almost didn't seem real to him. Daisy Hurley. He tried to dredge up a memory of her face, but it came only partially into his mind. He didn't even like her much; she was too needy. When they left town, he only felt relief.

And all along, Evelyn had known. Mason thought it had been filed away and long forgotten, this one indiscretion. Now, he searched his memory, trying to remember if Evelyn had changed in any way, if she had grown distant or cool toward him. But he could shake nothing loose that felt like an accusation or a judgment. She had been there, steady as a boulder all those years, supportive, loving, and strong. And all along, she knew. Mason shivered. What could he do now? Could he go on acting as though nothing had happened so long ago?

His rear end ached from the hardness of the couch arm. Finally, he rose and turned carefully, testing the strength of his legs. He needed to reach his chair where he could relax and remove his shoes.

The house had gone quiet again with young Pete's departure. The stillness descended like the chill of air conditioning. Mason sat back in his chair and drew a deep breath, then another. Why had she never brought it up? Certainly, there had been hard times and angry arguments when they traded cruel accusations. But they had weathered these; she had never taken the opportunity to lash out about his disloyalty. Yet all along, she had known.

He looked around the room. Everything had changed, yet nothing had changed. Now, he could only wait.

MARGE AND MAYBELLINE

Marge and Maybelline moved into the old Hackett place next door. As soon as she met them, my mother said, "That Marge. She'll be the problem." Not "a problem," but "the problem," as though trouble was inevitable, and my mother was already gearing up to deal with it. Why this nuance stuck with me all these years, I can't say, although I'm sure the subtlety of it eluded my fourteen-year-old brain, which was busy being swamped by the surging hormones of adolescence.

My mother's declaration on that long-ago day came back to me forty years later as we sat in the funeral parlor waiting for Marge to be reduced to ashes so Maybelline could carry her away like a carton of take-out Chinese food. Only then did I fully comprehend the meaning of what my mother had said—she was preparing herself as a force, flexing her muscles, so to speak. That force came to define her relationship with our two new neighbors. Like a polarized magnet, it pushed her away from Marge and pulled her toward Maybelline.

Maybelline pulled me toward her, too, and she knew it, although her perception of why no doubt differed from mine. Arousal fantasies percolated in my imagination as soon as I saw Maybelline. I had only recently discovered the joys of what my shrink now calls self-pleasuring. Back then, my buddies and I called it jerking off. It occupied a significant place in the ever-expanding discoveries of youth, and I indulged my passion for it with an enthusiasm previously reserved for building model airplanes.

Maybelline was oblivious to my desire. To her, I was merely a goofy kid who liked to hang around, offering to help, anything I could do to please her. She tolerated me with a kind of cheerful indifference, mostly ignoring me for long moments as though she had forgotten my presence, then rediscovering me with surprised amusement. Then she would smile. Now, I am a middle-aged college professor, nearing sixty, yet the memory of that smile still pierces me as it did then. And I wonder, as I did when I first met her in 1960, whether she knew her mere smile could cause the juices of sexual arousal to surge through me,

Marge arrived first in a U-Haul van loaded with belongings. Her dark hair had been cut short with clippers like a man's haircut so that her ears stood out. Closer up, you could see gray streaks in her hair. She was stout, almost stocky, and wore gray workman coveralls with pouches and belt loops for tools. At this point, this far away, you could not yet tell that her eyes were slightly mismatched in color: one blue, the other more brownish. Later, I realized this anomaly had a kind of mesmerizing effect when you looked her directly in the face. Not that most people did. The tightness of her jaw said, "Stay away." Few people faced her head-on. Except my mother, of course, later, when everything had changed.

I watched from our porch, bouncing my basketball, as Marge lugged boxes and small pieces of furniture into the house. Her strength impressed me. My mother joined me on the porch and carefully studied the scene. "She'll need help with the bigger things," my mother commented finally. Sure enough, at that moment, another truck pulled up, a larger one, and two heavily muscled men got out. The two movers hefted out a large sofa and carried it toward the house, where Marge stood, hands on hips, waiting to give directions.

"Now she can be the boss," my mother observed. She said this as though she already knew Marge had a domineering nature, something we found out over time. But how could my mother have suspected it at this point? Now I realize that women like my mother have a kind of radar for detecting the presence of a potential rival. Even before her cryptic remark about Marge being "the" problem, my mother had sensed something that bristled her fur and caused her to raise her head like a lioness sniffing out danger lurking in the grass.

All of this went over my head as I wallowed in the thick emotional syrup of desire. My first encounter with Maybelline happened when my mother sent me next door with a cherry peach cobbler, her specialty, as a welcoming gift. No one responded as I knocked on the front door with my right hand, juggling the cobbler with my left. Sounds of someone rustling about in the backyard came around the corner of the house, so I walked toward the back. And as I rounded the corner, I saw Maybelline. I had expected Marge—I hadn't seen another person arrive—so the fact that someone else stood there, hoe in hand, chopping weeds, surprised me. Especially someone blonde and beautiful, moderately tall (at least taller than Marge), with green eyes that probed me when she turned and saw me standing there, extending a freshly baked cobbler as a peace offering.

I wouldn't describe what I saw as a vision exactly, but the sun was shining behind her, casting a kind of halo around her head and shoulders, and it dazzled me for a moment. Then she shifted her head, and I could see her more clearly as she stared at me. There was a need in her green eyes that I could sense but, at fourteen, not comprehend. An elastic band pulled her curly blonde hair back from her face so that the hair tumbled carelessly down her neck and piled up on her shoulders. She left me breathless.

"Oh, hello," she said, startled.

I tried to respond, but as soon as I said "I'm," my voice failed me, and I gasped before being able to add, "Alex." Again, my voice cracked. "From next door," I finally managed to croak. My face turned hot, so I thrust the cobbler forward in self-defense. "My mom sent me over with this."

Maybelline looked at the cobbler, then at me, then back at the cobbler as it wobbled a little in my hands. For the first time, she smiled at me slowly, almost lazily, a smile that rattled my equanimity. I spent the summer trying to prompt that smile out of her in any way I could.

"Well, how nice. And thoughtful," she said, taking the pan from me. "Here. Let's go inside and show Marge."

She walked toward the back door, with me tagging along behind. At that point, I noticed what she was wearing, what she invariably wore when working in the yard. Rompers, my mother called it, a one-piece outfit with a short bottom and a sleeveless top, a kind of jumpsuit without arms or legs. Even I could tell it looked more like something a child would wear. But mostly, I noticed the fluid movement of her buttocks, blending smoothly into her bare legs as she walked. (Later, my best friend Leonard pointed out that she didn't wear anything under the thin material of the outfit.) At the time, I just followed her meekly into the kitchen.

Marge stood on a small stepladder, getting ready to roll paint on the kitchen wall. An acrid tobacco odor still filled the room, spreading throughout the house, the result of Mrs. Hackett's two-pack-a-day habit. My mother had said they would have to paint the whole place. "It stinks more from the cigarettes than the corpse," she said when the body had been discovered a couple of days after Mrs. Hackett died, and my mother went next door to help extract the remains.

"Marge, this is our new neighbor," Maybelline said, pausing for a moment as she reached back in her memory to remember my name. "Alex. From next door. Look what he brought."

She held out the cobbler, then set it on a clear space on the counter, cluttered with utensils waiting to be put away. She looked at me. "This is Marge. And I'm Maybelline." She shot me that smile, and I felt my face grow hot again.

Marge looked at us without comment. From her perch on the ladder, she appeared bigger than her actual size and more intimidating. Even before she spoke, she radiated a sense of animal strength, like an armadillo with a hard shell that deflected any warmth going in or coming out. As she climbed down, I first saw the streaks of gray in her hair. My mother had them, too; a curse of middle age, she called it. Any possible trace of gray would have been impossible to see in Maybelline's flowing blonde hair.

Marge looked older than Maybelline. But how much older, I had no idea; stages of adulthood weren't discernible to me until someone had become really old, like my grandmother or Mrs. Hackett. Anyone between twenty-one and sixty was simply a "grownup." But Maybelline's appearance soon clarified things. My friend Leonard enlightened me when I invited him over to assess Maybelline's finer qualities from the privacy of my bedroom window. Leonard's powers of observation were keener than mine—he figured out the absence of underwear, for instance—so I valued his opinions on all matters relating to the female sex.

"Yeah, she's pretty," he said after studying her for a while. "But, geez, she's an old broad." He continued to stare. "Maybe around forty. Like our moms." He looked for a while longer. "Nice boobs, though."

Leonard's comment surprised me. The fact that my mother's age defined her in any way other than making her grouchy every year on her birthday had never occurred to me. But "an old broad"? Could that be? And Maybelline as an old broad, with me lusting after her body, someone as old as my mother? The idea embarrassed me so much that I blushed. Luckily, Leonard didn't notice as he gazed down at Maybelline in her rompers, her butt moving nicely as she hacked and hoed. I quickly suppressed my embarrassment and resumed looking at her. She did have great breasts.

In the kitchen, at that first encounter, Marge walked over and looked me square in the face and said, "Thank your mother for us." A little impatience came across in her voice, more like annoyance than gratitude. I could tell that she viewed me and the whole business as a nuisance. Over that long, simmering summer, as I came around to their house more often, I increasingly felt Marge's irritation at being intruded upon. Soon, I recognized that she directed her grouchiness toward the world at large, not just at me. Teenagers are accustomed to being considered a nuisance, so I learned not to take it personally. Besides, Marge was of little interest to me. I focused on Maybelline in her flowered rompers, those needy green eyes probing my face when she looked at me. I was hooked.

That summer, I evolved into the regular yard boy, helping Maybelline hack away at the tangled garden and rebuilding the yard into a model of trimmed and cultivated perfection, which won even my mother's approval. During Mrs. Hackett's prime, she had built the small grounds around the house into a showcase of dazzling foliage. In time, Mrs. Hackett's arthritis and other infirmities handicapped her, and the weeds and overgrowth gradually took over the yard as she sat in her kitchen smoking cigarettes.

Maybelline planned to restore the yard to its former glory, adding her own special touches wherever she could. She later told my mother that the yard and its potential had been the key selling point of the house for her. "The yard can be a showcase again; the garden has good bones," she told my mother. "I'm going to put some meat back on them." And she set about doing it with determination and skill. Maybelline is a true gardener, my mother acknowledged as she watched the transformation from the kitchen window.

At first, nothing seemed unusual about my mother looking out the window; even I found the garden interesting. But it began to seem that my mother spent a lot of time there, ostensibly drying dishes or wiping up. Sometimes, when nothing occupied her hands, she simply stood with them resting on the edge of the sink while she gazed out at Maybelline busily chopping, pruning, and planting. My mother had no great affection for the kitchen or cooking. It did seem a little unusual to find her in the kitchen more and more, having gotten up from her writing desk (she ordinarily grumbled about interruptions) and going to the sink, where she would run a glass of water and not drink it, but just hold it as she watched from the window when Maybelline happened to be outside.

Maybelline managed the yard; Marge handled everything related to the house. It would have been unusual to see Marge in anything but overalls, often with a tool belt strapped around her hips, a hammer hanging in the loop. Once, I saw an axe stuck in there, and it looked vaguely ominous, like a weapon ready for use. She can fix anything, Maybelline told me. Marge worked steadily on the old house, rarely missing a day, patching, fixing, painting, or whatever might be needed. Once, I saw her on the roof, replacing shingles. Another time, she had squirmed under the crawl space beneath the house to hose out the sewer drainpipes.

Over the summer months, my presence established a sort of liaison between the two households. Maybelline kept me busy mowing the lawn with the ancient push mower she discovered in the garage, lugging tubs of garden waste to the curb for pick up, taking out garbage cans stuffed with refuse from inside the house where Marge was hard at work, and even being sent on errands to the hardware store three blocks away. But the directions mostly came from Maybelline; Marge seemed oblivious to my presence. She only spoke to me if I asked her a question, which wasn't often. Maybelline served as the living link, the life force that pulled me in. And also drew in my mother.

A week or so after I delivered the cherry peach cobbler,

Maybelline showed up at the back door carrying a plate of chocolate chip cookies. "We finally got the kitchen straightened up enough that I could do some baking," she told my mother, a little breathlessly, as though she had walked a distance, although her kitchen door lay no more than twenty yards away. "We thought you might enjoy these."

By now, early on, both my mother and I recognized that "we" really meant Maybelline alone, given Marge's chilliness toward us. But Maybelline's bubbling cheerfulness offset any negative vibrations from Marge. Maybelline soon became a regular visitor to our kitchen, where she and my mother would sit sipping cups of herbal tea, for which they discovered a mutual liking. "I'm Maybelline," she had said when she first met my mother, "but you can call me Belle." I remembered it because she hadn't said that to me on that first encounter in the backyard. No one else called her Belle except Marge.

In those days, two women living together stirred up interest in the neighborhood. Only the Anderson twins, ancient recluses who mostly stayed hidden inside their old Victorian house, provided an example of female cohabitation. They were sisters, so that made sense. No one understood the connection between Marge and Maybelline, and they never explained it. Mrs. Shaw from across the street, our cleaning lady and the leading local gossip, speculated about possibilities. Sisters? (They certainly didn't resemble each other.) Cousins or relatives of another sort? (That's possible, but distant surely, she said out loud as she dusted.) Just friends? (Do friends live together, especially middle-aged women?) Nothing seemed to explain it; you could hear puzzlement in her voice and the hint that something wasn't quite right. She tried to pry information from my mother, who shrugged it off. "Maybe they're roommates," my mother said indifferently, "like college." My mother hated gossip, so she refused to cooperate in the speculation. But people wouldn't let it go. There must be some connection, Mrs. Shaw said, shaking her head as she mopped. The murmuring went on.

My mother rose above it in the way she typically detached herself from the routine nosiness that preoccupied our neighbors. Her aloofness separated her from most people; even I felt it. She loved me as a mother should; I knew that. But she served it up at room temperature, neither too hot nor too cold. Motherhood suited her sense of command. To most people, especially other women, she seemed somewhat intimidating. Because she could talk straight out to men without flinching, they respected her. "I'm a writer, not a talker," she said (she worked for a technical electronics magazine, which allowed her to work from home). She had no time for titillating rumors or insinuations about other people's business.

(Part of the mystery about Marge and Maybelline concerned how they supported themselves, since neither seemed to be employed. Much later, my mother learned that they lived on an endowment from the estate of Maybelline's wealthy maiden aunt, who had raised her.)

Despite my mother's standoffish demeanor, she soon displayed an unexpected fondness for chit-chat at the kitchen table with Maybelline. Because she felt smarter than most people, she usually avoided small talk as much as she did gossip. Maybelline certainly displayed no conversational gift, but something she provided appealed to my mother. It became routine for me to wander in and find them deep in discussion, keeping their voices low, whispering as though sharing a secret. Now I realize that the connection between them—the polarizing force that pulled them toward each other while pushing Marge away—had started working. But my adolescent brain had no capacity to grasp anything other than two women chatting over tea.

That force came into play in the matter of the bird feeders and the squirrels. Maybelline got the idea of putting bird feeders in the yard where she could see them from the kitchen window. "We'll get chickadees, finches, goldfinches even. They're beautiful. And cardinals." She envisioned two sizes of feeders:

two smallish ones for the littlest birds, like the goldfinches, and two larger ones for the bigger birds, like the cardinals. She rhapsodized about seeing the yard swarming with birds, chirping, bickering, and pushing each other from the feeders as they fluttered around. "They'll be the finishing touch to the garden," she told me as she considered where to place the feeders so she could see them from her kitchen window. She drew me into the plan: "You can help me put them up," she said, her bright smile sealing the bargain.

Marge was dead set against it.

"Bird feeders bring in the damn squirrels," she said. "They'll dig holes in your flower beds. And the next thing you know, they'll be all over the roof." She let this sink in. "Then we'll have them in the attic, and they'll be hell to get out." Again, she paused. "Rats with furry tails," she said. "We don't need them."

"But nowadays, they have feeders that squirrels can't get into," Maybelline protested.

Marge snorted. "Baloney. Nothing can stop the squirrels. And even if they can't get at the feeders, the stupid birds scatter the seeds all over the ground, so that'll attract the squirrels."

I was hearing this exchange through the kitchen screen door; Maybelline had set me to spading up the ground next to the porch. I couldn't see the two of them, but I knew Marge's jaw had locked into place.

"I'm against it," Marge said finally.

There, the matter stood for the time being. After the argument, Maybelline had come back into the yard, her face flushed. She said nothing but started hoeing vigorously around the flower bed. I couldn't tell whether I would be assembling bird feeders or not; I had looked forward to impressing Maybelline with my engineering skills acquired from my model-making days.

Later, when I walked into our kitchen, my mother asked

me, "What have you been up to this morning?"

"Next door, working in the yard. Maybelline wants to put up bird feeders." I told her the story. "Marge is against it. She says it'll just bring squirrels."

The kitchen sparkled from my mother's newfound interest in it, something it certainly had never stimulated before. As I talked, she stood, rubber gloves on her hands, holding a cleaning sponge she used on the sink. She looked at me while I related what I had heard through the screen door: Maybelline's enthusiasm, Marge's adamant stance against the idea, Maybelline's attempt at reasonableness, and her red face when she returned to the yard.

My mother took this all in without comment. She turned back to the sink and resumed her cleaning. After a while, as I searched the refrigerator for the peanut butter and jelly, she said, "Well, I agree with Maybelline. Having birds around would be nice. We could see them, too." She paused in her scrubbing. "And I don't think the squirrels would be a problem." She worked on the already-polished sink some more. "Squirrels aren't so bad anyway."

Now, even from my fourteen-year-old perspective, this statement surprised me. My mother had always been indifferent toward birds. She had never shown the least interest in putting bird feeders in our yard or having birds around. Once, during one of my periodic bouts of lobbying for a pet, I had stooped to the level of suggesting parakeets, which my mother dismissed with derision. "No way," she said. "Their chattering would drive us crazy. And you'd lose interest, so I'd wind up cleaning the cage."

And she hated squirrels. On the rare occasions when a squirrel wandered onto our back deck, she would grab the broom, yank open the door, and swing madly at it, threatening terminal harm if she could get close enough to give it a whack. Which she never did, of course. But her vehemence impressed me.

My mother soon found a chance to express her opinion on the bird feeder issue. It happened a few days later when she decided to trim the bushes along the fence between our yards while Maybelline hoed away in her yard and Marge scraped paint on the porch nearby. Everyone worked in silence for a while until my mother got close to where Maybelline chopped away at the flower bed across the fence.

"I hear you're thinking of putting up bird feeders," my mother said. Snip, snip. "What a good idea. Having birds around would be nice." She pulled loose some of the clippings and threw them toward a pile behind her. "You can get the kind that keeps out the squirrels," my mother went on. "I hear they work really well."

Maybelline had stopped hoeing and stood looking blankly at my mother, who tossed me in as a finishing flourish: "Alex would be glad to help you put them up." The snipping resumed, and I could hear my mother quietly humming a tuneless song. "Just let us know when." "Us"—I noted that. My mother had never shown much interest in my yard work next door. Now, she wanted to be notified.

Marge stopped her scraping; she had said nothing as my mother talked, but I heard her issue a kind of growl. She backed down from the small ladder she had been standing on. When she turned toward the area where Maybelline and my mother were working, I could see cold ferocity on her face, glowering like an angry badger zeroing in for the kill. She moved steadily across the grass toward Maybelline, almost marching. Marge never looked in my mother's direction but walked directly up to Maybelline and planted herself in front of her. Her eyes never left Maybelline's face. Maybelline shrank back. Neither of them said anything.

Marge began to remove her work gloves, pulling each finger one at a time. When she had them in her hand, she held them for a moment. Then, Marge raised the hand holding the gloves—and slammed them down at Maybelline's feet. She didn't watch where they landed, but I could see that one of them rested on Maybelline's left foot. Without a word, Marge pivoted and stalked back toward the house. The screen door screeched as she yanked it open and disappeared inside.

The episode of the bird feeders established a new order between the four of us and our two households. Before, there had been a physical barrier, the fence separating us, Marge and Maybelline on one side, my mother and me on the other. Now, the significance of the physical barrier receded. A new, invisible boundary grew out of the bird-feeder confrontation, one that placed Maybelline, my mother, and me together on one side, with Marge alone on the other. I included myself in the Maybelline-mother group since I assumed I belonged there. But in reality Maybelline and my mother alone defined it because they had the ability to stand against Marge. I simply tagged along.

In some ways, little changed. Maybelline and I continued to trim and plant the evolving garden, which was growing into something even I could appreciate. I pushed the lawn mower back and forth, pulled, bagged, and dragged trimmings, and happily did whatever Maybelline asked for. Sometimes, I would just watch her as she worked. Occasionally, as her arm moved with the hoe, or she raised it as she lifted a shovel, I could catch a glimpse of her breast through the armhole of the rompers. Then, I couldn't look away until she changed positions, and I could go back to my work.

Marge continued to putter around the house, inside and outside, carrying her tools strapped to her sturdy body. Maybelline and I put up the bird feeders a few days after the confrontation in the yard. At the wild-bird supply store, we bought four squirrel-proof feeders to mount on high poles, exactly as Maybelline had envisioned. I assured her that assembling them posed no problem, and it didn't. Maybelline praised my work and complimented my skill, which made me puff up with pride. She bought the most expensive sunflower seeds. "Why not give them the best?" she said. She hummed as we worked, her happiness making me happy, too.

And it happened as planned. The birds flocked in, chirping and harassing each other as they fluttered about the feeders. Marge's prediction also came true: the scattered seeds on the ground became a mecca for the squirrels. They were everywhere, digging holes in the garden bed, scurrying around on the porches of both houses, staring keenly at my mother as she shooed them from the porch. Marge never again mentioned the squirrels or the bird feeders, at least not in my hearing. Maybelline took great pleasure in the birds flocking around the feeders and cheerfully said so. My mother barely noticed them.

The birds and squirrels joined the little imbalanced world composed of me, my mother, Maybelline, and Marge. Everyone pretty much stuck to what they had been doing all along, although the invisible boundary my mother and Maybelline had established separated Marge more clearly, the way a flock of sheep might shun one member and push it to the side, not driving it away exactly, but keeping it on the fringe. I accepted the new order of things without much thought since I had little grasp of adult behavior until the "discovery"—which changed everything.

The "discovery" happened when I returned from my annual two-week stint with my father. Usually, we took a camping trip, but this year, we went to the North Carolina shore, where he let me drive and drink beer, two aspirations I had eagerly expressed. My dad and I had a pretty relaxed relationship, a result of his "What the hell, it'll happen anyway" attitude toward me and the world in general. He was a professor at the state university in our town and liked his students well enough that he often talked about the most interesting ones. From what I could tell, they liked him too. He and my mother got along very smoothly, at least from what I could see. They had split up three years before without any apparent conflict. My mother didn't say much about it. "He likes living alone," she said, as though that explained everything. "You'll be able to see him whenever you want."

And I never heard them argue. He always asked about her and seemed honestly interested in what I said. It didn't seem particularly strange to me, or uncomfortable, that they got divorced and he moved out. I accepted it as just another part of the landscape.

My dad dropped me off in front of the house a couple of hours earlier than planned; it rained that last day at the beach, and he decided to get on the road. Gray clouds brooded in the sky during the trip and dripped moistly on me as I said goodbye to my dad and walked up the sidewalk. When I opened the front door to the house, the gloominess reached into the hallway as I entered. I considered turning on the hallway light but didn't. Neither did I call out that I had arrived. Instead, I moved quietly, thinking I would surprise my mother. Voices came from the kitchen, so I headed there.

From the dark hallway, standing out of their line of view, I saw this: Maybelline backed against the kitchen counter, my mother facing her and standing close, her legs slightly spread for balance, reaching up to touch Maybelline's hair, fingering it, stroking it lightly, as though gently testing its softness. She pushed her body against Maybelline, who stood quietly, motionless, her arms at her sides, as my mother pressed closer against her. I could see no separation between them as my mother played with Maybelline's hair, placing her fingers against Maybelline's cheek, then back to her hair, and repeated the action, hair, cheek, over and over, with a sensuality that radiated toward me.

Then, as slowly and carefully as someone might raise their hands to lift a butterfly from a leaf without scaring it, I watched

Maybelline's arms begin to rise and encircle my mother's waist, loosely at first, then more firmly; then she pulled my mother's body more tightly into her own. My mother shifted slightly within this embrace as though testing its intensity. She placed her hands behind Maybelline's head, pulling her face toward her own. When they came together, she opened her mouth slightly and kissed Maybelline on the lips. And I watched Maybelline kiss her back. When Maybelline moved her face away, my mother said only, "Oh, Belle." My mother's hands then moved again, this time sliding to regions of Maybelline's body I could not imagine being touched by anyone other than the owner of them, certainly not by another woman, and truly, inconceivably, not by my mother. But there it happened, right in front of me, my mother fondling every part of Maybelline's body, and Maybelline responding in kind.

You might think that a kid seeing such a thing happen would be stunned into shock. But it didn't happen that way. From my dark vantage point, I felt—well, nothing much at all. At best, I sensed a kind of hollowness swelling inside me, where the facts I observed could deposit themselves so they could drift, unattached to any part of me, filed away for future reference when I might be better prepared to process them. I felt as though I had eaten something that I expected to be bitter and had been surprised to find bland and tasteless.

Yet I knew, even then, that the emptiness, that inner void with the detached artifacts of the discovery floating inside, would somehow define me. In time, it would become a portal into my being that never closed, filtering every feeling, every sensation, every connection to people: those I loved, those I despised, and those who stirred nothing in me at all. Mostly, I had a sense of facing a mysterious opening into the future, the character of which I could only dimly fathom. The discovery had created a vast range of uncertainties, like opening a Scrabble game and finding every tile blank, which could be good or bad, depending on your point of view.

So that was my reaction to watching my mother having sex with Maybelline, something I had dreamed about myself. Now, I realized that mine were mere childhood fantasies, and I felt my own desire melt away in the heat of adult reality. Maybe I should have done something; maybe I should have yelled "Stop it," or ran into the kitchen, something like that. But I didn't; I couldn't. All I could do was back silently away into the darkness of the hallway until I bumped against the front door. I opened it loudly, then slammed it, as I called out, "I'm home."

I never told anyone what I saw in the kitchen that day: not my friends, not my mother or father, and certainly not Maybelline. And I never saw them being intimate again. All I knew was that I saw it once, and it forever shaped my image of my mother and Maybelline and, ultimately, of all people. It embodied a fundamental lesson of life that every person should understand—that things may not be what they seem. In time, I grasped its significance, but when it happened, I only sensed its importance. I did not comprehend it.

If I had to describe the mood that descended on our lives after the discovery, it would be somber, although subdued might be a more accurate term. We were the same people as before, yet it seemed to me that our world had become a different place, changed by the new conditions. All three of us who had taken part in the discovery now had to process the events from different perspectives. We shared a secret, but only I knew that fact. Only I knew that their secret was not a secret at all. We acted much the same toward each other, but only I knew that they were just acting, that they truly wanted to be something other than what they appeared to be. In time, I could absorb that reality; as a teenager, I could only experience it and leave it to gestate until it ripened in my grownup self.

I went back to school, so the yard work declined. Maybelline's garden had undergone a transformation, and I took a certain amount of pride in my contribution. Nothing much seemed to change in the behavior of the three adults in that universe of two houses and adjacent yards, at least not immediately. As the weather cooled, Maybelline changed her rompers for pants and shirts, and she worked less in the yard. I could hear banging and sawing from inside, indicating that Marge continued her renovations. She rarely worked outside now.

Maybelline's visits to our house began to increase until they became almost daily. When I came home from school, I often found her and my mother at the kitchen table, talking quietly, almost murmuring while sipping their tea. I tried not to reflect on what might have gone on during my absence. But I could not always avoid it. Sometimes, when the thought came into my mind, a chill would sweep through me, like opening a door into a wintry blast.

Leonard and I continued our visual surveillance of the budding womanhood among the girls at school. Leonard continued his sage commentary. What a set, he would sigh. And an ass to go with it. Boy, I'd like to hump that mound. I could not match his eloquence, so I usually said nothing.

For my part, despite the stimulation of Leonard's comments, a certain joy in self-pleasuring seemed to have left me. As I fantasized about girls to arouse myself, I often found the scene in my brain muddled. Maybelline suddenly began appearing at the edge of the fantasy, observing me. Sometimes, her image would not go away or would merge with the object of my desire, so my efforts collapsed, and I would sit back in frustration. Other times, out of nowhere, an image of my mother would appear together with Maybelline just as I reached the point of climax, and I would abruptly stop. Only days later did I have the nerve to start again. Then, the two of them, my mother and our beautiful neighbor, would intrude once more, watching me. Again, I would falter and stop. This repeated itself often enough that I came to expect it as two realities. The desire for sexual release came into conflict with the shame of being scrutinized by my mother and Maybelline. The tension unnerved me. Once, I even cried.

In March, as signs of spring began to appear and the tulips popped up in Maybelline's flower bed, she asked when I could resume my yard responsibilities. There's a lot to do this year, she told me one day in the kitchen as my mother looked on. I had helped a little during the winter, carting out waste from Marge's renovations, helping Maybelline fill the bird feeders, and so on. I thought about how it had been the summer before, her in her rompers, her ass waving as she worked; me mowing the grass, covertly ogling her. I wondered whether that scene could be revived.

But my heart wasn't in it. She no longer enticed me. I couldn't see myself acting as I had when I first met her and studied her body surreptitiously, watching her from my bedroom window. So, I said no: I planned to work as a stock boy at the local supermarket. Neither Maybelline nor my mother resisted the idea. Looking back, I think maybe they were relieved that I wouldn't be around so much during the summer. But I'm only guessing.

Marge disappeared. No one told me: I just figured it out. One day, my mother said Maybelline had called and said she needed to move a chest down from upstairs. Could I help? This surprised me because I had never been asked to do something like this inside. Marge and Maybelline always seemed capable of moving things themselves. When I walked inside, the house instantly felt different. At first, I couldn't figure out why. Then, details began to dawn on me. Marge's tool belt wasn't hanging on the peg inside the mudroom entryway as it usually was. The photo of Marge and Maybelline, smiling together at the beach, no longer sat on the shelf next to the herb rack where Maybelline had put it. The stack of home repair magazines and catalogs that Marge kept on a side table had disappeared.

The upstairs, where I had never been before, seemed even emptier of Marge's presence. When we walked into the bedroom, I could see a few items I recognized as Maybelline's: a sweater on the bed, a jacket draped over a chair, and a hairbrush with blonde strands on the dresser. But nothing associated with Marge. We hefted a cedar chest sitting next to the dresser and lugged it downstairs, panting as we carried it awkwardly down the steps. "Let's put it next to the front door," Maybelline said, breathless from the exertion. We plopped it down; it looked out of place, as though waiting for someone to pick it up later. Maybelline gave no explanation, but she did offer me a tip for helping. I turned her down.

With Marge gone, the little defensive circle that kept her out, that bastion of Maybelline, my mother, and me, became unnecessary; it slowly weakened and dissolved. The pressure of it had bound the three of us to each other. Now, the bonds loosened among us. I could feel it but did not understand the feelings since I had no experience of emotional withdrawal or words to express it. Years later, as an adult, I realized that when the strain of Marge's presence had been removed, a new stress filled the vacuum. The tension had shifted to me. Another circle emerged: one that bound my mother and Maybelline together and excluded me.

None of this meant much to me then. Life blew new breezes at me from all directions, and I responded to them enthusiastically. Regardless of the complications in my parents' relationship, they both paid a lot of attention to me, attention of a good kind. In the end, that's mostly what a kid really needs. My parents supplied it, and I am grateful for that. Whatever complications Maybelline introduced were still mostly kinetic, going over my adolescent head as I became absorbed in teenage-boy things: secretly smoking, drinking pilfered beer, and strategizing about how to get under the skirts of teenage girls.

Unbeknownst to me, however, the power of our blonde neighbor bubbled just below the surface, waiting to be energized. At the end of the summer, it burst forth to produce a sea change in my life.

The sea change began while my father and I hung out for two weeks in the mountains on our annual retreat. He brought it up over burgers and shakes: how would I like to live with him? he asked between chews. The idea caught me off guard. I had finally relaxed back into a routine living with my mother, and the thought of disturbing it momentarily unsettled me.

Not that the subject of living with my father was entirely new. It had been broached before, but only obliquely, as in, if you lived with me, we could go bowling more often, or we could shoot pool at Mickey's Pub on a school night or go to the beach in the winter without a lot of planning ahead, and so on. I never considered it a real possibility; I regarded it as a kind of father/son banter, more an expression of male bonding than a concrete proposal.

When it came up now out of nowhere, it felt like the shock of stepping into cold water. Reality had been laid on the table. As I bit down on my fries, I looked at my father and could see the seriousness in his mild eyes. He wasn't kidding. As he ate, he supplied some details: my mother thought she might be traveling more in her work or even possibly relocating to work in the headquarters of her publishing firm. She couldn't know for sure right now, but she and my father needed to plan ahead in case it happened suddenly. My fate had to be settled before school started so I wouldn't be disrupted by an abrupt midterm alteration.

I wouldn't have to change schools; my father had already checked. Transportation to school (he lived ten miles farther away than my mother) could be handled through a carpool with some other kids who lived in his neighborhood. Then, the kicker: Next year, when I turned sixteen, I could get my driver's license, and he would supply a car. I would be on my own; he trusted me. I could even pick up Leonard if I wanted to. What reasonably clear-headed, pimple-free teenage kid yearning for independence could turn down such an offer?

I liked my father, and the idea of a bachelor's existence with him had appeal. I even liked his lady friend, Alice, and she took to me. She had a great laugh and a way of messing my hair that made my loins tingle. It all sounded pretty good. For a few moments, I pondered the notion of not returning to my mother's house each day after school, of not seeing her or hearing her off-beat commentary on the world, of not encountering her and Maybelline, whispering to each other in the kitchen. And I realized I wouldn't miss it. I didn't have to give it a lot of thought. As I ate the last of my burger, I gave the most definitive response that came to me: sure, why not.

Life now centered on my father and me, with my mother receding into a support role. I took to it without looking back. The carpool worked fine. Since there were three other kids, my father had to do it only once a month or so. The emotional weight of my life now shifted to my father's world. At school, I made friends with a few older kids who had cars, so my social life stayed on the uptick. From time to time, my mother would pick me up for visits. My room in her house stayed pretty much the same, although all the important stuff, like most of my clothes and books, my basketball and baseball gear, and my airplane models, now resided with me at my father's.

As the school year moved along, I eagerly anticipated my sixteenth birthday. The fact that my mother did not adopt the two-week retreat approach to give us time together didn't register with me. When it did, I realized I didn't miss it. I don't want this to sound as though I had somehow lost my attachment to my mother or my affection for her. Our relationship remained pretty much the same: she was clearly in charge, but not in an overt way; I accepted the boundaries of privacy that had evolved. She still set the rules in the world we shared. Not until I reached twenty-one did I dare smoke in front of her; swearing never achieved acceptability. But she tolerated my friends and teenagers in general with friendly firmness. One of my friends called her "cool" in comparison to other moms. Even Leonard grudgingly agreed. Yet, at this stage, she still occasionally popped up in my mind as I worked to achieve satisfaction, and this disturbed me. It tended to happen after I saw her with Maybelline. After Marge left, that seemed to be the case whenever I visited.

In fact, gradually, Maybelline's presence in my mother's house seemed to swell, although nothing changed in the living arrangements, at least that I could tell. Maybelline did not change much as she aged; she was still youthful, with no hint of gray streaking as in my mother's hair. She worked away in her garden as always, her rompers on her fine figure, listening to music on the outside sound system she had installed (without Marge's help or mine), and often sang along. I knew things had undergone a drastic change when my mother didn't complain about it. She would have pounced on such an intrusion by anyone else. When I became curious and quizzed her, she said simply, "Maybelline likes music. It's okay."

As for me, Maybelline remained friendly in her somewhat detached way. I still helped her occasionally when I happened to be around. I could feel her green eyes on me as I worked. How did she regard me, her lover's son? I couldn't fathom. She invariably offered to pay now; I invariably said no thanks. I had become inured to her charms and responded to her only in the polite, deferential way that was expected of me. Being helpful to adults, as I had been taught to be, constituted a suitable relationship now. She could have been anyone, any woman, needing a bit of assistance, which I could provide. Just being neighborly, as a nice boy should be. I wanted to believe that. So I did.

That's how my teenage years evolved. I didn't speculate much about my mother's life. Over time, she didn't travel in her work much more than she had before, which wasn't a lot. And she certainly never gave any sign that she might move away. Things stayed pretty much the same while I went through high school. When I graduated, my mother said I should invite both Alice and Maybelline to my graduation; I did, and they both came, both bringing dress shirts as gifts. I went to college far enough away that I saw my parents only occasionally and increasingly less often. I traveled and took long sabbaticals, roaming around Europe as I worked my way indifferently through graduate school. Vietnam's chaos dominated the times, and I hid out from it successfully, eventually saved by a high number in the draft lottery.

As I matured, I felt the influence of both parents in me: my father's easygoing passivity and my mother's aloof superiority. Both were smart, and I inherited their brains. When I became a college professor (an expert in an obscure field few people knew existed and even fewer cared about), the combination of my father's mild-mannered abstractness and my mother's mindful independence combined to produce a kind of lonely detachment in me. I embraced this because I could imagine no other way. Mostly, I withdrew into solitude, dwelling inwardly, alone with my thoughts. While I did not think of those thoughts as secrets, I rarely expressed them; I lacked a vocabulary adequate to the purpose. Even though I lived in a world of words, they were rarely mine, about me.

I wandered through a first marriage, drifted around in a second, and never really embraced either. Over time, my therapist helped me understand how connecting vulnerabilities can strengthen people and help them bond. But that knowledge emerged only gradually over many years. And by then, it was too late. I had no ability to reveal the hidden parts of me that might have attached themselves to the inner lives of the women I married. They lacked that capacity, too. Maybe that's why we chose one another. Over time, the marriages blurred in my mind and canceled each other out as though they had never happened. All three of us were simply too fragile to establish emotional connections. Fortunately, no children arrived to muddy the waters.

On those occasions when I did visit my mother, her house had that same feel I had sensed as a teenager when I visited her after moving in with my father: the feel of someone else's presence, a presence that shared the space with my mother and defined her world. I felt like an intruder, and it made me uncomfortable enough that I kept my visits brief, claiming the press of work or giving some other excuse to leave. My mother never protested as some mothers might, so no oppressive grasping or sense of abandonment grew between us. I just no longer belonged there. I hadn't for a very long time.

That memorable first summer with Marge and Maybelline had happened forty years ago. Now, I sat with my mother and Maybelline, organ music playing during the short ceremony as some of Marge's friends drifted in to pay their respects. There were only a few. My mother had surprised me by asking me to join her at the funeral. There had been so little contact over the years I scarcely knew her anymore, so the request perplexed me. Maybe residual nostalgia, I thought when she called, a memory of the brief time when the four of us—Marge, Maybelline, my mother, and me—lived there, cloistered in our little enclave. I stopped speculating when I realized I would never fathom my mother's motives. I just said yes, of course I would come.

Marge had returned to live with Maybelline as abruptly as she left. This happened about the time I graduated from high school. As before, no one said anything to me; I happened to see Marge working on the house again, still in her gray overalls, as though three years had not gone by. I asked my mother about it. She said only, "You should say hello." She looked out the window for a moment. "And offer to help." She gave no explanation for the change.

Maybelline sat stiffly upright throughout the ceremony, her eyes focused forward. She had remained beautiful as she aged, a maturing kind of loveliness that reflected her seventy-plus years but with discernable strains of a more youthful, arousing appeal, the kind that drew men's attention. Her hair glistened as it had when I first saw her in rompers, hoeing in the yard. Now, she wore it shorter. There still was no gray. No doubt she colored it. The longing in her green eyes hadn't changed, but now, I could comprehend something of what it meant. She wanted to be loved, nothing more. As I sat next to her and she stared straight ahead, I hoped she had been.

My mother grew older in a more conventional way, age showing in the wrinkles on her skin, her graying hair losing its luster as it settled into drabness. But she retained her nobility of stature, that strong sense of self, of being a superior person but tolerant of the vagaries surrounding her. Experience had brought her wisdom, I suppose, and with that, a mellow quality that replaced the brittleness I recalled from my youth. She still held her chin high and gazed at life head-on. I admired her and realized admiration had replaced love.

Had I ever really loved her? Or had she already been too detached, too emotionally remote, when Maybelline suddenly appeared, and the ground shifted under our feet? I didn't know the answer then, when I first felt it, and have reached no conclusion in the years since. She was a good mother and parent. That was enough to keep me attached. I sought no other answers.

The answers came along anyway. Maybelline had ridden home with us, holding Marge in her little box. She thanked us quietly for being there and gave each of us an awkward one-arm hug as she turned to go inside her house.

"Come over when you feel like it," my mother said. Maybelline said she would.

I looked at the house and marveled at how trim and clean

it still looked, reflecting Marge's vigorous maintenance and Maybelline's inspired yard work. Our house paled in comparison, but it, too, had held up well, partly because of Marge. Not long after Marge returned, she abruptly started taking care of my mother's house, too. She never explained why. She would simply mention something she had noticed that "needed attention" and would proceed to address it. That was her way, my mother said. Marge could never express herself very well, my mother explained, except through actions. In time, the help spread to interior fixes: backed-up plumbing, balky dishwashers, peeling wallpaper, all the things Marge fixed in her own home. She's probably doing it to protect the value of her own property, my mother observed. But I don't think she really believed that. For my part, I think Marge saw it as a way to get inside the circle Maybelline and my mother had drawn around themselves, on whatever terms were required.

When we went into our own house, my mother made a pot of tea and placed it on the kitchen table between us. She began to tell me a little about Marge's last years, how the cancer had been discovered in her female parts, and how she had stubbornly refused to treat it. Years earlier, when menopause took hold, she had become even more difficult to tolerate, my mother said. But Maybelline stoically endured her. In time, Marge returned to a more familiar condition, still surly but no longer aggressively so. The edge had been taken off. Things were more peaceful after that, my mother said. When the cancer in her ovaries came along, Marge's grim comment had been, "I always knew those things would kill me." Now they had. It took fifteen months.

My mother said all of this as the early evening light in the kitchen turned gold, glinting on the gilded edges of the cups and teapot. For a while, she said nothing. She lifted the lid on the teapot. The tea surely had steeped enough by now, I thought. But she didn't remove the tea bags or pour tea into our cups. She simply held the lid in her hand without moving.

"All those years, I felt sorry for Marge," she said at last. The remark surprised me since I still remembered her quip when she first saw her. "She could never really adjust. Accept things." She placed the lid back on the teapot. "Maybelline will be selling the house," my mother said after a while. "She doesn't want to live there with Marge gone." For a while, she was silent. "I've invited her to live here. She shouldn't be alone."

She fell silent again, reflecting; I just sat, saying nothing. Then, she looked at me, and I sensed that she was on the edge of talking about herself and Maybelline. I wanted her to. All those years of blocking out information, of shielding myself from knowledge of how they lived—all that disappeared. Now, I wanted to understand.

She fiddled with the pot some more but still did not pour the tea. It had steeped for twenty minutes or so. Could she possibly like it this strong? I wondered, my mind skittish from the tension in the room.

Finally, she said, "Belle and I shared what we could. When we could."

She paused, this time picking up her spoon and placing it next to the saucer and the empty cup. She had lost interest in the tea. We remained as we were, thoughtful and quiet. A feeling of loss overwhelmed me, and I suppressed an urge to cry.

My mother spoke again. "We could do nothing else. That was all the times would allow."

We sat there in silence, waiting for night to give us an avenue of escape.

A RIDE HOME

All day, Callie hoped the rain would stop before school let out. But by three o'clock, it had gotten worse. She felt it lashing against the house in waves, almost horizontal at times. The sky had grown darker than it was an hour ago. She would have to pick up Russell at school. He wouldn't like it, of course. He preferred walking the three blocks home, even in the rain. Maybe, especially in the rain. His yellow slicker kept him dry enough, and he liked slopping through the puddles, splashing the water high enough to get his pant legs wet even under the raincoat. He had grown more independent, more like his father, not disobedient exactly, but stubborn. More and more, he had to be persuaded. He wouldn't let himself be pushed. Callie could picture the scene now. He would see her in the car, shrug his shoulders in resignation, and flop into the back seat, hunching down and staring out of the window. He might even say, "I'm not a baby, you know." It had become his favorite comment when she tried to mother him. But no matter. Today, it was simply too wet. He would have to put up with it.

By the time Callie arrived at school, the yellow school buses had lined up, nose to tail, along the street in front of the entrance. School had just let out, and the kids were grouping under the shelter of the overhang covering the entrance, momentarily stopped by the intensity of the rain. Some teachers at the top of the stairs tried to regulate the flow, but it did little to stop the children. Batches of them spotted their buses and ran raggedly toward them, laughing and shrieking in the rain, pushing through the open doors. Teachers with umbrellas were little help. Callie watched in fascination as the kids sorted themselves out for the buses, their raincoats a kaleidoscope of colors. There were no school buses in rural Tennessee where she first went to school. Kids walked or sometimes didn't go to school at all. It was the Depression. People were so poor; mostly, they just tried to survive. Callie shook her head slightly at the memory. Her long hair brushed her shoulders. She wanted to cut it short to make it easier to manage. But her husband liked it long, and she didn't want to disappoint him.

Many of the children had yellow slickers, like Russell's, so she searched carefully among them for his. He probably wouldn't wear the hat. He hated the look. A few kids ran toward other cars, which gradually began to drive away. One bus had departed by the time Russell appeared at the top of the stairs. Sure enough, he held the rain hat in his hand, his book bag in the other. He saw her and came toward the car, opening the back door and sliding across the seat. A surge of cold November air swept into the car through the open door, surprising Callie with its freshness as it drove out the stale, heated air inside. Russell hunkered down against the car door behind her. *He doesn't want me to be able to look at him,* Callie thought. She adjusted the rearview mirror, so he came into view.

"Before you start, it's just too wet for you to walk," she said to his reflection. Every day, he looked more like his father, with dark brown eyes and high cheekbones. Her husband bragged that he had some Cherokee blood, but she never knew whether to believe him.

"It's okay," Russell said. To her relief, he didn't complain. Sometimes, he could figure things out for himself. She liked that about him. Once he decided to go along, he couldn't resist. She felt a small thrill of love. He was a good kid.

Callie waited as the bus and car congestion around the school began to dissipate. Most of the cars were gone. Finally, the bus directly in front of her pulled away, allowing her to see the stairs at the entrance more clearly. A few teachers stood huddled back under the overhang, watching as the buses departed.

That's when Callie saw him: one child remaining on the top step, a boy, a small, gray figure in jeans and a jean jacket. That's not enough in this weather, Callie thought instantly. Where's his raincoat? The teachers seemed oblivious to the boy. Callie could see them shivering, anxious to return inside out of the weather. The boy just stood there, his arms at his sides, looking into space. Had he missed his bus? Was someone supposed to pick him up? The cars and buses were leaving. Callie didn't see anyone else driving up to the school. No one could expect him to walk home in such light clothing, could they? she thought. Why weren't the teachers doing something instead of chattering? A wave of anger swept through Callie. So irresponsible. Maybe she should say something. She looked again in the rearview mirror at Russell slumped in the seat.

"Who's that boy, the one standing at the top of the stairs?" she asked.

Russell raised himself slightly from his slump. "Oh, that's just Benny," he said, slouching back. "He never talks in class."

Callie studied the slight figure on the stairs. He reminded her of something, something about herself. "Benny who?" she asked Russell's reflection in the mirror.

For a while, he said nothing, pondering the question. "Taggart. I think."

Taggart. She knew that name. The Taggarts lived in a ramshackle house on Digby Road, on the fringes of town, so far out that the town board had debated whether to extend utility service that far. In the end, it did and created a headache for itself. Callie worked part-time in the municipal office. She had gone to the location when the board members went there to puzzle out the logistics, so she knew the house. The Taggarts were poor. No one in the office knew what Mr. Taggart did for a living, if anything. Shift work in the sawmills, most likely, and that was spotty. He drove around town in an old green pickup truck with a noisy muffler.

Mr. Taggart became the scourge of the utility district, chronically late in paying his bills. When the backlog became too great, they shut off the water service. Mr. Taggart stormed into the office, angry and red-faced, when he confronted Callie at the front counter. Everyone else shrank to the back, even the manager. But Callie steeled herself to face him, to overcome her fear of him and be as polite as possible, enduring his rants. When he finally paid the bill, after his rambling complaints, he thrust some wadded-up currency at her. She had to unfold the hot, sweaty bills as he stormed off. Yes, she certainly knew Mr. Taggart.

The buses and cars had departed, and the teachers had disappeared back inside. Silence settled in; only moments before, there had been a noisy swarm of children and idling buses spewing fumes. The emptiness engulfed Callie. Only three people remained: her, Russell, and the boy on the stairs. He hadn't moved since Callie spotted him. No cars were pulling up. Maybe he knew no one was coming. Maybe he was just waiting for the rain to stop so he could start walking home. The shabby place where he lived was at least four miles from the school.

As a girl, she knew how it felt to walk home from school in the rain. One time, she plodded along the muddy road in rural Tennessee, shivering, the charity raincoat from the church barely covering her dress. A neighbor, an old man with skin the color of the dark soil, came by in his wagon and offered her a ride. She knew him. He came to their back door with vegetables from his garden, saying timidly that he had so much and no one to share it with, so would Callie's mother please take some. Callie climbed up on the wagon, and the old man stretched the canvas tarp covering his head to cover her too. They creaked along in silence, the rain pouring off the flanks of the mules. Callie felt secure, sitting close to him under the tarp, smelling the odor of the farmland on him. She stopped him before her home came into view. She climbed down, thanking the old man, relieved that her father hadn't seen them. If he had, he would have exploded in anger about the dark-skinned man and her sitting next to him. She was grateful for the ride, but even more for the secrecy of it.

Four miles—in the rain. Why should Benny have to endure that? Why hadn't the teachers dealt with him? She would have to complain to the principal about it. She kept staring at the boy, transfixed. He looked so alone, ignored and forgotten.

"Russell, go get him and bring him to the car," she said to the figure in the mirror. Surprisingly, Russell didn't object. She had expected him to. Russell clambered out the passenger-side door and ran up the stairs. She watched as he spoke to Benny, reaching out to take his arm. For a few moments, the boy seemed to resist; then, he gave in as Russell tugged him toward the car. When they reached the car, Russell scrambled in, Benny following slowly behind him. Russell reached over and slammed the car door.

"Man, it's wet out there," Russell said. Benny said nothing. Callie turned to look at him. He had to be Russell's age, but he looked younger. His slight frame made him seem smaller than Russell. His hands rested on the washed-out denim of his jeans. Callie couldn't help noticing his fingers, slender, fine-boned and delicate. So fragile, she thought, like a little porcelain statue. Benny sat looking at her, expressionless. His blond hair lay wetly against his forehead. Drops of water ran down his cheeks. She wanted to reach back and wipe them away.

"Hello Benny. I'm Mrs. Brandt, Russell's mother. Did you miss your bus? Is someone coming to pick you up?" She realized she had never seen Benny's mother, or at least didn't know who she was. She would probably be a woman beaten down by her situation, navigating carefully around the inferno of Mr. Taggart's temper. Someone like her own mother. "Is your mother coming for you?" she asked him.

The boy stared at her. He didn't answer. Callie could read nothing in his expression: no gratitude, no relief at being out of the rain, not even fear. He hadn't moved since he followed Russell into the car and laid back against the car seat. How can he be so passive? Callie wondered. She tried to imagine Russell in the same situation. He would be curious, exploring the boundaries and asking questions. But this boy—this boy almost seemed unable to act. She thought about the world Mr. Taggart created: volatile, chaotic, frightening.

Maybe that was it: silence was survival. She understood the need to retreat inside yourself to survive like you didn't exist at all. Mr. Taggart reminded her of her own father, a sullen, forbidding drunk. She remembered how he ripped his family out of its roots during the Depression and hauled it to a sharecropper's shanty in Louisiana, then another in east Texas. They lived in leaky, mouse-infested shacks, where her father hounded her and her brothers and mother to work in the cotton fields. To earn whiskey money.

She hated the Louisiana and Texas schools. "Croppers," the other kids called them, taunting them for their threadbare clothing. Callie fought back the only way she could by being the smartest kid in class, reading the most books, and knowing the answers to questions the teachers asked. Shame burned inside her, but she learned to mask it. In time, the sharecropping failed, and her family joined the refugees from the Dust Bowl, fleeing to California, where they were called "Okies" no matter where they were from. White trash.

Yes, she could imagine what Benny's life must be like. The poverty, the humiliation of it. The least she could do was give him a ride home. "No one should have to walk in this weather," she said, almost to herself. "So, let's get Benny home." If Benny heard, he said nothing.

Digby Road wound away from the center of the small town, through the shabbier sections, past the sawmills near the railroad sidings. Callie rarely came this far on Digby Road. The noise and dirt unsettled her, the trucks heaped with pine logs, the screaming saws, the towering sawdust burners spewing ash and smoke into the air. The houses were spread out here, some scarcely more than shacks, drab and poorly maintained. Transplanted rural people, mostly poor, lived here. The houses reminded Callie of the sharecropper shacks in Louisiana and Texas, the shock of them on her young mind. She shuddered as she drove. At least things were better in the part of town where she lived. After the war ended, things got better. Now, in 1952, people could find work if they wanted it. She and her husband had managed to build a life for themselves and their children, a respectable life. Her husband had a good job at a construction company and a steady income. But somehow, prosperity had not reached the part of town she was driving through.

Now, they were beyond the houses and the sawmills, passing through the scrub oak and reddish-brown manzanita brush that grew in the dry, hard northern California ground. The Taggart house wasn't far now. Callie tried to imagine what it must be like for the small boy in the back seat to trudge along this road in the summer or when it was wet and rainy, like now. She wondered if Benny had brothers or sisters and considered asking Russell if he knew. Maybe there was some older sister who should have taken responsibility. She decided not to ask. She remembered how her own brothers suffered from her father's rages—and her inability to intervene to protect them. She realized she would rather not know if there was a sister.

As she rounded another curve, she saw the Taggart house. It sat in a slight hollow, back from the road about a hundred yards. A muddy drive filled with potholes led up to the house. The heavy rain splashed in the puddles as she drove slowly along, the car bouncing over the rough surface. She pulled up into the small turn-around area and stopped. The house sat there, silent, even more dilapidated than Callie remembered. She didn't see Mr. Taggart's truck, but that didn't mean anything. It could be anywhere. As Callie gazed at the house, she began to realize that it seemed empty. There were no lights in the windows, no sign of activity at all. The place looked abandoned.

Benny had said nothing as they drove up the driveway toward the house. Now, he spoke for the first time: "We don't live here no more." His voice rasped softly like he didn't use it often. Its edge surprised Callie. It seemed too harsh for a child.

Callie turned and looked at him. "What do you mean you don't live here anymore? Why didn't you say something?" Her irritation came out. "Why did you let me drive you all the way out here?" She spoke more harshly than she intended.

The boy had fallen silent again. Don't get mad and scare him, Callie told herself. She took a deep breath and tried to calm her voice. "Okay, then, where do you live?" Benny had withdrawn even deeper into the seat cushion, shrinking back as though to make himself smaller. He looked at her but seemed to have no comprehension of what she was asking. She leaned further back over the car seat, trying to get closer to him. "Benny, you must tell me where you live. Please." The boy just sat.

She felt anxiety rising but forced herself to resist it. An earlier worry suddenly flooded back: what if someone had been on the way to pick him up and had simply been late? Maybe his mother or a relative had been delayed. Now, Callie had ruined everything. Of course, that must've been what happened. They would be frantic now. Fear began to overwhelm her. Callie fought it off. No. If someone was coming, why had Benny gotten into the car? Surely, he would have said something to explain. Or would he? He had spoken only once, a clipped comment with no elaboration. How could he be so unresponsive? She shook her head again. The whole thing seemed crazy.

Callie leaned forward and rested her head where her hands gripped the steering wheel. Too tight, she thought and relaxed her hands a bit. Her stomach felt queasy. What had she done? Here she was, in charge of a small boy she didn't know, parked in the yard of an empty house, without the least idea of where to take him. There must be a way out of this mess. Maybe she should take him to the sheriff's office. That seemed excessive; it might just frighten him. What about going back to the school? It would be closed, the front door locked, everyone gone. But maybe, by chance, someone would still be there and hear her knocking. Maybe the principal, mild-mannered and rational, would be there. He would be easier to explain everything to. But even as she considered the idea, Callie felt hopeless. What would she do when she found the building empty, which was likely? Could she just leave Benny where she had found him, shivering alone as she drove away? Of course not. She had to resolve it.

She had to think harder to sort it out. Benny must know something he could tell her. She just had to get it out of him. Maybe he knew where Mr. Taggart worked. The idea of confronting Mr. Taggart, the boy in tow, chilled her. He might explode in anger. But she had no choice. She steeled herself against the idea of confronting him. Benny shouldn't have been left waiting in the rain, she would say, looking Mr. Taggart squarely in the face. She hoped she would have the nerve. She turned to look at the boy. "Benny, do you know where your father works? The mills, maybe? Or somewhere else?" She tried to make her voice as mild as possible.

Benny stayed silent. By now, he must be completely bewildered, Callie thought, even frightened. She tried to think of other ways to draw him out. What is your favorite class in school? Do you like baseball? The standard questions you ask children to get them to open up. But she knew it would be hopeless on this boy. He remained bottled up inside himself. Other kids no doubt bullied him. He probably knew better than to say anything, to keep his mouth shut when they taunted him. Complaining would only make it worse. Maybe he felt the same way now. Silence is safety against the unknown.

A lash of rain shook the car. It didn't rain often here, but when it did, it came in torrents. She watched the wipers trying to scrape the windshield clear. She had no idea what to do next. Worry tightened inside her, but she resisted it. There had to be something she could do, some way of getting information about the family. She realized Mr. Taggart had not been in the office on one of his tirades recently. Maybe a month or more. That must've been when they moved, deserting the place on Digby Road. Maybe she should have tried to know more about him and the family. If she had, maybe she would know what to do.

"Mom?"

The voice from the back seat startled her—Russell; she had nearly forgotten he was there.

"What, Russell?" She needed to say his name to bring him back to mind.

"I might know a place. You know, to look."

She slanted the rearview mirror so she could see him again. "What do you mean, 'a place to look'?"

"Well, a place where Benny might live."

Callie studied her son in the mirror. He had such a fertile imagination. Tales bubbled out of him. It wasn't easy to separate fact from fiction in what he said. She would tell him stories, and he loved telling them back, giving them a twist of his own that made them both laugh. Was he just making this up?

"Well, then. Where?"

"Out Allen Road. At the end. Some people live there."

Callie considered this. Allen Road twisted through the manzanita brush and dead-ended at the town dump. Callie had only been there once. She accompanied her husband when he took a pickup load of trash to discard. The stench hit her even before she could see the smoking mounds of garbage smoldering like some dystopian furnace. The scavengers descended on the truck as her husband was backing up, poking through the refuse, looking for something useful, at least on their terms. They were silent and rude, shifting things without asking permission. At first, their intrusion offended her. Then she thought, It is junk, after all. We're just discarding it. Why should they need permission? The place gave her the chills. She sat in the truck until her husband had finished unloading, and they left. It had been at least five years ago. She didn't remember seeing any houses nearby. Why would Russell think anyone lived there?

"Allen Road goes to the dump. People don't live out there. Why do you think that?" She stared at Russell in the mirror.

He squirmed and looked uncomfortable. But he stuck to his story.

"Well, kids at school. They talk about it. About spooky people, tramps, bums, people like that, staying at the dump. They poke fun at Benny and say he lives there, too."

It sounded to Callie like something Russell might dream up. She couldn't tell. She looked at Benny, who had stayed silent throughout this exchange. How unlike Russell he was—pale, withdrawn, lost in his own grayness. Did he understand what they had said? If so, he gave no sign. Callie had finally resigned herself to a sad fact. He must not know where he lives. Like it or not, she could only keep searching. At least Russell had provided a clue.

Allen Road lay on the other side of town. As she drove, Callie stared straight ahead, trying to empty her mind of anything except the small hope that Russell might be right. Not that she doubted him. He just had such vivid fantasies. She forced herself to keep her skepticism under control. They were well beyond the town boundaries now, out in the country. As they wound through the manzanita brush, the rain splattering against the windshield lessened. The wipers kept up their steady drumbeat. Callie stayed focused on the road and the rhythm of the wipers. At least they were doing a better job now that the rain had let up a bit. She could see the road ahead more clearly.

No one had spoken since they left the old Taggart place. Callie resisted looking at her watch. She didn't want to know how long it had been since Russell pulled Benny into the car. It seemed like an eternity. Everything else had receded from her mind, and she could think of nothing except the mess they were in. Because of her, her impulsiveness and lack of judgment. It was all her fault.

Five minutes later, over a slight hill, she saw the dump. No vehicles were parked around it. In the rain, the scavengers must have stayed away. As she drove toward it, she noticed a structure off to the right, barely visible above the brush and easy to miss. A shack with a tarpaper surface. It sat back a good distance from the road, connected by a muddy track worn into the ground by car tires. Could anyone possibly live in it? And then she saw it: Mr. Taggart's truck sitting there, partly obscured by the structure but unmistakably his. She stopped, uncertain what to do next.

She heard a sound from the back seat and turned to look. Benny had opened the door and was climbing out without a word. He didn't bother to close the door. She watched him trudge up the wet path toward the house.

The truth rose in Callie's throat, choking her. Just a ride home. Under the tarp. It changed nothing. The world went on. Everything stayed hidden inside; it was the only way to cope. She felt a sudden urge to cry but caught herself. She didn't want Russell to see tears.

For a while, she sat like that, looking out, seeing the rain splash into the car.

"Close the door, Russell," she said finally. "Let's go home."

THE WOMAN IN THE CLOSET

Barnes saw the woman the instant he moved his wife's coat aside so he could try to squeeze in his own. She stood in the corner of the closet, behind the jumble of coats. He jerked back. "Jesus Christ!" he said. If the woman heard him, she gave no sign. His brain struggled to make sense of it. Maybe he imagined it. Maybe there's nothing there. She certainly wasn't there when he went out earlier. A trick of the mind, he told himself. He shook his head to help clear it and breathed in deeply, letting the air out slowly. I'll try again, he thought.

His wife's coat had flopped back into place when he let go of it. Gently, he moved the sleeve just enough to see. A woman stood there, sure enough. A woman with pale skin and long, light-colored hair, wearing a white robe. Her eyes were closed. Thank God she's not looking at me, Barnes said to himself. She leaned against the wall, propped like a statue. Maybe she isn't real, he thought. Maybe she's a mannequin, like a dress dummy, that his wife Sybil put there without telling him. Then, the woman moved, just a little, her eyes still tightly closed. She moaned slightly. Oh my God, he thought.

Barnes backed carefully out of the closet, still holding his own coat, and pulled the door shut. He draped his coat around a dining room chair. Sybil was standing at the counter in the kitchen, chopping an onion with her big chef's knife.

"There's a woman in the front hall closet," he said.

"Don't start in on me." She pointed the tip of the knife at him. "I'm in no mood for jokes."

"No, I'm serious. There really is a woman. In the corner of the closet behind your coats."

She raised her head from the chopping and gave him a look full of meaning, baked-in by thirty-five years of marriage. "Did you remember the detergent?" Detergent. The idea of laundry detergent had flown from Barnes's mind the instant he walked out the front door. Once he stepped outside, the day washed over him, still chilly in the early morning but full of promise. At that moment, it seemed as though he had no particular reason for going outside except to take a morning stroll, as he often did since he retired.

"You forgot it, didn't you?" She pointed the knife at him again. He considered lying: they were out of the brand you wanted. Or Feldman couldn't leave the counter to go get it in the back room. But why lie? She wouldn't believe him anyway. "It slipped my mind. It was such a beautiful morning, I forgot." He imagined the knife slicing into his gut and thought of Norman Mailer stabbing his wife in the stomach just to see how it felt.

"I don't see how you could forget why you went out in the first place," Sybil said. "Honestly, Barnes, sometimes I think you're losing your mind." She put the knife down. "I can't do laundry until I have the detergent."

"Would you at least look in the closet?"

The baked-in expression returned to her face. Barnes sighed and turned to retrieve his coat so he could go for the detergent.

All the old boys were in Millie's Coffee Shop, sitting in a booth, when Barnes walked in. "Barnesy, sit your lazy butt," Larry

Wilmot said and slid over to make room.

Barnes squeezed onto the bench, trying not to press against Larry's leg.

"So, what's cooking in your stew pot today?" Matt Terrell asked. Barnes thought, should he mention the woman in the closet? It wasn't exactly the sort of thing you talked about. Then he decided, what the hell, he had nothing to lose.

"This morning, when I looked in the hall closet, there was a woman standing in there."

Eddy Barnett slapped his hands against the table. Everyone jumped. Eddy's hands were cupped and clasped together like he had trapped an insect. He widened his hands a crack, closed one eyelid, and peered down with his open eye.

"Yep. I thought so. Just caught me a whopper." They all laughed except Barnes, who sat expressionless. He should have known better—they thought he was joking. Barnes wrote novels. Sometimes, characters or plots going through his mind crept into his conversations with people. If he was lucky, he could keep a story that was germinating in his brain going for days before the boys caught on that it was fiction. They didn't always know when to take him seriously, and they didn't like being fooled. But they respected Barnes. He ranked as a local celebrity. A little eccentric, people thought, but a good guy. That's just Barnes-y, the old boys said.

"I've got her trapped right in here," Eddy went on. "What do you want to do with her?"

Barnes said nothing.

"You should call the deputy. Old Lew would know how to handle it," Billy Jones said. "He'd use his gun. Blow her all to hell." The boys nodded. That's how the deputy, Lew Kleiner, proposed solving all kinds of situations: demonstrations, protesters, smart-ass hippies, things he saw on television.

Barnes sat silently. Millie had brought him a cup of coffee, and he watched as she walked away. He wished he had never come in. For the moment, he just sat, listening to the old men's prattle. Of course, they didn't believe him; they hadn't even really heard him. Not much could penetrate their rituals, the humdrum repetition of their dialogue. Barnes sometimes found the predictability of their banter oddly comforting. He would drift with it, adding a jibe here and there, which mostly passed them by. But today it grated.

Jerry Lancaster had been silent. Now he said, "If she was in the bedroom closet, you could have screwed her." Everyone laughed again. Jerry never said much, so they were impressed that he spoke up.

"Not old Barnes-y," Eddy said. "He'd only do missionary. Nothing standing up." The men went quiet. The stale air of old age arousal hung over them like a fart.

Barnes slid off the booth seat and stood. "See you guys," he said. As he walked off, he could hear them urging Jerry to talk more. "How would you do it to her?" Larry said as Barnes left.

Barnes hung around Feldman's Grocery for a while, talking with Feldman. Boxes of open stock stood here and there in the aisles. Feldman got to them when he could. Feldman fussed about business now that Walmart had opened outside of town. "I'm finished," he told Barnes. "Won't be long."

"Your daughter and her husband won't be taking over?" Barnes asked out of politeness; he already knew the answer.

"No way," Feldman said, plopping the plastic container of detergent on the counter. "Not interested. A waste of time and money, they say."

To distract Feldman, Barnes told him about the woman in the closet. "I found a woman in our closet this morning," he said as he took his change from the counter. Feldman didn't react. He was lost in the apprehension of being at the edge and not knowing whether he would fall—or step—off. Barnes left him like that.

As Barnes walked back past the coffee shop, he could see through the window that the old boys had left. Millie got a brief respite between breakfast and lunch. Barnes preferred going into the coffee shop then so they could catch a few minutes to chat. Millie was level-headed about everything except the shop. "I know I should have sold it, or closed it, after Frank died," she told Barnes, "but I couldn't think of what else I would do. So, I didn't."

Millie wiped the cloth across the table at the booth where the old men had been sitting. She motioned that Barnes should sit there. She took the last of the dishes away and returned with two cups of coffee. She sat across from him.

"What did you do to rile up the boys?" she asked.

"It doesn't take much," Barnes said.

"It must've been something dirty. I could hear them talking dirty. They left when I wouldn't bring them any more coffee."

"No, I didn't say anything dirty." Barnes wondered whether he should tell Millie about the woman in the closet. She might not believe him, like the old guys. But she always talked sense, and right now, Barnes needed that.

"Actually, I told them about an odd thing that happened this morning." He stirred his coffee and hoped it wouldn't sound too nutty. "When I opened the hall closet this morning, there was a woman standing in it. Behind Sybil's coats. Scared the hell out of me." Millie studied him. They had known each other since the third grade. She had figured him out by the fourth. It gave her an edge for the rest of their lives, one he could never quite overcome.

"A woman?" Millie asked.

Barnes nodded.

"Are you sure you saw something? Were you wearing your glasses?"

She's trying to figure out if I'm balmy, Barnes thought. *Or just playing around.*

"Oh, I saw her. At first, I thought it might be a dress mannequin that Sybil put there. But she moved and made a sound. A moan, sort of." He waited while his words sank in. "At least her eyes were closed. She wasn't looking at me."

Millie's expression had turned serious. "Do you know who she is? Or how she got in there?"

"Well, she could have sneaked in through the front door, I guess. While I was out." They rarely locked the front door. That could explain it. But he had taken his own coat from the closet when he first left. He thought back: could she have been in there already? He had been distracted. Maybe he just overlooked her. "But, no, I don't know who she is."

"She could be a burglar," Millie said.

"Yeah, I thought of that."

"Maybe you should call Lew."

Barnes pictured Lew Kleiner, his big fat gut bulging over his belt, poking around in the closet. He dismissed the idea: Sybil would never put up with it.

"Well, if she's a burglar, she probably got away while I was talking to Sybil in the kitchen."

Millie nodded. "What did Sybil say about it?"

"I asked her to look in the closet. But she wouldn't do it."

Millie sat quietly. She appeared to be deliberating as though she had reached a conclusion and was considering what to say next. Barnes brooded. All the coffee he had drunk pressed on his bladder. He scooted out of the booth, leaving Millie to her meditation, and walked back toward the bathrooms.

"I was thinking," Millie said when Barnes returned. "Maybe you should try talking to her. The woman in the closet, I mean."

The suggestion caught Barnes by surprise. He hadn't thought of that. He hadn't even said, "Who the hell are you?" when he pushed back the coats and saw the woman. Now, he felt stupid for not saying anything.

"Talking to her?"

"Yes. If she answered back, at least you'd know she was real."

Barnes drank the rest of his coffee. It had gotten cold but tasted better, sweeter. "Gotta get going," he said, standing. "See you."

"Good luck," Millie said.

The door jangled as he pushed it, and cool morning air drifted in. Could he talk to the woman? Was it possible?

"You know, Barnes, sometimes the things you say are too complicated for the boys," Millie said behind him. "They can't always tell if you're just joking around."

On an early morning nearly forty years before, Barnes backed down the driveway into the darkness just before dawn, an hour earlier than usual. He needed to get to the college in Shepardsville to finish reading the papers of his senior English class. They expected them back; he had promised and didn't want to let them down. His classes were popular and always full. He's different, a little weird, students said. They liked him.

The fog thickened as he accelerated. Drizzling, not quite rain, but wet enough for the wipers to scrape some wetness away, then sweep dryly a few times before the water collected again, and they cleared it off. The wipers mesmerized him as he drove. His mind sometimes worked that way: a patch of thoughts to clear off, then dryness for a while until new thoughts emerged, and some lines he could write down came to him. Damn, it's dark, he thought. It had gotten too hot; he reached over to lower the heat, glancing toward the dashboard.

The world exploded in a dazzling sea of shimmering lights. He felt them piercing him as everything disappeared.

He awoke, lying on his back, his mouth so dry he could barely part his lips. Someone stood over him—a woman. He felt her doing something. Gripping his wrist.

"Water," he croaked.

A haze covered his eyes like goggles. He couldn't quite make her out.

"You're awake. Finally. That's good," she said. She pushed a glass straw against his lips and said, "Suck."

He sucked and felt the liquid flowing across his dry membranes.

"Where am I?" It came out as a whisper, barely audible.

"In the hospital," the woman said. He could see her dressed in white, with a white cap. A nurse: that's what she is, he realized. And drifted back to sleep.

When he awakened later, his brain felt a little clearer. He saw her again, doing something above him.

"More water, please," Barnes whispered, a little stronger now.

She handed him the water with the glass straw. "Try holding it yourself."

Barnes sucked in the water. He managed to place the glass on the table next to the bed.

"What happened? Why am I here?"

"You and a deer tried to occupy the same space at the same time," she said. "Technically, you won."

Barnes moved the muscles in his face and flexed his jaw.

"You mean I hit a deer? I don't remember it."

"You sure did. A buck. A beauty. Came right through the windshield and sat in your lap. Had huge antlers. Tangled up in everything. They had to cut off its head to get it out of the car." For a while, she looked at the intravenous bottle hooked up to him. "They thought you would be dead." She walked to the end of the bed and took up a clipboard hanging there. "But here you are. Bright as a summer day."

"I don't feel very bright." The words sounded almost normal. Maybe he would survive after all.

"You will," she said.

A day later, when the wooziness wore off, he recognized her. Sybil Boone, daughter of Cyrus Boone, publisher of the local *Boonetown Tribune*. She had been a senior in high school when he was a freshman, a glittering star on an unreachable horizon. He did not exist in her universe, but she ranked first on his list of unfulfillable longings. Their paths had never crossed, even after he grew up and achieved a modest level of notoriety for his books, which the *Tribune* wrote about in complimentary terms.

"You're Sybil Boone, right?" he said when she returned.

She nodded. "Yes. And you're John Barnes. I know your books."

The comment pleased him. "Do you like them?"

A doctor interrupted doing rounds, so she didn't have a chance to answer.

The courtship lasted as long as his recovery. He had a fractured pelvis, a splintered right femur, and broken ribs so painful he cried out in anger even through the narcotics they pumped into him. After Sybil's shift ended, she would sit next to the bed, soothing him, shushing him like a child when he groaned loudly. It helped. In time, the bones healed, the pain in his sides receded, and they could talk of other things. She asked why people called him "Barnes" instead of "John."

"When I was in elementary school, there were three 'Johns' in the room," he told her. "One was the class bully. The teacher, Mrs. Wilson, called him John in a way that sounded like an accusation. The other was a little timid kid who cried if you talked to him. She called him Johnny. That left me. I was the smart one, bookish. So, for some reason, she called me by my last name—Barnes. Maybe it sounded literary to her. The kids picked it up—'Barnes-y, go read a book.' I begged Mrs. Wilson: call me John, too. But she ignored me."

He shifted against the pillow to ease his neck. "My mother still called me John, but she died when I was so young it didn't matter. My father never used my name at all. He didn't care what I was called. So, Barnes stuck. After a while, I accepted it too. Sometimes, at a meeting or a conference, I don't recognize myself when I'm introduced as John Barnes."

He relaxed back on the bed and felt fatigued like he did

after physical therapy. He had never explained about his name to anyone. No one remembered the story. Now Sybil knew, and somehow, he felt he had told her everything she needed to know to know him.

Sybil sat silently as he spoke. When he finished, she reached over and took his hand. "I'll call you John if you want me to," she said. The warmth of her hand penetrated his, and he felt something different in her touch.

"No, Barnes is fine," he said. "Otherwise, I might think I'm someone else."

When he had recovered, Sybil took him home with her to the large Victorian home on Main Street, where she lived with her retired father. The wedding surprised people: Sybil had been considered an old maid at thirty-eight. To work, Barnes settled into a small room at the back of the house, looking out over the yard, where he could write his books and read the stories his students produced. In the evenings, he played chess with old man Boone.

Gradually, his new life absorbed him, and its rhythms became familiar. At first, it had been a shock. It came from out of the blue, like the deer through the windshield. How had he gotten here? he wondered.

"Why me?" he asked Sybil a year into the marriage when he awoke one day and fully realized it had happened. Sybil studied him, and he felt like an unfinished sculpture, a work in progress being carved from stone. "We needed each other, Barnes," she said finally. Later, she added, "You needed help."

Had he needed her? he asked himself as he lay sleepless in the dark. There had been other women, mostly aspiring writers like him, with strong opinions and fragile egos. None had stuck long. Sybil was different. She had none of the abstract fury of the women who had come and gone in his life. He felt the common-sense determination in her hands when she first touched him as he lay broken in the hospital. She dealt with the problems that faced her—helpless patients, often in pain. She handles things, he thought as she moved efficiently around him. Like me. He realized he had entered her reality and left his own. He had been alone so long that he accepted his isolation as normal. Sybil found him in his solitary state, he believed, and salvaged him.

Now, after she took him home and they were married, he felt solitary still, but with companionship, a combining of spirits that intertwined and mingled but did not blend. He considered his condition and concluded that he could not expect more. He could not say as much to Sybil, of course. Instead, he eventually wrote about it in a novel. Reviewers praised the book for its sensitivity to the vagaries of human relationships, especially marriage.

Sybil understood it, too, when she read the final draft. She had handed it back to him without comment. Days later, as he watched her on her knees, troweling in her garden, she said to him without looking up, "You understand us, Barnes. At least on paper."

Wanda surprised people, no one more than Barnes. Sybil, a mother at forty, Barnes a father at thirty-seven. Conception seemed like a miracle to him. No technical or scientific explanation covered it sufficiently: the sheer, magical improbability of it. He marveled at it, just as he marveled at the wiggling form in his arms when he held her. Even changing her diapers seemed like an expression of transcendental bonding. Barnes knew love for the first time. It sent thrilling shockwaves throughout his body. He realized Wanda had replaced Sybil on his internal scale of importance, and he worried that Sybil might sense it. But it seemed that Sybil had also been transformed. They felt a new chemistry between them, brought on by the life they had created.

Wonder Girl—that's what Wanda named herself as a child. "I'm Wonder Girl; you can't catch me!" she would yell as Barnes chased her around the backyard. He fashioned a cape for her from an old sheet. It waved behind her as she ran giggling across the lawn. Barnes worried about her tripping, and she did. His heart rose into his throat, and sometimes she would have a scrape or a bump. But she never cried. Even as a child, she shook it off and jumped up to run again with a determination she would later show in facing every risk.

Sybil taught Wanda to swim when she was two. (Sybil was the athlete in the family; Barnes had been too awkward to catch a ball as a child.)

"It's too deep," he warned when Sybil let Wanda float on her own. "She'll drown." He envisioned her limp body being lifted from the water.

Sybil laughed. "She's like a porpoise," she said. "She's alive in the water."

Barnes could only watch, imagining the worst.

In high school, Wanda became a gymnast and threw herself around with abandon. Her mother's heart, Barnes thought, tough as they come. And the force of love surging through him would tighten the muscles in his arms and legs. He wanted to enfold her, envelop her in his own strength to protect her from the battering of life that lay ahead. But he knew she would have to face it on her own. He would be a helpless bystander. She went through her adolescence and became a beautiful young woman. Dating brought its own challenges to his peace of mind, but she laughed it off and had boyfriends galore. Her date that last night seemed no different from any other. Wanda in a silky dress, her bare arms tanned and strong. She kissed Barnes goodbye, and he thought, Wonder Girl, as he watched them drive off.

The sheriff came to the house to tell them: a dark road, speeding, the deer came out of nowhere, through the windshield. Wanda dead at the scene, the boy okay. The sheriff seemed embarrassed as he held his cap in his hands. Barnes remembered that detail as the words soaked through him like an acid bath eating away his heart. He wanted to comfort the sheriff: it isn't your fault. It isn't anyone else's fault. Only mine.

The media picked it up, the cruel irony: a deer through the windshield nearly killing Barnes a generation ago, a deer killing his only daughter now. People shook their heads. Poor Barnes, they said. Like something from his books.

Afterward, he would jerk awake in the night: it wants me. It didn't finish the job the first time. I should have been there, not Wanda.

As Barnes left the coffee shop, on impulse, he crossed the empty street to the opposite side, something he rarely did. He walked slowly along the sidewalk, past Lenore's vacant stationery store. A notice of a reading at the library, dated years before, still hung taped to the inside of the dirty window. Good tape, he thought, as he paused to look at it. He leaned slightly to study it more closely. It was a notice about him and his last novel, his final reading at the library. The book flopped. By then, he didn't care. He stopped writing after that without saying so. People just assumed he was working on something new. He continued teaching for a while until his momentum ran down, and he retired.

Barnes walked slowly along the sidewalk, noticing the grass pushing its way up through the cracks. This block had been abandoned, like much of the old downtown. Maybe towns decay like people, Barnes thought. Old age brought the insight that not everything is fixable. What's gone is gone—the old stores, the Tribune, Wanda dead fifteen years.

The bag holding the detergent bottle weighed on him now. He hefted it in his arm to relax. He had little desire to return home. Would the woman still be in the closet? How would he handle that? If she was a burglar, she had probably escaped by now. Somehow, Barnes doubted that. She had seemed comfortable in the closet. Talk to her, Millie said. Barnes tried to think of what he might say. "Hello. How do you happen to be in my closet?" The humor of it struck him, and he made a sour laugh.

"What's the joke?" a voice asked. Barnes looked around and realized he was standing next to the bench for the shuttle to Walmart. Butch Potter, the editor of the *Tribune*, involuntarily retired when the paper closed, sat sprawled there. Butch still stubbornly lived near the old newspaper office, carless, amid the closed stores and decaying storefronts.

"Have a seat," Butch said, moving his arm to make room.

Barnes sat and let out a sigh. The image of the woman wouldn't go away.

"What's up, Barnes? You seem mopey today."

Barnes thought about what to say. Butch might be sympathetic about the woman. People considered him the town philosopher.

"This morning, I found a woman in our closet. In the hall."

Butch looked interested. "A woman?"

"Yeah. Standing behind the coats. Startled the hell out of me."

Butch straightened up. "Who is she? How did she get in there?"

"Who knows? Maybe she sneaked in when the front door was unlocked. I don't know."

"Did Sybil see her? What did she say about it?"

"I told her, but she wouldn't look in the closet."

"I don't blame her. Sounds spooky." Butch chewed his lip for a while. "Who else did you tell?"

"Millie. The boys in the coffee shop."

"The boys? Those stupid bastards. I'll bet they laughed at you."

Barnes didn't respond.

"What did Millie say?"

"She said I should talk to her. To the woman."

Butch sat silently again. "Well, Barnes, it's awful strange. Are you sure you didn't just dream it? Maybe a little too much vino last night?"

At least he isn't needling me, Barnes thought. "No vino. At first, I figured it might be a mannequin Sybil put there. But it moved a little. And made a sound. I know it's not a dummy."

Down the block, they could see the Walmart shuttle approaching. Butch stood and stretched. "Well, Barnes, it sounds like something from one of your novels."

"I don't write novels anymore."

The shuttle door opened, and Butch stepped up. "Maybe you don't. But your brain might. And the rest of you just hasn't caught up yet."

The shuttle pulled away.

Barnes continued to sit on the bench, feeling the hardness and the coolness of the wood underneath him. In his pocket, his cell phone buzzed. Sybil. Wanting to know where he was. When he would be back. He didn't answer it. She'll leave a message if it's important. She would also know that he might not remember to check the messages. He believed it to be mere forgetfulness. Sybil thought he didn't want to know what the message might be.

Honestly, Barnes, sometimes I think you're losing your mind.

Sybil said that as she stood pointing the knife at him. He worried about it too—had worried about it for years. After Wanda's death, numbness had shielded him from feeling anything. He collapsed into a state of near paralysis, almost unable to rise out of bed, or to dress himself. He struggled to make sense of things. Sometimes, his imagination overwhelmed him: the deer wanted to finish the job.

"It wanted me," he told Sybil. "I should have been there, not Wanda."

"It was an accident," Sybil told him. "A coincidence."

"It wanted to finish the job," he insisted. "If I had been there, she would still be alive."

Sybil studied him as only she could. Even through his pain, he sensed her frustration. She held his hands in hers, and he could feel the strength that had once healed him.

"It's shock," Sybil said. "It will wear off in time."

He tried to believe her and waited for mere sadness to settle in. But the weight grew heavier. His doctor began to hint about hospitalization—temporary, of course, a rest. That scared him, so he struggled harder against the pressure of Wanda's loss. Somehow, he managed to return to teaching, surprising himself that his mind and body worked together to get him to the college. He felt the flow of shy sympathy from his students but had no idea how to respond. He simply moved ahead, picking up where he had left off a few months before.

When he tried to write, he realized he no longer could. It felt like he had lost some essential part of himself that functioned on its own, like walking or eating. He had been a long way into a new novel and felt good about the draft. Then the motif of his life—a deer through the windshield—would grip him, and the words froze. His stories seemed pathetic next to Wanda's ironic death. He tried forcing the words to come out of his fingers onto the page. Just type something, he told himself. But without success. He quit trying.

Barnes heard something. He looked up and realized that the Walmart shuttle had returned and waited there, its door open. He hadn't noticed the rattle of the engine. He waved the bus away. The driver gave him an irritated look as he closed the door.

How long had he been sitting here? Barnes looked at his wrist but had forgotten his watch. It happened a lot; he had no recollection of where he had taken it off.

Honestly, Barnes, sometimes I think you're losing your mind.

The day had gotten warmer, and he felt uncomfortable in his sweater. He should go home; Sybil needed the detergent. But he continued to sit, unable to move. He remembered the cell phone and took it out. Sybil had left a message. He clicked on it to listen: "I'm going out," she said. Barnes felt relieved. Just "going out," not "going away." "Going out" could mean anything; "going away" would mean the end, that she had finally given up on him.

It had nearly happened once before. She found out about Amelia. Amelia—Amy—his best graduate student, one of the few over the years who had real ability. He met her at a reception for new students.

"I'm Amelia Longstreet," she said, extending her hand. "Amy. I love your books."

She wanted to be his student; he remembered seeing her name on the registration list for his graduate seminar. He shook her hand, and felt her strength, a strong grip, confident. He released the pressure of his own hand, but she held on an instant longer, long enough for it to register with him. A sensation spread through his body, something he hadn't felt in years.

Barnes looked at her, at her dark eyes, and saw the same confidence he felt in her hand. She's taking a risk, he thought, but she's sure of herself. As though she already knows the outcome. Wanda had that confidence, too, pushing to the edge, certain that she could draw back when she needed to. He remembered watching her on the balance beam in the gym, his apprehension choking him as she leaped around with no fear of falling. Amy struck him like that: the risk of falling didn't frighten her.

He felt the pull and push of Amy. An affair with a student, he told himself. Ridiculous. A cliché. Something he would never do. Yet, as he got to know her better, it occurred to him that he could draw on her strength to energize himself. He invited her into his office to discuss her interests and plans. She came willingly, eagerly. Soon, she began coming on her own, bringing her work for his review. "It's good," he would tell her. "Very good." He began to feel liberated, like a captured animal being released into an unfamiliar forest, a new world waiting to be explored.

The affair took place mostly in his office, on his couch,

the door locked, drinking the bottle of wine she brought. He remembered the whiteness of her lingerie the first time he watched her undress. After making love, she said to him, "I want to write about characters that come alive, people that you understand the instant you see them on the page—exactly like people you recognize from reality. The most important thing is to give them life, make them different from each other, like real people, who are living and loving and struggling." The people in your books are alive like that, she told him.

She proved she could do it. He praised one of her stories and told her it deserved to be read by the public. She sent it off to be published with his endorsement, and her success inspired him. Slowly, his own words began to come back to him. His fingers began to work again, hesitant at first but with increasing confidence. Early on, he had figured out that his life unfolded through words and that without them, he would not exist at all. He returned to his novel but decided to start over. Amy had given him a new life. He felt the strength of it, and the story flowed easily.

But, when he had finished, he realized his writing had changed. His readers saw the difference, too. His characters had always earned praise for their complexity and depth. Now, the people in his book seemed flat, one-dimensional. "Every character seems to be the same person," one reviewer wrote. "There's no difference among them. You expect them to think and feel the same way, the same words to come out of their mouths." Barnes is finished, burned out, some reviewers said.

Barnes knew why. The story was really Wanda's story, barely concealed. Every character was Wanda in some disguise. Each one said, "Yes, you will love me, and I will betray you and leave you adrift and alone." He could write about nothing else. She lived in every sentence, every phrase. His writing became a repetition of the same tired eulogy. In time, he realized his pain explained the affair with Amy—he wanted to bring Wanda back to life. The feeling shamed him. He told himself he had to give Amy up. But he did nothing.

Sybil saw it in the book, too. "You only write about Wanda," she said. "You think she can live in your words."

"I can't help it," Barnes said.

"You won't accept her death."

"She's gone. I know it," he protested.

"No, Barnes. You don't even try."

"I do try." But he knew she was right.

When Sybil discovered the affair, he almost felt relieved. Amy had come with him to a conference. He absent-mindedly left the boarding passes in a suit jacket pocket, and Sybil found them when she sent it to the dry cleaners. She laid them on the table in the kitchen, where he sat drinking a cup of coffee.

"Her name is Amelia?" she asked. "I assume she's a student."

His cheeks flushed. Lying wouldn't help; he knew that. "Amy. That's what we call her."

"We?" Sybil said, and he could feel her sarcasm. "Is there more than one of you?"

"I just mean, that's what she tells people to call her."

"Spare me the details, Barnes. I don't need to know them."

She turned her back on him. A week later when he returned from teaching his classes, she said, "You can stay. But not in the bedroom." He moved his things into the study, which had been unused since old man Boone died. He felt grateful. She had been a part of him for too long for him to consider another way of living. Amy resisted the breakup, but, after a while, she gave in and told him goodbye. Sybil began her new life. Barnes struggled to save his own.

Sweat trickled down his neck. It's time to go home, he thought. He stood up, a bit shakily from sitting so long, his rear end sore from the hard wooden bench. He picked up the detergent. Thankfully, Sybil wouldn't be there to criticize him for being gone so long. Then he remembered the woman in the closet—she would be there.

Or would she? It had been hours since he saw her; he barely remembered what she looked like. A white gown, he remembered that. And long hair. She had startled him; he hadn't noticed details. Now, as he reflected on the moment of discovering her, she had seemed like a statue. Not real, not alive. The movement she made, the sound, could have been his mind playing tricks. He must've been mistaken. She must have been placed there by someone playing a joke. Something like that.

"Talk to her," Millie had said.

When he reached the house, he wondered whether he would need his key. Maybe Sybil had been spooked and locked the door when she left. But it opened when he tried the latch. The stillness of Sybil's absence swelled inside the room and seemed to swallow him. He wondered if Sybil had looked in the closet. She didn't need to go into it just to get a coat; she had others.

He opened the closet door. Sybil's coats hung there; he couldn't tell whether she had taken one. Only a few hours ago, they had jarred him like something lunging out of the dark. But now the closet seemed so normal. He stepped further in and reached back to the last coat and pulled it aside.

Barnes saw the woman, just as before, her eyes still closed. His nerves held; the shock had worn off. He studied her, admiring her marble-like perfection.

"Hello," he said.

Her eyes blinked open.

"Hello," she replied.

DON'T YOU KNOW?

When Carlton asked Joanne to marry him, her mind was elsewhere, so she hardly heard what he said. She had been thinking about an occasion following the death of her husband, Gordon, when her Aunt Hazel had taken her for a long ride in the country. Aunt Hazel was worried about Joanne's state of mind. She believed in confronting sorrow head-on: pandering to grief would only entrench it more firmly. Joanne was used to Aunt Hazel's take-charge approach and did not object. Her aunt had a very practical mind, and Joanne knew that she would urge sensible activities. Digging in the garden was one of Aunt Hazel's standard therapies for someone who was worried or sad. On the ride, Aunt Hazel made her case. Don't wallow in self-pity; use your time constructively; find something to do to keep your mind occupied. You have a good head on your shoulders. Make use of it.

Joanne had considered what Aunt Hazel said. Was she depressed, as her aunt believed? She couldn't tell; her feelings were a mystery to her. The mood that settled on her in the weeks following Gordon's death was not terribly different from her usual equanimity. But Aunt Hazel's advice made sense: she should be active. What could she do? Years before, she had been a schoolteacher. She retired when Gordon wanted to travel, and they could afford it. She had never worked in Gordon's insurance company and, in any case, had sold it soon after his death. At least she didn't need money. She didn't have a garden, so her aunt's usual tonic for depression wouldn't work. All she had was her bridge group, her quilting circle, and her books. She wondered if that would be diverting enough to satisfy Aunt Hazel.

Her aunt kept talking as they drove along the country road. She had an idea: Bernice wanted to stop working in her husband Arnold's pharmacy. She was tired of dealing with the public, she told Aunt Hazel. Arnold got to dispense the drugs; he didn't have to face the public across the counter. Bernice wanted to retire and breed miniature poodles. Joanne could take Bernice's place, her aunt suggested. The pharmacy was on the town square, and Joanne could walk there from her home. She wouldn't even have to look for parking. Arnold was a good pharmacist but an indifferent businessman. Joanne could be a real help. Each of them would benefit. It was the kind of solution that appealed to Aunt Hazel: straightforward and practical.

Joanne thought about standing behind the counter at the pharmacy. How would it feel? She would be handing over the prescriptions, handling transactions, and exchanging small talk. She wasn't exactly shy, but she wasn't much of a conversationalist; it might be a little uncomfortable. And what about working with Arnold? She had known him since high school when he was one of the serious students. Nowadays, he would be called a nerd. She couldn't recall what serious-minded kids were called back then. She liked him well enough, but strictly on a "how are you?" basis when she saw him in the pharmacy or ran into him at the market. He and Bernice were not among her regular friends. In reality, she scarcely knew them. Maybe that would be an advantage; there was no baggage.

Joanne said nothing while Aunt Hazel was describing the benefits of working in the pharmacy. Her aunt clearly liked her idea; she was getting more enthusiastic by the minute. She interpreted Joanne's silence as a sign of uncertainty. Well, she could certainly fix that. She would investigate it on Joanne's behalf. Joanne wouldn't have to stir herself. Satisfied with her solution, she drove along the country road, humming a tune, while Joanne gazed at the passing landscape. Joanne felt a sense of relief. Let Aunt Hazel figure it out.

Carlton had given an elaborate rationale for the marriage proposal. Life must move on. They were both alone now. They had been friends for years and were neighbors to boot. Besides—and Carlton said this shyly—he had always been drawn to her and thought she was the most beautiful woman in town. Marriage would be good for them and help them to build a happy new life. He swallowed; she could tell he was nervous. And I would love you very much, he said in closing. (So, love is his trump card, Joanne thought.) Carlton had finished on a high note. His speech had rambled a bit, but he finally got to the point. Now, he was waiting for her answer.

Joanne almost forgot he was there. Carlton was the type who would wait patiently. Gordon would have done something to rouse her, rattle the newspaper or shift in his chair. Marry him, she thought. *Marry him?* Where did he get such an idea? She couldn't recall doing anything to entice him; she never flirted with anyone. But she knew she was still an attractive woman; Gordon had reminded her often enough. She aged well compared to many of her friends. She was slightly taller than they were, and she carried herself well, with a certain graceful quality. The gray streaks in her dark blonde hair were not as prominent as among her darker-haired friends. She knew she still looked good. At fifty, she could hold her own with the forty-year-olds.

It was not necessarily a surprise that Carlton was attracted to her; it had simply caught her by surprise. Carlton was just a neighbor who lived alone in the house next door after his wife left him. He was Gordon's friend more than hers. Gordon died in the process of doing Carlton a favor by climbing onto his roof to dislodge a tree limb that was tangled with his satellite dish. Something happened, and Gordon tumbled from the roof. He landed directly on his neck, and that was it. No one blamed Carlton for Gordon's death, least of all Joanne. Just an ironic accident, people said, shaking their heads. Poor Gordon. A victim of his own helpfulness.

Carlton was an accountant and a partner in the town's largest accounting firm. He and Gordon referred clients back and forth between them. Joanne found him pleasant but quiet, at least compared to Gordon. She had never considered Carlton as a distinct individual, just as someone they knew, certainly not someone who would have the nerve to ask his dead friend's widow to marry him. Maybe he feels guilty about Gordon's death, she thought. The marriage proposal could be an act of contrition.

The phone was ringing. It was Aunt Hazel. "Arnold thinks it's a good idea," she said. After a pause: "Bernice said it was okay." Joanne thought about Bernice: breeding yappy little dogs would suit her. "He wants to know how soon you can start."

Joanne considered what her aunt was saying. Maybe going to work wasn't such a bad idea. She had noticed recently that she sat at the kitchen table long after she had finished her breakfast. She could sit for extended periods without feeling a need to move. Even putting the dishes into the sink seemed unnecessary, something that would not have been true while Gordon was alive. He favored neatness. That was okay with Joanne. She made a point of keeping things neat: dirty dishes in the dishwasher, scattered papers stacked, closet doors closed. Now, it didn't matter. Sometimes, moving just to tidy up didn't seem worth the effort. Seeing dirty dishes on the kitchen table didn't bother her. At first, it felt relaxing. Now, it was more like lethargy, which concerned her. Getting out of the house and going to Arnold's pharmacy might invigorate her. Why not give it a try?

She told Aunt Hazel she would think about it and hung up the phone. Carlton was still sitting in the same position. He had said nothing during the telephone conversation. He was still waiting, a look of expectation on his face. Joanne had no idea what to say. She almost wished her aunt would call back to give her something to do. Maybe she should offer Carlton something to drink. At least that would give her a few minutes to think. "Can I offer you something?" she said. "A cup of coffee or a beer?"

There was a flicker of annoyance on Carlton's face. But he smiled and said he would have a beer. Joanne rose to go into the kitchen; leaving the room broke the tension, and she relaxed a little. She still had no idea what to say to Carlton. She thought about Gordon's proposal of marriage years before. They were in Bermuda, a romantic weekend. The setting seemed perfect for a marriage proposal, and she assumed Gordon had arranged it that way. He was fastidious about such things.

It seemed to be a foregone conclusion that she and Gordon would marry. All their friends assumed it would happen. Gordon would sometimes talk about the future as though they were already married. Joanne remembered wondering whether it was an unusual way for a marriage to occur—just drifting into it, a simple evolution from an existing condition. They were sitting on the veranda of the beach house where they were staying. It was a beautiful, warm evening. The day had been hot, but it was cooler now, with the palm trees swishing in the wind. The moon was moving in and out of view with the swaying trees, its reflection bouncing on the small waves splashing lightly on the beach. She listened to the slight hissing sound they made as they slapped the sand over and over. It had a kaleidoscopic effect on her mind; her thoughts were random patterns, congealing for a moment, then dissolving, one after another. Gordon had put his arm around her shoulders and said how much he loved her. He wanted to be with her forever. Would she marry him?

She had expected the proposal; she could sense that something was coming. But she surprised herself by being a little *surprised*. Maybe it was a kind of emotional self-defense, she had thought, to avoid having to take it in all at once. They had been together since college. They assumed they would return to the small town where they had grown up. Gordon was ambitious. He had plans to take over the small insurance company where his father sold fire and automobile insurance. Gordon had grander plans. He believed he could sell annuities, life insurance, and other pricier products. People had more money; the country was prosperous.

She had thought about their small town and how it was reinventing itself in the image of a quaint holdover from some idyllic past, with a village square and a gazebo where a band played summer concerts. A landmark committee was created; it came up with a plan to restore the square as it had been designed in the 1890s. Standards were set for storefronts on the square. Merchants had to consult an architect appointed by the committee on their awnings and storefronts. Even the parking meters were designed to look old-fashioned. Gordon capitalized on the local enthusiasm. He became a leader in the effort. We'll make it look like something from *The Music Man*, he said. He had a lot of support; restoration would reflect the town's prosperity and increase property values. People admired his effort. His business was flourishing, especially after he eased his father out. "It's a good place to live," he told Joanne, "and now is a good time to get married."

Joanne sat silently as Gordon spoke. If she were to be married, it could only be to Gordon, of course. But she realized that she had thought little about what marriage involved. She had no objection to the life they now led: an easy relationship, a relaxed attitude toward life. Even their sex life was free of stress. They enjoyed each other's company, dressed or undressed. Joanne taught her pupils; Gordon ran his insurance company. Everything was fine. It occurred to her that marriage would change the equipoise of their lives. Marriage would mean children, wouldn't it? Wouldn't that be a natural consequence? Children would change everything. Did she want that? She didn't know. She could think of nothing to say to Gordon's proposal: not yes, not no, not even "I'll think about it." She had no good argument either way. The yin and yang of it was a blur to her.

She sat, pensive, Gordon looking at her expectantly, the question—will you marry me?—hanging there. He would become impatient soon. She had to say something.

So she asked, "Don't you know?"

They were married in April after the tulips were gone and before the peonies had bloomed. Joanne would have liked peonies at the wedding. But they wouldn't be available until June, and Gordon wanted to be married now. Once he made a decision, he didn't like to wait. It was a pleasant wedding, well attended, and they were both satisfied. They sold Joanne's small bungalow, and she moved into Gordon's home, one of the oldest in the village.

Gordon's business grew. His enthusiastic volunteerism became his trademark. Anything that concerned the community involved him. He helped paint the community center, read stories to the old people in the nursing home, and flipped pancakes at the annual park fundraiser. He was always ready to help a neighbor—that was why he made his fatal climb onto Carlton's roof. It's good for business, he told Joanne. But Joanne knew that it also reflected his true character; he was a relentless optimist, eager to improve things. When something needs to get done, go to Gordon, people said. They didn't need to ask; he would have shown up in any case.

Despite Gordon's good reputation, the town was divided about him. Most people accepted his helpfulness as an indication of his natural friendliness and a caring neighbor. After all, why would he spend so much effort and energy if he wasn't a good guy? But others gave it a negative spin. He needs to be in charge, the complaint went; he wants to be the boss of everything. This view was articulated on behalf of the anti-Gordon faction by Agnes Felt, whose flower shop was next to Gordon's business on the square. He's too domineering, it was said; he won't take a back seat to anyone. Gordon's partisans countered that Agnes was just being jealous. She wanted to run things herself.

True or not, the conflict resulted in many tense exchanges at community meetings. Words could grow heated. Tempers flared; people would storm out, as happened in the matter of the holiday decorations on the town square. The Gordon faction favored a lavish display, lights on all the trees and bushes and along the fence. The Agnes faction took a minimalist approach: we don't want it to look like some nutty suburban house, they said. The controversy raged for days. In the end, the Agnes faction won. Its plan was less expensive, a fact that tilted the decision in its favor. Gordon took the defeat with good humor. He wasn't one to hold a grudge. He even served Agnes an extra pancake at the fundraising breakfast.

Joanne taught her fourth-grade students, and she and Gordon were happy in their own way. No children arrived over the years, which surprised her. They had an active and affectionate sex life, so she assumed that she would become pregnant in time. But it hadn't happened after two years of marriage. Finally, she consulted her gynecologist. "We must do tests," he told her, "on both of you. Once we have determined the cause, we can decide what to do; there are options." He patted her shoulder reassuringly. Joanne liked her doctor and believed the problem was solvable—if that was what she wanted. Gordon would need to be involved. Joanne would have to initiate the conversation. But wouldn't that make it seem that she wanted children? She couldn't decide. She never brought the subject up, and neither did Gordon. Twenty years later, that was still how it stood.

Carlton put the beer glass down on the coaster Joanne

had put on the coffee table. The situation was becoming awkward. Soon, she would have to say something. But what? The proposal was so unexpected. And she couldn't stop thinking about her conversation with Aunt Hazel. Did she really want to be a pharmacy clerk? And what about being around Arnold all day? Maybe Bernice wouldn't really like the idea, although Joanne could think of no reason why. They got along well enough. Joanne had taught their son Henry in the fourth grade. But who knew how Bernice felt about someone taking her place; maybe she would resent anyone who took over, especially a woman. Joanne could ask Bernice directly how she felt about it, but that would be presumptuous; she hadn't even talked to Arnold yet.

Carlton broke the tension by standing up. Joanne could tell that he was embarrassed, and her silence hadn't helped. "I think I've caught you off guard," he said. "I should have thought of that. Me being Gordon's friend, you know. I mean..." His voice trailed off. "And all." He was standing, half-turned, as though uncertain whether to step toward her or the door. Finally, he reached out to shake her hand; Joanne took it. Carlton turned to leave. "I think we would be very happy together," he said over his shoulder as he left.

Joanne talked to her friend Annie about Aunt Hazel's idea as they rode the train into New York City. She didn't mention Carlton. Unlike most of her friends, Annie wasn't totally absorbed in the lives of her children and grandchildren. She saw them occasionally, and that seemed sufficient. She was levelheaded and soft-spoken. Joanne knew her perspective would be thoughtful. She raised the subject to Annie as they rode the train into the city. Joanne had gone to the museums and theaters since childhood when she went with her parents. Gordon was less interested in art and music, so she went alone when he was doing something else. When she met Annie, who had joined her bridge group, she discovered that Annie shared her cultural interests. They often went together, especially for matinees at Lincoln Center, which Annie particularly liked. Their trips became more frequent now that both of their husbands were gone.

As Joanne explained Aunt Hazel's plan, Annie listened quietly. For a while, she said nothing as the scene outside slipped past. Finally, she asked, "Is it something you really want to do? It sounds like a lot of work." She didn't know Arnold, so she couldn't say how she thought it would be to work with him. She liked the store itself, and especially its location on the square, but didn't get her prescriptions there. She had chatted with Bernice a few times; Arnold was always buried in the back. She couldn't remember whether she had ever spoken to him. But if Joanne really wanted to work, even if just for something to do, maybe it wasn't such a bad idea. The question was whether it would make her happy. If not, she could quit if she didn't like it. On balance, it seemed worth a try.

Joanne went to work in the pharmacy a week later. She enjoyed the short walk to the store and liked the store itself. Bernice was active in the restoration effort, and she decorated the store to give it a vintage look that had the clean, friendly feel of an old-time drugstore. But it was technologically up to date. Everything was computerized: the inventory, the accounts, the business contacts. Joanne soon mastered the complexities of inventory control and kept the database current so that Duncan, the man who placed orders and stocked the shelves, could always find what was needed. Aunt Hazel had been right about Arnold, too. He was a brisk, efficient pharmacist; he kept up with the literature and counseled his clients carefully. But he was oblivious to what went on in the rest of the shop. When Joanne suggested adding a new product to the shelves, Arnold invariably agreed with a little wave of his hand. He seemed to have no interest in the business side of the pharmacy beyond complaining about the cost of drugs and commiserating about it with his customers.

But work at the pharmacy was problematic from the start. She and Arnold kept bumping into each other. This shouldn't have happened; the store was spacious enough. Collisions should have been easy to avoid. Despite that, Joanne would turn from the cash register and knock into Arnold, who would be reaching under the counter for something. Sometimes, when she went into the room where the drugs were stored, he would follow her into the aisle, searching for something on the shelf, and she would have to squeeze past him.

On one occasion, as she was squeezing past, he turned and put his arms around her. His hands held her clumsily at the waist. He placed his head against her neck; she felt his breath. "Oh, Joanne," he said. Oh, Joanne—just that. Joanne was stunned; she felt trapped. She pushed his hands away and backed out of the aisle. She stumbled to the closet where she had hung her summer jacket, took it from the hook, and struggled to put it on as she went out the front door without closing it behind her.

She had no idea where to go. Her mind was flipping around; she couldn't focus as she tried to figure out what to do. What had he been thinking? He was a nice enough man; it seemed so out of character. Should she have said something? Should she have been more forceful, pushing him away and expressing anger? But she felt more surprised than violated. His action seemed pathetic. She wasn't afraid of him at all. It felt more like pushing away a boy who got too close at a high school dance. That was how Arnold always seemed to her, like someone still in high school, an awkward, lonely boy, too shy to ask her to dance. As she thought about it, she couldn't help feeling sorry for him. Bernice was certainly no softy; she had a hard edge, useful in business. Poodles were her passion. They probably slept on the bed with her.

Joanne crossed the street to the square. Only a few people were there, mostly nannies and mommies with their children in the play area. Joanne sat on a bench and watched the children playing. How different her life with Gordon would have been if they had children. They would be adjusting to his absence, just as she was. There might even be grandchildren. Grandchildren. She had barely thought about children, let alone grandchildren. Her friends talked constantly about their children, sometimes obsessively. It was hard letting go. Some children were separating with clinging rips, like velcro. Others seemed to seek as much distance as possible. Whichever it was, none of the mothers seemed satisfied. They bragged that their children were creating their own lives, but the bragging lacked sincerity.

Joanne was puzzled by the complexity of their relationships. Grandchildren were coming along, and they doted on them as grandparents are supposed to do. But even that didn't displace an undercurrent of dissatisfaction they seemed to feel toward their children. Sometimes, they didn't even seem to like them very much. When Joanne was teaching, she liked her students well enough. Some of them became attached to her and still sent Christmas cards from distant places. Her own children would have attended the school where she taught, she supposed. How would that have been? The issue had never arisen.

It was summer now, and the square was in full bloom. Gordon had been on the garden committee, which was responsible for overseeing park maintenance. But Agnes controlled it. Joanne wondered how Agnes felt now, with Gordon out of the way, no longer a challenge to her authority. Gordon favored bright flowers—tulips, petunias, things that would give the square a medley of colors. Agnes preferred a more formal look, with a carefully designed rose bed and manicured hedges and bushes. As a florist, she had good taste, and the square reflected it. People were proud of the square; they always showed it off to visitors. But even from a distance, Joanne could see paint peeling on the gazebo. Gordon would have been on it in an instant. Agnes cared mostly about the plants.

Joanne had not been thinking about the episode with Arnold, but now it came to her mind. What in the world was going on? Now, she had two men after her. She had been a widow for a year. Perhaps the void around her just drew them in. She felt more bewildered than troubled. She never thought about men seeing her in this way, particularly men who were just around in the milieu of her life, some of whom, like Arnold, she had known since she was a child. Now, it was happening, whether she liked it or not. Somehow, she would have to deal with it.

The sun was hitting her, and it was becoming too warm where she was sitting. She left the bench and walked home.

That evening, Arnold came to her front door. He had two of Bernice's poodles with him. Joanne had often seen Bernice walking the dogs, but never Arnold. The dogs seemed confused by the change and were milling around his feet. Arnold looked abashed, like someone who was about to say that he had accidentally driven over her flower bed. "I was out walking the dogs," he said, "and thought I should stop by to apologize." The dogs continued to mill. "I don't know what got into me. I've never done anything like that before." The dogs were circling him in opposite directions, curious about the new surroundings. Arnold went on, "You have a right to be offended, and all I can do is apologize." The leashes were intertwined now, wrapped around his feet. He looked ridiculous standing there, unable to move until he unraveled them. He seemed exactly like the awkward boy she knew when they were children, Joanne thought. She could at least invite him in.

He walked gingerly into the hallway, almost tiptoeing, like he was afraid he might step on something and break it. The poodles pulled in different directions; he was having a hard time controlling them. "Please, sit down," Joanne said. Arnold perched tentatively on the edge of the couch. One of the dogs jumped up next to him; the other sniffed around the coffee table. Arnold's nervousness calmed her. He was pitiful, no threat of any kind, just out of his element, uncertain of how to act in this unfamiliar place for an uncomfortable reason. Should she offer him something to drink, as she had Carlton? At least it would give her something to do. But Arnold said no thank you; he had to get the dogs home, or Bernice would worry.

He stood and stepped toward the door. The dogs had lost interest in the room; they were now tugging at the leashes to get back outside. Arnold turned to face her at the door. Was he going to shake her hand, she wondered, as Carlton had done? Arnold was saying, "If you want to come back, nothing like that will ever happen again. I don't know what got into me. Believe me, you could feel entirely comfortable." He paused. "We were a good team." He opened the door; the dogs rushed out, straining to go. I hope you will consider it, was the final thing he said.

On Saturday, Carlton saw Joanne across the fence. She was reading a book, but it lay open on her lap. She had been thinking about her life with Gordon and the encounters with Carlton and Arnold. Her feelings about Gordon had mellowed, less sharp, shaded at the edges. She had felt the loss intensely, but in a somewhat abstract way, as though she didn't quite know what to make of it. Her mind was clear; her heart was opaque. At Gordon's funeral, she felt more drained than bereaved, and she remembered hoping that no one could tell. Some people were openly crying. Gordon had been much loved; his loss was deeply felt throughout the community. The mayor and town council had issued an official statement. At least she could be proud of that.

Carlton was saying something: he had just picked fresh tomatoes from his garden. They were spectacular this year. He planned to make a salad for dinner. Would Joanne like to join him? It was the first time they had spoken since the proposal more than a month before. In fact, it was the first time she had seen him; he seemed to have disappeared. Her memory of the proposal was less intense now. She hadn't forgotten it, but it was less present in her mind. She still had not thought of a response. Fortunately, it hadn't been necessary. Maybe speaking to her was a way of getting his courage back up. But she felt less pressured now. At the least, it would be nice to be friends with Carlton; they were neighbors, after all. If the subject came up, maybe she could deflect it in a way that wouldn't feel like letting him down. She said, "All right. I'll come."

That evening, she walked through Carlton's front fence gate and went around the side of the house to the backyard. She had done that only a few times before; over the years, she had mostly seen his yard across the fence. Carlton had set dinner places on the picnic table. He had become very domestic since his wife, Beverly, left, he said, almost apologetically. Beverly had certainly never seemed very domestic to Joanne, not that she knew her that well. Beverly was intense and self-absorbed, silent much of the time. She acted in the local theater company, and rumor had it that she had left with another actor to live in the East Village. No one seemed to know exactly where she had gone. If Gordon knew, he didn't mention it. The question hung there, like a plant hanger without a pot in it. As they sat at the table, Joanne admired the garden. It was lush and well cared for. She liked the fact that he grew things to eat rather than just admire. She might have done the same if she gardened.

Carlton was being excessively cordial; Joanne could tell he was trying to reduce any awkwardness she might feel. She appreciated that; she wasn't entirely sure why she was willing to face him again. Maybe it was just part of being a good neighbor, which she certainly wanted to be, especially for someone who had been such a friend to Gordon. He fussed around to make her comfortable. Would she like a glass of wine or iced tea, perhaps? (Iced tea would do.) Would she prefer to sit facing the yard or the house? (The yard would be fine.) They ate in relative silence; there was little to talk about. At least he was right about the tomatoes, Joanne thought. They were delicious.

Carlton broke the silence. He wanted to talk about Gordon; he hoped it was okay. He said he hadn't wanted Gordon to go onto the roof that day. He was just showing him that the wind had blown a tree limb against the satellite dish on the roof. It was entangled with the dish. He was thinking about how to extricate it when Gordon said he would climb up and take it off. (Carlton was afraid of heights; he certainly wasn't going to do it himself.) But Carlton said no, don't do it. It's dangerous, the roof's too steep. I'll call the tree guys; they can handle it. But Gordon had already gone into Carlton's garage to get a ladder. Now, he was propping it against the edge of the roof. Why spend the money, he was saying; it will be easy. Just like Gordon, Carlton said, looking at Joanne—jumping in to solve a problem before anyone figured out what the problem was.

The limb was clinging to the dish and the wires that secured it. Gordon was tugging on it, which made Carlton nervous. Maybe I should get a saw so you can cut it into pieces, he called up to Gordon. Better yet, let me get the tree guys. You are making me nervous, he said. But Gordon kept pulling. "I think I have it," he shouted. Suddenly, the limb sprang free. Gordon fell backward. He plopped on his rear end at the edge of the roof, bouncing his feet in the air as he toppled off and landed with a thud directly on the back of his neck. The paramedics took Gordon away; they knew he was a goner but had the decency not to say so. Let the doctors at the hospital deal with it.

Carlton's eyes had misted; he touched each one with his

finger. Joanne understood what he was feeling. He had been so close to Gordon. How could he not feel responsible? Carlton was speaking again: he felt so guilty; he should never have let Gordon go up there; he should have insisted—no, demanded—that they wait for the tree removers. Why did this happen? Why should Gordon have to die for such a trivial thing? I should have insisted, Carlton repeated. Joanne knew that would have been pointless. Once the idea was in Gordon's head, no one could have stopped him. That was just Gordon's way; Carlton wasn't to blame. The guilt would wear off in time, she thought sadly. Carlton was quiet now. Lacking words, Joanne reached over and patted him lightly on the hand. They had both loved Gordon. They could at least share some grief.

The pat on his hand revived Carlton. He was embarrassed and didn't look directly at her. "It's just that I miss him a lot," Carlton said. "I can't even imagine how you must feel. I hate the fact that I have caused you such pain. I thought that telling you would make it better. But now I'm not sure." He looked at Joanne and smiled a little. "It's just that I feel so"—he searched for the word—"lonely, I guess." He sat for a moment, thinking, and continued, "You know, it's strange; I didn't feel that way when Beverly left. I don't think we cared anymore. But we must have provided something for each other—I just don't know what it was." He looked at Joanne again. "I don't miss her, but I feel her absence. It's like discovering that whatever you were bumping up against is no longer there, so you miss the resistance."

Joanne was touched. Carlton didn't seem embarrassed that he missed his friend more than his wife. Joanne knew people who felt that way about their dogs, like Bernice. Arnold was probably just a fixture. But Carlton's feelings for Gordon seemed so deep. She thought about his statement: he felt Beverly's absence but didn't miss her. Did that describe her feelings about Gordon? No, she thought instantly. She and Gordon had loved each other; she felt the pain of his loss acutely. But she also sensed the absence Carlton described. She and Gordon had the complex routines of a long marriage. In some ways, the loss of those routines was as numbing as the emotional loss. She realized that she was struggling, silently, to establish a new framework, one in which Gordon's absence was a given but not the dominant force.

Carlton was speaking again. "I feel so empty," he said. The word grabbed her; it was exactly what she felt. For the first time since Gordon's death, she had a name to put on her feelings: emptiness. Gordon's presence was gone from her life; now it was empty. Emptiness more than loneliness: that described what she was left with. It was so obvious; why hadn't it occurred to her before?

The thought played around in her mind. Then it came to her: it was because she had been focusing on Gordon, not herself: she had been thinking about what was missing, not what now existed. Their house seemed empty without him, just as her life felt empty. The emptiness would have to be dealt with like a hole in the yard being filled in. She realized that this was what Aunt Hazel had been trying to tell her: deal with it by taking action. It was as though she had changed her seat in a familiar room and had a new perspective on the contents. She could not fill the emptiness in the house by herself; maybe she should sell it and travel. This was a new idea. It hadn't occurred to her that she was now free to do as she wished. And the idea of another man in her life was new, too. It even felt possible. She felt a growing kinship with Carlton now. They were both alone. Maybe she should marry him.

It was cooler now; the sun was almost gone. Carlton had been silent for a while, looking at his wine glass and swirling it. He seemed to have nothing else to say. The subject of marriage had not arisen; perhaps he had decided to let it drop or simply didn't want to bring it up in the circumstances. His little speech about Gordon and Beverly and how he felt had moved her. She realized there was more to him than she had previously seen. He was so different from Gordon: less forceful but more insightful, maybe more sensitive about life and its nuances. Could Gordon have spoken about his feelings the way Carlton had? Somehow, she couldn't imagine it. Gordon had been good and kind, but he expressed himself through actions rather than words. She was the opposite: words and ideas, communication, mattered more to her than deeds. Carlton was like that, too.

She stood. "It's time to go home," she said. She thanked Carlton for the evening, and he walked with her to his front gate. He didn't go further, but just stood as she walked the short distance to her door. On the steps, she looked over and said good night. He said good night and went into his own house.

A week after the dinner with Carlton, Joanne was still thinking about the pharmacy and whether she should return. She hadn't told Aunt Hazel about the problem with Arnold. Her aunt knew something was wrong, of course, when word got around that Joanne wasn't there anymore. She asked, but Joanne said that Arnold was giving her time to decide whether she really wanted to work at all. "Well, he's making do with someone from a temporary agency, and the place is a mess," her aunt said. "The woman can't seem to find anything. The customers are complaining." But she let the subject drop. Joanne had considered telling Annie. She would be sympathetic. But she didn't discuss it with either of them. She also had not told them about the proposal from Carlton. These were things she would have to deal with on her own, she decided.

The evening with Carlton had given her a new perspective on him and Arnold. She realized that both were struggling. Yet each had shown resilience. Speaking about feelings, especially embarrassing ones, is hard, especially for someone who isn't used to doing it. It took courage. Carlton had spoken openly and honestly; he seemed different to her now, in a good way. Arnold had looked ridiculous as he sat on her couch with the poodles crawling over him. But he had the nerve to show up and try to make things right. That took strength, too. She believed him when he said it wouldn't happen again. But she realized that Arnold wasn't the issue: it was about her and her command of her own situation. She didn't know how she would feel, standing at the counter again, with Arnold behind her filling pill bottles. But she had concluded there was only one way to find out. The next day, she called Arnold and said she would come back.

Life was settling into a pleasant new routine; she felt it as she was walking to the pharmacy. She felt herself adjusting to Gordon's absence. Yes, there were the intertwined connections of many years together, like strands of DNA. But the memories of them were becoming less intense. She felt more settled now that she was finding ways to shape her time without him. She saw Carlton across the fence, and they chatted about various things—politics, the weather, events happening in the town. Their relationship was amiable, with a growing, easy familiarity. She invited him over, and they sat in the yard in the evening, watching the sky turn dark and hearing the insects singing. She felt good about this. Her feelings were changing; they were deeper somehow. But why, and for what? They were still a mystery to her. Carlton surprised her by showing an interest in what she was reading. He followed books in the *Times Book Review*. He read *about* books more often than he read them, and he laughed. But he had an interesting mind. It was a side of him that had been absent or suppressed when Gordon was around.

One evening, as she left her house to walk to the square where the summer concerts had begun, Carlton came out of his front door. "I'm going to hear the music," he said. "So am I," Joanne replied. "Let's walk together." The still summer evening rested gently on her, warming her body and soothing her mind. She could feel the transition beginning between day and night, when the sun settles slowly but seems to hang slightly as though reluctant to leave. The insects were tuning up, humming, not yet ready for the full-throated chorus of nighttime. She loved this moment, the brief suspension of time, neither coming nor going, the sense that the sunset wanted to hesitate for a moment, pausing to reflect briefly before moving on, the past behind it, the future ahead—just like the mood of her new life, poised and ready, Gordon in the past, the future waiting for her.

At the square, she and Carlton chatted with the people who were there. When the concert began, they sat together. She sat next to him without consciously deciding to do so. He might have been any of her neighbors. As the music played, it occurred to her that people must have noticed her sitting next to Carlton. It had truly been a chance encounter on the sidewalk, at least for her. Only later did it occur to her that Carlton might have planned it. Most of the people there certainly knew the circumstances of Gordon's death. She wondered whether they thought it was peculiar for her to be there next to the man who was involved in her husband's death. Perhaps she and Carlton would become the subject of gossip.

A week later, she and Carlton went to lunch at a nearby country inn on a Sunday afternoon. Carlton had suggested it to her over the fence. It was a casual place, a kind of hangout for the town. People often wandered in, alone or in pairs, and sat together in unplanned groupings. As they entered, Joanne thought people might assume that she and Carlton had just run into each other on the way in. But they were seen coming in together: planned or unplanned; that was the real point, she realized. We are neighbors, Carlton explained to a friend who stopped by their table. He repeated it to others as though being neighbors provided an excuse for being together that had no other implications. Joanne knew Carlton's explanation didn't matter. People were obviously curious; Joanne knew they would draw whatever conclusions they wished.

She and Carlton drifted along; the subject of marriage didn't arise, but she couldn't help thinking about it. An easy relationship had developed, amiable, with a growing closeness. The proposal was still there, even if he had not repeated it since that night on her couch. Joanne could now see that the issue was not so much responding to Carlton's proposal as deciding whether she wanted to be married at all. She had been married to Gordon for so long; she couldn't tell if she really missed it. The habit seemed stronger than the emotion. What would Carlton be like as a husband? She saw a new side of him now, and it appealed to her. He was a good man and an interesting person, very different from Gordon, but attractive in his own way.

And what about sex? Could she have sex with Carlton, Gordon's friend? How would that feel? It occurred to her that Carlton's attraction to Gordon might be sexual. It wasn't a far-fetched idea. Carlton had clearly loved him in some way. He and Beverly had two children, but, these days, people were coming out of the closet after long marriages. She rejected the idea. Gordon was straight, clearly. And if Carlton was gay, why his attraction to her?

On the train, Annie had asked whether she could be happy at the pharmacy. Happiness: Joanne wasn't even sure what it meant. Over the years, she had felt many dimensions of happiness: as an emotion, as a pleasurable mindset, and simply as an absence of stress. Her happiness with Gordon had been all those things and more. She thought about her relationship with Carlton; it was growing stronger, and she liked that. He was becoming a companion; did she want him as a husband? She could feel the emptiness caused by Gordon's loss. Could marriage to Carlton help fill that void? As she considered that possibility, she began to see merits that had previously escaped her.

But as she reflected on it, she still had uncertainties about what lay behind Carlton's proposal. It continued to seem somewhat improbable to her. Was it mostly guilt? That thought had occurred to her at the start. He said he loved her, but love was a nebulous term, like happiness. It could mean almost anything. When she was young, the word "love" was rarely spoken. Now, it was thrown around so casually that it had lost any real meaning. She thought about whether she could love Carlton or whether it would even be necessary. They certainly were attracted to each other and had developed a strong friendship. Maybe that would be enough. At their age, perhaps it wasn't even an issue. Maybe love was something reserved for the young when the need for reassurance was strong. She knew she didn't need to replicate her feelings for Gordon. She had the freedom now to feel whatever she wished. Maybe that would be enough.

A week after lunch at the inn, Carlton called: would she like to go to dinner in the city and maybe see a show? Joanne felt a slight twinge of anxiety; the invitation felt more like a real date. Was she up for that? How would Carlton react if she said no? Would it hurt the friendship that was developing? She didn't want to undermine that. She thought for a moment. Carlton was quiet; he had gotten used to her hesitations. Then she said, "Yes, that would be nice."

As she dressed for the evening out with Carlton, she reflected on his motives. Did he regard it as a step toward something more serious? If so, dressing up might make him think she felt the same way. On balance, it would be better to dress in her usual understated way, as though it was just another friendly outing. She went to her jewelry box. When she opened it, she was surprised to find Gordon's gold watch, the one she had given him for their twentieth wedding anniversary. She must have put it there after his death, even though she didn't remember doing so.

In the weeks and months following his death, she had roamed through the house looking at the things and places she associated with him. She struggled to see a pattern that defined him but could not find one. She touched things: his pocketknife on the kitchen counter and his hairbrush in the bathroom. Sometimes, she put things in drawers. Others, she could not bring herself to move: the magazines and books in his reading nook, for instance. He grumbled when he had to look for something he thought was there. She thought of him sitting in his corner, the newspaper scattered around him, like a child playing with its favorite toys. He could sit for long periods like that; it was one of the few things that could contain his restless energy. She loved seeing him there and loved him for being the way he was. She left it undisturbed. There would be plenty of time to put things away.

The gold watch had always been on Gordon's dresser. She wondered why she hadn't noticed its absence before. Luckily, he was not wearing it the day he died, so she did not have to retrieve it, as she had his wedding ring. Perhaps she had seen it when she returned from the morgue, still numb from seeing his body, and had absentmindedly put it in her jewelry box so she would not have to look at it. Now, she took it out and laid it on the dresser next to the box. It was a beautiful watch, and he was proud of it. She looked through the jewelry—the earrings, the bracelets, the watches—in her jewelry box. At the bottom, she found a pair of dangling earrings, white gold, with intricate patterns of woven vine. They were longer than anything she normally wore. Gordon had given them to her when she had her hair cut short. She had always worn it moderately long, which Gordon liked. But as she got older, she grew tired of it.

At one point, when she was at the beauty salon, she decided to cut it off. The decision thrilled her a little. It was unlike her to act on impulse. But the result was a success. The women in the salon said it made her look younger. It emphasized her tallness and her long neck. Her young hair cutter said, you are gorgeous now. Another woman said, "You look great, but now you'll need new earrings." And Gordon loved it. He became so enthusiastic that she wondered if he was trying to convince himself. But he seemed sincere. He bought her the dangling earrings: these will look wonderful with your new haircut, he said. They were expensive but not gaudy. They suit you, he said, they are perfect. One night, she had put them on when they made love.

She had not worn them for years. Most of her earrings were simple, small and inconspicuous. She laid the long earrings on the dresser next to Gordon's watch. She had always associated earrings like this with younger women: women who were seeking attention, who were presenting themselves in a certain way. Should she wear them tonight? They would make a statement. Why shouldn't she show off her good looks? She abruptly rejected the idea: she wasn't sure what signal she wanted to give. She selected a simpler set of pearl earrings and began to put them on. The left one was in. She paused for a moment and took it out. Then she put on the dangling earrings.

At dinner, Carlton couldn't stop looking at her. You are so beautiful, he said. She realized she wanted to hear him say it.

Carlton called the next evening after the date. Could he come over for a minute? He had something to say. He sat on the couch where he had sat before, the same place where Arnold had tried to manage the milling poodles while apologizing. Joanne could tell what was on Carlton's mind. He was more relaxed now. He began by saying how much he enjoyed her company and appreciated the fact that they were becoming friends. Even just talking across the fence made him feel close to her. He thought he could see inklings of the same in her. Now, he knew that he had been hasty by surprising her with a marriage proposal so early on. He felt sorry for that and apologized. He sat up a little straighter. But it had been a serious proposal. He truly did want to marry her, even more so now. Together, they could fill some of each other's emptiness. Two would be stronger than one, he said, almost with a flourish. I wish I could say it more eloquently, he said, but I truly love you. He was renewing the proposal. Would she do it—marry him?

This time, Joanne wasn't surprised; she had expected it. Carlton's mind was made up; he had overcome his nervousness and brought it up again. She admired his courage. His simple declaration charmed her. He was looking straight at her now, but it didn't make her uncomfortable. She found herself liking him very much. Maybe she could even love him. She remembered Gordon's proposal so many years before. Then, she could only respond with a question, a question that left the decision to him. Now, her confidence had grown; she felt stronger and more decisive. She had handled the situation with Arnold by overcoming her usual uncertainty about herself. Throughout her life, she had preferred to leave the choices to someone else. Now, she felt the determination to decide, and the choices were clear to her. She believed that she could have a good life with Carlton, maybe even a happy one. She also knew she could go on alone if she chose to, as she felt herself changing and becoming someone new. The situations were distinct: either could work.

Yet, as she sat there, Carlton facing her, she realized that the choice was not easier now because she was stronger. It was harder, harder because each possibility was desirable. Choosing one meant losing the other. She could not have both. She hesitated; her thinking faltered; her will faded.

At last, she could only ask, "Don't you know?"

Carlton sat silently for a moment or two. She could not tell what he was thinking. His expression had not changed at first, but now there was a look of something she couldn't interpret on his face, something ambiguous and uncertain. Then, she realized it was resignation. Carlton rose, and she could see the sadness in his eyes. I'm sorry I brought it up again, he said. It just seemed like such a good idea to me that we would be good together. It wasn't meant to happen, I guess. We can still be friends. I hope we will be. And he left.

In the morning, Joanne brought the big suitcase up from the basement. It was the one she and Gordon used on long trips. In the bedroom, she also took out her smaller case. For now, two would be enough. She packed mostly fall clothing; summer was ending, and it was getting cooler. She would leave her winter things. By winter, she didn't plan to be anywhere they would be needed.

She wrote a note to her friend Doris, a member of her bridge group, who was a real estate agent. Please put the house on the market, she said. My lawyer has power of attorney; he can sign anything that needs signing. His office can also pay the bills. She included a list of everything, including the yard man. You can reach me by email. I will send a forwarding address later. She did not plan to use her cell phone; she would not be at the other end of the line until she was ready. She put the note and her house key in an envelope. She would slip it under the door of the real estate office as she left town. She thought about whether she should send an email to Annie but rejected the idea. Emails were not her favorite way of communicating. They seemed like shopping lists: useful but unimaginative. She could never have said anything meaningful in an email. She would write letters to Annie and Aunt Hazel later.

She carried the two suitcases down the stairs and out the back door. They weren't heavy, which satisfied her. She was traveling light; that was best. She thought Carlton might see her as she opened the garage door and put the bags in the trunk of the car. But he was nowhere to be seen. It would have been all right to see him. She would have felt no embarrassment. It was also just as well that it wouldn't be necessary.

She thought about how different Carlton was from Gordon. He had little of Gordon's self-confidence. She would have been the stronger of the two: she could see that now. That was a unique, new realization, an idea of what she could be: the stronger partner. Marriage to Carlton would have been nothing like her life with Gordon. She and Carlton could have had a good life together. She was confident of that. But it would not happen, and she had no regrets, no matter how the decision had been reached. She could feel her new strength, and she liked that feeling.

Joanne backed down the driveway and into the street. She would go to the inn near Bennington that Gordon loved. The inn on the green, he called it. From there, she could decide what to do next and where to go. There was no hurry. She would probably go south; New York winters had always worn her down. Now there was no reason to suffer through them. She would stay close to the ocean, somewhere near a beach. Wherever it turned out to be, she would eventually find it. She was confident of that. As she drove out of town, she felt halfway there already.

THE MAN ON GANU MOR

Maybe the dog sniffing at Hogan's ankles should have warned him. A moment before, he had glanced back along the rocky trail up the mountain and saw nothing. It surprised him to discover a small white terrier at his feet, its clipped tail wagging energetically. He had been distracted, studying the landscape stretching up the mountain, his thoughts lost for a while as he peered into the twisting Scottish fog. It took concentration to make out a route as the mist swirled, playing with the visibility ahead.

"Ha-llooo!" a voice called. Hogan turned. A man coming up the trail had almost reached him. The man seemed to have materialized out of nothing, appearing from nowhere. Hogan shook his head to clear his mind. That's ridiculous, he told himself. I just didn't notice him approaching. How could he have been so distracted that he missed seeing someone coming up the trail? Maybe the fog was getting to him.

The man called to the dog, "Get back, Simon. Leave the poor fellow in peace." Now, as the man stood a few feet away, Hogan could see him better: a person of middle height, a head shorter than Hogan, with brown, wavy hair and dark eyes deep-set in a smiling face. Pretty ordinary-looking, Hogan thought. Definitely a Scot. The man wore khaki hiking trousers and a safari jacket with scuffed boots. His hand gripped a long walking stick; he leaned on it. He had an Australian bush hat in his hand, which he now placed on his head. "A nice day," the man said, extending his hand. "If a bit gray."

For an instant, Hogan hesitated. Something about the man made him cautious. He had to will his arm forward to take the man's hand. He released it quickly; it had a clammy feel. "I've seen worse," Hogan said.

"Ah. An American. I hear it in your voice. Although I might have guessed." The man pointed his stick at Hogan's boots. "Master Peak high-tops. Americans favor those." Hogan bought the boots in Fort William three days ago; he had no idea they would tag him. The shopkeeper had praised their long tops, well-padded and close-fitting, to guard against ankle injuries. "You need them for these rocky trails," the clerk said as he laced them. Now, Hogan looked down at his boots, then back at the man, and said nothing. The man seemed not to have expected a response.

"So, you are challenging our mountain. Our Ganu Mor."

The possessive struck Hogan. "'Our' mountain?" he asked.

The man laughed. "A figure of speech." He waved his hand as though to sweep in the entire landscape. "One of our beautiful Scottish peaks."

Beautiful it is, Hogan thought. He had studied the mountain from across the loch where he parked his car. Foinaven was the name on the map. But the locals called it by its Gaelic name: Ganu Mor, the Big Wedge. Eons of erosion had eaten away the surrounding rock, leaving the mountain standing alone, singular and isolated. Hogan felt an instant connection to it. It missed being a Munro, one of the famous British hiking peaks 3,000 feet or higher, by only twelve feet. It was enough to keep it off the hiking beaten track. That near miss appealed to Hogan: a loser by a nose, otherwise flawless. Like placing second in a beauty contest. And its location here in the distant northwest, remote even by Scottish standards, made it less traveled. As Hogan studied its angular shape, it reminded him of a humpbacked whale, with a long spine cresting at the head and a sharp drop off down the face. He imagined how he would approach it: up the spine to the crest on the head of the whale. The top looked flattish before the drop-off down the face. Then what? What was the face like, the way down? The maps were ambiguous. It was not a well-hiked mountain, and information was sparse. No one he asked could tell him much.

The man sat on a nearby stone and rested his stick against it. "A pleasant day for a walk. But wettish. It might rain."

Hogan looked at him. Might rain? What does he think this stuff is? Hogan wondered. The heavy mist came close to being a soaking rain. For some reason, Hogan could not get a clear fix on the man's face. The outline was there, sure enough, and eyes that had a fixed quality, reminding Hogan of black dots on a domino. But the face itself seemed indistinct, blurred as though seen through a rain-streaked window. Each time Hogan tried to focus more clearly, the man's features seemed to shift a little, like a kaleidoscope re-jiggling the jumbled pieces ever so slightly.

At that instant, Hogan decided to abort his climb. He couldn't see a trail clearly enough; the drifting, erratic mist was too misleading. His uncertainty had started as he gazed at the mountain from across the loch. Now, a third of the way up it, his nerve failed him. He hiked alone; he had to be cautious, especially in this remote place. An accident could leave him helpless. He looked at his watch: 10:45, two and a half hours since he left the lodge, and he had barely started up the mountain. He should be further along by this time. "Don't kill yourself," his ex-wife's phone message at the hotel said. "You shouldn't take chances." She liked to leave messages stating the obvious, like cautioning a child. He was used to it; even years after their divorce, she enjoyed pointing out his inadequacies. This time, he would take her advice. Too much risk, he decided. The maps had failed him; he didn't know the trail.

Now the weather had settled it: he would quit and go back to the lodge where a bottle of Glenfiddich waited.

Hogan shifted his backpack slightly and turned to face down the trail the way he had come. "Going back?" The man seemed surprised. "Why, the walk ahead is delightful. One of our best." He gestured toward the slope. Hogan hesitated, then took a step back down the trail.

"A little too wet for me today," he said. He lifted his hand, about to wave goodbye to this stranger and his dog.

"Yes, Scottish weather can do that to you." The man's eyes scrutinized Hogan. "Your first time here?" The question grated on Hogan. This guy thinks I'm a tenderfoot, he thought. He had been to Scotland before; of course, he had. He knew the Scottish mountains and the weather. He had been up Ben Nevis two different ways, in fact. And Canisp, Quinag, and others. Ganu Mor couldn't be that different.

"I've climbed a bunch," Hogan said. "But now I'm going back."

"Wait," the man said as he stood, lifting his arm in a halt signal. "You've come this far. Why give up now?" Again, the man's tone rankled Hogan. "I don't know the trail," Hogan said, trying to keep the irritation from his voice. "The maps are unclear. And I can't see much in this fog."

"Oh, the fog will burn off higher up," the man said. "And the trail?" He gave a dismissive wave. "It's simple. A passable up. Just follow the spine to the top. You can't miss it. Once there, you'll be able to see the road at the base of the mountain. Then, zigzag down the face to reach it. A breeze." He chuckled. "Those fine boots deserve it." The dog had returned to Hogan's ankles, ready to herd him back toward the peak. The man went on, "Two hours to the top. Three at most and an hour down the other side to the road. It'll be easy to catch a lift back to your car from someone driving by. You'll be home for tea." The man's tone was firm, reassuring.

Hogan stood, his body half-facing downhill. The dog

blocked him; he would have to step over it to proceed. Three or four hours, a total of seven or eight since he started. A typical hiking day. What did he have to lose? If he turned around, what was back there waiting for him? Just a message at the lodge from his lawyer. He hadn't returned the call yet. The man stood quietly, waiting for Hogan's decision. Why should the drizzle stop him? Hogan thought. He liked Scottish weather, so unlike New York's suffocating summer heat. Here, high on these remote, lonely trails, the cool air sedated him; the gloomy sky induced a relaxed peacefulness. He had come for this, after all. And he liked this mountain, this wedge-shaped monolith.

"If you head up to the top, perhaps we'll join you," the man said as though to clinch it. "Simon and I hadn't planned a long walk today. But we would enjoy the company. Maybe we'll go along to help show the way." Hogan considered this. Here is someone who knows the mountain, he thought. The idea reassured him; it would be unusual to have a guide. He wasn't used to it. Hogan looked back at the man, standing there, stick in hand, then looked at the dog, planted firmly in his path. Okay, he said to himself, I'll do it. He turned toward the trail heading upward and shrugged to help the backpack settle in between his shoulder blades.

"What are we waiting for?" he asked.

An hour later, his legs were hurting and his lower back throbbed. His thigh muscles quivered as he scrambled awkwardly from one rock to the next. A half-hour before, he realized that the path was not a trail at all but simply a sequence of rocks that were low enough for him to step from one to the next, like crossing a stream on steppingstones. He had encountered Scottish trails like this before and hated them. The heavy mist made the rocks slippery. Hogan had to place each foot carefully to balance before shifting his weight. It took concentration. The uncertain footing focused his attention downward to his feet; he could see no further than the next rock as he struggled up the steep slope. In this jumbled terrain, it was easy to become disoriented. He had no chance to look around to get his bearings. Not that he would have seen much. The cloudy air hung sullenly around him, backing off now and then just enough for him to see a few steps forward, then locking in behind as though sealing him off from a retreat. "The fog will burn off higher up," the man had assured him. Apparently, we aren't high enough yet, Hogan thought sourly. He could hear the man up ahead but could not see him through the haze.

Finally, he reached a space level enough to pause. As he stood, panting from the exertion, he realized he could no longer pick out the steppingstones before him. Ahead lay a new maze of rocks and crevices, with no way to distinguish the path. Anxiety pressed on him. He had feared this uncertainty, a sea of choices, at risk of losing his way. He peered ahead, trying to make out the route the man had taken. But the stranger had disappeared into the damp, leaden air.

"Let's take a rest," Hogan called out. And the man appeared, already in motion, descending toward him out of the haze as though he had anticipated Hogan's words.

"Okay," the man said and settled himself on one of the large boulders along the path.

"I thought you said the fog would lift," Hogan said, still breathless from the climb. The man nodded.

"Yes, it is thick today," he agreed. "But a little higher should do it. Nearer the spine."

Hogan considered this: higher up, further into this fog, with little sense of where he was headed. His resolve had started to waver a half-hour before when he realized the way would not get easier. One rock to the next, then another: that's what this hike meant. He was tired of it. He should have turned around earlier. Now, the lodge was an hour further back, and he would have to find his way in this gray syrup. But this is too much, he told himself. I'm heading back. Another time, perhaps, when the weather improved, and he felt better. He stood and adjusted his backpack.

The man seemed to sense Hogan's hesitation. "Having second thoughts?" he asked, his tone mild. "You shouldn't worry. You can do this."

A familiarity in the man's voice annoyed Hogan. What did he know of Hogan's abilities, his determination? How could he judge what Hogan could or could not do? For the first time, Hogan felt a flicker of apprehension about the man. He knew nothing about him, some stranger he met on the trail. Maybe the man wasn't familiar with the place at all. Maybe he had been bragging, or even lying, about knowing the way. Hogan had accepted the man's words without question; now, doubt began to settle in.

"Going down on these wet rocks is harder than going up," the man went on. He rubbed his chin and looked intently at Hogan. "And you might get lost in the fog."

Hogan considered this: descending was riskier, that was true, especially for ankle injuries. He had learned this the hard way on Ben Nevis; he sprained his ankle badly as his foot slid from a rock just as he shifted his weight to it. He could barely hobble the two painful miles back to his car. And the fog showed no sign of letting up now; behind him, it seemed even denser than before. What did he have to go back to anyway? His lawyer's call still waited. Looking ahead beat looking back, he figured, even with the uncertainties.

The man stood and picked up his stick from the rock where it leaned. "The spine's not far ahead," he said. "From there, you'll be able to see the peak." Further up, the dog had already begun to leap from one rock to the next.

So effortlessly, Hogan thought, like he knew the way. The man, too, had started moving, his stick clicking on the hard surfaces. Without looking back again, Hogan followed him.

It took another hour to reach it. The spine: a narrow ridge stretching from where they now stood, a half a mile or more to the peak up ahead. The fog had lessened a little, as the man predicted. As they ascended, it gradually dissipated enough for Hogan to make out the crest ahead, still draped in mist but undeniably there. But, below him, the thick clouds still burrowed into the valleys surrounding the mountain, making it seem like an island in a turbulent gray sea. Hogan could not grasp what the neighboring landscape looked like or the elevation they had reached. The mountain seemed to dwell in its own universe, isolated from the world, with two men and a small dog trapped on its top. The way up had been completely unclear to Hogan; any semblance of a trail had vanished. He could only follow the man when he could see him through the haze and listen for the sound of his footsteps when he could not. An uneasy sensation grew in him: he was lost. He had no way out except where this man, this odd stranger, took him.

The man was eating a sandwich as Hogan reached the small plateau at the start of the spine.

"Lunchtime," the man said and waved the sandwich at Hogan. The way up had not gotten easier; Hogan's own hunger grew as he struggled up it. He found a nearby rock, sat on it with a grunt, and opened his backpack.

"You said the trail was easy." Hogan's irritation came through. "It's anything but."

"I said 'passable,'" the man replied. "Is anything worthwhile ever easy? In life, I mean."

"You can skip the philosophy," Hogan said. "I don't have an opinion on that." Nothing in his life was easy. It pressed in from every side, choking him. He tore his sandwich apart and stuffed pieces into his mouth.

The man appeared thoughtful. "So why do you come here?" he asked finally. He took a toothpick from his shirt pocket and began poking at his teeth, up and down. "Trying to avoid something?"

Who is this cheeky bastard? Hogan asked himself. Why did he come? Because he loved Scotland, that was why. The emptiness of the Highlands absorbed him. When he stood gazing at the landscape, the wind churning the air and rippling the long grass at his feet, he felt his spirit flowing from his body, escaping into the vastness, connecting him seamlessly to the endless expanse of sky and beyond.

"I come because I love Scotland," he said. "That's all."

The man persisted. "Something wrong at work, perhaps? Or home?"

How could Hogan respond to that? He considered his job. The investigation, the subpoenas, everyone clamming up. Someone ratted; that much was clear. Hogan had pushed the boundaries, like everyone else. But he covered his tracks carefully. He stopped trading altogether just to give himself some distance from the whole mess. "I don't think you'll be indicted," his lawyer told him, with an uncertain wobble in his voice. Who knew how it would play out? Who knew anything? And what news would be waiting for him when he returned his lawyer's message, waiting back at the lodge? Anyway, it was no business of this stranger.

"My work is none of your business. Let's drop it."

But the man pressed on. "Your children, probably. You look old enough to have grown children. They can be great disappointments."

"Disappointments," indeed, Hogan thought. Two children who treated him like toxic waste: Alice, cynical, contemptuous of him and his world, like her mother, his first wife, and Daniel, his son by his second wife, years of boozing and drugs, mental breakdowns, arrests. Hogan shied away from them when they were growing up. They were so needy, and he had nothing to give. At least nothing he could identify. Mostly, he struggled to ease his own torment and fear. Fear of what?

he often wondered. Failure: demands he could not meet; the gnawing sense of exposure? Yes, I failed you, Hogan brooded. I meant to protect you. But I couldn't; I didn't know how. I didn't know it would turn out like this.

"I don't have children," he lied. "And you ask a lot of damn questions."

The man smiled. "Yes, I'm a little nosy. Always have been. I can't help it. People interest me." He looked sheepish. "No offense intended." The man's embarrassment took the intensity away. Nosy people are usually harmless, Hogan thought; he could deflect it.

"No offense taken." He stood. "Can we get going?"

The man smiled again and put the toothpick back in his pocket.

"Yes. Let's go."

Hogan confronted the spine. The pathway stretched precariously along its top, barely wide enough to walk on. He gave it a worried look. On both sides, the ground fell sharply away, down steep slopes of rocky ground, disappearing into the clouds below. Like edging along the blade of an axe, Hogan thought. Falling down either side would be a headlong plunge into gray emptiness. He shuddered. "Are you sure it's—walkable?" His courage waned again: why was he doing this? It had stopped being fun.

"Yes, I know it looks risky," the man said. "But you'll find your footing once you start across." His voice sounded confident. "To the top. Then, from there, down to the road and back. Isn't that what you came for?"

Once again, the man's questions irritated Hogan. Would this character never let up? "My reasons are my own," he said flatly.

"There I go again," the man said, shaking his head. "Didn't

mean to presume. It's just that you seemed interested in hiking the trail the whole way. Up and down. And I wanted to help."

Somehow, the man's tone had begun to change. His words had a sharper edge; his probing seemed more intrusive. Apprehension trickled through Hogan's stomach. He tried to shake it off. So far, this screwball's help had only led him deeper into a situation he couldn't quite understand. This hike should not be so difficult; nothing about Ganu Mor warned him of these conditions. Now, he had only the man to count on. He felt another urge to turn back. But he steadied himself. His stubbornness took hold: the man's gibes shouldn't play into it. Maybe the fog was just getting to him. It had disoriented him before on other mountains, making him lose his bearings and rattling him until he wanted to turn back. Just like now. He took a deep breath and forced himself to calm down. Don't show your fear, he told himself. He squared his shoulders; he would not give in to it. His head ached from the tension. He massaged the rigid muscles in his neck and stood.

"Let's just do it," he said.

At least the spine was relatively flat, unlike the steep grade leading up to it. Hogan watched as the man moved forward into the mist, the dog at his heels. The gray drizzle quickly enshrouded the man, but Hogan could hear him, his boots crunching on the gravelly surface. Hogan stepped carefully ahead, testing the surface, relieved to find it solid. Below him, on either side, the fog brooded in the valleys, concealing the bottom far below. He warned himself: don't get dizzy. Keep your head down and concentrate on your footing. Balance, balance: he made it a mantra, matching his careful footsteps, first one foot, then the other, one step at a time. He moved slowly, aware of the man's stick hitting the ground up ahead, lost in the mist.

"Just keep moving," Hogan mumbled.

He could barely hear the man now; he's moving fast, Hogan thought. He felt ashamed of himself for going so slowly. He'll probably mock me, call me a greenhorn, Hogan thought bitterly. But he could feel the surface becoming increasingly unstable. Stones bounced loose as his feet jarred them, unnerving him as he heard them cascading down the hillside. At least it isn't windy, he told himself as he plodded ahead. A breeze came up as though summoned by his thoughts. He cursed quietly. If it got stronger, it would be harder to keep his balance. His legs felt wobbly now, partly from fatigue, partly from anxiety. Why had he started across such dangerous, tricky ground? He should have turned back two hours ago. For a moment, he paused and listened for the sound of the man's footsteps up ahead. Nothing. No sound. He's reached the other side and is waiting, Hogan reassured himself. But his stomach churned. Just keep moving, he thought. There's no choice.

Right, left, right, left; steadily, he moved on, focusing only on placing his next step. Then, abruptly, the trail narrowed further. The firm surface seemed to dissolve; his footing became shaky and loose. The fog lifted slightly, enough for him to make out the route ahead. For fifty yards or more, Hogan could see a ridge of loose stones and pebbles stretching along the spine. Can it hold my weight? he wondered. He imagined the whole thing crumbling, like gravel sliding from a dump truck, spilling him into the canyon below. Uncertainty rose inside him; he struggled to suppress it. Get a grip, he lectured himself. Figure this out. There was no way he could cross it upright, on his feet—not with the wind growing stronger. It pushed him one way, then quickly switched directions, threatening his balance. Oh, Christ, he said to himself, I'll have to crawl on my hands and knees. Desperation pounded in his gut; maybe he should still turn back. But the man said the summit lay just ahead. Then the way down the other side. He had only to cross the next fifty yards.

He lowered himself into a crouch, then leaned forward onto his hands and knees. The sharp stones ground into his kneecaps, sending shocks of pain through him, hurting his palms as he groped ahead with his hands. The wind pushed and pressed against him as though trying to dislodge him from the path. The steep sides falling away on either side tugged at him. Even in his desperation, he felt foolish, crawling along like an animal. He inched awkwardly ahead, scraping each knee painfully, his hands reaching for something firm to grab onto. Behind him, he heard rocks falling, a cascade of them sliding down the steep slopes. He realized the ridge was disintegrating behind him. He didn't look back. He didn't need to. He could feel it happening. Now, there could be no turning around, not now, not ever. He could only grope his way forward. Don't think about it, just move, he told himself over and over.

Then he was across. The ground became firm again; a small, grassy knoll stretched before him. He rose shakily to his feet, his knees aching and his palms pulsing from the pain of pressing on the sharp stones. Up ahead, he saw the man sitting on a rock, his boots off, massaging his feet.

"These stones are tough on the feet," the man said cheerfully. "I suppose yours are hurting too." He looked at Hogan's feet. "Especially in those new boots. You should have broken them in some more." He continued rubbing his toes. "Anyway, I'm glad you made it. I wasn't sure you would."

Anger seized Hogan. "I don't give a shit what you think of my boots. You lied about the trail, about being passable. It nearly killed me."

"Yes, it can be hard," the man replied. He lounged backward, extending his legs. "Frankly, I'm a little surprised you took it on." He wiggled his toes inside his socks. "Not like you to face up to tough things, is it? Hard choices. No, not like you at all." He flexed his feet, stretching out his toes again. "Maybe you should have turned back a couple of hours ago. Like you wanted to."

Hogan flared. "How the hell do you know what I can face up to? You don't know me. And it wouldn't be any of your business if you did." Sweat soaked his palms. He resisted an urge to wipe them on his pants. "Who are you anyway?"

The man chuckled. "By now, I thought you would have figured it out."

Fear swelled in Hogan. He stepped backward until his legs felt the hard surface of a large rock half-tripping him, and he sat awkwardly. The man's words alarmed him. He struggled to regain control of himself.

"Well, I haven't figured it out. I don't know who you are, only that you keep asking me these obnoxious questions. How could you know anything about me?"

"Just a guess," the man replied calmly. "The kind of thing that might be true of anyone."

"Well, I'm tired of the intrusion. Maybe I'll ask the questions."

"Fair enough," the man said. He seemed to be enjoying himself. "Fire away."

"First off, who the hell are you, and where are you from? I'm beginning to wonder if you know this mountain at all."

"Oh, I know it all right. I was born around here." He lived in a cottage near the base of Ganu Mor with Simon, a true Scottish pup, who joined him as he walked about the countryside. He loved the mountains in this part of Scotland—"hills," he called them—but Ganu Mor most of all.

"Ganu Mor's challenge is not its size or altitude. It's no mere Munro," the man went on. "No, it's the surface, the landscape, ever-shifting, ever-changing. Each time up is different. You must focus and concentrate to find the path."

"Yeah, I got that part," Hogan said. He thought of stepping from one slippery rock to the next on a course nearly impossible to follow.

The man laughed. "But that's the challenge, isn't it? Searching out the right path. Finding meaning through seeking." He rubbed his chin. "Isn't that what makes life worth living?"

"I don't spend a lot of time seeking deep meaning in everything," Hogan said.

"Maybe you should," the man said. "It might help."

Hogan bristled. "Help what?"

"Oh, I don't know. Help you find yourself, perhaps."

"I don't need help with that," Hogan said curtly.

But the man's statement rattled him. The right button had been pressed: Hogan knew it. He did feel lost, felt that he no longer knew who he was. For years, he had felt himself drifting, losing control of his life. He struggled to regain it, to rouse himself like a bull shaking itself to restore its strength. But inertia took over. Gradually, he surrendered to the torpor, becoming more guarded, less able to reach out to people, shielding himself, protecting what lay inside him. His family, never close, fell further away; his few friends lost touch. And he could do nothing to counter it. As he aged, he felt his world tilting toward finality, the pull of the downward slope gently but persistently tugging at his ankles, dragging him toward the edge, with only darkness beyond.

He realized he had been talking and abruptly stopped. Why was he revealing himself to this strange man, saying things he had never said to anyone else? Just shut up, he told himself. But something urged him on; maybe it was the place, being stranded on this odd mountain, the isolation and loneliness, the sense of desolation. He felt a need to talk.

"Sometimes I feel that I'm on the edge," he said after a while. "And there is nothing beyond it."

The man listened closely to Hogan's words. "Is that why you wander these trails? Alone. To avoid facing that abyss?"

Hogan considered this: hiking to escape. From himself. How odd, he thought. He had always believed the mountains forced him to confront reality, a tangible reality under every arduous footstep. In fact, he was escaping a harsher reality: his own. He had never thought of it that way.

"Yes, that could be it," he said quietly.

Suddenly, uneasiness came over Hogan again. Somehow, this conversation had gotten out of hand. How had he been lured into intimacy with this stranger? He needed to regain his composure and get back on track quickly before the man could respond.

Hogan stood abruptly. "No. I meant I don't know what you're asking. The question is nonsense."

The man did not stand but lounged further back on his perch. His body seemed to flow into the curves of the stone surface. He gave another quick laugh.

"I think you understand perfectly. You are hiding from what you are. What you've chosen to be." His gaze remained fixed on Hogan. "Now you don't like it. You have only regrets." He shifted again on the rock and seemed to meld further into it. "Well, this is a good place to hide. Here on the edge of nowhere."

"I'm not hiding from anything." Hogan's voice shook despite his effort to control it. "And you know nothing about me."

"It's not easy to escape the truth," the man went on coolly, ignoring Hogan's response. "You just run into something else. Usually something worse." He gave a mirthless chuckle. "You are smug about your life, your success. But you've come to realize how empty it is. Based on lies mostly. Deception is second nature to you, a sort of reflex." He paused while Hogan took this in. "You are always on guard; you can never relax. You've gone through life in a defensive crouch."

The man's fierce black eyes bore into Hogan's skull; he felt his confidence unraveling.

The man went on, "That's why you come to these mountains and hike these rocky trails by yourself, because you think that might redeem you. Give you strength and the courage to change yourself inside. Something to compensate for the lies, the dishonesty." The man sat up and leaned over to locate his boots. "Help you find your soul perhaps." He pulled the boots on, lacing them tightly and giving each a final tug. "Yes, it is about your soul. That surprises you, doesn't it? But that's the truth: you are trying to save your soul."

He stood, placing his hands on his hips and arching backward. "Oh, these old bones. They've gotten so creaky." The man stood for a while, silent. Hogan felt the sweat dripping inside his shirt, even as the cold wind chilled his skin. He couldn't stop shivering.

"I had you nailed from the first," the man said finally, looking directly into Hogan's eyes. "A phony." He pointed his stick at Hogan's feet. "Those boots gave you away. You thought they would set you apart. Make you look special, a real hiker." He stomped his feet to get his circulation going. "But you can't handle boots like that. They're too good for you." His voice became pleasant. "You're like a beggar in a Mercedes. It wouldn't suit you. Out of place, that's you. You're wearing a disguise. But in the end, it can't hide what you are."

The dog had stood also, and now waited next to the man's feet.

"Frankly, I'm surprised you made it this far," the man said. "We'll see how you do at the top. It isn't far." He pointed his stick up ahead, where the fog had settled back in, obscuring the summit. "But you'll have to find the way now. I won't be here to guide you."

"What the hell are you talking about?" Hogan felt queasy. "Where are you going?"

"I'm tired of your company," the man said. "You'll have to go on alone."

Hogan's mouth was dry; he could hardly pull his lips apart to speak.

"How can I do that? I'm lost. I just followed you." The

man's words made him lightheaded. "I didn't have a choice."

The man snorted and flicked his wrist, like batting away a fly. "Of course you had a choice. You could have chosen to turn back. Like you wanted to. Instead, you let me lead you up here."

Hogan's heart pounded. "I don't know the way. How can I find it?" He paused. "Without your help."

The man stood for a moment, considering this.

"All right. I'll take you the rest of the way if you want me to." Again, he fell silent. The dog sat, no longer impatient to leave. "Or you can proceed on your own." His tone turned mocking. "You wanted a choice. Now you have one."

Hogan gazed up at the man, now sharply defined against the misty backdrop. Control yourself, he thought. Don't panic; think this through. In fact, he had chosen to follow the man up the mountain. And, yes, he could have turned back. What should he do? Maybe he could still turn back. Then, he remembered the sound of the crumbling trail behind him. He could only go forward. But how? He was sick of the man's company, the intrusive questions, and the cutting remarks. The man had misled Hogan about the trail; why trust him now? But doubt gripped him: wouldn't the wise course be to stick with him? They had gotten this far, after all. And the man had to reach the top, too, so he could get down the other side. Hogan could tag along; he could tell the man off later, after they were safely down.

The man waited patiently, not moving, as Hogan pondered his situation. His head ached from the tension. An alternative plan began to take shape in his mind; he rubbed his temples to bring it into focus. Even in the gray shroud surrounding him, it felt as though the peak couldn't be far. The man said as much. Hogan reassured himself: every route will begin to converge on the peak. Just keep heading upward. You can't miss the crest the closer to the top you get. Why should he need the man now? Following him had created this mess. Why stay tethered to him? Who knew what other problems might arise if Hogan stuck with him. No, he needed to get back into control. He would be better off on his own—alone, the way he was used to, like he had always done everything. He needed to cut himself loose.

"I'll make my own way up," he said, trying to sound confident. "You go on."

At that, the dog stood, ready to leave, as though he understood Hogan's words.

"So be it," the man said. He turned and stepped forward without looking back as the fog reached down to collect him. He disappeared into it, and the dog, too.

Hogan shivered. He peered into the gray mist that had swallowed the man. His heart pounded. Not from exertion, he realized, but fear. Never had he felt so detached from his surroundings, from the world itself. The man's absence pressed on him. Hogan shook himself, trying to break free of its force.

Everything had begun to feel unreal, as though the man and his dog were merely products of his imagination. Had they really been there? Or had the loneliness of the trail simply deranged him for a while as he struggled up the unstable ground? He had felt this kind of disorientation before when he hiked alone and saw no one for hour after hour. It's just the isolation, he told himself, that's all. These barren Scottish mountains disturb your peace of mind. They scare you a little. Yes, he had felt it before: a distorted perspective, a sense of unreality. It's easy to imagine things that aren't there.

In any event, he would soon be back to the real world. Just ahead was the top. Then down the other side to the road. You can see the road from the top: he remembered the man's words distinctly. He would catch a ride to his car, then back to the inn. At this point, he had to press ahead, reach the peak, and satisfy himself that he had done it without help from a mysterious man and a spooky dog, real or not.

As he hiked, the ground became steeper. A good sign, he

thought. I'm nearing the top. He panted from the exertion. The haze had cleared; he could begin to see the summit. As he approached, the slope became gentler, ending in a small, flat plateau. Even from this perspective, he could see the edge, the pinnacle, up ahead. That wasn't so hard, he told himself, relieved as he moved forward. Not so bad at all. Soft meadow grass covered the ground. It felt springy under his feet, a welcome relief from the rocky pathway up. Tiny yellow wildflowers scattered about the grassy surface, snuggled close to the ground. The wind had grown still; the serenity of the scene soothed him. This is a beautiful, peaceful place, he thought. And I've made it.

Not far ahead, only twenty yards or so, he could see the crest.

"All downhill from there," he said aloud.

He felt a rush of joy; the panic had gone now. He could remember the fear, but it had congealed into a cold lump in his memory. He had confronted danger and conquered it. He felt calm, satisfied that he had made the right choice. No reason to follow anyone or anything, he told himself, real or imagined. He had made it. On his own. That's all that mattered. He laughed and slapped his leg as he walked the final few steps to the edge. If the dog were here, he would pat its head and say: good work.

Then he was there, standing on the edge. He looked down along the face of the mountain, anxious to see the road and the pathway descending to it.

Instead, he saw a sheer vertical wall of granite falling away at his feet, disappearing into the rolling mist. His brain strained to adjust as he took it in, the reality creeping through him.

There is no way down, he realized.

He stared into the emptiness below and could see no end to it.

ABOUT THE AUTHOR

W. A. POLF (WILLIAM) is a native Californian who has spent most of his adult life in San Francisco and New York City. He holds a BA from San Francisco State University and a PhD in American history from Syracuse University. He worked for the New York State American Revolution Bicentennial Commission and the Speaker of the New York State legislature. He was an executive at Columbia University and spent thirty-five years in the Columbia University – Presbyterian Hospital system in New York City. He retired as a Senior Vice President at New York Presbyterian Hospital in Manhattan. He lives in Pittsboro, North Carolina, with his wife Robin Eisner, an artist and retired journalist.

His stories have appeared in various publications. He has been a finalist or semi-finalist in several short story competitions. In 2018, he won second place in North Carolina's Doris Betts Short Fiction competition, awarded by the North Carolina Writer's Network. His story was published by the North Carolina Literary Review Online and was nominated for a Pushcart and for The Best Short Stories Online. The editors of the *New Yorker* wrote that "there is much to admire" in one of his stories. He published his first book of short stories, *Magical Ballyglass and Other Stories*, in 2012.

ABOUT ATMOSPHERE PRESS

Founded in 2015, Atmosphere Press was built on the principles of Honesty, Transparency, Professionalism, Kindness, and Making Your Book Awesome. As an ethical and author-friendly hybrid press, we stay true to that founding mission today.

Always feel free to visit Atmosphere Press and our authors online at atmospherepress.com. See you there soon!

Milton Keynes UK
Ingram Content Group UK Ltd.
UKHW042015300724
446162UK00008BA/117/J

9 798891 323377